"Are you a witch?" Navarre whispered against her lips. "Tell me truly—are you in league with Richard and Locksley?"

Kendra buried her hands in his hair and pressed his face next to hers, even as she laughed aloud. "Oh, my brave knight," she said softly, "if I were a witch, I would enchant you and bind you to me forever. I would keep you tethered to my bed and you would fulfill my every wish. Richard and Locksley could never compare to you."

Navarre jerked back from her embrace, and with a roar rolled away from her and sprang to his feet. Startled, Kendra raised up on her elbows.

"Wrong answer, huh?" She smiled. "Well, that's what I get for trying to be poetic. Now–" she lifted her arms to him, "come back here. I'm freezing."

Navarre towered above her, his hands curled into fists at his sides. "Witch!" Navarre hissed. "Soon you will be warm enough, for you will burn when we reach Nottingham!"

Kendra sat up, arms wrapped around herself as she shivered, her teeth beginning to chatter. "I am getting very tired of this. This is my dream and I would think I should be able to have things my way. So cooperate or I might just turn you into someone who will be—like Mel Gibson."

Kendra started to laugh, but the laughter died in her throat as she saw Navarre's face pale at her words. His strong jaw tightened and the gold in his eyes burned, not with desire any longer, but raw anger.

He stalked over to the fire where her clothing was stretched across rocks to dry, grabbed them, then turned and threw them in her face. "Dress, before I end your worthless life."

Other *Love Spell* books by Tess Mallory:
JEWELS OF TIME

CIRCLES IN TIME

TESS MALLORY

LOVE SPELL **NEW YORK CITY**

For my sister, Cassie-Renaissance woman, artist, editor, friend.

LOVE SPELL®
May 1997
Published by

Dorchester Publishing Co., Inc.
276 Fifth Avenue
New York, NY 10001

Printed in the United States of America.

ACKNOWLEDGMENTS

This is my favorite part, thanking my friends. Much love goes out this time to all the folks who still believed this year in spite of everything: my children, Erin, Heather and Jordan, without whom I could not exist; and the rest of my family, Papa Daddy, Bill, Cassie, Jan-Jan, Jewell, Meg, Pat, Tommy, Jason, Julie, Linda, Tom, Marci, and Blake. Thanks to my wonderful friends Laura, Melissa, Greg and Ellen (and their six kids whom I adore), Shannon the faithful, dear buddy Rick, and my friends at the Point. That means you, Leatrice!

Special belated thanks this time around to science-fiction author Warren Norwood, my long-ago writing instructor, who told me again and again (with an exasperated sigh), "Just finish something, T.C., and it'll sell." I clung to those words then and they kept me going. They still do. Thanks, Warren, now and always.

There are many more people to thank, and I hope to write many more books so that eventually I'll be able to include them all. Much love.

Drowning in the darkness, grasping at the light,
healing, holding, unspeakably bright;
come now appear, knight on white steed,
gracious, precious, finally I'm freed.
   —Erin Mallory

Silhouette upon the glass, that used to hold the time,
Shadows of my memories, the hours not as kind.
The fallen sand still haunts me, within that hourglass,
So tell me now, where are we—the present, future, past?
   —Heather Mallory

Prologue

It was a dark place where the old one lived, a place of mystery. In the glow of a dim candle's light, Celtic artifacts—Christian and pagan—fought for dominance on the narrow, cluttered shelves of the circular room. Stone crosses kept company with gargoyles; elaborate knotted designs whirled on the face of a dirty cloth tacked over the solitary window of the hovel.

The man crouching at the feet of the old one did not notice his surroundings. His attention was riveted on the woman whose wisdom he had come seeking, and on the carved, rectangular stones she now rubbed between the palms of her hands. Silence permeated the musty room, undisturbed, even when she threw the stones to the dirt floor. They fell noiselessly and loose soil rose, marking their communion with the earth. The woman's eyes shut and a low keening sound from deep inside of her echoed through the stillness.

The man's gaze, shadowed by the hood of the dark cloak he wore, never moved from the woman who now rocked on her knees, wrinkled face distorted as if in agony. At last the motion slowed, then ceased altogether when she opened her eyes. Pale gray, almost colorless, they focused on the one who silently waited.

"There is danger," she said, her voice low and harsh.

"What danger, Magda?" he asked.

The corners of her thin lips tightened slightly, then slackened again.

"Betrayal."

"By whom?"

11

The one called Magda bent her head over the stones, peering more closely at them. Her lank, gray hair tumbled over her thin shoulders. "By an old friend. A lion." Her voice lowered into a whisper. "It means your destruction. Yours—and another, who also bears the name of lion."

"The king?"

She nodded. The cloaked man stood, hands clasped behind him, and began pacing the small confines of the room. "An old friend, a lion—why speak in riddles? Give me information I can use to stop this betrayal. A time, a place, a name!"

"These things are not told to me," she said, still hunched over the stones. She frowned down at them, then glanced up and smiled. "But there is hope."

"What kind of hope?" He knelt down beside her once again. "You must speak more plainly, Magda."

The solemn eyes gazed at him in rebuke for his impatience and the man sighed, jerking the hood from his head. He exposed an aristocratic face, the sharp angles of his cheekbones framed by curling light brown hair.

"Forgive my impatience, but there is no time to lose!"

"You have time." She gathered the stones back into her hands and stared down at them thoughtfully. "In a fortnight, when the moon is full and high, your salvation will be brought to you—by powers beyond our ken—to the mystic field of Abury."

He paled at her words. "Abury?"

The old woman nodded. "Aye, there is magic there still. "Both the catalyst and the catastrophe await you. Salvation comes, yet with it comes destruction. This salvation alone can prevent the danger that it brings, for England, for Richard." She lifted her head and pierced the man with her pale-eyed stare. "And for you, Sir Robin-of-the-Hood. Guard it well."

Robert of Locksley, knight of the realm, outlaw and thief, stood again and moved away from her. He lifted the filthy cloth over the window of the hovel and stared out, his gaze determined.

"You speak in riddles I do not understand. Nevertheless, I shall go to Abury," he promised, one hand resting on the hilt of the sword belted across the plain brown tunic he wore. "I shall find Richard's salvation and guard it with my life.''

Outside Magda's home, a solitary figure slipped stealthily away from his hiding place below the window. Navarre de Galliard glanced quickly around him as he moved with cat-like grace through the darkness, smiling without humor. His old friend Locksley had been foolish enough to come alone. It would prove to be his undoing.

Navarre reached the edge of a clearing and mounted his black stallion which awaited him half-hidden in a small grove of trees. The wind whipped up suddenly, lifting the man's own black mane of hair from his shoulders. For a moment, fragile tendrils danced in feathery contrast about the stern, unyielding face, and he glanced up at the sky, his golden eyes narrow with wariness.

The moonlight carved shadowy plains into the man's hand-some, rugged face, giving him a wild, almost feral look. In that moment, there was not a man in England who would have failed to recognize the knight once known as the Black Lion, once King Richard's most loyal follower.

Navarre watched the hut thoughtfully. So, he mused, the witch knew of Richard's danger. How much more did she know, and what was the meaning of her cryptic message to Locksley? He glanced up at the half-moon above him.

"In a fortnight," he whispered to the cold night air, "I shall take Richard's salvation, old friend, and make it mine own. But first, I will make sure that you never reach Abury."

Silently, Navarre drew his sword from its sheath, easing his horse toward the hut. The wind danced wildly about him, as though it would push him back from his goal. His fingers tensed around the hilt. He would wait until Locksley left the witch; then he would kill him. Like lightning, a picture of him and Robin fighting side by side against a gang of cutthroats during a long ago trip to London flashed through his mind. Navarre pushed the thought away. There was no room left in his life for sentimentality or softness. Robin had chosen the wrong side. He must be eliminated. It was as simple as that.

Navarre drew his mount beside the hut, then jerked his head up as the wind suddenly stopped and the air around him fell still. He was not a superstitious man, but the sudden, eerie stillness sent chills down his spine. His horse stirred restlessly and nickered softly toward the open field beyond the witch's home. Movement in the distance. Woodsmen. Navarre could see them now, dimly, a dozen or more heading toward the hut.

Cursing under his breath, the Black Lion quickly resheathed his sword and headed his horse back toward the sheltering grove. Locksley had not been as foolish as he supposed. Once again hidden by the foliage, Navarre watched for a moment as his old friend clasped arms with a huge bear of a man, then turned to greet a slim youth.

"Another day, Robin," he promised softly and disappeared into the forest.

High above Magda's house, too distant for human sight, a cluster of tiny blue lights flickered with the regularity of a heartbeat. They swirled brightly for a moment, then slowly, one by one, disappeared.

Chapter One

"Just what is this supposed to mean, Mac?"

Kendra O'Brien slammed the sheet of paper faceup on the startled newspaper editor's desk. Arthur Mackenzie recovered quickly, however, and glared back at the woman standing in front of him, hands on her hips, blue eyes flashing. He met the fire in her gaze with a flame of equal proportion.

"You want to walk out that door and come back in like a civilized human being?" The gray-haired man folded his arms resolutely across his chest. "Then maybe we'll talk."

"Damn right we'll talk!" Kendra pushed her long auburn braid of hair back behind her shoulder, resolving to get the unruly mane chopped off to her ears at the first opportunity. Things had been getting a little out of control lately, beginning with the problem she'd had during her last story, and ending with Mac's little surprise that morning. It was time to take charge of her life again, something she'd become very good at in the last three years.

"What—is—this?" She demanded, punctuating each word emphatically.

Arthur Mackenzie, editor of the *New York Chronicle*, gave the crumpled paper a cursory glance. He stood and crossed casually to the entrance of his glassed-in office and closed the door, effectively shutting out the sounds of the clattering newsroom beyond. He returned just as casually and took his place behind his desk, leaning back in his chair and lacing his hands behind his head. "I believe it's a notice of your promotion to editor of our latest new venture. Congratulations."

"Promotion? New venture? Mac, I'm warning you, I'm not going to stand for this!" Her rush of words tumbled over each other and Kendra caught herself, counting to ten. Mac didn't like it when she got this way, and it could only make matters worse.

Her Uncle Mac had written the book on stubborn, but as his best reporter, who happened to be his favorite niece, Kendra could get away with matching his obstinance glare for glare. This time she sensed things were different. In fact, as she gazed into the steady eyes that presently resembled circles of steel, Kendra knew she was treading on shaky ground.

He stood slowly, his bushy eyebrows colliding over his pear-shaped nose. Mac was a large bear of a man, six feet tall and twenty pounds overweight, and suddenly he seemed to fill the room.

"Do you have a problem with being promoted, O'Brien?"

Swallowing the hesitancy she always felt when confronted with an angry Mac, Kendra's blue eyes flared to life as her own temper rose to the occasion.

"You know I do!" She pointed to the paper on his desk. "This says that I'm supposed to go to England and investigate one of those phony baloney crop circles. C'mon, Mac, this is *National Enquirer*, 'I Was Stolen by a UFO' tripe, for Pete's sake!"

"And people love it. Besides, I think you've oversimplified the situation. If you'll look at the information I gave you, you'll see that this isn't just another crop circle." He leaned forward slightly. "A man has disappeared—not your typical UFO groupie either."

"So what?"

"Well, I thought you would particularly be interested in the story because the man happens to be Ian McKay."

Kendra's anger faltered for a moment. "Professor McKay? He's missing?"

"He was in Wiltshire, testing a theory he has about the formation of crop circles and after this last one formed . . ." Mac shrugged ". . . well, he hasn't been seen since. Something strange is going on over there, O'Brien, and every major paper

16

has someone covering it. The Chronicle isn't going to be left behind."

Kendra hesitated, then lifted her chin, the fire returning to her eyes. "Don't think you can play on my sympathies about Professor McKay. Just because I took one physics class from him doesn't make me his keeper. Send Esteban—he loves this kind of garbage."

"I'm sending you. Listen, brat, the paper isn't doing so well right now financially and we're counting on this new tabloid to perk up circulation."

"So perk it up—but not with me."

"Don't fight me on this, Kendra. You're the new editor and my decision is final." He picked up a sheaf of papers from his desk and began absently sorting through them as he talked. "*Galaxy* will cover stories about celebrities, lifestyle/features, and the unusual, things like this crop circle occurrence."

Kendra stared at him in disbelief. "I can't believe you'd do this to me," she said. "I can't believe that you'd put me in charge of a new national "I-Had-Elvis's-Alien-Baby" rag-sheet!"

Mac's gaze was even. "Believe it."

Kendra lifted her chin in challenge. "And what if I say no?"

His eyelids flickered briefly but his expression didn't change. "Then you're fired."

Kendra gasped. He couldn't mean it. This was just another one of Mac's ploys to get her to slow down, to take some time off. She took a deep breath and forced herself to speak in a more civil tone.

"Look, I am all set to catch my flight to China to cover that student riot. I promise when I get back, I'll take some time off like you've been nagging me to do, okay, Mac?" Her shoulders relaxed and she laughed. "You've made your point." She pulled up the only other chair in the cluttered office and sat down, running one hand down the side of her jeans. "But I owe you for scaring me half to death. You'll be telling this one around the office for days."

"I mean it, Kendra."

Kendra stared at him, the amusement fading from her face.

"You're serious about this." Shaking her head in astonishment, she leaned toward him, her voice tense. "Mac, the word around is that I may be nominated for an award for my story on Northern Ireland, maybe even the Pulitzer. Do you know what that could mean for the paper?" Her face was flushed, her square jaw locked with determination. "Last year I was recognized for my work in Russia and—"

Mac cut her off abruptly, slamming both hands down on his desktop, his voice level rising to match her own.

"And a year before that, you did a bang-up job on the mess in the Middle East. I'm your editor and the closest thing to a father you've got, Kendra, so don't start waving your resume in my face—I taught you every damned thing you know!"

"Then why are you sending me on this cock-and-bull story when I could be covering real news?" she shouted back, standing to meet him nose to nose.

"Because you have a death wish!"

Kendra felt the muscles in her back tighten.

"Just what is that supposed to mean?"

Mac moved to the window, hands clasped behind his back. He sighed, then ran one hand through his generous shock of white-gray hair.

"Sit down."

For once Kendra didn't argue. She sat, wondering why she suddenly found it so hard to meet her editor's eyes.

"I don't want to hear this, Mac," she said, twisting her fingers together in her lap.

"I don't give a damn whether you want to hear it or not. For once you're going to listen to me."

Her head jerked up. "I'm not going to listen to more of your armchair psychology."

"Yes, you are." He turned, his gaze pinning her to the chair like a butterfly to poster board. "I told you on your last assignment that if you took any more unnecessary risks I was going to pull you off the international beat."

"I didn't—"

"You did. You're just lucky that you didn't end up getting shot again."

"It wasn't that big of a deal."

"My God, woman, you were held hostage by the IRA for two weeks!" He held up one hand to stop her protest. "I think that's a big deal. And it was totally ridiculous. There was no reason in the world for you to place yourself in that position."

"I thought there was, or I wouldn't have done it, Mac."

He shook his head and paced away from her. "You always think there's a reason to risk your life. You take more risks than anyone else in the business!" He whirled. "Did you know that they call you Crazy O'Brien?"

Kendra flushed. She'd heard about the nickname and laughed it off. Now, however, hearing Mac say it aloud made her feel childish and unprofessional.

"And why do you take these risks?" Mac was still talking, his voice becoming more forceful as he circled around the desk toward her, one index finger stabbing the air for emphasis. "Because you still haven't gotten over James and Nicole's deaths, and deep down, you want to get yourself killed so you won't have to deal with living without them." He paused, and when she didn't respond, he shook his head and sighed. "You've got to get over it, deal with it somehow."

Kendra stood and turned away from him, her arms folded tightly across her chest. She stared out at the almost empty newsroom through the glass walls of his office. A throbbing pain began in her left temple.

"Tell me something, Mac," she said as her fingers bit into her upper arms. "How do you 'get over' losing your husband and baby?" She whirled to face him, her eyes narrowed and hard. "Does it just happen one day? Do you wake up and decide, 'Oh, I think I'll get over this today'? Tell me, Mac, how do you get over it?"

"You begin by getting on with your life," he said softly, looking away from her piercing gaze.

Kendra sighed and spread her arms in exasperation. "Isn't that exactly what I've done?"

"How? By becoming one of the *Chronicle*'s best reporters?" He shook his head. "You haven't gotten on with your life through your work. You're using your work to run away from life—and toward your own death!" He paused, letting his words sink in. "Have you taken a look in the mirror lately?

You've got circles under your eyes, you're pale, your clothes hang on you—''

''Are you speaking as my editor, Mac, or my fashion critic?'' she asked drily.

He shook his head. ''Make all the jokes you like. I'm not going to continue to be a party to your experiments in attempted suicide! I—''

A sharp knock at the door interrupted his speech. ''What is it?'' he shouted.

The door opened and an older woman with salt-and-pepper gray hair and a tight, harried look on her face stuck her head in the door.

''Excuse me, Mr. Mackenzie, but I was wondering if there was anything more I could do for you or Kendra before I leave.''

Mac glanced at his watch. ''There is one thing I needed mailed, Olivia,'' he said, moving toward the door. ''Let me get it from the other office.'' He pointed his finger at Kendra, his expression stern. ''I'll be right back, O'Brien. Stick around.''

The door shut behind him and Kendra sagged back against the scruffy chair. She cradled her head in her hands as her anger drained away into a familiar heaviness. Mac was all the family she had left. After her father's death when she was eighteen, his brother, Mac, had offered her a job on the *Chronicle*. By the time she was twenty-two he'd put her through college and taught her everything there was to know about the newspaper business.

When her mother died, not long after that, Mac had been there to grieve with her and help her make arrangements. The next spring, he had walked down the aisle at her side and given Kendra Miller away in marriage to James O'Brien. A year later he attended the christening of Nicole Mackenzie O'Brien, Kendra and James's precious baby, and his new great-niece and namesake.

Kendra closed her eyes, wishing she could shut out the memories as well. Tears pressed with a terrible heat against her eyelids, but she ignored them, even when they slipped down her face and burned salty across her lips.

Two years after her daughter's birth, Mac had helped Kendra plan two more funerals. Standing before the caskets that held her husband and daughter, she had buried her face against her uncle's broad chest and screamed with impotent rage. She had been working late. Mac had offered to run her home, but James wanted to take her and Nicole out to dinner. She had been waiting for them to pick her up when the call came from the hospital.

A drunk driver had smashed into her family head-on and the occupants of both cars had been killed instantly. Kendra's life suddenly broke into shattered fragments—fragments that could never be put back together again.

She knew that over the next few months Mac had felt as helpless in the face of her overwhelming grief as she did. She couldn't eat, couldn't sleep, couldn't work—until the day she picked up a rival newspaper and saw that a senator, arrested for drunken driving, was suspected to have Mafia ties. That was when her life had irrevocably changed.

Storming into Mac's office she had demanded he back her in an investigative attempt to prove the story's allegations. Mac had refused. She'd covered the story anyway, uncovered the truth, almost gotten herself killed, and won the respect not only of her editor, but of the publishing world at large.

After that she had requested every dangerous, exciting assignment that came across Mac's desk, and he'd granted most of them to her. Her obsessive passion for her job hadn't waned in three years. It had given her a way to go on, a reason to live.

And now he was telling her she really wanted to die.

Well, do you? she thought. Kendra's innate honesty compelled her to consider the question. It was true she sometimes took incredible risks. Could it be Mac was right? Was her bravado simply a subconscious way to end her life and join her husband and baby?

No! Angrily she pushed the ugliness of Mac's accusation away. Mac was an old man, almost seventy, locked into old ways. She was a woman, and his niece, and those two factors were enough reason for him to decide her job was too dangerous. He'd been tolerant while he thought she needed the

Tess Mallory

change in order to get on with her life, but lately he had begun acting like an overprotective maiden aunt. There were no dark, psychological secrets lurking in her closet. She simply loved her job, that was all. It had given new meaning to her life. And now Mac was asking her to give up that new meaning— as if he had the right.

A cold realization settled suddenly in the pit of Kendra's stomach. She opened her eyes and felt the moisture flooding her cheeks. If Arthur Mackenzie didn't have the right to ask something of her, then no one did.

The door opened and she dashed the tears from her face. As Mac crossed to his desk, Kendra noticed for the first time that he hadn't shaved that day. It gave him a tired, haggard look, and she felt a swift stab of guilt as he sat down at his desk and started shuffling through one of the many piles of paper stacked there.

"Look, Mac," she said quickly, "I appreciate your concern, but just because I've investigated some dangerous stories, doesn't mean I have a death wish."

He looked up, one gray brow raised knowingly. "Doesn't it? Not long after James died you insisted on investigating that senator and almost got yourself blown up when a bomb went off in your car!"

"But I wasn't in the car," Kendra reminded him firmly, "because my contacts warned me. I'm a good reporter, Mac, and you know it."

"Being a good reporter didn't protect you when you were shot in Iraq," he said. "You were lucky you know, you could have died."

"It was a flesh wound!" she retorted. "Besides, if I remember correctly, you're the man who assigned me to most of these so-called dangerous stories."

"Yes, I did, and if you'd handled them correctly I wouldn't be making this speech." His hand tightened on one of the papers he held and he shook it at her. "You are a damn good investigative reporter, Kendra, but you're reckless. That kind of recklessness has no place on my paper. It could cost you not only your life, but someone else's."

"But, Mac—"

22

"I've tried very hard not to let our personal relationship interfere with your career. I needed your passion for this area of newspaper writing and I also felt that you needed it at the time. But I've realized that I'm not helping you. I'm hurting you by allowing you to keep running away from reality."

"Reality!" Kendra bolted out of her seat. "I've seen more reality than most people could ever bear!"

"Which is exactly my point. You're numb, O'Brien. You're running on empty. When is the last time you felt anything, besides grief or anger?"

Kendra spun away from him. It was true, working on stories often under traumatic circumstances had caused her to harden that part of herself that could still feel, still hurt. She liked to think she had her emotions under control, packed into a neat little bundle that she could set aside at will. Before she had seen it as an asset to her profession, like a doctor's objectivity. Mac's accusation threatened her defenses.

"I want you to live, Kendra, not blindly rush toward destruction. I want you to date, get married again, have more children—"

"That's enough, Mac!" Kendra searched frantically inside herself to find her cool, controlled self, the self that was able to keep the walls up that prevented anyone from ever touching her unbearable pain. She was losing her protection, and feeling a slight panic, she turned and strode to the door, shoulders stiff with anger and determination.

"Kendra . . ."

The tenderness in Mac's voice stopped her. She didn't look back at him as he began to talk, the crusty newspaper editor suddenly becoming simply her uncle.

"Look, sweetheart," he said, moving to stand behind her, "you're like a daughter to me. Can't you understand? I don't want to lose you."

Kendra turned, feeling her resistance ebb away as she searched his face. When had the 'worry' line between his brows gotten so deep? When had his gray hair grown so white? When had the laughing eyes filled with such pain?

Closing her own eyes, Kendra leaned her head against his shoulder and felt his strong arms wrap around her in a familiar, comforting gesture. Summoning the last ounce of strength she possessed at that moment, she pushed down the emotions about to flood over her, and pushed herself away from her uncle at the same time.

"All right," she said, folding her arms across her chest and moving to stare out the window. "All right, Mac. I'll write your Elvis and the UFO stories for six months—no longer." She glanced back and saw him beaming at her. She couldn't help but smile back at the sight of his obvious relief. "But, there have to be two conditions."

His smile faded and his gray brows collided. "What conditions?" he asked warily.

Kendra sighed and turned away from the window, squaring her shoulders. "You don't tell anyone about this—not yet, at least." He started to speak but she held up her hand. "*And* I have complete editorial control."

Mac ran one hand over his rough face as if in solemn consideration, then nodded. "You drive a hard bargain, but you've got a deal."

Kendra's lips curved up and her eyes flashed with challenge. "You may live to regret this, Mac, I hope you realize that."

The older man shook his head, his gray eyes steady. "Just as long as you keep living, O'Brien, I won't regret a thing. Now . . ." He quickly crossed the room and handed her an envelope. "Here's your airline ticket, plus travel expenses. Call me and let me know what the situation is once you get there." He hugged her tightly and in spite of herself, Kendra found she was hugging him back.

"The situation?" She laughed harshly, tossing back her braid as she gazed up at him. "What else can it be but another stupid trick being perpetrated against mindless idiots who read drivel on supermarket racks? I'll write you a story, Mac, but trust me, it won't be what you expect!"

"It never is, O'Brien," he said with a chuckle. "It never is."

Chapter Two

Kendra shifted in her uncomfortable squatting position and eased the strap of the camera case away from the back of her neck, hoping desperately that the large, neolithic rock she was hiding behind wouldn't decide to come crashing down on top of her.

She had arrived in England only twenty-four hours after her talk with her uncle, eager to get to work on her assignment and be done with it. True to her disciplined nature where her job was concerned, Kendra had gathered all the information on crop circles she could find in the short time given her before leaving New York, and had read it all on the plane on her trip over the Atlantic. Expecting to be bored, she had been amazed at how interesting the subject really was.

She learned that in the late nineteen-seventies and early eighties, huge circles of flattened wheat and barley, the stalks pressed down in a curious swirling pattern, began to appear in fields in southern England. And no one had ever seen what caused the circles. A field could be completely untouched one evening, and the next morning sport two, three or even four circles.

By 1987, so many circles had appeared, many of them in elaborate geometric designs, that the name pictograms was given to them. Researchers had flooded the areas where the circles usually appeared, and for years had tried to capture the making of a circle on film, to no avail. Also fascinating were the reports of popping sounds, coupled with sightings of UFOs and flashing blue lights that often danced above or within the circles.

Reading further, Kendra found that many theories had been espoused in connection with what came to be known as the "circles effect." She dismissed the UFO-type theories, but found herself intrigued by one scientist who believed the circles to be caused by whirlwinds. When she stumbled across an article by none other than Ian McKay, she read with rapt concentration his premise that the phenomenon was caused by magnetic waves that he believed were capable of disrupting the time-space continuum. It was a fascinating article and made a sort of sense, at least to anyone who had studied with this brilliant teacher, as she had.

She still believed the circles were the work of men—and not little green men from Mars, either—and more recent research would seem to back her up. There had even been a contest to see if the circles could be duplicated. The results had been highly debated and varied conclusions reached. But Professor McKay's theory was very interesting to say the least, and she was intrigued that he had disappeared at the same time the crop circle appeared.

Perhaps Professor McKay had been kidnapped, she reasoned, although why was a mystery. He wasn't that well known, or rich, or as controversial as some. One thing was certain—at least in Kendra's mind—the crop circle had absolutely nothing to do with his disappearance. How could it? There was a logical reason for his disappearance and as soon as she did her bit to satisfy the crazies that liked this sort of goop, she was going to find the real story.

After a leisurely bath and a good night's sleep in a good London hotel, Kendra felt prepared to investigate the newest of England's famed mysterious circles. She arose early, hired a car, and drove straight to the site of the latest sensation.

When Kendra reached the field, near the ancient Avebury monuments in Wiltshire, she'd discovered that reporters had been banned from examining the circle close up. Too many people tramping around would apparently destroy the find. TV cameramen, photographers, reporters—all sat outside the fenced-off area grumbling their discontent. But Kendra hadn't made a name for herself in reporting by taking no for an answer. Now from her cramped position, she glanced over at Sean Taylor.

She'd met the wiry, small-for-his-age, fifteen-year-old in the crush of people outside the fence. The boy sported a wild hairstyle that left half of his head shaved and the other half with hair to his shoulder. His clothing was a trifle ragged and only slightly outlandish. Tight-fitting jeans with holes in the knees covered black boots. A plaid shirt hung down to his thighs, and a black leather jacket studded with metal completed the picture.

His cockney accent added to his overall charm, that and the fact that he continually called her "love." His appearance was nothing compared to characters she'd met in New York, and yet nevertheless, Kendra's caution radar had gone on alert as the boy pulled her away from the teeming crowd of spectators.

"Wanna see the thing close up, love?" he had whispered into her ear. "For five pounds I kin take you right up to the bloomin' thing's elbow."

Sure that circles didn't have elbows, but somehow charmed by the boy's eagerness, she'd nodded agreement then followed him on a thirty-minute trek that had led distinctly away from the crowd of onlookers at the site.

When they had entered a dense forest glade, Kendra had begun to grow a little uneasy at being in such an isolated spot with this curious guide, but a few minutes later they had broken free of the trees and were on the other side of the conglomeration of photographers and reporters. Sean had led her to a large, strange-looking rock and they were now hunkered down behind it, waiting. For what, Kendra wasn't certain.

"Great view from here, eh love?" the boy asked in his thick brogue, smiling eagerly at her. "In just a few short steps ya could practically be inside the circle yerself."

She smiled at his exaggeration. They were a good twenty feet away from the circle. "Thank you, Sean, I should be able to get some great pictures from up here—if anything happens."

"Cor, something's gonna happen," he said. "Ya can feel it in the air, can't ya, love?"

Kendra didn't answer. The truth was, she could feel something in the air—a heaviness, coupled with an awareness she could only describe as electric.

She glanced up at the sky. It was late June, but the day was overcast, cloudy, cool, and gray. She'd worn comfortable clothing: a long colorful tunic with black, blue and teal designs over tight black leggings and ankle-high boots. She'd brought her favorite denim jacket in case the weather turned cooler. Kendra squinted up at the sky again. More likely she would need the raincoat folded at her feet.

"It's a grand day, ain't it?"

Kendra looked over at Sean and quickly slipped the lens cap off the camera around her neck. The young man sat gazing at the circle, his thin face ruddy with the wind, looking delightfully English and at the same time, like something out of a heavy metal rock video.

"Pictures!" He chirped as he heard the click and spun around. His blue eyes were round with excitement. "Kin I 'ave one to take to me ma? Please?"

"Well, these have to be developed, but—hang on a minute." Kendra rummaged in the pack at her side until she found her camera that produced instant pictures. She took several shots of the boy and a few minutes later smiled as he beamed down at the photographs in his hands. Again she was amazed at the contradiction in the lad, so innocent, yet with a streetwise assurance.

"Thanks, love. I hope you see something tonight. I seen all kind of strange things out 'ere."

"Here? In this field?"

He nodded. "Me ma told me this be a place where the old 'uns used to do their magic—back ages ago."

Kendra cocked a doubtful eyebrow at him. "Oh, come now, Sean, surely you don't believe in that sort of thing?"

The boy flushed. "It sounds daft to someone like you, but you ain't seen the things I seen 'ere. No need ta worry though, I'll protect you."

"You will, eh?" Kendra said, unable to stop the amused smile from spreading across her face. "And how do you propose to do that?"

"With this." The boy reached inside his jacket and to her astonishment pulled out a Smith and Wesson .357 Magnum.

"What in the—" she burst out, then recovered quickly. She had to figure out some way to get the gun away from the boy without alienating him. It was silly, but she liked the kid and hated to injure his apparently newly budding masculine ego. "Wow. That's pretty amazing. Where'd you get something like that in England?"

"My brother," Sean said, smoothing his hand lovingly over the barrel of the weapon then sighted down the length of it, his finger causally resting on the trigger. Kendra shifted nervously beside him. " 'E lives in London 'e does," Sean went on. " 'As a sort of business there where 'e acquires stuff like this, if ya know what I mean." He winked at her and Kendra summoned a knowing laugh, though her brows puckered worriedly together.

"What are you doing with it?" she asked. "I mean, isn't it kind of dangerous to carry it around? If you were stopped by the police—"

"Aw, I ain't scared of the police," he scoffed, straightening his shoulders proudly. "My brother taught me how to get around them boys."

"I see," Kendra said thoughtfully. "You know, Sean, I'm very glad you brought this along because I wasn't able to bring the gun I usually carry on assignments and I feel very unprotected. Do you suppose you might lend it to me until I leave England? I could even pay you a rental fee."

Sean's face dropped at her words until he heard the words "pay" and "rental." "Cor, love, o' course you can. I trust you."

He turned the gun toward her and Kendra hastily reached out and took the weapon from him, pointing it toward the ground. He grinned at her and she tried to return the gesture but found her response shaky at best.

"Thanks," she said, shoving the gun into the satchel bag she carried. "I promise I'll return it to you at the end of the week." *After I have a little talk with your parents*, she told herself grimly.

"Just keep it handy, love. No tellin' what may happen here tonight."

Kendra nodded absently, then peered around the large stone again. It was centered at the top of a small rise, and from her vantage point she could see the entire circle. The circle was about sixty yards in diameter, with a wonderful swirling pattern that began at the center, flowing out with perfect symmetry to the tall growth at the edges.

From her research she knew that this was a very large circle, perhaps the largest ever discovered. She itched to get a closer look and find something to expose it as a man-made hoax. Once it was completely dark, she intended to sneak down and take some close-up shots with her new camera, then sit there and wait out the night.

She turned the camera over, admiring it for a moment. It had been a long ago gift from Mac. Kendra smiled and ran her fingers across the metal plate on the back that had her name engraved on it for identification. It wouldn't be long before she'd be back on the international beat. Of that, she was certain. In the meantime, she'd do her best. Maybe she could write an exposé called, "I Spent the Night in a Crop Circle."

Kendra lifted the camera and peered through the lens. One way or another she was determined to wring an exceptional story out of this assignment, preferably by finding Professor McKay. It wasn't Pulitzer material, but she had to admit, begrudgingly, she was enjoying herself. For the first time in a long time, she felt relaxed, except for the tension of anticipation, of course. If she ever lost that, she'd give up journalism forever. She shifted position to sit on her knees and glanced up at the overcast sky. Almost dark enough. She lowered the camera, then picked up the instant camera and slid its strap around her neck too, before settling back to wait.

She guessed she'd dozed off, for how long she wasn't sure, but suddenly a tremendous roar in her ears shook her awake. Instantly alert, Kendra sprang to her feet and saw the sun had completely disappeared and all the other reporters and media people were gone. The wind swept across the field with a sudden intensity, sending a cold chill down her spine as a fine rain began to mist and the clouds above her head rolled like angry combatants on a churning sea.

She reached beside her for the raincoat she'd brought along.

"Here, Sean," Kendra said over the rising sound of the wind, "put this over you."

"Cor, not unless you gets under it too."

Seeing the sense of his generous offer, she huddled beneath the disposable plastic coat she'd bought at the airport, shivering with the boy whose eyes had grown large and round.

"You aren't scared, are you, Sean?" Kendra asked, trying to keep the tone of amusement out of her voice.

"Me?" He shook his head. " 'Course not." The next crack of thunder made him jump and he glanced at her sheepishly. "I ain't scared," he said again, more forcefully.

She laughed. "Well, I am," she lied. Actually Kendra felt exhilarated, buoyed up, the way she always did when in the midst of covering an exciting or dangerous story. Her pulse quickened as she looked up again. The moon had risen, full and bright, but now, cloaked in the mist of rain, it seemed mystical and surreal.

"If we can just hold out a little longer," she said into Sean's ear, "I think that—"

At that moment, lightning split the sky in half. The wind, howling like a wounded dog, kicked into high gear and churned the air, tearing across the open field, sending Kendra sprawling to her knees.

"Cor, love," Sean whispered, "here it comes."

Kendra wiped the back of her sleeve across her face. "H-here comes what?" she stammered, stumbling to her feet.

"Hold on to the rock!" the boy cried, his fingers biting into the stone.

Without questioning the order, Kendra flung herself against the huge outcropping and clung to it as a sudden, incredible force swept down upon her as though determined to sweep her away.

Seeing her distress, Sean inched his way around the rock toward her, until his young, wiry arm encircled her waist. She was grateful for the support, but worried about his own precarious hold.

"I've never seen weather like this in England!" she shouted, trying to be heard above the tumult.

"I've seen it here, lots of times!" he shouted back.

Deciding to save her strength to hang onto the rock, Kendra pressed herself more solidly against the hard surface, when everything went suddenly still. As abruptly as the wind and rain had begun, the turmoil ceased.

Kendra released her death grip on the stone and took an unsteady step from behind it. "Wow. Are you all right?" He nodded. "C'mon, let's see if the circle's been damaged by the wind."

"I don't know if that's such a good idea."

Kendra laughed. "Oh, don't be silly, Sean. This is an adventure." She started walking down the incline and then stopped and glanced back at him. He stood fidgeting a moment, then bolted.

"I'm sorry, miss, but I think I hear me mum callin' me!" he shouted as he tore down the incline, across the adjoining field and down the road. Kendra stared after him openmouthed. She burst out laughing and it took a good minute to bring herself under control.

"Tough guy, huh?" she taunted aloud. "Well, at least I have the gun and if I run into any unfriendly aliens I'll be well armed. Thanks Sean, for the tour."

With a sigh Kendra hefted her bag onto her shoulder. Reaching inside, she took out a small flashlight and turned it on. She headed down the incline, looking for one of the tramlines left by the farmer who had planted the field. If she walked down its path she wouldn't disturb the overall picture of the circle. Trudging along, wishing she'd worn heavier boots, Kendra found the tramline and was soon striding resolutely through the waist-high barley, toward the infamous circle. A crackling sound behind her made her draw up short and whirl around.

"Sean?" She smiled into the misty haze now settling over the field. Maybe the boy had regained his nerve. "Is that you?"

Silence answered her, along with a sudden surge of wind that briefly lifted the wisps of hair escaping from her long braid and used them to tickle her face. Kendra pushed the hair away from her eyes, and giving one last searching glance behind her, headed toward the circle again.

As she got closer to the patch of pressed-down grain, Kendra began to feel a little light-headed and she paused, fighting the sense of vertigo. Shaking her head to dispel the dizziness, she moved forward, but found that with each step she took, her body seemed to grow heavier, her steps slower. She heard a crackle behind her. Laughing nervously, Kendra shot a cautious glance back over one shoulder.

"Sean, it's all right that you were scared. But you've got to feel this. I think I've discovered one of your 'strange happenings.' " Her heart beat a little faster as her gaze swept the smoky semidarkness. Was it Sean playing a practical joke on her? She liked the boy and found it hard to believe he would trick her this way unless—she turned around thoughtfully—unless the whole thing had been some kind of set-up.

Holding herself perfectly still, Kendra took a deep breath and waited. A misty breeze curled around her face and in her nervous state of mind, Kendra imagined ethereal fingers touching her. She swallowed hard, then began to scold herself aloud.

"Don't be absurd," she said brightly, breaking out of her statuesque pose and moving laboriously toward the circle. One more step, and then another, and she was at the edge of the circle. "This is nothing compared to—"

This time the sound came from in front of her. A popping sound, like a lightbulb being thrown on cement, Kendra thought. She took a step backward and her flashlight went dead.

"No . . ." she whispered into the blackness as a mélange of blue lights appeared in the center of the circle. They moved upward, hovered for a moment, then moved twenty or so yards to the left of the crop circle and began to spin.

She stood frozen for a moment before the reporter inside took control and propelled her into action.

A crop circle forming! No one on earth had ever photographed a crop circle as it formed. Maybe Mac was sharper than she gave him credit for and this story might be worth something after all!

Kendra hurried across the field, her satchel bouncing against her bag as she shed her instant camera and shoved it into the zippered opening. Careful to stay within the tramlines, she stopped about thirty feet away from the lights, where she lifted her camera toward the shimmering blue orbs above.

"Wow," she breathed, unaware she'd spoken. Unconsciously she lowered the camera as blue lights danced in a silent choreography. It was the most beautiful, mesmerizing sight Kendra had ever seen. She stood, mouth open, like one paralyzed, as the incandescence swirled above the ripe grain. Shaking herself out of her reverie, she lifted the camera again and pointed it at the phenomenon, when all at once she felt something tug her forward sharply until she was sprawled five feet closer to the forming circle.

She gasped and felt it again, but this time it was a steady force not unlike the wind a few moments before, propelling her forward.

Except there was no wind.

Magnetic was the only adjective Kendra could lend to the sensation in her mind, coupled with a feeling similar to static electricity, only multiplied a thousand times over. The hair on her arms and the back of her neck, on the edges of her already unruly hair, were all standing on end. Wide-eyed, her camera dangling from its strap, she allowed herself to be drawn beneath the dazzling array of light.

Awestruck and immobile, Kendra watched the azure lights descend and begin their whirling dance anew, this time around her. Entranced, she lifted one hand to touch the lights, but they danced away from her. Without warning, lightning cracked the sky again and Kendra cried out as the gentle tornado around her suddenly became a roaring cyclone.

The blue lights deserted her as the storm tore at her clothing. Kendra dropped to her hands and knees, bowing her head to the ground. Her fingers touched smooth stalks of vegetation, spiraling out from the center core of the forming circle. Almost unconsciously she traced them, clung to them as the tumult cried out in terrible cacophony above her.

I'm going to die, she thought. Suddenly she knew that everything Mac had said was true. She had rushed, headlong to this moment in time, and now that it was here—she did not want it.

Struggling to her feet, Kendra stood, unconsciously lifting her arms as if to plead with the forces sending tingling rushes of light into her innermost being.

I don't want to die! She tried to shout the words, but couldn't.

As if in answer to her silent plea, the blue lights descended once again, encompassing her within their whirling vortex. Kendra threw back her head and cried out as the sensation of icy water being pumped through her veins flooded over her. Closing her eyes she felt an incredible torrent of crystal-clear understanding course through her mind and body, and in that instant, Kendra knew all, felt all, was all.

She tried to take a deep breath and couldn't. The pounding of her heart ceased. Kendra opened her eyes and knew she was dying as suddenly the wind rushed down again, sucking her into its maelstrom. The power wove itself around her and she felt consciousness going along with her ability to see and hear. Kendra managed one last breath, one last glance upward before the darkness came upon her, twisting her down into the circle as the twinkling blue lights slowly disappeared, one by one.

Chapter Three

Navarre de Galliard pulled back on the reins, knees pressed firmly against the heaving sides of his horse, his gaze wary behind the slits of the flat topped helm he wore. His chain mail, combined with the leather hauberk covering it, was bulky and heavy. He was grateful for the warmth on this cold February day, but wished fervently he had not worn the armor. While it would protect him against whatever danger might lie in wait for him, he did not expect an army to be assembled on the Abury plain, and he cursed himself for riding into trouble laden down with unnecessary weight, and a vision-obscuring helmet.

With an oath, Navarre removed the metal helm, running one hand through the long hair plastered hotly against his face. His tunic, golden with the emblem of a black lion in the center of it, was sleeveless and split down both sides, covering his mail and hauberk. His eyes, the same color as the tunic he wore, gazed around again, this time unimpeded by the clumsy battle gear.

He'd come dressed for war, but the English countryside seemed quiet and peaceful as he observed it from his vantage point. Under the full moon's light the frost glistened on the field, lending the stubble of grain that once grew there a fanciful appearance. Mostly rolling farmland, Wiltshire stretched in frozen waves to the horizon in either direction. Here and there a grove of oak or ash trees dotted the fields. In the summer, it was a rolling checkerboard of wheat and barley waving in the gentle breeze. Right now, however, it lay cold and silent.

Navarre drew in a deep breath and forced himself to expel it slowly. He had ridden hard from Nottingham. The diversion to keep Locksley busy and away from Abury had taken several days longer than he'd planned, but at last he had diverted the outlaw and arrived at the ancient site on time, exactly one fortnight from the day he'd overheard Magda make her dire prophecy.

Now he waited at the edge of a woods near the largest of the mystical mounds. If anything were going to happen, if anyone—or anything—were going to come, he would see before being seen. Perhaps he had been foolish, coming alone, but taking a large contingent of men would have aroused curiosity, and Richard's spies were everywhere. Besides, with the sheriff away he could not leave Nottingham unprotected. Locksley would most surely seek to retaliate for the deeds that had kept him busy in Sherwood instead of here at Abury.

The moonlight created eerie shadows across the fields, and Navarre resisted the sudden urge to cross himself. He no longer believed in God or magic, but sometimes he had to remind himself of those fairly new revelations.

He'd had time on the road to think about Magda's words, and the more he thought, the more he believed his first inclinations were true, that he had overheard a coded message from one spy to another. By using the pretense of the woman relating a "prophecy," they could speak freely. Locksley could not be blamed for listening to a woman's mad ravings, could he? It was a very clever way to warn the outlaw that a plot against Richard's life had been discovered, and that an ally would meet him at Abury in a fortnight. Accordingly, Navarre had come well armed. When Locksley finally arrived, he'd find Richard's "salvation" had suffered an ill fate.

The hint of a smile lifted one corner of his lips. He had enjoyed harassing Locksley and his band of outlaws before leaving for Abury. As *custodis pacis*—keeper of the peace— Navarre had the authority to order the soldiers of the garrison to ride into Sherwood and capture as many of the infamous "Robin of the Hood's" forces as possible.

They hadn't captured any. Locksley's men were too quick, but it had been good sport. He'd left enough men guarding

Sherwood to keep Locksley trapped, but he had no doubts that when he returned the dungeon would be just as empty as it had been when he left. He sighed. Garrick was growing impatient with him. Old friend though he might be, the Sheriff of Nottingham wanted Robin Hood and he wanted him dead. He expected Navarre to take care of that little deed, just as he expected his friend to take care of Richard.

Navarre closed his eyes briefly, allowing his thoughts to flicker over the memory of a time when he and Richard and Locksley had been united, brothers in a holy quest. But that was long ago, and of no consequence now. He had made his choice, and they theirs.

His horse moved nervously beneath him and Navarre reached down to stroke the stallion's silky black neck.

"Easy, Kamir," he murmured softly, "what is it?" The stallion nickered and shook his coarse mane. "Aye," he agreed, shifting into a soldier's alertness, "I feel it too."

Just as the night outside Magda's hut the wind had seemed almost alive, this night the air around him felt heavy, almost tense. Suddenly it was as though a hundred invisible bumblebees were buzzing around him, within him, rippling beneath his skin like tiny, pulsating waves.

He glanced up through the leafy treetops at the sky. Overcast. A moment ago it had been clear. Kamir shifted again and whinnied, the sound harsh against the stillness.

"Quiet, my friend," Navarre whispered, replacing his helm and sliding his sword from its sheath in the saddle. He'd fought a Saracen with a saddle like that, in Outremer. The man had been able to draw his blade so quickly that Navarre had almost lost his head. When he'd returned to England he'd had a saddle made with the unique feature. If he wanted to live to fight Richard, he reasoned, he needed every possible advantage.

Kamir shook his head as if in protest to their vigil, but Navarre no longer noticed his horse's nervousness. A storm was brewing, a storm unlike any he'd ever seen before. A light fog had rolled in, and a fine rain with it, nothing unusual in that, but a brisk, oddly circular wind also began to churn around him, sending bits of frost and dirt into the air. Temporarily distracted by the swirl of frozen chaff, Navarre was unprepared when lightning split the sky and the resulting thunder sent Kamir's forelegs into the air, pawing frantically.

Navarre dropped his sword and just managed to keep his seat. After a moment's struggle, he brought the horse under control. Sliding off into the now wet earth beneath his feet, he picked up his sword.

"Two years in battle," he muttered fiercely, "two years of dodging arrows and blades and now you bolt because of a storm?" He patted the dark neck. "My friend, you must be growing old." Kamir shook his head and Navarre laughed in spite of himself. Then he stopped laughing and stared at the spectacle taking place in the field below.

The wind was gathering itself—that was the only way he could describe it—and settling into an area of the wheat field. Then a stillness settled over the plain and the real show began.

"Holy Mother of God," Navarre whispered. His hand moved to make the sign of the cross, something he hadn't done since Acre. Blue lights, like tiny stars, fifty or more, danced above the frozen field. Like a tiny, colorful whirlwind they swirled downward. As if in a trance, Navarre remounted his horse, then walked Kamir toward the lights, his eyes fixed on the luminous orbs spinning above the ground.

Kamir neighed a warning, but Navarre did not hear. As they grew closer to the circle, the bumblebees under the knight's skin grew frantic, until, in some distant, still coherent part of his brain, he thought his insides might be about to burst forth. Instead, he reached the dancing lights and looked up in time to see them descending toward him.

They hovered above Navarre, the bumblebees tearing at his stomach, his chest, his face, until he thought he would go mad. He tried to turn Kamir but to his horror, found he could not move. He was trapped, caught in the throes of some otherworldly power.

Arrogant fool, to come alone to this ancient, mystical place known for its mystery and power! Suddenly every story of magic and sorcery flooded his mind, as well as his own fall from grace. He had turned his back on the church—was God going to kill him now for his unbelief, allowing the forces of evil to consume him? As the blue lights came within inches of his face, Kamir threw his powerful front hooves into the air and let out a cry Navarre had never heard a horse make. The stallion's hooves came down and plowed into the earth, pulling them out of the enchanted circle. Navarre felt the strength of his horse beneath him, felt the effort it took for the animal to pull them free.

Instantly, the buzzing of the bumblebees shifted away from him. Navarre felt his breath leave him, and he crumpled forward against Kamir's mane. Navarre's own sweat assailed his nostrils as he pulled himself upright in the saddle, gasping as he tried to draw air back into his lungs. When he could breathe again, he cautiously opened his eyes.

The lights still twinkled nearby, and as Navarre watched, the blue orbs began to spin, faster and faster, until he had to look away from the blinding blur of light. When he looked back, they were gone, and on the ground lay a woman, dark red hair tumbling across a chalk-white face.

Kendra's brain had exploded. At least that was her first thought as she tried to open her eyes and could not for the searing pain behind them. Trying to calm herself, she concentrated on using her other senses. She could smell the dampness of the earth. It smelled like England. Funny, she thought dazedly, how places had their own particular smell. England smelled like rosemary: green, fresh. And cold. Why was it cold?

Kendra's fingers moved and she could no longer feel smooth, spiraling stalks of wheat beneath her. Instead, her fingers met with icy stubble and she blinked, trying to clear the confusion from her mind. She was conscious of an aching weariness permeating her bones, as well as the pounding pain inside her skull.

Don't think about that, she ordered herself, her reporter's instincts beginning to function. Get your eyes open. Find out what happened.

The storm. The last memory she had was of a terrible wind, followed by lightning and thunder and—the circle. Something had happened when she went inside the crop circle, but what? She couldn't remember.

Slowly, feeling as though twenty-pound weights were attached to her eyelids, Kendra managed to pull her eyes open. Her vision blurred and she could make out only hazy images of muted colors. It was still night, the moon was still full and bright. She couldn't have been unconscious for too long. With a groan she heaved herself to her knees, feeling dizzy and disoriented; she shivered as a cold wind blew across the field. The camera around her neck thumped heavily against her chest and she steadied it, wishing she could steady herself as easily.

The sound of a rapid pounding coming toward her brought Kendra's head back up, then she relaxed as she remembered her young companion.

"Sean?" she called, squinting to see the person approaching her. "Thank goodness you came back. You weren't kidding when you said strange things happen around here, were you?" Kendra stood, swaying, her knees threatening to buckle beneath her. "Did you see what happened? Was I struck by lightning or something? I can't see very well and—"

She looked up and her words trailed away.

Her sight was still blurred but it didn't take twenty-twenty vision to know that this wasn't Sean. This was a man—a big man—riding a horse, and the two of them towered over her like the ancient Minotaur. Kendra swallowed hard as the rider drew nearer. The man fit the horse as if he were part of it, and they both seemed exceptionally large. The man had big biceps and shoulders as broad as her outstretched arm. But the head—the head was what sent her heart suddenly into her throat. The head of this man was made of metal.

Kendra took an involuntary step backward. The man—thing—halted the horse and slid easily to the ground. He approached her confidently and to her astonishment, walked up to her and grabbed her by the wrist. The warm touch of his hand on hers reassured her that he was, indeed, flesh and blood. She screamed anyway.

"Let me go!" she cried, twisting away and lashing out with a well-aimed kick at the man's shin. She winced as her soft booted foot connected with something that felt like steel. Steel. Steel enclosed her wrist too, in spite of the warmth. She looked back up at the monstrous form, but still could only see a marred outline of his face—if it could be called a face. Thin slits instead of eyes, horrifying slats instead of a mouth. She shuddered, then gasped as the apparition reached up . . . and took off his head.

The scream she'd been preparing died in her throat as she found herself staring up into a very human face. Kendra narrowed her eyes and her vision cleared slightly. Before her stood a man with the most unusual golden-brown eyes she'd ever seen. A stark contrast to the black hair falling in waves to the man's shoulders, the effect was provocative and disturbing to her dormant feminine senses. She'd not looked at a man with anything other than mild interest since her husband's death.

Too tongue-tied for a moment to speak, Kendra continued to gaze at the man staring down at her. Dark brows frowned in a high arch above black-lashed eyes that in a woman would have been considered feminine. He was anything but. His face was square at the jawline, the nose aquiline, and the chin—stubborn, Kendra decided. His lips, firm and full, at the moment were pressed tightly together.

She pulled herself together and glanced at the metal object he held in his hands. It was supposed to be some kind of helmet. A welder's helmet maybe? Or—she shifted her gaze to his chest. It was covered with a loose, black shirt of some kind, with a giant gold emblem emblazoned on it. She squinted again. A lion? Beneath the tunic the man wore a blur of silver. His arms were silver too. Kendra reached out and touched his arm. Metal links. Chain mail. Armor.

Kendra took a step back. "I must have been hit harder than I thought."

He didn't speak but just kept staring down at her, still holding her wrist. She looked at his hand rather pointedly and lifted one brow. "Do you mind?"

He let go of her abruptly, but didn't speak. Kendra ran one hand through her disheveled hair, feeling a familiar signal course through her body: danger. Who was this man and why was he dressed like a knight from the days of old? She took a step back and suddenly remembered the gun in her bag. It certainly wouldn't hurt to have it in reach, now would it?

42

"Look," she said, backing a little farther away and keeping her distance from the man, "did you see a boy about fifteen years old around here? Small for his age?" She brushed her hair back from her face. Somehow it had come loose from its braid. The wind. She remembered the wind had gone crazy just before she lost consciousness.

Kendra looked away from the man and was frustrated by the continuing haze obscuring her vision. She turned, looking frantically for her bag, while trying to maintain a semicasual air. There it was, or at least what looked like it might be the soft satchel, a few yards away. She took a step toward it, her foot crunching down on ice, and suddenly, Kendra looked around and really saw, for the first time, her surroundings. She opened her mouth and shut it several times before the fear completely wrapped itself around her heart.

The Abury plain was like a sheet of crystal and looked nothing like it had before she passed out. Oh, it was still night, and the fields still as bright as noonday by the full moon's light, but there were no waving sheaves of grain rolling across the countryside. Instead, there was stubble covered with a thin sheen of ice. She shivered, from cold and from sudden fear.

The man didn't speak and she turned back to him, remembering dazedly that she had asked him a question. What was it? Sean. Yes, where was Sean?

"I said—" Kendra didn't finish her sentence. She looked up into golden eyes that trapped her where she stood. Long used to sensing danger, Kendra knew without a doubt she was staring it squarely in its well-chiseled face. All at once she realized the man was holding something in his other hand. She squinted down at it. A sword. And he was lifting it to her throat. Kendra swallowed hard, then turned and made a dash for her bag.

"Hold!" cried the man.

Kendra risked one astonished look over one shoulder. Did he really think she'd be crazy enough to stop? She caught the bag up in her hand and kept running, her breath coming more raggedly as she ran faster, legs pumping, head pounding as though it would shatter as she stumbled across the wheat stubble, the short, thick stems stabbing through her soft boots into

43

her feet. She could hear him mounting his big horse and turning it to race after her. Frantically she began looking for a tramline. On the tramlines—the empty furrows left unseeded by farmers in order to walk their fields without damaging the grain—there would be no stubble. Kendra ground to a sudden halt and stared around, bewildered.

There weren't any. But that was impossible. She remembered distinctly that all of the fields in Wiltshire had tramlines. She just couldn't see them, that was all. Her vision was too blurred. If she kept moving, she'd find one. The farmers left them at regular intervals. Ignoring the fact that not only were there no tramlines, but no wheat—the weather had suddenly turned from a cool English summer's day to freezing winter—Kendra started across the field again, stumbling over hidden clumps of dirt. Up ahead was a small woods. If she could reach it. . . : She stopped again. There were no woods near these fields. Copses of trees here and there, yes, but no real woods or forest.

"I said, hold, witch."

Kendra turned. The crazy knight was three feet away from her, back on his horse, this time brandishing his sword. It was funny, but he almost seemed to be afraid of her. Squaring her shoulders she composed her thoughts. She'd once talked a man out of jumping off a building, and another into releasing a hostage. This couldn't be too different, could it?

"Look," Kendra said, keeping her voice calm even as she slid the strap of her bag onto her shoulder and slipped one hand inside the satchel. "I don't know what your problem is, but calling me names isn't going to help. Now, just put down the sword and we'll try to work this out, okay?" As he hesitated, she tried a haughtier tone. "I'm an American citizen and if you dare hurt me you'll have the FBI and the CIA down on you faster than you can say—"

"Silence!" the man roared. Kendra's mouth snapped shut. Okay, so it was different. This man wasn't some criminal desperate to cut a deal—yet—or a man who seemed out of control. On the contrary, he seemed to be very much in control, both of himself and the situation. Her trembling fingers closed around the hidden pistol.

Navarre stared down at the woman standing in front of him, his sword hand shaking. A woman! When she had suddenly appeared in front of him, he'd thought he was going mad, seeing things—then she'd opened her eyes and he'd known she was real. She wasn't beautiful by his standards. Her face was too strong to be considered fair, with its square jaw and pointed chin, but her hair was incredible, long and thick, auburn and gold curls intermingling almost to her waist. It was the kind of hair a man wanted to bury his face in, to twine around his hands while making love to her. Her eyes, the color of the English sky, had been dazed when they opened, her long lashes wet with mist as she gazed up at him in sudden horror.

If she'd been a man he'd have killed her on the spot, had intended to do so at once. Richard's salvation. Was she a witch? A changeling? Her clothing was that of a page or a serf, and a masculine one at that. She wore a blue tunic with strange black patterns on it, black leggings, and soft, ankle-high black boots.

Her words, too, were spoken in the Saxon tongue, not Norman, so she likely was no one of consequence. Yet, she had an unusual box that looked quite costly hanging around her neck by leather straps. He'd shaken himself out of his stupor and grabbed her. When she shrank away from him, her eyes wide with fear, he'd realized it was his helm that frightened her.

She'd calmed as soon as he removed it and, still dumbstruck, he'd released her when she'd asked. He realized her vision was somehow impaired as she squinted at him, then listened in perplexity as she began to chatter in a nonsensical way, saying things that made little sense.

Was she trying to enchant him? Weaving some kind of spell with her strange, disjointed words? FBI? CIA? Navarre prided himself on not being a superstitious man, but the last few minutes had sent him plunging backward in his thinking. He could find no other explanation for the strange and mystical way the woman had appeared in front of him but magic. In spite of his past devotion to the church, he had never ceased to believe that forces he could not ken still worked in the world. This woman must be a witch and she must be silenced before she enchanted him. His sword at her throat had produced the desired effect. It had also sent her running as though facing all the demons in hell.

He'd thrown himself and Kamir after her. Richard's salvation must not escape to aid him. Now as he stood a few feet away from her he knew he should kill her and be done with it. He could take no chances. He . . .

A face, brown-eyed and gentle, swayed in front of him and Navarre clenched his eyes shut to dispel the illusion, but she was still there, behind his eyelids, pleading with him. Talam. He felt cold beads of sweat break out across his forehead and shook himself back to the present. Was this the witch's magic as well? Had the witch sent his dead love's face to his mind to stay his hand? He opened his eyes.

The woman walked toward him, one hand behind her back. He watched her warily. It wouldn't do to get too close. She had touched him before. Did her touch give her power over his mind?

Navarre was shaken. His mother had been an educated woman and he had been raised a good Catholic. However, as a boy he'd had a nurse who believed without question in fairies, elves, and other nonsensical beings. He'd believed in them too, as a child, until he'd grown up and away from such nonsense. Though there were many in the Crusades who had carried charms and talismans with them to ward off evil spirits, Richard had scorned such things as ridiculous. According to the king, a man needed only his faith in God to withstand any enemy. Except perhaps the enemy who calls himself friend, Navarre thought bitterly. He passed one hand over his face as the image of Talam danced once again in his mind. He had come home to England, turned his back on the new ways, come home to the old ways, and magic was one of the oldest ways of all.

"Stay away from me," the woman said, her voice low and cultured, though oddly inflected. "I don't want to have to hurt you."

He shook away the hesitancy and noticed that the woman had something in her hand. Something silver, made of metal, yet it wasn't a knife or dagger. What was it she had said? She didn't want to hurt him? He snorted to himself and resolutely moved Kamir a few paces toward her, his face set in grim lines.

"Don't come any closer," she warned, waving the small lump of metal in her hand.

"You will not escape me," Navarre said, pulling Kamir up short in front of her. Suddenly a sound unlike anything he had ever heard before—louder than thunder, deeper than the tumult of a raging waterfall—rang out between them. At the same time something struck his chain mail with the force of a mace's blow, and his upper arm began to burn in the deepest part of the muscle. He looked down to see blood pumping from his arm. Incredulous, he looked back at the woman and saw she had begun to run, glancing back over her shoulder, tears streaming down her face, the lump of metal clutched to her chest as she sped away from him.

Navarre swore roundly and wheeled Kamir to follow her. She was headed for the forest and once there, she would be easily lost. He didn't know what had happened but he knew he could not let "Richard's salvation" escape. Kamir pounded across the field as the woman tossed one frightened look after another back over her shoulder. Navarre had almost caught up with her when she reached the edge of the forest and disappeared into the dense foliage. Throwing himself off the back of his horse, the knight plunged after her, cursing Magda and all of her ancestors as the branches snatched at his hair and tore at his body. He needed to staunch the increasing flow of blood from his arm but could not take the time as he hurried after his quarry.

Fool, he thought silently. Be still and she will lead you to her.

Stopping in his tracks, Navarre listened and was not disappointed as the sound of another person crashing through the underbrush reached his ears. She was to the left of him, and if he remembered correctly there was a rather wide stream nearby. She would have to slow down, if only to cross it.

Quickening his pace, Navarre parted the forest, then paused and grinned as the sound of a woman cursing then screaming, followed by a terrific splash and more screaming, filled the forest. Navarre pushed through another yard of bracken and he had found her. The auburn-haired wench sat in water up to her waist, shivering with cold, the lump of metal on the bank of the stream, her face twisted with anger and fear.

"Cold, isn't it, milady?" the knight said, giving her a mocking bow. After a moment of enjoying her predicament, Navarre took pity on the woman and crossed to her side, extending his arm to her. "Here, let me—"

Before he could react, Navarre saw the woman hook her feet around his heels and jerk with all of her might. He fell backward into the stream as her laughter pealed out around him. Navarre shouted as he hit the icy water, his back thumping against a sharp rock, his ankle biting into an extended tree root. Cursing and groaning, he hauled himself quickly out of the freezing stream and unceremoniously jerked the woman to her feet, his fingers biting into her arm. She glared up at him, but as he reached down and picked up the lump of metal beside the stream and shook it in her face, her arrogance faded and her lips began to tremble.

"You are coming with me," he said, his voice little more than a growl. "And if you run again, I will kill you."

Kendra studied the man sitting across the fire from her and sipped water cautiously from the wooden bowl he had handed her moments before. The blanket he had given her after the stream episode was coarse and rough and kept slipping off of her bare shoulder. She felt more than a little disconcerted to be sitting naked, except for the blanket, facing her captor.

As soon as he had hauled her from the icy water, he had first dropped the gun into a bag that hung from his saddle, then without warning, collapsed. Kendra had hurried to his side, her heart pounding as she examined the bleeding hole in his arm, trying to gauge just where the bullet had entered and if it had exited or was lodged inside of him.

She hated guns, always had, but especially after the time she'd spent as a reporter in battle-weary lands, she hated them. Even now she could scarcely believe she had actually fired the pistol. She'd only intended to frighten the man into stopping, but she hadn't counted on him ignoring her command to halt. Pulling the trigger had been a reflex action, a survival action, and as the bullet exploded from the gun she was immediately sorry. Kendra had prodded the wound and found that the bullet had apparently struck the man in the upper part of his arm, then passed cleanly through the other side.

"Lie still," she had ordered, one hand on his chest. "You'll be all right, but I've got to find something to bind this with."

Kendra had gasped as the knight's hand closed around her wrist. Their eyes met for a long, breathless moment, then the knight reached inside the heavy leather tunic he wore and pulled out a kerchief. He handed it to her wordlessly, sweat pouring down his face, the skin around his lips white.

Quickly Kendra had tied the makeshift tourniquet around his upper arm, noting the strength in the bulging muscle there. She had no more than finished tying the knot than the crazy knight stumbled to his feet, picked her up and carried her— kicking and screaming—back to his horse. There he had mounted the huge, black stallion and balanced her in front of him, both of them dripping wet, one strong arm encircling her waist in a viselike grip, apparently none the worse for having been shot with a .357 Magnum and dumped into an icy stream.

After a while Kendra had given up fighting, realizing that all she was doing was wearing herself out against this magnificent hunk of a man who even a bullet couldn't fell. The smart thing to do was bide her time and use the skills that had gotten her out of worse situations than this. He stopped long enough to extract a blanket from behind his saddle and wrapped it around both of them, but Kendra was still freezing, clad in her soaking wet clothing. She tried to protest but soon gave up even that, since her shouted entreaties were met with silence.

As they rode, Kendra had begun to grow increasingly alarmed. She was in England, but something was desperately wrong. She had passed out when it was summer with sheaves of grain waving in the wind. When she had awakened the stubbled ground was covered with frost. A strange weather distortion? An unseasonable cold snap? Then, there was the matter of Innusbury. She had passed through Innusbury on her way to investigate the crop circle and had read a very impressive marker about what was left of the one-time village.

Innusbury had been abandoned in the year 1340, by order of the local aristocrat, Lord Somebody-or-other. Apparently the lord needed the land for his sheep and it was easier for the remaining few inhabitants to seek other housing than to rebel against their liege lord. When Kendra had passed through on her way to the hotel, there had been nothing left of Innusbury except the stone foundations where the village had once sat.

But the Innusbury she and the dark knight had ridden through only hours ago was a bustling little village filled with houses, a chapel, and a dirty inn, which in no way resembled the empty remnant she had visited the day before.

Kendra shifted her position near the fire and eased the pressure on her bottom. Riding on a horse for five hours, bouncing against a man encased in metal, had done little to improve her humor or her backside. Almost worse than the ride was the strange feeling she had that as long as the crazy knight had his arms around her waist, she was safe. She'd leaned back against him with no doubt that he would support her and never let her fall.

Eventually though, even his strong chest grew uncomfortable. She'd hoped he'd stop at Innusbury—or wherever they really were—and let her rest at the inn, let them dry their clothes and get warm. But the dauntless knight had dragged her across the countryside for two more hours before making camp in a secluded, rocky crag. He had then proceeded to build a roaring fire, for which she was very grateful, and ordered her to take off her clothes.

When she'd hesitated, he'd snorted, thrown her a blanket and stalked off to deal with his horse, staked a good ten yards away. After she'd stripped and wrapped herself in the blanket, her jailor left her for a few minutes, though his own lips looked fairly blue with the cold. He returned with a dead rabbit, skinned the hapless creature, and cooking it over the open flames, prepared a meager meal. Even with the memory of its dismemberment fresh in her mind, Kendra had pounced on the meat hungrily.

Now she glanced around her, feeling incredibly tired. The sun was just beginning to rise above the tall rocks surrounding the campsite, and with a shiver, Kendra realized that this was the perfect place to kill someone. *How long would it be before her body was found?* she wondered. *Would Mac ever get over it?* She pictured his craggy face drained of color, twisted with grief. All her reckless chances, her thoughtless risks had been the epitome of selfishness. Too bad she'd never realized it before. With a pang, Kendra suddenly understood what her death would mean to her uncle. Just as James and Nicole's deaths had shattered her life, so would her death break Mac's gentle heart.

Taking a deep breath, she set aside the bowl the knight had given her. There was no sense in growing maudlin. She had to get away from this madman. She would keep her wits about her until the right opportunity for escape presented itself.

Kendra glanced over at the silent figure crouched in front of the fire. Thank goodness his wound had stopped bleeding and he seemed fine, except that he was shivering with the cold and likely to catch pneumonia from the icy plunge in the stream. Since he'd thrown her on his horse, he hadn't spoken a word to her, and no matter how she begged him to tell her where they were and what he wanted with her, he had remained stone faced and silent. Kendra knew from long experience that there was no way to negotiate with someone if the person wouldn't talk to you. It was time for questions—and answers.

"Listen," she said in a soothing voice, "I'm sorry I shot you. I was frightened, I mean, look at the way you're dressed. Pretty menacing." She tried to smile to soften her words but the knight with the golden eyes simply stared at her and continued to eat the last of the rabbit. Her smile faded and she cleared her throat nervously. "Look, I don't know what your problem is, but I'm sure I could find you some help. This is really common these days, you know."

He stopped in mid movement, the meat in his hand halfway to his lips as he stared at her across the fire.

Kendra stood, laughing nervously. "I mean, everybody wishes at one time or another that they could run away, join the circus, become part of a fairytale." She moved slowly around the perimeter of the stone-enclosed campfire, hands behind her back, until she was only a few feet away from him. "And I know that you don't really want to hurt me, do you? You've probably been under a lot of pressure on your job, under a lot of stress and—"

"Silence!"

She had just reached his side when the man barked the command, flinging the meat to one side, rising to tower over her like Atlas preparing to shoulder the world. Kendra gulped and, feeling her kneecaps melt into jelly, sank down at his feet.

"Sorry," she whispered.

Navarre picked up his sword and strode a few feet away from the woman. What was the witch trying to do, get information from him? For witch she most certainly was. Her words made no sense. Circus? Stress? Job? He glanced up at the sky as daylight stretched pink-gold fingers across the fading gray of night. It would take another day of riding to reach Nottingham, but before he arrived he wanted to know exactly what the witch had to do with Richard and Locksley.

He had traveled at night in the hopes that if no one saw him with his beautiful burden, Locksley wouldn't know he had taken Richard's salvation from Abury until after they had safely reached Nottingham. They would spend the day in the crag, and at sunset, start out once again.

Navarre wiped the back of one hand across his face and his shoulders sagged. He was weary, exceedingly weary, and his arm ached where the witch had pierced him with her sorcerous weapon. Zounds, it had hurt like the very devil! *How had she done it,* he wondered? *How had she burrowed a hole in his arm from such a distance with only the help of a strangely shaped lump of metal*? He wanted to examine the lump but was fearful she could cause it to hurt him again, even kill him, just by his holding it.

Magda had said in her prophecy that Richard's salvation would also bring with it the king's destruction. Was the lump of metal that destruction? Or was it the woman? Which was salvation and which the danger? Or were they either? He drew one hand cross his face and released his pent-up breath. He would lie down, he would rest, and when they arrived in Nottingham, he would seek Garrick's counsel.

With one eye on the woman, Navarre moved back to the fire and shrugged out of the open-sided tunic he wore, wincing at the pain that laced down his arm as he did so. He unfastened his leather hauberk and bent over, letting the heavy armor fall straight down, trying not to disturb his arm again. One side of the leather brushed the wound and he grunted as the piece slid to the ground, then turned away from the woman's open curiosity as he began unfastening the chain mail he wore. Used to having his squire remove his armor, he struggled with the small fastenings at the side, his fingers too large and too square and at the moment, too cold, to accomplish much. His arm pained him more than he wanted to admit even to himself.

Kendra watched the knight struggle for a minute, shivering with cold, then, resolutely stood and crossed over to him, mildly slapping his hands away from the straps at his side.

"Here, let me help you," she said, her smaller hands making short work of the latchlike apparatus. She had quite a time keeping the blanket from falling off and totally exposing her nakedness, but at last she had the metal sheath unhooked and the man grunted what could have been thanks, as he pulled the long tunic of chain mail off. "Honestly," Kendra went on, "men take the simplest things and turn them into major—"

She stopped, her voice catching in her throat. He looked back at her, almost defiantly, his long, black hair rumpled around his face. But it wasn't his face that commanded her attention. Under the mail he wore a long-sleeved white tunic with no collar and straight sleeves, which currently lay plastered coldly against his skin, and leggings which molded themselves to thick, muscular thighs. The costume showed his magnificent physique to its best advantage, and as she watched, with her blurred vision, he shed the undertunic as well, giving her an unobstructed view of his wide, well-muscled chest.

Kendra took a step back from the knight, running her tongue across her lips as she gazed up at the slightly blurry, yet still incredible specimen of manhood standing in front of her. No man on earth really looked like this—and particularly no nuts-for-brains psycho who thought he was a knight in shining armor. Kendra sat down again, feeling as though the air had been knocked out of her.

Suddenly she knew the answer to the strange things that had been happening since she blacked out. The reason there was no wheat, the reason Sean had disappeared, the reason Innusbury was now a bustling little village, the reason it was cold, the reason everything had this strange, hazy, dream-like quality to it. Because it *was* a dream. She had been knocked out, maybe hit by lightning, and was probably at this moment being rushed to the nearest hospital in Wiltshire.

Chapter Four

It all made sense now: a tall, dark, handsome, silent knight in shining armor appears out of nowhere, sweeps her up on his black stallion and makes her his prisoner. C'mon, O'Brien! This is the stuff dreams are made of! Even as the realization she was probably unconscious, maybe even in a coma, sent a wave of fear through her, the thought of sharing a dream with this now apparently harmless, handsome apparition seemed suddenly very attractive.

Kendra gazed up at the knight and felt her heartbeat quicken. It had been a long time since she had felt attracted to a man. After her husband died, it was a year before she even acknowledged there *was* an opposite sex. Mac had begun "fixing her up" with blind dates, but every one of them had been a disaster. She'd never again met a man who could thrill her the way James once had, just by walking into the room. Until now. Too bad he wasn't real.

Her sudden silence got the knight's attention in a way all of her ranting and questions hadn't been able to accomplish.

"Are you ill?" he asked, kneeling beside her. Kendra blinked at the sound of the deep, husky voice next to her ear. She turned and found her lips inches away from his. He was wearing only the blanket now over his leggings. His chest was broad, smooth except for a dusting of dark hair that ended in a V between his pectoral muscles. His scent was heady, masculine. It should have repelled her, but somehow it did the opposite.

"What the hell," she whispered, never taking her eyes from his mouth, "it's my dream."

Slowly she ran both hands beneath the blanket and up the front of his bare chest. He stiffened and drew away from her.

"What—what do you think you are doing?"

"This," she said softly, pulling him back to her and taking his face between her hands. Opening her mouth slightly, Kendra brushed her lower lip against his and the knight's golden eyes turned to burnished amber. Thanking her subconscious mind for its attention to detail, she moved to deepen the kiss. He jerked away from her and jumped to his feet as if she had branded him with a hot iron. Hot iron, she thought languidly, is what I chiefly need right now. Navarre moved quickly away and in a matter of moments was brandishing his sword again.

Kendra tossed her long auburn hair back from her shoulders and frowned up at him. "Give it a rest, will you?" she said crossly. "This is my dream and if I want to kiss you I will."

The man looked genuinely puzzled and took another step back from her. "You will not use your witch's wiles against me," he said.

Kendra stood, clutching the blanket to her chest, moving toward him with a slight roll to her hips. Boldly, she pushed aside the sharp sword he had raised to make a barrier between them. The knight stood openmouthed as she reached up and linked her arms behind his head. He was so tall she had to stand on tiptoe to curve her hands against the back of his neck, but she managed. The blanket slid to the ground behind her and his sudden intake of breath was quite gratifying. His eyes were golden—golden! Kendra felt laughter bubbling inside of her. Those eyes should have been the first giveaway she was dreaming. No one on earth had golden eyes!

"Do you have a name, Sir Knight?" she asked softly, wondering absently how a dream could feel so intensely cold.

"N-name?"

Navarre ran his tongue across his lips and saw the witch's gaze follow, her own mouth curved up in a satisfied smile as she pressed her lithe, naked body against him. He was being seduced—no, bewitched—by a woman who didn't even come up to his shoulder, by a woman he could crush with one hand, by a woman he suddenly wanted to possess with every fiber of his being.

"My name is Kendra. What's yours? You know, your name?" she said huskily, pulling his head down closer to hers. "You know, what your friends call you when you aren't busy slaying dragons?"

"Navarre," he whispered, then dropped his sword.

Kendra gasped as, with a groan, the man gathered her into his arms, crushing her against his chest. His lips devoured hers like a white-hot flame licking through a building made of straw. He swung his blanket around both of them, enclosing them in a tent of sudden heat as the mad knight possessed her mouth. From the way his hands were moving, Kendra realized he had no intention of stopping with a kiss, and that was just fine with her. She arched against him, pulling him closer, his touch sending tremors of desire coursing through her. His hands roamed over her body, caressing, stroking, and Kendra found herself responding with an eagerness that should have shamed her—even in a dream.

His tongue continued to warm her mouth as deft fingers moved over her body. Kendra had always prided herself on being broad-minded, liberal in her thinking, but the truth was she had grown up in a small Texas town where even sex after marriage seemed to have certain limitations. She had tried to shake off her inhibitions, but since James didn't seem to mind that she was often a little shy with him, she had settled into patterns of lovemaking that seldom changed.

As she stood clasped in a stranger's arms totally naked, Kendra felt a sudden freedom and exhilaration, and the hungry look in the knight's hooded eyes filled her with a heady sense of power she'd never known before. His hands moved over her, sliding down her back, cupping her buttocks, then around and up to caress her breasts.

"Like lily-white pomegranates," he whispered.

Kendra gasped as he bent his head and his hungry mouth moved to rake the tender skin that had for so long been neglected. Her eyes slid shut as a euphoric lethargy swept over her. She scarcely noticed when Navarre scooped her into his arms and lowered her to the earth, her blanket beneath them, his atop. She was conscious only of the incredible utopia of feeling, of long dormant emotions breaking free as his lips, two searing flames, moved to caress her mouth once again.

Kendra clung to Navarre and suddenly she became the aggressor, as though to assert her own equality in their dance of passion. Her fingers tangled in his long, dark hair and she arched against him, her breath hot and fevered, her hands touching him intimately even as she was being touched. Kendra lifted her mouth to his throat, almost sobbing from the relief of being touched, of having someone hold her again, kiss her again, love her again. Then suddenly, the mad knight stopped. He drew back from her, staring down at her, his golden eyes confused, his face troubled.

Kendra smiled up at him and, lifting her heavy hair from beneath her, spread it behind her head like a waving, red-gold fan. She was freezing, but the fire between them was warmth enough. She reached for him, for her knight in shining armor, but he just stared at her, his eyes burning with an inner fire. He made no move to touch her again.

"What is it?" she said softly.

"This changes naught," Navarre said, his jaw tightening. "You are still my prisoner. You are still my enemy."

Kendra smiled again and without a word, lifted her hand and caressed his inner thigh with her fingertips. With a groan, Navarre covered her mouth with his own, her body with his, and Kendra knew he was as lost as she was, lost to the heat driving him, lost to the enchantment weaving around them, lost to the fire burning between them.

Kendra closed her eyes. She wanted him, like nothing she had ever wanted before in her life. And because it was a dream, she could have him, in a way that in real life she would not allow.

Hot iron, she remembered suddenly with a gasp, as their flesh collided. Hot iron. Tears filled Kendra's eyes as she felt the burning flame that was Navarre begin to chase away the cold emptiness that had been her constant companion since James's death. Warmth, dark and desperate, danced through her veins and she clung to the knight, her hands caressing his back, feeling the hard muscles beneath the skin, the scars that told too much and yet so little.

She opened her eyes and for a moment their gazes locked as something strangely tender passed between them. Navarre stopped his movement again, and Kendra felt bereft until a rough laugh brightened the harsh lines around his mouth. Then her face was between his hands and laughter was forgotten.

"Are you a witch?" Navarre whispered against her lips. "Tell me truly—are you in league with Richard and Locksley?"

She buried her hands in his hair and pressed his face next to hers, even as she laughed aloud. "Oh, my brave knight," she said softly, "if I were a witch, I would enchant you and bind you to me forever. I would keep you tethered to my bed and you would fulfill my every wish. Richard and Locksley could never compare to you."

Navarre jerked back from her embrace, and with a roar rolled away from her and sprang to his feet. Startled, Kendra raised up on her elbows, her expression one of bemusement.

"Wrong answer, huh?" She smiled. "Well, that's what I get for trying to be poetic. Now," she lifted her arms to him, "come back here. I'm freezing."

Navarre towered above her in all of his naked, outraged glory, his hands curled into fists at his side. "Witch!" he hissed. "Soon you will be warm enough, for you will burn when we reach Nottingham! I should have listened to my instincts—think you to ensorcell me by possessing my body? Or do you seek a child from me by which to bind my soul to yours?"

Kendra sat up, arms wrapped around herself as she shivered, her teeth beginning to chatter. "I am getting very tired of this. This is my dream and I would think I should be able to have things my way. So cooperate or I might just turn you into someone who will—like Mel Gibson."

Kendra started to laugh, but the laughter died in her throat as she saw Navarre's face pale at her words. His strong jaw tightened and the gold in his eyes burned, not with desire any longer, but with raw anger.

He stalked over to the fire where her clothing was stretched across rocks to dry, grabbed them, then turned and threw them in her face. "Dress, whore, before I end your worthless life."

Kendra's eyes flashed rebelliously and her chin lifted. "I am not a whore, or a witch."

The knight raised both dark brows and one corner of his lips lifted sardonically. "You've just admitted to being a witch and your wanton behavior proves you a whore as well. Now be silent before I finish what you started, in a manner which, I assure you, will leave no doubt in your mind who has been possessed."

Kendra glared up at him, then began jerking her clothes back on with quick, angry movements, thankful they were almost dry, as she grumbled to herself. "Why can't I even have what I want in my own dreams?"

Navarre began pulling on his clothes, never taking his eyes from her. When she finished dressing, the woman stood, her lips swollen from his kisses, her chest rising and falling with indignation. Navarre swallowed hard. The witch was even more alluring now as her azure eyes glimmered with anger instead of seduction. Navarre realized with a dawning comprehension that from now until they reached Nottingham he must guard himself every moment, or else kill the woman and be done with it.

He pressed his lips together grimly as he finished tying his leggings, remembering the way her gentle hands had worked a wondrous magic of their own without spells. He frowned as his desire quickened once again at the thought. To kill her would be the smartest thing to do, but to do so would be a mistake. Who knew what information she might have concerning Richard and Locksley's plans? Prince John would never forgive him if he killed her before questioning her thoroughly.

Navarre ran one hand through his long, dark hair. It was obvious that someone else was going to have to do the questioning. He couldn't trust himself around her. Even now, fully clothed and with six feet between them, he felt the desire wrapping itself around him, twisting his insides as though they were as supple as the mass of tangled auburn curls she was trying to braid. She lifted her gaze to meet his and Navarre narrowed his eyes as the force of her power hit him again.

"I want to know who you are," he said. "Who you are, where you come from and whom you are working for."

Kendra sighed and dropped her hands to her lap in resignation. "My name is Kendra O'Brien, I'm from New York, I'm a reporter and I work for my uncle who is the editor of the *New York Chronicle*."

"Chronicle?" Navarre frowned at her. "A chronicler? What do you mean? Are you a scribe then?"

"A scribe, yes, that's what I am, a scribe."

"What value is a scribe to Richard?" he muttered to himself as he paced around the small area. "How does his salvation lie in one that knows how to write?" Navarre shook his head. Then he glanced down at her, his eyes keen. "But I do ken what destruction you have brought with you." He lifted his hand to the bandage on his arm. "What manner of weapon did you burn me with? With what spell do you control it?"

"I'm tired of this dream," Kendra said, moving closer to the fire. "I need to get out of it." When he continued to stare down at her, a puzzled expression on her face, Kendra released her breath explosively. "I say, fair knight, I need to rest awhile and I am freezing."

Navarre strode over to his horse and jerked another rolled up blanket from behind the saddle. "Here, lie down," he ordered, "and take your rest. We ride at dusk. Do not think to overcome me with your spells again. You may be Richard's salvation, or his destruction, but you are still mortal. And do not think you have escaped from my questions. You will answer them, eventually."

"Why," Kendra muttered as she plopped herself down in the dirt, "why couldn't I have at least conjured up a mattress and pillow in this dream?" She pulled the rough blanket around her and put her satchel bag under her head for a pillow, then looked up and saw the fire in the knight's eyes quicken at her words. "Sorry," she corrected herself, "I didn't mean to use the word 'conjure'—maybe 'created' would be less dangerous around you."

Navarre picked up his sword from the place he had dropped it. "There is one Creator," he said with disdain. "Even a witch would not dare to compare herself to Him.''

''I didn't mean—oh, what's the use?'' Kendra jerked the blanket around her shoulders and tried to get comfortable on the rough bed of dirt and rock. This was the way most of her dreams ended, she reminded herself. She lost the guy and went to sleep. Then when she awoke again, she was truly awake. Maybe all this nonsense meant that back in the real world she was beginning to fight her way back from the state of unconsciousness to which the lightning—or whatever—had plunged her. With a sigh, Kendra closed her eyes.

Navarre stretched out a few feet away from the woman, feeling spent and troubled. Who was she really? And what was the sorcerous weapon she had wielded against him? He wanted to examine the metal thing again, but there would be time enough the next day, time enough to force her to show him how it worked. He watched the rise and fall of Kendra's chest as she slipped into sleep, watched and envied her cheeks the touch of the long eyelashes against the skin. How would it have been, he wondered, if he had not stopped their joining? How would it have been to experience the full consummate fire of their union? Angrily, he shook the thought away.

He watched the woman for quite a while, expecting some last-ditch attempt at escape, but finally he decided she was, indeed, doing as he had bid her. Even witches needed sleep he supposed. Only after her breathing slowed did he allow himself to relax. At nightfall they would journey on to Nottingham and once there, he would turn her over to the sheriff and be done with her. Navarre was unable to suppress a shudder as he envisioned what his friend, the sheriff, would do to the beautiful witch. What had she said her name was?

Kendra.

Resolutely, Navarre cleared his mind, determined to dispel the ridiculous feeling that he should protect this woman who had injured him, who had tried to ensorcell him, this fascinating woman who was his enemy, and England's. He should tie her but somehow could not bring himself to, which of course, was even more proof of her power. The throbbing in his loins had not ceased entirely since he had pushed her away from him, and he burned with the want of her. A sudden, paralyzing thought seized him.

Had he stopped their lovemaking too late? Had the partial possession of their passion resulted in his total enchantment? With an oath Navarre rose and began to pace around the crag. One thing was certain, he must stay awake, and he must not allow the witch to touch him again. He moved to his horse's side and for a moment leaned his head against Kamir's rough mane. His arm pained him but it was nothing compared to the burning need inside of him.

Even now, the memory of her skin against his, her touch, the smell of her hair, made him want to turn and take her in his arms.

He lifted his head. He was a soldier, used to facing grim realities. Somehow the auburn-haired witch had enchanted him, and somehow he must find a way to quench the fire in his loins. He groaned softly. Even now he felt fear wash over him. He must not allow her to control him, and yet, he was just a man. If she indeed were a sorceress, this searing, overwhelming desire she had created inside of him might forever rule his destiny, place him at her beck and call. What was it she had said—"I would enchant you and bind you to me forever, I would tether you to my bed and you would fulfill my every wish."

Navarre pressed his lips tightly together as his fingers unconsciously reached up to brush against the crude bandage she had tied around his wound. If he could not conquer these feelings, this fervent desire, there would be no other alternative— the woman must die.

Kendra awoke with a smile on her face. She didn't open her eyes right away because she wanted to savor the sensual aftermath of the very intense, highly remarkable dream. It had seemed so real, so vivid, and had starred none other than herself and a huge, handsome hunk of a knight in shining armor.

She shifted in the bed and winced as her body ached in protest, then she shivered as a cold gust of air swept over her. Moving restlessly, she felt the roughness of the blanket against her skin and decided drowsily to change hotels as soon as possible. Granted, she'd had a wonderful dream, but sleeping in this bed was like sleeping on rocks and the blankets were awful, not to mention the lack of heat and—

Kendra opened her eyes. Six feet away lay a man, broad-shouldered, dark-haired. He lay with his eyes closed but she knew they were as golden as the sun that even now was setting quickly below the distant horizon. Navarre. The knight in her dream. She squinted, her memory returning swiftly. The haze that had permeated her vision ever since the storm had knocked her senseless, was gone. Nothing marred her view of the handsome man who, in her dream, had almost ravished her on the ground.

On the ground. Kendra sat up, a twig beneath her leg biting sharply into her skin. She stared around her. The crag. The campfire. Navarre. Kendra passed a shaky hand across her eyes, then smiled hesitantly. Of course—she was still asleep. She'd had many dreams within dreams in her life. That would explain the fact that it was the middle of winter when it should be summer and that a mad knight had captured her. Of course it was a dream.

Sure, O'Brien, she scoffed at herself, feeling a rush of fear sweep over her as she slowly stood and moved toward the sleeping man. When did you ever have a dream like this?

"This is no dream," she whispered, feeling the blood rush away from her head and the strength from her legs. She sat down, quietly, quickly, where she stood.

What have I done, what have I done, what have I done? The frantic thought echoed through her mind. This was not a dream. This was real. That meant yesterday had been real as well. She had almost made love to a man holding her hostage, a man who thought he was a knight!

Stupid, stupid, stupid!

Kendra ran her tongue across her lips and tried to bring her racing thoughts back under control.

All right, so it isn't a dream. It's real. He's real. No harm done. No harm done? Are you crazy O'Brien? Count yourself lucky he didn't decide to go through with it, although given how far you actually went can you honestly say you didn't make love?

Kendra felt a quick flush of shame and fear warm her
cheeks, but she pushed away the emotions. There was no time
for such considerations as pride or modesty. She had to get
away from this lunatic. He had become quite violent toward
the end of their encounter. She grimaced. What was it he had
kept yelling at her? Something about being a witch. Who was
he? What did he want? Those were the questions she had to
find an answer for.

Kendra knew she had made enemies on her way to the top
of the investigative reporting racket, enemies who might pay
someone to get rid of her. Or was this man working on his
own? Even now a ransom note might be winging its way to
Mac in New York, demanding a few hundred thousand dollars
for her safe return. Or perhaps ''Navarre'' was involved in
some sort of terrorist activity and wanted to exchange her for
a political prisoner. It wouldn't be the first time.

But it would be the first time her captor had thought himself
to be a medieval knight.

She groaned inwardly. She had to get away, but Navarre's
long form was stretched across the entrance to the rocky crag,
his head butted up against one tall stone and his leather-clad
feet against the other. Kendra rose from her sitting position,
uncurling herself slowly. If she could step over him without
waking him, perhaps she would have a chance of escaping.

Kendra wiped her sweating palms down the sides of her
thighs, ignoring the dirt clinging to her leggings. Grabbing her
bag, she crossed to the knight. He lay with his hands comfortably folded over his broad chest, which rose and fell in
rhythmic movement. His sword lay at his side and she could
see the bag he had taken from his saddle and put the gun in
was underneath his head. Kendra traced the harsh angles and
planes of his face with her gaze, noting how the hard lines
around his mouth had softened with sleep; how his lips were
still tense, as though a part of him remained ever vigilant, ever
ready for battle.

Tiny wrinkles radiated from the corners of his eyes. Laugh
lines? Somehow she had a hard time picturing this stern-faced
Goliath ever cracking a smile, much less indulging in a hearty
laugh. Still, he had smiled briefly she remembered, in the midst

of their lovemaking. Lovemaking. Kendra groaned softly.

She jumped as the knight suddenly yawned and stretched his arms above his head. He froze, then, as if sensing her gaze upon him, turned slowly to face her, the full brilliance of his golden eyes stunning her. Once again Kendra reminded herself that she faced a dangerous adversary, a lion waiting to pounce.

"So, you are awake, witch," he said, his voice like rough gravel. He rolled to his feet in one quick, lithe movement. "Did you think to escape me—or did you intend to try to seduce me again?"

"Please," Kendra began softly, "there's really been a terrible mistake. I thought—" she flushed. "I really thought I was having a dream and you were—I mean that's why—" She released her breath explosively. "Please, just let me go home and I promise I won't press charges."

Navarre stared down at her for a long moment, then lifted his hand to touch her face, drawing one finger lightly down the side of her jaw. He stood as one transfixed and Kendra felt, with horror, the slow burning flame of desire beginning anew within her. The knight must have felt it as well, for something flickered in the depths of his golden eyes and he lowered his hand from her face.

"We ride for Nottingham," he said softly.

Nottingham. Kendra's hopes had risen when Navarre finally told her their destination. There was no way he could parade her through that city on horseback without attracting immediate attention. Hopefully her captor's brains really were so addled he would do exactly that and her rescue would virtually be assured by his actions. At that thought, Kendra felt a little of the tension ease away, even though she was forced to ride in front of Navarre, turned sideways in the saddle, her body crushed against his. It didn't matter. Once they reached Nottingham, everything would work itself out.

Night settled across the land like a velvet cloak, and as the gentle sound of the stallion's hoofbeats began to lull her to sleep, Kendra had the strange sensation that she and the knight were somehow caught in time, suspended between reality and fantasy. Wearily, she allowed her body to relax completely against the heat of Navarre, the swaying motion of the horse's step rocking her to sleep. Kendra found herself wishing this crazy adventure *had* turned out to be a dream—with Navarre as a noble knight in shining armor, not an escaped lunatic in tinfoil.

She should be frantic, upset, but the promise of finding help in Nottingham had somehow calmed her fears—or was it the shelter of Navarre's arms enclosing her so completely, with such strength? Kendra closed her eyes, her thoughts drifting into a confused jumble of fantasy and reality. In some rational part of her mind she wondered how long this strange calm would last.

It lasted until they reached Nottingham.

Kendra stared in horror at the dim, dank cell Navarre had just unlocked using a heavy, ancient-looking key. He had pushed her inside and now stood silhouetted in the open doorway, his face hidden in the shadows.

"You are not going to leave me in here," she said, in a tone that, in the course of her career as an investigative reporter, had shaken presidents and press secretaries alike with its tenacity. To her horror he backed out of the door and slammed it suddenly shut in her face.

" 'Tis only for a time, witch," he informed her through the small window at the top of the door, "until the sheriff sends for you."

"No!" Kendra threw herself against the wooden door, feeling splinters gouge her fists as she beat impotently upon the barrier. "Don't leave me here, you bastard!" she cried. There was a silence, then she heard his footsteps echo down the stone corridor. Panic swept over her with the same cloying strength of her prison's stench.

Wide-eyed, Kendra turned to face the cell. A dim light from the tiny window stretched across the room, exposing clumps of straw in various stages of decomposition, as well as three dead rats. The stench of urine and filth rose up to assault her senses and Kendra covered her nose with her hand even as she fought the urge to vomit. A dark form the size of a kitten scurried across the room and with a gasp she backed away, colliding with the solid frame of the door. Leaning there for a moment, eyes closed, Kendra tried to still the thundering of her heart and took a deep, shuddering breath.

They had arrived at their destination just before dawn. Kendra had known immediately something was desperately wrong. She had been to Nottingham before, once as a child, and later on her "trip abroad" after college. It was an industrialized city, with over a quarter of a million people. There were many tourist attractions, including a statue of the legendary Robin Hood. She had been disappointed to find there was no castle, only a manor house which had been renovated into a museum and art gallery. Kendra had loved every minute of her time there.

But when Navarre's horse had carried them through gigantic wooden gates and he announced they had arrived in Nottingham, Kendra had stared around in disbelief and confusion. Flanking a large, open square of mud were dozens of shops crammed together, most of them looking like a good stiff breeze would send them tumbling. Signs hung outside a few, apparently depicting by picture the type of service the shop provided. There were no words. A wooden boot swung outside one, a crude anvil above another.

Here and there a few early risers shuffled along what passed for the village street, wearing ragged tunics and dirty cloaks, barefooted or wearing sandals, their faces so coated with dirt and grime as to be scarcely recognizable as human beings.

Numbly, Kendra had stared as the knight's horse picked its way through the rutted street, leading them past the shop where the anvil sign hung outside. Inside, the blacksmith pounded on a length of metal, the crude beginnings of a sword. Hawkers began calling out their wares and suddenly Kendra's calm facade crumbled into hysteria.

She began to scream and fight a startled Navarre, and as she did, several people came running out into the street. They gawked for a moment at the sight of a young woman struggling with a knight on horseback, then simply turned and walked away.

Kendra stopped screaming out of pure shock. The people had come as she'd hoped, but acted as though there wasn't anything wrong with what was taking place. What was going on? When she finally stopped struggling, Navarre had tied her wrists to the saddle and continued through what was not an industrial city, but a bustling village. When they arrived at the gate of a huge castle, Kendra knew something was terribly wrong. When she'd visited the castle museum she'd seen pictures of the original Nottingham Castle. This was it.

Faint with hunger and exhaustion, Kendra had closed her eyes and sagged limply against Navarre. When she finally opened her eyes again, they were no longer on the horse. She was lying near a trough of water and Navarre was using a cold, wet cloth to wipe away the dirt of the road from her face. Kendra caught a glimpse of concern in his eyes before his mask of implacability slid into place. Once she had revived somewhat, he had given her a cool drink of water and produced a kind of meat pie. She wolfed it down without any pretense of manners. After she licked the last crumb from her fingers, the knight had picked her up and carried her down several flights of stairs, then through a long hallway illuminated only by the light of occasional torches held in iron sconces embedded in the stone wall. He had stopped in front of a large, thick wooden door with bars at the top, and looked down at her with something like regret in his eyes.

Now, Kendra turned and beat her fists against the rough door until she felt her hands bleeding from the impact of splintering wood. Standing on tiptoe, she grabbed the iron bars in the small window at the top of the door and hoisted herself up.

"Let me out of here!" she shouted, barely able to see over the window sill. "My editor will pay you well for my release, but not if you leave me in this pigsty for another minute!" Kendra couldn't stop the trembling of her voice and it infuriated her. Nor could she hold herself up for long, and as her feet touched the floor again, she spun around in dismay.

Kendra O'Brien, top investigative reporter for the *Chronicle,* never lost control of her emotions or the situation. Never.

Right, O'Brien, you were really in control when you tried to seduce your crazy knight, she thought.

Pushing the embarrassing memory away, Kendra paced

back and forth in the small area in front of the door, shivering, wishing Navarre had at least left her the blanket, her aching hands clutched behind her back. There had to be a way out. There was always a way out. He would come back. Of course he would. He had to. There was no reason why he shouldn't come back. After all, he couldn't hope to gain anything if he left her down in this cesspool.

Unless—her pulse quickened—unless he didn't hope to gain a thing and was simply a crazy man who wanted to keep her locked up for some twisted reason of his own. Now that she thought about it, why would a sane man refuse a woman who wanted his body? And why would he spout all of that nonsense about witches and Richard? She'd thought at the time it was just part of his plan to confuse and frighten her. But now . . .

Her heart started pounding, throbbing through the skin of her chest even as she stared down at the nasty piles of infested straw. Willing herself not to panic, Kendra focused on the stream of light pouring through the window and took several deep breaths in an effort to slow her rapid pulse.

"Concentrate," she ordered herself aloud in a trembling voice. "You will get out of here. You will! Say it, O'Brien! Believe it!" She spun around and faced the door. "I'm going to get out of here!"

"Save yer strength."

Kendra jerked in surprise at the sound of the croaky voice outside her cell. Her fingernails bit into the narrow sill of the door's window as she pulled herself up to the opening again.

"Who's there?" she cried, her words echoing down the stone hallway. "Where are you?"

"Over here," the voice said, "jest acrost from yer lovely chamber."

Kendra squinted through the window, torchlight illuminating the space between her door and the identical one opposite. She could barely make out what appeared to be the top of a head, then caught her breath as two hard, black eyes appeared in the opening.

"Ye kin tell yerself lies 'till yer gullet's raw but ol' Ben knows the truth. There ain't no way out of 'ere—'cept the noose or the blade." The black eyes squinted at her. "Or the fire, mayhap. Pretty 'un, ain't ye? But t'won't matter a whit when they drag ye before the sheriff. I 'eard the keeper say ye be a witch. Is ye?''

"No." Kendra retorted. "I was kidnapped by that big ape. He probably means to try to ransom me from my uncle.''

"Aye, that happens. Why then is 'e saying ye be a witch?''

"Because he's crazy," Kendra said, lowering herself from the window and flexing her fingers. She glanced around the cell. He would be back any moment. "How long have you been here?'' she asked, raising her voice slightly.

"Me? I been in the dungeon for a year now, I figures.''

Kendra went cold. A year! Dear God! Was it possible that a person could simply disappear for a year and not be found? But in her case she knew someone must be looking for her by now. Mac had surely called the hotel and discovered she was missing.

"Why are you here?'' Kendra asked. "Are you a political prisoner or are you being held for ransom?'' She held her breath as she awaited his answer.

A cackling laugh echoed through the stone and Kendra shivered, involuntarily rubbing her hands up and down her arms. The chill of the cell was beginning to seep into her bones, along with a terrible fear.

"Ransom? I be no one of fortune. Po-lit-i-cal? What be that? Nay, wench, I be in this pisshole for thievery. The sheriff has forgotten me, and likely I'll never see the light of day again. And neither will ye. The sheriff 'e 'ates witches—fears 'em 'e does—an' e's a bloodthirsty bastard, make no doubt o' that.''

Kendra leaned against the door, then wearily turned and grasped the bars above her head, once again pulling herself up. The man's black eyes were curiously bright in the dim light. "Where am I?'' she said across the hallway, her knees braced against the door, her voice now a defeated whisper.

"This be Notting'am," the man answered, "Notting'am Castle.''

"Nottingham," she repeated with a sigh. So the game continued. This man had probably been planted in the opposite cell purposely to frighten her. Of course, that was it, just more of the insane play acting that Navarre had subjected her to from the beginning. Mac would start a search for her soon. Sean Taylor, the boy that had guided her to the crop circle, would report she had been missing since . . . Kendra rubbed one hand across her eyes. What day was it? Since this adventure had started the days had meshed together until she was no longer sure just how long she'd been missing. The night she'd crouched in the field of the crop circle in Wiltshire had been July 16.

"What day is this?" she asked her unseen companion in the darkness. There was a pause, and Kendra could hear the man counting.

"It be the Sabbath."

Kendra closed her eyes and swallowed hard, her fingers tightening around the iron bars, her arms aching with the effort, her heart pounding fearfully.

"What date?"

Another pause, then the rough voice spoke again, this time its tone wary.

"Date?" The question seemed to puzzle him. "This be about the middle of Feb'wary," he said at last, his voice thoughtful. "Aye, Feb'wary, in the year o' our Lord, 1194."

Kendra felt her hands uncurl of their own volition and the bars slip from her grasp. The rough surface of the door scraped her face as she slid to the cold, stone floor, oblivious to the sound of scurrying rodents in the corner of the cell.

Kendra stared into the blackness and began to tremble, nausea choking her with its intensity, terror seizing her as the full import of the man's words struck her with the force of a hurricane.

The year of our Lord, 1194.

Chapter Five

Navarre gazed out of the narrow window of his chamber, hands clasped behind him, dark brows knit together above stormy golden eyes. Dawn broke softly in Nottingham. Pale pink fingers of light shot through the mist-gray sky illuminating the castle walls, shadowing the hodgepodge of houses and hovels scattered within those wooden barriers. Normally Navarre enjoyed watching the sun rise over his adopted city, but not today.

He had not slept as he intended after throwing the witch into the dungeon. Instead, he had lain upon his bed and thought about the softness of her skin. Over and over again the scene in the crag replayed itself in his mind and he tasted of her lips, caressed her soft breasts, sheathed himself in the dark, giving warmth of her body. He knew it was sorcery, yet some irrational part of his being did not care.

Eventually he had forced himself to leave his daydream and his warm bed to pace the room in hope that the cold would shock him back to his senses. He had finally slept for a few hours, only to awaken feeling more unsettled than before.

Now Navarre looked wearily at the dawning sky of their second day in Nottingham, knowing full well he should forget the witch and get on with his usual duties. He should put the thought of her fear-filled eyes as he locked her into the dungeon out of his mind. He should forget the sound of rats squealing in the darkness. Navarre squeezed his eyes shut against the image of rodents tearing at Kendra's soft white skin.

Kendra.

Navarre ran one hand through his dark hair, spinning away from the window and the tendrils of dawn. He had tried not to think of her as Kendra, a woman, but only as the witch who sought to ensorcell him. Even during his vivid fantasies of the night he had not called her name in his mind. But today, in the cold light of morning, he knew that when he brought her before Garrick and related the story of Magda's prophecy and all the details of Kendra's strange appearance, and the fearful weapon she had brought with her, the sheriff would think her a witch and order her death.

And knowing Garrick these days, it would be a decision he would enjoy making. Navarre frowned and began once again to pace across the stone floor of the small room. Garrick had grown increasingly cruel of late. It would seem that the power of becoming both sheriff and Prince John's advisor had begun to affect his friend's thinking. Navarre had tried to remind him, when they were alone and had no need to keep up the pretense of being sheriff and *custodis pacis*—keeper of the peace—that their mission in Nottingham was not to persecute helpless serfs and villains, but to bring a revolution to the heart of England. Garrick had only laughed.

Why did the thought of Kendra enduring Garrick's idea of justice cause him anguish? Why did her face continue to haunt him like Talam's? Would another woman die because he couldn't protect her? Did she deserve to die? Perhaps she spoke the truth. Perhaps, after all, she was a victim of bizarre magic or events over which she had no control.

Navarre stopped pacing. Could he successfully evaluate the situation himself before the sheriff arrived? He had a little time. John and Garrick were still in London where they had gone to seek secret support for their plans of usurpation. They were not expected to return to Nottingham for yet another week. Given what he knew now, Navarre would have no choice but to bring Kendra before them for judgment once they arrived. But what if he could prove his own suspicions wrong before that time?

He sighed and sank down on his bed, running his hands absently across the coverlet. It was golden, the color of the lion, the color of his eyes. Richard's mother, Eleanor, had given it to him after he had been knighted, just before he left for the crusade. Navarre glanced around the small room. He had purposely taken a smaller chamber, for he didn't think it proper for a knight to wallow in comfort. His life was one of sacrifice and moderation, and he felt his living place should reflect those duties as well. But between Eleanor's gift and the lady Marian, it was not an uncomfortable room at all.

His bed was not large, but it was ample, even for his big body, with simple but stately lines and the relief carving of a lion at the head. Fanciful, he had called it, but Marian had insisted on giving it to him for his birthday. He had laughed and told her that young ladies should not give men such things and she had smiled her shy smile and told him she wasn't a young lady yet, so made it all right. That had been years ago of course, and now Marian was a young lady.

The rest of the room was fairly austere, a table and stool for writing on the rare occasion that he did, one tapestry on the wall depicting a crusading soldier—Marian's needlework. Luxurious drapes, the color of his coverlet, flanked the one window in the room. He had brought the material back from the holy lands and given it to Marian as a present. She had surprised him a month later with the window hangings.

He frowned as he glanced around the room again. New decorations had been added, he saw, since he had been gone— dried broomweed had been fashioned into a wreath and hung above his door, bright ribbons dangling from the top. A new rug brightened the stone of his fireplace hearth, and on the mantle was a wooden statue of a lion. Marian's handiwork again, of course. No one else in the world cared whether he lived or died—with the exception of Garrick.

At the thought of the sheriff of Nottingham, Navarre shook himself from his reverie and crossed to the chest where he had left his saddlebag. The weapon must be examined, even though he feared touching it again. The one time he had held it, the cold, dull metal had frightened him in a way a sword never had. Foolish, superstitious nonsense, he told himself sternly, and opened the bag.

A sharp knock came at the door, sounding several times

before Navarre shook himself from his reverie.

"Come."

The door swung open, and a young woman, slight of stature and plain of face, timidly slipped into the room. Her russet dress was unadorned and an overdress of dark brown only served to make her already sallow complexion seem even muddier. She wore her dull blond hair twisted into a haphazard bun at the base of her neck.

"Navarre," she said softly, hovering just inside the door, "is it true?"

Navarre sighed. "Marian, what are you doing skulking about the castle at this hour? You should still be asleep in your bed like all good children."

The fleeting grimace of irritation across her plain face did not pass unnoticed, and Navarre masked the beginnings of a smile by turning away from her. Lady Marian, the king's sixteen-year-old ward, thought herself a woman fully grown. Were it any other maid in the city Navarre would have agreed, but Marian . . . ah, sweet Marian lived in a dream world of her own making filled with heroes and fairies. Although she had been of marrying age for almost two years, Navarre had discouraged Richard from promising her in marriage. But that was two years ago, and all had changed, except Marian. Marian was still the same sweet child. Navarre hated deceiving her.

"I heard you brought back a witch from Abury and threw her in the dungeon." Her pale blue eyes widened and the hesitancy disappeared as she moved quickly across the room to lay one hand lightly on the knight's arm. "Is it true, Navarre? What does she look like? Does she have a horrible face with warts and discolored splotches? Did she try to cast a spell on you?"

Navarre sighed indulgently. Marian was the only part of Richard worth tolerating. He had known the ward of the king since she was a child, and although Navarre was but a bastard who had bought his knighthood at the auction block, Richard had welcomed him into his family as well as his army. Navarre had spoiled the child, treating her as though she were his own daughter, and even Richard's fall from grace in Navarre's heart could not change the knight's love for her. At the moment, however, she was trying his patience.

"Marian, where do you hear such nonsense?"

"From the servants, of course." She lifted her chin. "From whence else would I hear it? No one in this household knows that I exist except the servants. Faith, I believe they think perhaps I am a servant."

"I shall try to be more attentive in the future," Navarre said dryly. "Now, off with you. Back to bed, or if you have so much energy, go help cook with the morning meal."

Tears welled suddenly in her eyes. "Do you see? Even you order me about as though I were a serf. I am the ward of the king—is it so much to ask to be treated as such?"

"You have everything you could possibly desire," Navarre said impatiently.

The pale eyelashes blinked and two tears trickled down her cheeks. She quickly brushed them away. "Yes, of course. Forgive me, Navarre. Being alone so much, I fear I grow melancholy."

Navarre felt a brief prickle of guilt and he patted her shoulder awkwardly. "You need to get out more," he said. "I'll talk to the groom about taking you for a ride twice a week."

"I'm afraid of horses," she reminded him, her voice once again faint and listless.

"You need to overcome that fear, sweetling." Navarre turned away from her to a small chest at the end of his bed where he kept his extra clothing. With his back to her he shrugged out of his filthy tunic and lifted the lid, reaching into the chest for a cleaner one.

"And you need a bath," Marian said softly, the trace of a smile in her voice. She gasped, then, and Navarre spun around.

"Your arm!" she cried, rushing to his side. "What happened?"

He shrugged and turned back to the chest. "A scratch," he said. "Do not worry about it."

"It must be bathed—you must be bathed," she added sternly.

Navarre glanced over his shoulder and his granitelike countenance split into an answering grin.

77

"Aye," he agreed, "that I do. Well, Maid Marian, who would rule the household of Nottingham if only we mere men would let her, why don't you bring me something to eat and then I promise I will scrub this journey's dirt from my body."

"I shall, and I shall put a fresh, clean bandage on your wound," she said, a brief spark of mischief lighting her eyes, "if you let me see the witch."

He sighed. "There is nothing to see," he said, as he chose a golden-colored tunic and pulled it over his head, his back still to her.

"Of course there is—is she the one? Is she Richard's salvation?"

Navarre spun around in time to see Marian clap her hand across her mouth and her eyes fill with sudden terror.

"What did you say?" he demanded, crossing the short distance between them and glaring down at her.

The fear in Marian's eyes quickened as the black lion glared down at her.

"I . . . nothing, Navarre. I was only jesting."

"Nay, 'twas not a jest." Navarre gestured toward a small stool sitting in front of the fireplace. "Sit down." The girl obeyed immediately.

"Tell me where you heard this," he said. She started to speak and he lifted one hand to silence her. "Take care that you do not lie to me, for I know when you are lying, little girl."

"I am not a little girl," Marian protested, then lowered her voice. "I am a woman—something no one around here seems to realize."

"Enough. Where did you hear these words, Richard's salvation?"

Navarre stood beside her, one foot balanced on the edge of the fireplace hearth, hands folded over one knee. Marian met his burning gaze, then dropped her own to her folded hands.

"I overheard it."

"Where? From whom?"

"In the forest. From Magda."

Navarre straightened, his foot coming down to the floor with a thud. "Magda! How do you know of her?"

Marian looked up and her light brows rose in a silent plea for mercy. She found none in the gaze of the furious knight.

"Answer me, girl. How do you know of Magda and how did you hear of Richard's salvation?"

Her voice trembled as she answered. "I . . . followed you."

"You did what?" Navarre stared down at the girl, thunder-struck by her admission. Marian was sixteen years old, an age at which many girls were married and already bearing children, but to Navarre she was still little more than a child. Besides, Marian had always been a shy, timid little thing, and the idea of her having the gumption to sneak out of the castle and follow him to Magda's hovel was incredible.

"I followed you to Magda's home," she said, then sighed. "I am tired of being treated like a child," she said, echoing Navarre's thoughts. "I know you and John and Garrick are plotting against the king and I wanted to find out what you intended to do."

"We are not plotting against Richard," Navarre said carefully. "We are trying to keep England safe in his absence, and that involves doing things you cannot possibly understand."

Marian stood and walked slowly toward the narrow window. She stopped, her back to Navarre. "Things like spying on Robin and Magda?" she asked.

Navarre frowned. "You say their names as though you know them personally."

Marian glanced back at him. "You forget, Robin of Locksley was once a welcome member of this household. In any case, I did follow you, I did hear Magda's prophecy, and I do want to meet the woman you have banished to the dungeon."

"I should turn you over my knee and spank you," Navarre said, folding his arms across his chest. "Now, go back to your room before I do exactly that—and no more arguments."

Marian opened her mouth, then clamped it shut again as Navarre raised both brows in warning.

"Very well," she said, lifting the hem of the long gown she wore and making her way toward the door. She stopped and looked back, her eyes filled with a firm, yet gentle plead-ing. "But know this, dear Navarre—either make me your ally, help me understand why you wish to destroy Richard, or," she paused eloquently, her pale eyelashes fluttering down, "I shall become your enemy."

Without another glance, she slipped out of the room. Navarre stared after her, speechless for a moment, shaking his head.

"Women," he said finally, under his breath, then jumped as a second pounding shook the door. Scolding himself for his jittery nerves, he jerked open the door to find a buxom young woman smiling up at him. He recognized her as one of the scullery maids he had tumbled once, not too long ago, when the demons inside of him had driven him to seek out a woman for the night. She had been lusty and enthusiastic and he had tipped her well.

"Sir," she said with a bob of a curtsey, her dark eyes twinkling boldly, her rosy complexion deepening under his gaze. "I am so happy you have returned safely. Lady Marian says you desire food." She licked her lips provocatively. "What may I bring you, m'lord?" She tossed her flaxen, none-too-clean hair back from her shoulders and moved a little closer to better display her ample cleavage to the keeper of the peace.

Navarre wasn't seeing the heavy breasts practically spilling out of the wench's tattered blouse, nor her round, healthy peasant face so eager to please. He was seeing Kendra, auburn-haired Kendra, slim and firm, elfin-faced, writhing beneath him, her eyes closed, her passion unrehearsed, unrestrained.

"I am not hungry," he said flatly, "neither for food nor your earthy wares. Get you gone."

The pleasant look on her face changed swiftly to pouting insolence and with a flounce she turned and started back down the hallway. Navarre watched her go, feeling a terrible sinking sensation in the pit of his stomach. Before he found Kendra he would have happily bedded the wench. Now he had turned her down simply because she did not compare with the woman from Abury.

He turned away from the door and strode to the window, his fists flexing in frustration, his eyes staring out, unseeing, at the distant horizon. Was there no way to be free of the witch's spell? Would he always desire her? Would the insanity of his need pound through his blood throughout eternity?

Navarre shook his head, passing one hand across his eyes shakily. Nay. Why was he so concerned? There would be an end to this, and very soon, once John and Garrick returned. If he did not prove to himself that she was not a witch before they arrived, he was duty bound to present her to Garrick's court of justice. Navarre closed his eyes as a wave of nausea and pain swept over him. He did not want her to die.

Enchanted.

His mind whispered the word and it echoed into his soul. Expelling his breath raggedly the knight spun away from the window and picked up a pair of leather gauntlets from the long, narrow table nearby. He pulled them on. A hard ride, that was what he needed. Physical exertion would chase away these superstitious remnants of his old beliefs.

Enchanted.

Navarre scowled and with a savage oath, strode out the door of the chamber and headed for the stables.

Kendra screamed as another rat touched the edge of her boot. She lashed out with her foot and sent the animal squealing and scampering off into the dark corner from which it had come, like all the others that had dared to venture over to her side of the tiny cell during the night.

After the prisoner in the other cell across the dark corridor had announced that it was 1194, Kendra had first sat stunned, until she began to cry, haltingly, later hysterically. At first she thought she had gone insane. Then again wondered if perhaps she was still asleep, dreaming. But she knew the truth even as she tried desperately to deny it. This was no dream. The pungent smell of rotting hay, dead rats and human waste was too intense to be any mere dream. If she had been honest she'd have admitted to herself during the sensuous interlude in the forest that it couldn't be a dream.

And she could not, would not accept insanity as a possibility. If losing her husband and child had not driven her crazy, nothing could. All at once she realized she felt just as she had when they had died—adrift, anchorless, teetering on the edge of hysteria.

James and Nicole. How long had it been since she'd allowed

Tess Mallory

herself to think of them? How long since the whirling merry-go-round she had made her life had paused long enough to picture their faces in her mind? Kendra leaned her face into the palms of her hands and let the hot tears flow unimpeded for once by any noble thoughts of self-restraint. She conjured them now into her mind, a tall, thin man with deep-set blue eyes and thick brown hair, a tiny little girl, redheaded like her mother, dimpled face and sparkling blue-green eyes.

She clung to the hazy photograph in her mind, connecting herself to the fragile memory, tying herself to the reality that once had been, that was no more. As though she viewed the two through a director's lens, Kendra brought James's face into a close-up. Lovingly she traced the fine lines around his lips and knew, with a pang, that she had put them there. He had never wanted her to be a reporter, had resented it so much. They had fought almost daily their last year together.

Kendra frowned. She had forgotten that, had not thought of it since before the funeral. All the pain, the trials of their marriage, their problems, had dissolved into a misty watercolor that continued to fade as the years passed until the memory of their lives together had been enshrined in her thoughts, pure and perfect and whole. Still, she had loved him, and he had loved her, and if he had lived . . . Kendra bit her lower lip. If he had lived, would they have stayed together? She'd never thought about it and even now shook the question away. It didn't matter. James was dead.

Next she traced Nicole's features with her thoughts. Disturbingly enough, this picture was hazy, her daughter's face fuzzy and indistinct. Kendra sighed and let the image of her child's smile disintegrate into nothingness. She had not opened the photo albums she collected since Nicole's birth, since the day of the funeral. She couldn't stand to view photographs of happier days. Was it any wonder then that she recalled her baby so poorly? And now she couldn't ever look at the pictures of her daughter again and refresh her waning memory. Never again would she have the opportunity to open the taped up box filled with Nicole's little dresses and shoes and favorite doll and remember her child.

As quickly as they had begun, Kendra's tears stopped as the

full implications of what had happened to her sank in. She sat for a long time in the darkness, her tears dried upon her cheeks, her mind carefully blank. Then at last, she felt her breath quiver inside of her and, using every last ounce of strength she possessed, Kendra unhooked the lifelines she had tossed around the memories of her family and once again, shut the door to her past. The present was what she had to concentrate on now. She shivered. The present, 1194 the present? She closed her eyes and drew in a deep breath, fighting for composure.

Evaluate the situation. That was what Uncle Mac had taught her when she first became a reporter. If and when a reporter found herself, or himself, in a precarious situation, Mac said, the first thing to do was evaluate the situation and gauge one's options. Kendra had spent the rest of the long night and all of this endlessly long day evaluating her situation. Now as she stared at the stone walls of her cage, she realized she was no closer to an answer than she had been when she started. All she had was the same suppositions she had turned over and over in her mind throughout the night. With a sigh she began the process again.

The storm on the Avebury Plain had not been just any storm, that was obvious. She thought back over Sean's words about the mystic fields. Was it possible that the myths and legends surrounding the ancient place were based on reality? Was it possible that some kind of time portal existed there? No, how could it? If that were true, then people would be disappearing left and right. Avebury was a big tourist attraction. No, it had to be something else, something more transient.

Concentrating to shut out the sounds of the rats in the corner and the man across the hall who had begun an eerie kind of singsong chant, Kendra forced herself to remember the details of the strange storm.

There had been blue lights hovering above her, she remembered that. But wait, before the lights appeared she had felt a strong, magnetic current that seemed to pull her across the field and into the crop circle. The crop circle! Of course, it all made sense now. Hadn't she read the theories of scientists who believed that England possessed the strongest magnetic poles on the planet? Hadn't she even read Ian McKay's belief that the magnetic "storms" that formed the circles disrupted the time-space continuum?

Suddenly it all made perfect sense. Whatever the power was, whatever the blue lights were, they were the source of the mysterious crop circles that had appeared in England for decades, perhaps centuries. If indeed they had created some sort of time portal—which suddenly seemed altogether reasonable given the events of the past day—then she had actually been taken back in time to the year 1194, to medieval England, to the days of knights and crusades and the burning of witches.

"Oh my God," she gasped. Running her tongue across suddenly dry lips, Kendra forced the panic from her mind. All right, if she had done the impossible and traveled through time, then she could do the impossible again and travel back to her own time. If she survived that long.

Kendra's hands turned suddenly clammy. Navarre had made it plain she was his enemy. She frowned, thinking back to their days together. Not only had he accused her of being a witch, but he had called her "Richard's salvation." What did that mean? He had mentioned the name "Locksley" too. She wasn't an expert on history, but as a teenager she had loved stories about medieval times, especially the days of Robin Hood, and Robin had been the Earl of Locksley, hadn't he? Robin of Locksley. Robin Hood. Richard. King Richard the Lionheart?

Kendra shivered and kicked out with her feet just to insure the vermin inhabiting the cell kept their distance as she thought about her hunch. Locksley and Richard. Navarre's accusations revealed that he believed she was working for the two men, or with them. That in turn had to mean that Navarre was *not* one of the guys wearing a white hat in this scenario.

She grimaced and shifted her position on the rotting haystack she'd been forced to use as a bed. The fact that Navarre was obviously not a hero came as no surprise to her. What she couldn't understand was how she could have been attracted to him. The image of Navarre, naked and hot against her, flashed through her mind and resolutely she pushed the picture away.

Locksley and Richard. But those were just fairy tales, weren't they? At least, the ones about Robin Hood. Of course there really had been a King Richard. She bit her lip, trying to recall the college class she had taken on medieval literature. Richard the First, so courageous he was known as the Lionheart, had journeyed to the Holy Lands to make war on the Muslims, leaving England unprotected and unguided. His brother John had tried to take over in his absence, initiating unfair taxes and harsh penalties. According to legend, Robert of Locksley had become an outlaw, called Robin Hood, sworn to defend England from John and the Sheriff of Nottingham until Richard returned. Wasn't that how the story went?

She shivered again, rubbing her arms vigorously against the dank chill of her prison. How long would he leave her in this hellhole? she wondered. How could he have left her there at all after what they had almost meant to each other? One corner of her mouth quirked up, and she was glad that in spite of the madness of the situation she still had her sense of humor. Or was she simply losing her sanity? That would be easy to do under the circumstances, and yet, she'd never felt so sharp, so clear minded, now that she knew what was happening.

It was the reporter in her, she supposed. Strange, even in the face of this incredible danger, every bone in her body screamed out "What a story!" It was silly, because even if she could get back to her own era, who would ever believe she had journeyed back in time? She'd be just another tabloid headline: "Journalist Travels Back In Time—Meets Robin Hood!" Kendra smiled. At least it would give Mac's fledgling paper a boost in the right direction.

Her smile faded. What was she thinking? She would likely never see Mac again. In fact, it was very likely that within the next twenty-four hours she would be burned at the stake or however they executed witches in 1194. Or maybe they would just let her starve to death in this horrible pit of despair. Kendra closed her eyes and shuddered. To die amid the stench, the filth, the rats, that would be the most terrible fate she could imagine.

"Navarre," she whispered aloud, "don't leave me here to die."

"I will not."

Kendra jumped to her feet at the sound of the deep, familiar voice. She almost rushed to the door but stopped, reminding herself that this man was not her rescuer but her captor.

"Why are you doing this to me?" she asked, hating the trembling sound of her voice. "I haven't done anything to you."

She could hear a key grating in a lock, then the door swung open. Navarre entered and the cell suddenly seemed much smaller. Kendra swallowed as the intensity of the golden eyes flickered in the light of the torch he held, boring through her.

"You have done much to me," he said softly. Reaching up he slid the torch into the metal wall socket designed to hold it, then moved through the dim light to her side. "You have done all you set out to do."

One hand lifted to cup her face, tilting her chin toward his, and before Kendra could protest, she was drowning once again in Navarre's embrace. His mouth plundered hers with a tenderness that, under the circumstances and considering the things he had accused her of, made little sense.

No! her mind shouted, as desire began to churn inside of her. He was her enemy. He was the bad guy. He had thrown her in a dungeon, how could she possibly want him?

But she did. When Navarre gathered her more tightly against him, she twisted her fingers into the dark texture of his hair and met him, passion for passion. His mouth devoured hers, his hands burned as they slid down the sides of her face, her shoulders, her breasts. His legs, hard and muscular pressed against her, forcing her backward until her spine touched the cold stone wall of the dungeon. It was the cold that brought her to her senses.

"What have I done to you?" she said breathlessly, pushing away from him, only succeeding in separating them slightly. "What have I done?"

"Bound me to you," he whispered, crushing her against him once again. "Made me burn with a fire that only you can quench. I cannot be near you without touching you. I cannot sleep for thinking of how I long to make love to you. I went into the forest to try to escape the thought of you. I cannot."

He squeezed his eyes shut. "God have mercy on me—you have ensorcelled me."

"No." Kendra heard the plea in her voice and fought for control. If she didn't know better she'd think it was the other way around—that he had used magic on her. Never in her life had she felt such passion, such flame, such raw desire as the knight pressed himself against her. "What I said about casting a spell on you, it was a joke—" she choked out "—a jest. I told you, I thought I was dreaming. I had hit my head, I didn't know I was awake!"

"No," he said, their faces inches apart, his golden eyes like a living flame. "You are a witch and you have enchanted me."

He turned away from her abruptly, leaning the flat of both hands against the wall in front of him. Kendra saw the tension in the set of his shoulders, the muscles straining taut beneath the soft fabric of his tunic. She longed to reach out and touch him, caress the knotted muscles.

"When I do my duty and bring you before the sheriff," he said, his voice low and muffled, "then I must watch you die and it will be like a knife thrust deeply into my heart." He sighed and Kendra saw the tension ease from his shoulders with the admission. "I beg you, in the name of God, release me from this torture. Repent and go to your death in a state of grace. I can fetch a priest." He lowered his hands from the wall and straightened, lifting his head with a kind of stoic resignation. "He will hear your confession."

Kendra moved to stand beside him. "I haven't enchanted you—I swear I haven't. I am not a witch. Let me go, Navarre." Kendra reached up and touched his face lightly. He closed his eyes and the look on his face was that of a man going through a great tribulation. "Let me go back to where I belong. Please, Navarre." Her hand slipped to rest lightly on his forearm.

"I cannot." He tried to move away but Kendra tightened her grip. With obvious reluctance he looked down into her face. For a long moment suspended in time they gazed at one another until at last Navarre shook his head slowly. "Nay," he said hoarsely, "I cannot."

"I am not what you believe me to be," she whispered. "I

am not a witch, nor am I Richard's salvation. I am . . ." she stopped, aware that if she began babbling about being from the future he would no doubt think her completely mad. What did they do with madwomen in medieval times? The word "bedlam" crossed her mind, and with it pictures of dungeon-like rooms inhabited by the insane.

"I am just a peasant girl who got lost." She lowered her gaze. "Please, Sir Navarre, please let me go home."

"Nay," he said softly, then turned and to her surprise, took her back into his arms. "But neither will I treat you in this manner. Your sorcery will at least insure you of a warm place to sleep and decent food."

"I'm not—" Kendra broke off, too tired to pursue the argument further.

"Come with me," he said, pushing the rough planked door open. Stunned for a moment, Kendra quickly recovered and hurried out of the dank cell, not daring to question why her captor was releasing her. She stopped abruptly and went back inside, searching the floor of the cell in a kind of panic. Her bag. Her bag contained all she had left to her in the world, all that she was.

"What are you doing?" Navarre said crossly. "Do you wish to remain here?"

"No, I'm just looking for my—there it is." Kendra pounced on a pile of straw, remembering belatedly that she had hidden the bag under the filthy covering and sat on it in the hope that the rats would not find and destroy it. One was gnawing on the strap as she crossed the cell and she kicked it away, ignoring its squeal of protest.

"Give it to me," Navarre ordered, holding out his hand. "Where did it come from? I do not remember you having it when I brought you here. Did you conjure it from the air?"

Kendra clutched the bag to her chest obstinately. Then, with a sigh, she held it out to him.

"No, I did not 'conjure' it," she said, spitting out the word. "I've had it with me the whole time. Can I help it if you aren't very observant?"

"Be silent," he said, almost casually. Slinging the bag over his shoulder, he motioned for Kendra to walk in front of him.

When she hesitated, Navarre glanced back into the cell and with a muttered curse, she complied. Silently they walked down the dark corridor until they reached the end of the hallway where a flight of steps led upward.

Clenching her fists tightly to keep herself from making a futile attempt to escape, Kendra could hardly contain herself when they reached the top of the stairs. Daylight streamed through a long, narrow window and Kendra rushed over to it, drawing in great, ragged breaths of the clean, extremely cold morning air, so different from the putrid stench she had endured all night. She sighed with relief.

"Where are you taking me?" she asked, as Navarre took her by the elbow and began propelling her up yet another flight of stairs.

"To the tower." His square face was taut with resolve. "It is clean and has a place for a fire. I will bring food to you." He wrinkled his nose. "Or have it sent. Zounds, what a stench you make, girl."

Kendra blushed, then lifted her chin defiantly and stopped in her tracks halfway up the stairway. "It isn't as though I asked to be thrown into that pigsty," she said. "I need a bath."

Navarre glared down at her, but all at once one corner of his mouth twitched and a slight smile crossed his stern features. "Aye," he said, "that you do."

"You could use one yourself," she said, tossing the now leaden mane of hair back with as much impudence as she could muster, then drew in a quick breath as the hard gold of his eyes softened to liquid fire.

"Aye." His husky voice slid across her shattered nerves like a soothing balm. "That I could."

For a moment she thought he might smile again, then the sternness returned to his lips, but the heat did not fade from his gaze.

"Come," he said.

"Where are we going?"

One dark brow arched upward. "Why, to take a bath."

"Both of us?" Kendra demanded.

This time a true smile stretched across his handsome face

and it was a wicked sight to behold. Kendra shivered and wondered again just who was bewitching whom.

"Afraid, my little sorceress?" he asked softly. "Do not tell me you have never bathed with a man."

She opened her mouth to speak but once again Navarre took the advantage. Kendra felt the hot flame of passion course between them as his lips covered hers, coaxing them apart, burning into her with a fire that was almost painful in its intensity. She moaned aloud and felt Navarre's arms tighten around her, his own breath catch in his throat as he suddenly released her and took a step back, almost stumbling down the stairs. Kendra reached out to steady him and he stared down at her hand on his arm, a dazed look on his face.

"All right, witch," he whispered, his golden gaze flashing back to hers. "This time we will finish what you began in the crag, but this time it will be you who are ensorcelled and not Navarre de Galliard."

Chapter Six

Navarre led Kendra to the bathhouse, a building the sheriff had devised for the specific purpose of always having warm water available when he wanted to take one of his daily baths. People in the village whispered among themselves about Garrick's preoccupation with cleanliness. If he had been a commoner, he probably would have been accused of witchcraft.

Most of the villagers seldom bathed, except perhaps in the heat of summer when the bathing was actually secondary to swimming. Those of higher standing bathed more regularly, but to bathe every day, and especially during the winter months, it was unheard of and invited death, on that everyone in Nottingham agreed. Navarre was amused by Garrick's obsession but enjoyed an almost daily wash himself. He and the sheriff had learned new customs during their tenure in the Holy Land, new customs and new horrors.

Navarre shook the thought away. Of course, bathing often in winter was something he had not yet braved, but an occasional bath was a pleasure he now looked forward to. And yet he knew it wasn't the thought of that particular pleasure stirring his senses as he escorted Kendra into the building.

A large room, Garrick had designed it well, with one large, oval tub sunken into the flooring. A hole had been dug for the wooden tub to fit snugly below the surface of the ground, devised with a quite revolutionary device that allowed the tub to be drained daily and fresh water pumped in. Garrick had designed the tubes that carried the water to and from the tub, and the blacksmith had made the tubes from bronze. One tube

91

Tess Mallory

was connected to an outside cistern where rainwater was caught. The tube brought the water from the cistern into the building where it flowed into another, smaller cistern. There it was heated, then pumped by a servant into the tub. The other tube took water away from the tub, taking it under the building and out into an open field nearby. The sheriff had seen one in Rome during his travels, and had vowed to build one himself someday. John had approved and even dipped into his own pocket to help pay for the expensive extravagance.

Torches ensconced around the walls lit the room, but the center of light and warmth was the round fireplace in the middle of the room. The stone chimney went straight up through the ceiling and the hearth opened on two sides, giving warmth to the bathers.

"Kin I assist the lady, sire?"

Navarre looked down at the old woman plucking at his sleeve. She was almost toothless, but her gray hair was clean and combed back in a neat knot at the base of her neck. Respectfully she lowered her eyes as she awaited his response. Garrick always had someone maintaining the bath. It was an extravagance John often complained about, but he loved the baths himself and his objections never lasted long.

"Yes," Navarre said at last. "She must be bathed to be presented to the sheriff and Prince John."

The woman began peeling the layers of filthy clothing off of Kendra who opened her mouth as if to protest, then snapped it shut and glared up at the knight.

Navarre stood, legs apart, hands clasped behind his back, and watched as the servant disrobed his prisoner. His gaze locked with Kendra's and silently he dared her to object. A flicker of response flashed across the blue eyes and her chin lifted in challenge as she allowed the woman to complete her ministrations. In a matter of moments Kendra stood completely naked before him.

Navarre felt the now familiar fire kindling inside of him and found himself unable to look away from her. A sheen of perspiration broke out across his brow that had nothing to do with the warm water steaming up below him. She was lovely, there was no other word to describe her. Breasts, soft and full, were the color of fresh cream, with peach-colored centers and a smattering of freckles scattered across her chest. Her waist was small, with lush hips complementing her ample bosom, and a triangle of fiery red hair stark against the paleness of her skin.

Navarre began to tremble. Their brief, almost frantic attempt to couple in the crag had not afforded him this view of his seductress. She continued to gaze up at him, as though she, too, felt mesmerized by the mysterious force drawing them together.

"Here, love," the old woman said, breaking the moment, "just step down here in the nice warm water." She took Kendra by the hand and helped her into the tub. Kendra went in wordlessly, still looking at Navarre. "And you, my lord," the attendant said, "kin I help you undress as well?"

Navarre didn't answer at first, didn't take his eyes from the auburn-haired woman. Then slowly, almost imperceptibly, he nodded. He watched the outrage form in Kendra's eyes and could no longer contain the smile that flashed across his lips. The old woman didn't bat an eye as she pushed him down onto a nearby stool and slipped his tunic over his head. When she would have removed his braes, however, he stopped her.

"Leave us," he ordered. Kendra sank a little further down into the water. Her eyes no longer burned with arrogance, he saw, but with a kind of fear, and apprehension. It made him feel, at last, that he had the upper hand—that this woman who had made him feel so completely out of control, could be made to feel the same way. It gave him a sense of power. Perhaps, after all, the way to be free of her was to prove to himself, and to her, that in spite of her spells, Navarre de Galliard remained his own man, a man who would not be controlled by a woman's wiles or a witch's spell.

The old woman hurried out without a backward glance. Navarre stood and began to tug at the cord holding his braes about his waist.

"What do you think you're doing?" Kendra asked.

"I have been giving it much thought," Navarre said as he matter-of-factly untied his braes and slid the dusty black material over his hips and down his legs before kicking them aside. He noted that Kendra kept her gaze stubbornly fixed upon his face in spite of his nakedness, and he almost chuckled aloud.

"This fire you have ignited inside of me burns most uncomfortably," he went on, "and I have decided that the only way to conquer it is to quench the flame." He stepped down into the water and felt an intense satisfaction at the real panic he saw leap into her eyes. The water felt wonderful on his weary body and he silently thanked Garrick for being such a sensualist.

"Don't come any closer," she said, in her curious dialect.

"Ah, but you have drawn me closer." He moved slowly through the waist-high water until he stood only inches away from her. He cocked one dark brow. "It is you who have cast a spell upon me. But if you think that by causing me to lie with you, you may control me, I bid you think again. My strength is greater than you know."

Her blue eyes flashed as Navarre lifted his hand and brushed his fingertips across her bare, wet arm.

"You didn't think so in the crag," Kendra said, shivering against his touch.

"True." His fingers traced a droplet of water across her collarbone and down the creamy expanse below. He felt her stiffen beneath his touch. "However, the fear I now see in your eyes convinces me that I may have been hasty in pronouncing you a witch, in which case, there is no reason not to avail myself of your abundant charms."

The woman stiffened as he brushed his fingers across her collarbone, up to one shoulder and then down her arm. His lips followed the path he had just traced and then moved from her arm to the center of her breastbone where his tongue painted a new pattern upward. He glanced up and saw she had her eyes closed, her lips pressed tightly together. She was trembling and the knowledge quickened his desire to possess her fully. Instead, Navarre brought his mouth to hers, pressing a burning kiss to her cold lips as he slid his hands lightly across her breasts, barely touching them as he continued to move upward, moving his fingers gently up either side of her neck and plunging them into her hair. She winced as his fingers met with a matted tangle.

"My lady is in need of a good brushing it seems," Navarre said softly. Kendra started to speak and he laid one finger against her lips. "I will play lady's maid." Slowly he began to unwind the long, matted braid she had fashioned during her night in the dungeon. His fingers hit another snag and Kendra reached up reflexively to grab his wrist.

"That hurts."

"I will be gentle," he promised, gazing down into her eyes, "in many ways." Again, her lips parted with words she did not utter, then she pressed them together and looked up at him.

Navarre drew his fingers through her hair, his gaze locked with hers as he separated tangled strands. Inch by inch he worked his way through the lush jungle of red and gold, forcing himself to ignore the way her breath came more quickly at his touch and the fact that her bare breasts, taut and aroused, grazed his chest. He ignored his own arousal even as he savored the feel of his rigid skin against her soft belly. Gradually he worked the tangles out of her hair, then turned and picked up one of the special soaps Garrick insisted the tub be supplied with, and began working up a lather between his hands.

"Lavender," Kendra said, her voice husky.

Navarre glanced up from the froth in his palms and smiled. "Stolen," he whispered, "from Madagascar pirates."

Her face was flushed as Navarre moved toward her again, his lathered hands extended slightly in front of him. Kendra blinked, then took a step back. There was nowhere to go. She stretched out both hands to either side of the wooden pool for support. Navarre froze at her motion and drew in a long, shuddering sigh.

Kendra stood, arms apart, creamy breasts exposed for his view, his touch, her sweet lips lifted to him for his kiss. He could see surrender in her eyes, in the very tremble of her breath. Forcing himself to advance slowly, Navarre moved until his chest was barely touching hers, then, lifting his lathered hands, he eased them into her auburn hair and lowered his mouth to hers.

She cried out against his lips and he longed to echo her utterance. The sweetness of her mouth was as he had remembered, and as his hands caressed her luxurious mane of hair, his tongue caressed her mouth and made its own sweet plunge into the depths of the fire that was Kendra. He was possessor, he was possessed.

Navarre lowered his hands to her shoulders and massaged the gentle lavender froth into her skin, then slid his fingers down to caress her breasts. Closing his eyes, he allowed himself to think only of the way she felt, the weight of the peach-tipped jewels he held in each hand. He bent his lips to pay homage to each and was rewarded by Kendra's quick intake of breath.

"Navarre," she whispered, sliding her hands around his waist.

He pulled her away from the side of the tub and leaned her down into the water, one hand supporting her back as he used the other to spill the warm liquid over her hair. Kendra closed her eyes with a sigh as the warmth cascaded over her hair and trailed between her breasts. With a touch more gentle than he knew he possessed, Navarre massaged her scalp, again drawing his fingers through the tresses until every knot and crimp had melted into flowing silken threads.

Navarre lifted her head and Kendra opened her eyes. He saw surprise mirrored there and something akin to trust. It was the trust that stirred something long dormant inside of him as Navarre lowered his lips to the hollow of her throat. He did not stop to examine the new emotion. The sudden realization that her arms were around his neck sent a wave of delight shuddering through him as Navarre drew her firmly against him and closed his eyes.

This is a mistake. The knowledge came to him with swift and brutal intensity. This time he could not blame her; this time he alone was responsible for the seduction. Why had he believed he could make love to this enchantress and still preserve his own soul? He could not. He knew now that if he availed himself of her sweet warmth as he longed to do, he would lose himself forever, for he would never be able to give her up—not for Garrick, not for England. And yet, the inferno raging inside of him could no longer be denied. The fire in his loins cried out to meld with the molten lava that was woman— this woman. Navarre groaned aloud. He must feel his seed burn inside of her or be devoured by his own flame.

"Sweet sorceress," he whispered against her hair, the scent of lavender encompassing him. "I must make love to you or die."

"Death is so final," she said softly, "and I think I would miss you sorely."

Her arms tightened around his neck and Navarre cradled her face between his hands, his gaze searching hers.

"Now that is a scene more befitting my old friend Navarre than I have seen for quite some time." A deep voice filled with amusement echoed around the enclosure.

Instantly alert, Navarre turned, blocking Kendra from the intruder's view. Nay, he thought as a sense of panic threatened to overwhelm him. 'Twas not fair. He needed more time—time to discern if Kendra was witch or merely desirable woman. Time to quench this terrible fire.

"Garrick," he said, trying to disguise his frustration. "You have returned."

"Aye," the voice said from the shadows. "Do introduce me to your friend."

Navarre felt Kendra's hand suddenly against his back—in warning? In fear? He felt her shiver, and for some unfathomable reason, a cold tremble of premonition shivered through him too.

"Kendra," he said reluctantly, "may I present the Sheriff of Nottingham."

Back in his chamber, Navarre hurried to change his clothing. He donned a split-sided sleeveless tunic the color of a lion's mane over a black undertunic that had long, full sleeves. The black matched his braes and soft leather boots, as well as the lion that danced in miniature repetition across the golden tunic. Navarre lifted his hand absently to touch one small beast. Bastard son of a Norman nobleman, Navarre de Galliard had become a wealthy mercenary in his twenties but had no title, no future, until he heard King Richard was raffling off nobility, titles, and estates for enough gold to enable him to wage war on Outremer, the Holy Land.

Richard had befriended Navarre, as well as Garrick, Na-

varre's childhood friend, whose mother had also borne a nobleman's child out of wedlock. Richard soon assigned Navarre
to ride at his side in battle and the knight became the king's
bodyguard, protecting him on the field and off. Richard was a
courageous warrior, called the Lionheart, and soon Navarre,
because of his dark hair, golden eyes, and fierce demeanor,
came to be known as Richard's shadow, the Black Lion.

In a small but solemn ceremony one bright April morning
near Jerusalem, Richard had paid Navarre honor by declaring
him knight, this time by merit, not by coin. At that time Richard had signed over several small estates to his protégé, much
to the distress of his advisors. The next day a messenger de-
livered a golden tunic with the handsome silhouette of a black
lion rampart upon it, a gift from Richard.

Navarre lowered his hand from the material, and reached
down for the sword he always wore at his side. Another life,
he thought idly. Another Richard—a man I loved like a
brother—who no longer existed.

He ran one hand through his hair, then picked up the saddlebag that contained the witch's strange weapon. It was time to
face John and Garrick, time to tell them that the woman who
held his heart in her hands was most likely a witch, sent there
to destroy them all.

Kendra took a deep breath and tried to slow her racing
pulse. When the man Garrick appeared in the bathhouse, inadvertently saving her from her own folly, Navarre had fled
from her side like a fox being pursued by a thousand hounds.
He had thrown on his clothing and hurried his friend to the
door, but before the two men left, Garrick had turned back,
his gaze sweeping over her naked form appreciatively. He had
laughed as she quickly covered herself with her arms, then
with a dramatic sweep of his black cape, followed Navarre out
of the bathhouse.

In a matter of moments, the old woman had returned, her
arms laden with clothing. Kendra had spent the next hour being dressed, primped and prodded by the woman whose lips
might as well have been made out of stone, for all the information she was able to pry out of her.

Now she stood before three men who were seated at the huge trestle table in the great hall, muttering to one another in French. She was terrified. All of her reporter's skills, her investigative calm, and her bravery, seemed to have disappeared in the midst of this impossible scenario. Where was her courage, she wondered, the kind of courage that had seen her through two hostage situations, a fire and an earthquake?

She smoothed her sweating palms against the unfamiliar garment hugging her tense body. She was clean at least, and her hair was—no, better not to think about her hair, for if she did she would think of Navarre's hands and the incredibly sensual shampoo he had given her, and *that* would cause her to remember his mouth on hers, hot with passion, and that would make her remember the width of his shoulders and chest and the way his body felt pressed against hers.

Enough. She tossed the long neat braid behind her shoulder, aghast at her reaction to her captor. Granted, the sexual attraction between herself and Navarre was incredible, but that was no reason to cast aside every ounce of morality or pride that she had for a chance to tumble him in the tub.

Kendra took another deep breath and glanced at Navarre. He sat behind the table speaking to a tall, blond man whom she recognized as Garrick, the man from the bathhouse, the sheriff of Nottingham. She smoothed her hands against her gown again. Dressed now in the fashion of the day, coupled with the events of the last few hours, Kendra felt a dizzy, terrifying sense of unreality sweeping over her.

The woman had given her a long dress to wear made from a slightly coarse material, brownish in color and quite unattractive; nevertheless, it fit the contours of her bodice and waist snugly before widening at the hips and falling freely to her ankles. The sleeves were long and tight and ended in points at the wrists. Over the gown she had been given a sleeveless, open-sided tunic, called a surcoat, that was really rather lovely, soft, and forest green, one of her best colors. Over that went a girdle or "kirtle," which amounted to a kind of sash worn low on the hips and knotted on the lower part of her belly. She had dressed, marveling in one part of her mind that she was truly experiencing the phenomenon of wearing medieval

clothing, while another section of her brain screamed for someone to wake her out of the nightmare.

She had been brought to a huge room called the great hall.
A gigantic fireplace adorned one of the longest walls and long,
narrow tables filled the room, benches on either side. It was a
room capable of hosting a large contingency of guests, however, this night it was empty, save for the three men and herself. The table where Navarre and the other two men sat was
placed on a level of stone that was slightly higher than the
others. Platters of food were being placed on the table by servants, and Kendra began to tremble as the two strangers smiled
at her, as if relishing what was about to take place.

"Now, Navarre," said a young, dark-haired man seated in
the only high-backed chair behind the table. "We shall speak
in English as you requested, but please do tell us about this
wench. You have my curiosity quite aroused, as well as other
parts of me."

Kendra nervously shifted her attention back to Navarre. He
was seated on one side of the short man, whom she assumed
to be the infamous John Lackland, the king's brother. The
Sheriff of Nottingham sat on his other side, smiling at her in
a manner she found disturbing. For some reason the man
frightened her more than all the other dangers she had encountered. Navarre looked up at her, and suddenly Kendra
found herself lost in the depths of his golden eyes.

He stood slowly, his gaze locked with hers, and Kendra
shivered as she felt the electricity—the magic—flow between
them. She saw an answering tension in his face as he left his
place and moved to stand beside her.

"There is not that much to tell, actually," Navarre said,
resting one hand on the hilt of his sword. "Acting on a report
from one of our spies in the village, I followed Robin of Locksley to the hut of Magda." The knight paused and glanced at
Kendra.

"Yes, yes, the strange woman who talks to trees," John
said in a tolerant voice. "Go on."

"She read the runes—"

"The what?" John interrupted, his brows knit together in
confusion.

"Runes—stones with strange symbols upon them," Navarre said impatiently. "Long ago it was said the druids used them to reveal the future."

"Then this woman, Magda, is a witch!" John plunked his goblet down indignantly. "You have always said that she was not, that she was only a madwoman."

"And so she is, my lord," the knight agreed. "However, she is also one of the last druid priestesses in the land and is greatly revered by the Saxons. She is not a witch; she does not cast spells or wish evil on others. She simply believes that she can tell the future."

"And can she?" Garrick asked, nonchalantly flicking a bit of food from the front of his perfect teeth.

"The Saxons think she can. In any case, Robin was at Magda's hut and I overheard her tell him of a prophecy."

"Prophecy?" John lifted his goblet once again and took a deep draught from it. "This sounds most sorcerous to me, Sir Navarre."

"She told Locksley that great danger awaited Richard, and that in a fortnight Richard's salvation would appear on the plains of Abury."

"And what did she mean by that—Richard's salvation?"

"I do not know. At first I dismissed it as nonsense, as a madwoman's ravings, but then I began to think perhaps it was a way to cleverly pass on information under the guise of her babbling."

"If so, an excellent ruse," the sheriff said, popping a plump piece of meat into his mouth, never taking his gaze from Kendra. Indeed, his attention had been riveted on her from the moment she had been escorted into the room by Navarre. Kendra shifted her position uneasily, wishing they would at least let her sit down before they burned her at the stake.

"A fortnight later I managed to create a diversion that kept Locksley from arriving at Abury on time," Navarre went on, his brows knit together. "I hid myself, expecting perhaps an assassin sent to destroy John. While I waited, a storm blew up, but unlike any storm I have ever seen. It whirled with such intensity, and it seemed I could almost see some kind of light in its center."

"Light? Like a torch?" John said, leaning forward. "How curious."

Kendra waited for Navarre to describe the light, knowing full well the sighting of a blue light would brand the incident as something highly unusual, surely magical. When he continued his tale without alluding to the blue lights, Kendra felt both relieved and puzzled.

"Aye, it was that, but then the storm blew away and I found this woman."

"Odd." Garrick's gray eyes were no longer languid and casual, Kendra noted, but clear and cold. He rose and circled around the table to Navarre's side. Kendra shivered again as the sheriff stopped directly in front of her and let his gaze sweep over her with calculated ease.

The sheriff was a handsome man, she decided, as she made her own appraisal. Not as ruggedly attractive as Navarre, but very handsome. Garrick was the epitome of the pretty boy, she thought, lifting her chin slightly to meet his challenging eyes. She saw little character, but she bet he had lots of charm when he wanted to use it.

"A bold wench," Garrick said with a laugh. "Still, she hardly seems the type to be an assassin—or a spy." A slow smile stretched across his features. "I would more likely grant her the role of . . . seductress." He darted a glance at Navarre. "Is that the way of it, old friend? Did she seek to seduce you into revealing our secrets?"

Kendra heard the quick intake of breath, saw Navarre's hands knot into fists at his side, then slowly relax.

"Nay," he said quietly. "She is but a woman. I do not yet know her part in this affair."

"Strange the manner in which she appeared after the storm," John said, "almost as if it were some type of magic." He tapped one finger against the side of his face, reflectively. "Magda predicted her arrival there. How know you, Navarre, that both Magda and this woman be not witches?"

Kendra tensed herself as she waited for Navarre's answer.

"I know not," she heard him say, his voice filled with hesitancy. " 'Tis best, perhaps, that we keep her our prisoner until we are able to discern her function in this matter."

A loud laugh startled Kendra and she looked up to see Garrick leaving his chair and crossing to her side.

"Ho, my friend, methinks I already know one very apt function the wench can fulfill, and it takes no discernment to name."

Kendra took a step back from him. This was it. Time to exercise the strength she was famous for. She swallowed hard and took a deep breath.

"Am I to be allowed to speak?" she asked, glaring up at the man towering over her.

Garrick glanced over at Navarre and one corner of his mouth quirked up in amusement.

"No," he said. "At least, not now. For now, you shall sit beside me and partake of the best that Nottingham has to offer.

"But I—"

"God's teeth, Navarre, is this your witch?"

Kendra and Navarre both turned, open-mouthed, as a slight girl of about fifteen glided across the stone floor to stand beside Navarre. The girl was slim, her face colorless, her hair muddy colored and ill-kept. She stared openly at Kendra and Kendra stared back, biting back a smile as the girl tried to appear haughty and failed miserably.

"Hold your blasphemous tongue, young lady, or I shall send you to Father Tucker for confession," Navarre said sternly. The girl hung her head and murmured a polite apology, but Kendra saw a small smile tugging at the corner of her mouth and found herself immediately drawn to the teenager.

"What is all this about witches, Marian?" John asked, rising to stare at the girl in front of him.

Kendra raised one brow. Marian? Maid Marian, and Robin, and the Sheriff of Nottingham? She closed her eyes. This was really too much.

"Everyone in the castle is speaking of it," Marian said, moving to take her seat behind the table after looking Kendra up and down quite openly. She reached for a golden pitcher and, with an air of refinement, poured a dollop of wine into a goblet.

"What are they saying?" Garrick asked.

Marian took a sip of her drink. "That Navarre has captured

a witch.'' She lowered the wine and returned her gaze to Kendra. "I must say that I am disappointed. No warts or anything. What is your name?"

"Kendra," Kendra said quickly with a smile, happy to be spoken to as a person instead of an inanimate object. "Kendra O'Brien."

"This woman is no witch, Marian," Navarre said, his voice hard. "She may be a spy, but she is no sorceress."

"Oh, well, then she is of no interest to me." Marian promptly turned her attention to two fat birds a servant had deposited on her plate.

"Come, my dear," Garrick said, offering Kendra his arm. "You must be starved after your long journey. I do apologize for your unnecessary stay in our dungeon." He glanced at Navarre. "Tsk, tsk, my boy, have you no sense of chivalry? To place such a lovely blossom down in the dungheap—'tis a travesty."

Kendra felt Navarre stiffen beside her.

"I thought it the proper place for her at the time," he said shortly. "After all—"

"Tut, tut," Garrick waved one hand dismissively. "One maid can hardly hold any danger for us. Therefore, we shall enjoy her as a welcome diversion—but first, we shall dine."

Kendra let the man take her hand and tuck it into the crook of his arm. She followed him meekly to the chair beside his, all the while her mind racing ahead. There had to be a way out of this, a way to keep the sheriff from using her as a "welcome diversion." What that way might be she had no idea. She glanced over at Navarre and saw with surprise that his jaw had tightened and the golden eyes shifted to molten stone as she took her seat beside Garrick. Turning on his heel, he strode back around the table, slamming himself down into the chair beside Marian's.

The sheriff smiled at him. "Don't worry, my friend, you shall taste the lady's pleasures as well as I. But, of course, you already have, haven't you?" He waved one hand. "Enough of this. John and I have much to tell concerning our journey to London."

"Aye," Navarre agreed. "But I suggest we discuss it in private. Marian, finish your meal and retire."

"I am sick of staying in my room," the girl said, pouting. "I have waited and waited for everyone to come home so that I might have my evening meal with someone besides the cook!"

"I would be delighted to have you stay," John said. "Really, Navarre, you do forget yourself betimes. One would think Marian was your ward instead of Richard's." He lifted a goblet of wine and tossed it down, then drew the back of his hand across his lips and poured himself another glassful. "I have been giving it much thought and I have decided that in Richard's absence, as his brother, I shall adopt Marian as my ward."

Kendra felt rather than saw the tension that sprang into Navarre's body with John's words. "I beg pardon, my lord," he said, "I have grown to think of Marian as much my ward as the king's—"

"As Richard's, you mean," John said, the perpetually boyish look shifting suddenly to one of warning.

"Aye, as Richard's. I have known the girl since she was but a child and in Richard's absence have taken on the responsibility of her well-being." He bowed his head respectfully. "So, while your offer is most kind, you can see, my lord, there is no necessity for it."

"You overstep yourself, Navarre," John said, his voice harsh. "I have said the girl will be my ward and that is what I mean." He turned to Marian. "That would please you, would it not, my dear?"

Marian glanced at Navarre, glowering. Then she shifted her gaze to the leering face of John. "I am quite honored, my lord. However, Navarre has always cared for me, even when Richard was in England."

Kendra lifted one auburn brow and shot Navarre a knowing look. He had the effrontery to glare back at her.

"Now that honor falls to me," John insisted, leaning back and gesturing for a servant to take away his plate. "And what is this "my lord" nonsense, Navarre? I am Richard's brother, ruling in his stead. Shall you not call me 'sire' as is my due?"

Navarre's face tightened and Kendra caught the subtle exchange between Garrick and the knight.

"As you are not the king, my lord," Garrick said smoothly. "And lest someone misunderstand your desire to help Richard in his absence," he said, looking meaningfully at Marian and then at Kendra, "I suggest we leave titles as they are presently. You must remember, John, that your lady mother, and her minions, rule in Richard's stead. You serve as her ambassador of good will."

"Dear, dear mother," John said mockingly, his full lips thrust forward in a babyish pout. "That will all change, Garrick, very, very soon."

"Yes, my lord," Garrick said, tapping his long jewel-bedorned fingers on the tabletop. "Now, shall we move on to other topics of interest? Mayhap Marian will be interested in the matter of those people."

Navarre frowned. "What people?"

"Ah, yes," John said, losing the pout and turning to Navarre angrily. "Those moneylenders. Really, Sir Navarre, I insist that we purge England of these heathenish Jews."

Navarre sighed in a tolerant way. Kendra watched him, weighing his reaction to John's petulant request.

"My lord, I have talked with you of this. The Jewish moneylenders do us no harm, in fact they do us a great amount of good. They keep a good deal of gold in circulation—gold that we would not have in England without them, thanks to Richard."

"Still," Garrick interjected, placing a thin morsel of meat on his tongue and winking in Kendra's direction, "they are such inferior creatures, such unbearable heathens, that I think it detrimental to our cause to tolerate such people." He waved his hand again. "Take a squad of men and find them, Navarre. Kill them, ship them to Normandy, I care not. You agree, John, do you not?"

"Indeed, indeed I do."

Kendra seethed inwardly at the bloodthirsty, yet casual command. To speak of killing people as though it was of no more consequence than killing a hill of bothersome ants! She leaned forward slightly to watch Navarre's face. His jaw was even tighter now and the flame in his eyes fairly danced.

"We have talked of this," he said again, his voice deceptively quiet. "I will not make wholesale slaughter against a group of people simply because they are of a different race or religion than I am." He took a deep draught from his goblet, never taking his eyes from Garrick's as he set the heavy glass down with deliberate slowness. "You must have me confused, old friend. I am the Black Lion, not the golden one who murders women and children in Acre and leaves England to outlaws and thieves."

"Outlaws and thieves," Marian said dreamily. "I do like the sound of that—outlaws and thieves." She smiled. "It quite rolls off the tongue."

Kendra hid a smile behind her hand and decided once again that she liked Marian. She was obviously shy, and yet, there was a quality about her that pointed to a strong character and personality under the timid exterior. The girl seemed lonely. Kendra caught her breath. Perhaps she could use that loneliness to her own advantage. If she could find a way to befriend Marian, maybe the girl would help her escape from Nottingham! A long shot, but at the moment it was the only idea Kendra had.

"You'd not think it so romantic, my fairy, if you had to deal with the ruffians as I do," Navarre said. He glanced back at John. "Is it really your wish that I should massacre these people?" Before he could answer Navarre hurried on. "Remember, if England should happen to have need of funds, the Jews have gold and are willing to lend—unlike our own people."

Kendra watched John. He was much younger than she'd thought at first, no more than twenty, but already his face showed signs of dissipation and an indulgent lifestyle. He stroked the short goatee he had trimmed to an impressive point as his brown gaze flickered to Garrick, then back to Navarre.

"We should not be too hasty, I dare say, Garrick," he said hesitantly.

"Ridiculous nonsense." Garrick shoved his chair back and stood, fingers pressed against the wooden table. "We can wipe them out, take what they have, and add it to our coffers."

"Aye," Navarre agreed, rising slowly from his seat, "we could, if we were thieves and murderers. I, however, do not consider myself either." He cocked one dark brow. "Do you, Garrick?"

Silver eyes locked with golden and Kendra shivered, feeling the tension between the two men. It was an uncomfortable moment; then a slow smile spread across the sheriff's face. He sat down and picked up his goblet.

"As always, my friend, you bring me back from the brink of my own barbarous nature." He waved one hand. "Keep your precious Jews."

Navarre hesitated for a moment, as if he wanted to say more, but shook his head and sat down, his gaze darting to Kendra. The frustration she saw mirrored there surprised her, and suddenly she found herself wondering what a man like Navarre de Galliard was doing with this sleazy pair of back-stabbing scum.

"Why are you and Robin enemies now, Navarre?" Marian asked abruptly. Kendra glanced at her, half holding her breath at the mention of the legendary outlaw. To think he was alive and real. What a terrific story it would make—an interview with Robin Hood. She blinked and shook her head slightly as the now increasingly familiar sense of unreality threatened to close in on her.

"Little girls should mind their own business," he said shortly. "Now, run along, we have much to discuss."

"I am not a little girl." Marian lifted her chin. "I am a woman. Perhaps I should go where I may be treated as such."

"And where would that be?" Navarre asked, his lips curving up in amusement.

Marian glared at him. "Perhaps in Sherwood Forest."

The knight laughed without humor. "Aye, they would treat you as a woman all right, but not as your romantic heart supposes. Go to your room, Marian, before I turn you over my knee."

Marian's brief flash of spirit died quickly and she lowered both her gaze and her voice. "I protest your treatment of Robin, Navarre."

"Do you now?"

"Aye. He is a hero, not an outlaw. It is only because of him that England has not fallen into unsavory hands." She made her statement with an air of innocence that quite took away the sting of its meaning. The men exchanged glances and John frowned.

"Marian," Navarre said warningly, "go to bed."

With a flounce, the girl stood and swept away from the table, her long dress dragging across the dusty floor.

"Very well, but don't say I didn't warn you. Someday I shall run away to Sherwood."

"Marian, dear," John said warmly, standing and following her. "Do not rush away feeling slighted." He lowered his voice. "Not everyone sees you as Navarre does." He took her hand and patted it in a brotherly way. "I find you very charming. Now, please, allow me to escort you to your room."

Marian smiled up at the young man and Kendra saw a dark anger leap into Navarre's eyes, then just as quickly disappear as he rose from the table.

"Do not trouble yourself, John. I shall see Marian to her chambers. I have something to discuss with her anyway."

"No, no." John firmly steered Marian away from the table—and Navarre. "You and Garrick have much to talk about, and I believe you should question this woman about her involvement with R— with our enemies."

Marian turned back. "I do hope you won't kill her," she said dispassionately. "I am tired of having no one to talk with, and besides, she has lovely hair. See how it shines?"

Kendra felt herself blushing as all three men turned to stare at her. Navarre looked quickly away and Kendra almost burst out laughing in spite of herself. She saw a glimmer of mischief in the dowdy Marian's eyes, and she sensed the young woman was trying in her own way to help her. Now Kendra was even more hopeful of enlisting Marian's aid. John and Marian drifted out of the room and the sudden silence quickly became oppressive.

"Well." Garrick rose. "If you will excuse us, my friend, I believe I shall take our lovely guest to my chambers where I plan to become much better acquainted with her."

"You mean you plan to interrogate me," Kendra said sharply.

Garrick pursed his lips and shook his head. "What an ugly word, my dear. I say I want to know you better and that is what I mean. I must know where you are from, what brought you to Aveury—if the skin of your inner thighs is as creamy as your lovely face and your hidden curls as fiery as those you openly display."

Kendra could not help gasping at his crassness, and Garrick laughed at her discomfort. He leaned down and slipped one hand under Kendra's elbow, his thumb surreptitiously caressing the side of her breast. "Come, my dear, let us retire."

Kendra had two choices. She could stay where she was and hope Garrick wouldn't pick her up and carry her to his room, or she could give in gracefully and let Sheriff "Pretty Boy" introduce her to sex—medieval style.

Kendra pulled her arm out of his grasp. "Thank you," she said politely, "but I haven't finished my dinner."

"Oh, I think you have." Garrick bent down until his lips touched her ear. "It grows late, my love, and I, too, have a hunger."

Kendra felt the panic welling up inside of her, and yet that terrified thudding was almost drowned out by the roar of anger thundering in her temples. She fought for control. Losing her temper now would do her little good. She glanced at Navarre and saw that he had his lips pressed together, his fists clenched on top of the table. Still, he did not speak and made no move to save her from Garrick.

"I will not come willingly," she said, trying to use the syntax of the day, "for I am not a whore to be used for your pleasure."

Garrick feigned a small gasp and straightened, spreading his hands apart. "Of course you are not a whore, my dear. But I am the Sheriff of Nottingham, second in power only to John, the next king of England." He trailed his fingers down the side of her neck. "Surely you can see the advantage of bedding a powerful man like me."

"I am the daughter of an important man," Kendra said desperately. "I have been trying to tell you but you would not allow it. My father will be very angry if you defile me.''

Garrick chuckled. ''An important man? And he allowed his daughter to roam the countryside alone in the clothing in which you arrived?'' He cocked one brow. ''You speak no French. A noble's daughter? I think not. A merchant's? Perhaps. I assure you, your father will see the advantage of cultivating a close relationship with a man such as I.'' His fingers moved lower and Kendra steeled herself as he slipped his hand beneath her tunic and caressed the top of her breast.

The sound of Navarre's low voice suddenly next to her startled Kendra and she jumped. Garrick removed his hand slowly from beneath her gown, giving a little caress to the side of her cheek as he did so.

''I thought we were going to discuss your trip to London,'' Navarre said through clenched teeth.

Garrick turned, his eyes dancing with amusement. ''Jealous, my friend? I know, I know, you saw her first, but even though I interrupted you in the bath, surely you gave her a bit of a tumble on your journey here.''

''Mayhap the lady was not willing,'' Navarre said.

Garrick laughed out loud. ''You are *custodis pacis*, keeper of the peace, you have the authority to do as you wish.''

''Again, you confuse me with another,'' Navarre ground out. ''Just as I do not murder, I do not rape.'' Kendra watched in fascination at the subtle play of a muscle flexing in his jaw. ''And I remember a time when you did not either. What has happened to those days, Garrick?''

The good-natured look of amusement faded from the sheriff's countenance as he brought his hand down roughly on Kendra's shoulder.

''Those days ended when we agreed to free England, my friend.'' His voice was filled with warning.

''If freeing England means I must deny every value I ever held dear,'' Navarre said softly, ''then England must remain forever shackled, for I shall not rend her bonds by cutting the throats of innocents.''

Garrick's mouth twisted in a smirk. ''You think her innocent? You have grown soft, Navarre, and foolish. Now, if you will excuse me, I must 'interrogate' this lovely blossom of womanhood. Meet me early tomorrow to discuss our business.''

"Nay." Navarre's hand came down on Garrick's where it rested on Kendra's shoulder. The sheriff turned, his gray eyes filled with astonishment.

"We will discuss our business tonight, Garrick," Navarre said. "I shall send the woman to the tower since you object to her staying in the dungeon. Perhaps tomorrow you and I shall interrogate her together." Garrick's face went stony and Kendra could see the violence just below the surface. She waited, trembling, as the two men glared at one another.

"As John said, you go too far, my friend." The tone of the sheriff's voice sent a cold chill down Kendra's spine.

"Do not think that you may treat me in private as you treat me in front of John," the knight said in a low voice meant only for Garrick's ears. "I am not your lackey. Take care you remember."

The fury faded suddenly from the sheriff's eyes and he nodded, a slow smile curving his lips. Lifting one long strand of Kendra's auburn hair from her shoulder, Garrick sighed.

"Ah, yes, I will remember. I find I am quite weary after all. Let us discuss London tomorrow, shall we?" He made a slight bow toward Navarre, then straightened and clapped the other man on the shoulder and laughed. "Let us not have a wench come between us, Navarre. Here, take her, enjoy her. My turn will come soon enough. Good night, my dear." Lifting her hand briefly to his lips, Garrick smiled a filthy smile and strolled casually to the entrance of the great hall.

Kendra watched as he paused at the doorway and spoke with one of the guards, then left. As soon as he was gone, she rose and turned to ask Navarre why he hadn't told them she was a witch, and maybe even more important, why he hadn't shown Garrick the gun.

Instead, she found herself swept into Navarre's arms, lost once again in his embrace. His lips burned against hers, lowered to her throat, then caressed her cheeks, her forehead and back to her mouth again. No, it was not a kiss, she thought in some rational part of her brain. It was a possession.

Kendra felt herself sinking, falling, pitching headlong into that gentle ecstasy Navarre kept promising. Linking her arms around his neck, she let herself fall. When at last he broke the embrace and lifted his face from hers, his golden eyes pierced her with their feral intensity.

"His turn will never come," he said softly, "I promise you that." As abruptly as he had taken her, Navarre broke their embrace, dropping his arms to his sides. "Guards," he commanded, his eyes never leaving Kendra's face. "Take her to the tower."

Chapter Seven

Kendra was marched up a flight of stairs and down two dark corridors before coming to a halt in front of a huge door. Kendra gazed up at the gigantic portal, which must have been over twenty feet tall, and forgot for a moment her anger at Navarre's cursory dismissal. The door swung open, creaking with the effort, and Kendra lowered her gaze to meet that of the sheriff of Nottingham's. Suddenly she knew why the man had paused to speak to the guards before leaving the great hall.

"Do come in," he said, executing a slight bow. "I have everything ready for your comfort."

"My, what short towers you have here," Kendra said dryly. "I counted only one flight of stairs, or perhaps funds at Nottingham are so meager that you must build your towers meagerly as well."

Garrick chuckled. "A witty woman, how droll. Again, do come in, my dear."

Kendra felt the sharp prod of a spear at her back and smiled graciously. "Thank you so much, my dear sheriff, and will Navarre be joining us?"

His cool gray eyes were surprisingly warm as he smiled at her. "Unfortunately Navarre has other duties to attend to. Please, have a glass of wine while I excuse myself. I will be but a moment." He walked across the room and opened another, smaller door, then glanced back at her. "Oh, there are guards outside my chamber at all times, so please, do try and relax."

As soon as the door closed behind him, Kendra took a survey of her surroundings. First, a quick look out the huge door, which she had trouble even getting to budge. Cautiously, she peered around the edge of the doorframe and found Garrick hadn't been bluffing. Two armored guards stood on either side of the door. Neither turned his head to even look at her, but she knew instinctively they were both aware of her perusal. With a sigh, she pushed the heavy door shut and turned to consider her other options.

The walls of the room were stone of course, with almost every square inch covered by ornate tapestries, bright with color. Once again, torches were the major source of light, although only two of the six in Garrick's quarters were presently lit. A gigantic fireplace took up most of one wall, a fire flickering there now, warming the hearth. A tapestry above the mantle depicted none other than the Sheriff of Nottingham in full crusade battle gear: white surcoat over silver chain mail with a crimson cross blazing across his chest.

Kendra stared up at the cold gray eyes and felt the ice of his flat smile chill her blood with new fear. Deliberately she turned away and came face to face with Garrick's bed.

Massively built, it occupied center stage in the chamber. Huge posters, two feet in diameter, adorned each corner. They had been carved into gargoyles with lurid smiles and bulging eyes. A coverlet of what looked to be heavy black silk lay across the bed, golden tassels around the hem. Sheer black curtains flowed forth from a large golden medallion set into the wall above the bed, the material falling on either side, while a wealth of red and gold pillows completed the picture. Kendra shivered at the sight of it, then scolded herself for her timidity. She'd been in much worse situations, she reminded herself.

But never in medieval England, her inner voice whispered.

She ran her tongue across her lips and immediately regretted the movement. Garrick, garbed in a loose-fitting robe, open down his chest, had silently reentered the room and was watching her, his eyes gleaming in the dim light like a predator's.

"Admiring my colors, I see," Garrick said, moving toward her with a dancer's grace. "The house of Neushaw has always decorated in red and black with just a touch of gold."

115

Tess Mallory

"Rather sinister," Kendra said, feigning a nonchalance she didn't feel as the sheriff stopped directly in front of her.

Garrick chuckled. "If only my dear father could hear you. He prided himself on his charity, you know, except to the women he impregnated outside of his sainted marriage, of course." He lifted his hand to her face and drew the knuckle of his index finger down the side of her jaw.

Kendra swallowed hard. "Then you're a . . . that is, your mother wasn't married to your father."

"Bastard, my lovely. That's the word you are thinking and that is exactly what I am, just like my good friend Navarre. Both bastards who will achieve greatness and nobility by their own hand, and in spite of their absent, most noble fathers."

Kendra's mind raced as Garrick's finger moved to trace the outline of her lips. If she could keep him talking perhaps she could buy some time. She slipped away from his touch and crossed the room to stand in front of the fireplace.

"Have you and Navarre known each other long?" she asked, turning her back to the fire. She was grateful for the warmth. She hadn't felt really warm since she'd arrived in England a week ago. *A week ago.* The thought sent a wave of panic coursing through her. A week ago in the future. A week ago that had never even existed yet. Kendra closed her eyes, feeling faint.

"Forever, it seems."

Her eyes flew open. Garrick stood directly in front of her, his pale eyes flickering casually from her breasts to her face and back again. Too late she realized she had given him the advantage by placing the fireplace behind her. It left her with nowhere to go. Kendra drew in a quick breath as he reached for her, then she relaxed slightly as she saw he had reached for the end of her long braid.

"Navarre and I grew up in Normandy, bastard sons of two of England's aristocratic best. Unfortunately, although our births were acknowledged, our birthrights were not." He tugged at the leather tie binding her hair and tossed the thin strap aside, then slowly began to unbraid the auburn locks.

"Normandy," Kendra said, trying to maneuver past him toward the right. He moved slightly, his eyes on his work, and

116

blocked her way again. "How is it you speak English?"

Garrick shrugged. The braid was undone and he combed his fingers through her hair, spreading it around her shoulders. Kendra forced herself not to shudder at his touch.

"We speak the Norman tongue when we are alone—that is, speaking of John and Navarre and me. Many, like our good King Richard, speak only Norman. However, Navarre and I were unfortunate enough—or fortunate depending upon your outlook—to spend enough time in poverty to learn the Saxon tongue as well. I admit it has aided us more times than not over the years. As the daughter of a wealthy merchant you should not only know these things, but converse in the Norman tongue as well. Interesting."

"You didn't believe my story anyway, did you, Sheriff?" Kendra said, fighting the tremor in her voice as Garrick's gaze moved from her hair, back to her face, "I heard what Navarre said about the priestess and the prophecy," she blurted. "I swear to you, I know nothing about it. I do not know this woman, Magda, and I do not know King Richard or Robin Hood."

"My dear," Garrick said, cupping her head between his hands and pulling her toward him, "I care not whom you know or know not. This night, you shall know me—in every sense of the word."

Kendra opened her mouth to tell him it would be a cold day in hell before she bedded him. It was a mistake. Garrick covered her lips with his. His kiss was hard, demanding, and absolutely terrifying. Using both hands, she pushed against his chest as hard as she could. Off balance, Garrick stumbled back a step and Kendra made a mad dash for the door, then stared up at it, stupidly remembering the guards beyond. He was on her in a matter of moments, his chest against her back, his hot breath raking against her right ear. She could feel his hardness through the cloth of her gown and felt bile rise to her throat.

"I'll scream," she said, feeling hysterical laughter bubbling up inside of her at the sound of her own voice declaring the age-old feminine cliché.

Garrick laughed softly. "Scream away, my dear. No one will come to your aid." He placed the palms of both hands flat against the door, one on either side of her face, then pressed against her until Kendra could smell his heat. He began kissing the back of her neck and she swallowed hard, fighting back a wave of nausea.

"I am the Sheriff of Nottingham," he said, enunciating each word slowly against her ear. "Here, my word is law. Here, I do whatever I wish and there is no one who will stop me." He jerked the back of her gown up above her waist. "No one at all," he whispered.

Kendra fought down the scream welling up in her throat and instead turned in his arms, meeting his gaze, fighting to keep the fear from her eyes. If she were going to be raped, it wouldn't be without a fight and she couldn't fight with her face against a door.

"Do you always have to threaten women into your bed?" she asked, pushing the words out past the lump in her throat.

With an oath, he jerked her away from the door. Fighting and kicking, Kendra was dragged across the room and thrown across the huge bed. Before she could scramble off the thick coverlet, he had thrown himself on top of her and seized her by the throat. Gone was any semblance of the polite, amused nobleman, and in its place was a ruthless madman.

"You will not fight me," Garrick ordered, tightening each finger around her throat until Kendra's own hand shot up and encircled his wrist in mute protest. "You will lie quietly and let me do as I wish, or I will kill you."

Kendra tried to speak but couldn't. She was strangling, dying at the hands of this monstrous man, dying in a land far from her home, far from her time.

"Will you cooperate?" he asked savagely through his teeth, his face pressed close to hers, his fingers hard bands around her throat.

Second order of business according to Mac: survive. The thought raced through Kendra's mind just as tiny black spots began to invade her vision. She closed her eyes and forced herself to nod. The pressure around her throat immediately eased.

"Splendid."

She drew in a deep, ragged breath and began coughing.

118

Garrick gave her only a moment before he began his next attack.

"Now, my dear, just relax," he said, leaning over her, trapping her legs with one of his. "I assure you there is really nothing to fear. I am certain you will prefer my lovemaking vastly over that of my good friend, Navarre."

Garrick moved his fingers to the neck of her tunic and with one quick gesture, jerked. Kendra jumped as the material tore easily, then closed her eyes as he ripped away the cloth of her underdress as well. Trying to remain calm, she told herself she was tough, could endure even rape if it meant surviving. But when she felt the cool air strike her thighs, and heard Garrick groping to shed his own clothing, something inside of her snapped. With the instinct that had served her through two wars and countless disasters, Kendra brought her knee up hard between his legs.

Garrick doubled over, his roar of rage echoing around the room. His eyes clenched shut and Kendra felt a momentary satisfaction at the sight of actual tears on the man's cheeks. She didn't waste time watching him, however, but ran to the door. Using every ounce of her strength she pulled on the door handle, managing to budge it open a mere six inches. That was all she needed before the sheriff untangled himself from the bedclothes and stumbled to her side. She had one chance, one uncertain chance.

"Navarre!" Her scream echoed down the stone hallway, startling the guards at the door and causing them to turn toward her, spears lowered. Garrick reached her first. Kendra turned to face him, terrified at the anger in his eyes, the twisted grimace of rage about his lips. He lifted his hand and brought the back of it down across her face. With a cry Kendra fell to the floor, the jolt the stones gave her knees nothing compared to the pain lacing through her jaw.

"I shall kill you with my bare hands," Garrick whispered, circling around her. Kendra cried out in fear like a wounded animal, terrified by the violence of the man. Something told her Garrick's blow had been very minor compared to what it could have been and if she didn't give in, he would make good his promise and kill her.

Survival, a voice in her mind shouted. *Give in gracefully and beg for mercy.*

"So this is the great Sheriff of Nottingham," she heard herself say, almost looking around in horror to find who had spoken. "The man who rules England, some say, reduced to bludgeoning a woman into having sex with him."

"Silence!" he roared, reaching down and jerking her to her feet. "You will be silent!" He pulled his arm back again and Kendra closed her eyes, bracing herself for the blow.

"Garrick, what in hell is going on?"

Kendra's legs almost collapsed with relief as she heard the voice at the crack in the door. Navarre.

"Navarre, help me!" she cried, all pretense of control cast aside. Garrick's gray eyes bored through her, commanding her to be still, but instead she struggled against him, succeeding only in bruising her arms where his hands held her in an iron grip. He spun her away from him and she fell to her knees as he moved to shut the door completely.

"Navarre, in the name of God, help me!" she cried.

"Kendra?"

The door was shoved open seconds before Garrick could slide the inside bolt home, shoving the sheriff back as well. Garrick stumbled backward as the black-haired knight burst into the room, his tall form framed in the doorway, his golden gaze shifting to Kendra's crumpled form on the floor.

"Navarre," she whispered, "don't let him do this to me."

His furious glare took in the swelling evidence of Garrick's temper on her jaw as well as her torn clothing and exposed flesh. His jaw tightened and his eyes darkened.

To her astonishment Kendra found herself blushing with shame. When she'd stood before Navarre naked, at his bidding, she'd felt no shame, but Garrick's violence, which was in no way her fault, made her feel ashamed. Tears burned against her eyelids and one slid, unbidden, down her cheek as she tried to pull the edges of her tattered gown together. Navarre bent down on one knee and stopped her, one hand covering hers.

"Did he hurt you?" he asked, lifting her chin gently. "I mean—besides your face." She looked up at him, unable to hide the pain in her eyes. "Did he . . . damn you to hell, Garrick," Navarre said, stumbling to his feet.

Garrick had shut the door to the outer hall and now stood, arms folded across his chest in front of the fireplace. Navarre stopped a few feet from him and drew his sword from its sheath. The hushed sound of metal against metal echoed through the stillness of the room, and Kendra held her breath. The last thing she expected was for Garrick to throw his blond head back, sending a peal of laughter to follow the sound of steel.

"Do you draw your sword against me, old friend? Over a wench?"

"What did you do to her?" Navarre demanded, taking a menacing step toward the sheriff.

"What does it matter to you what I did to her?" His lips were still twisted in amusement, but his eyes burned like pale charcoal.

"If you have used her as you used the women in Outremer—"

"What will you do?" Garrick crossed the room to where two swords were mounted, crossed, on the wall. He jerked one of them down and the other fell to the floor with a loud crash. "Will you fight me?" he said, spinning back to face the knight, the sword slashing the air between them. "Will you kill me? All for the sake of this woman? Does our time together then indeed mean little to you, our quest become as nothing? What has happened to you, Navarre? Has this whore bewitched you?"

Kendra saw Navarre's face grow pale and knew she was lost. He lowered his sword, then flung it to one side, the crashing sound shattering what little hope she had left.

"Nay, I will not fight you," Navarre said, his voice somber. He shot Kendra a look that chilled her to the soul, then glanced back at the sheriff. "Come with me, friend. There is much I have not told you concerning this woman."

Kendra cried from relief and didn't seem to be able to stop. She buried her face in the pillows on top of Garrick's luxurious bed and let the tears come. At last, when it seemed the last moisture had been wrenched from her body, she sat up and wiped her face on the edge of a silken coverlet, taking great pleasure in blowing her nose on the expensive material. Composing herself, she tried the door several times only to find it had been locked from the outside after the two men had stalked into the hallway.

Exhausted, Kendra buried her face again in a large, soft pillow, realizing her tears were not just a result of the harrowing experience she'd just had, nor were they solely because she was trapped in time with an uncertain future. She had wept because Navarre had turned his back on her.

She realized that she had painted the dark knight into the hero's role, and he was anything but a hero. In the bathhouse she had thought for a while that perhaps Navarre was truly beginning to care for her. Then he had failed to protect her from Garrick, knowing full well how much the sheriff lusted after her. When Navarre had seen her bruised face she had known he would not leave her, that he would rescue her. In fact, she had feared he might kill the sheriff and be imprisoned himself. Instead, he had tossed aside his sword and betrayed her.

"Dear God," she whispered into the darkness of the pillow, "please help me."

"I will help you."

Kendra flung herself over at the sound of the soft voice and sat up. The Lady Marian stood at the end of the bed, and at the sight of Kendra's bruised face her own gentle features twisted, first in astonishment, then in outrage.

"Who has done this to you?" the girl asked.

Kendra brushed the moisture from her cheeks and tried to still the tremble in her voice. "The sheriff," she whispered.

"And Navarre did not stop him?" she demanded.

"He started to, but . . ." her voice trailed away. "He thinks I am a witch and now he has gone to tell Garrick how I appeared magically at Avebury and bewitched him." She laughed, a little hysterically. "What's funny is that Navarre doesn't even know the truth of how I came to be at Avebury, and even if I tried to tell him, he wouldn't listen."

Marian moved to her side and with a very maternal air for

one so young, smoothed Kendra's tangled hair back from her tear-stained face. "I have been sent to escort you, along with the guards, of course, to the tower." Her pale blue eyes bored into Kendra's. "Once we are there, I promise you, Kendra O'Brien, no one else will harm you, and I will listen."

With great care Marian helped a muscle-sore Kendra change into fresh clothing before leading her into the wide corridor past the guards, who fell into step behind them. As she walked down the great hallway behind the thin young woman, Kendra felt at least some of her strength returning. She was still alive, she told herself, trying to bolster her own spirits, and had not been subjected to the trauma of rape, nor to great physical harm. She had tossed aside the last vestiges of belief in Navarre de Galliard. The last item in itself was a great accomplishment.

Of course, Navarre was no doubt at this moment telling the sheriff of her witchery where he was concerned, and no doubt the good sheriff—angry at her rejection of his attentions— would sentence her to be burned. She had to escape, and the thought sent a fresh wave of panic coursing through her. Her only chance of escape lay with this teenaged girl, who didn't have the gumption to say boo to a mouse. Or did she?

"In order to reach the tower," Marian explained as they walked, "we must walk outside the castle itself. The steps spiral up the sides of the turret and guards are posted at the bottom. It is impossible to escape from the tower," she added.

Without help, Kendra thought, but she nodded outwardly and gave Marian what she hoped passed for a submissive look of defeat.

Walking out of the castle and through the muddy streets of Nottingham was an experience in itself and once again the sensation of unreality, of being trapped in an unending nightmare, coursed through Kendra's innermost being. People were everywhere, dirty people who stared at the two women and their enclave of armored men crossing through the outer realm of the castle. As they passed through the outer gate, Kendra felt a sudden urge to run, to lift her long skirt and take her chances, putting as much distance between herself and this crazy castle as she could.

"Do not even think about it," Marian said softly, close to her ear. "The guards would cut you down without a second's thought." Kendra stared at her, open-mouthed. The girl smiled. "I could see the idea forming in your eyes. Come."

Kendra followed her meekly, realizing there was much more to Marian FitzWalter than met the eye. When they reached the base of the tower, however, she almost turned and ran anyway, in spite of Marian's words of caution.

"I'm supposed to go up there? On those stairs? With no railing or anything?"

"It is safe," Marian said. "Just stay close to me."

Kendra didn't remember much of their ascent. She ended up keeping her eyes closed and clinging pathetically to Marian's hand as she half-slid, half-crept up the narrow stairway that led to her new prison.

Once inside she was able to relax. The room was small but comfortable. A fire burned warmly in a curved niche of a fireplace in one wall while a bed piled high with coverlets and pillows occupied the major portion of the room. A woven carpet covered the stone floor.

"This is a prison?" Kendra asked, feeling confused. "But the dungeon—"

"The dungeon is for thieves, murderers, common criminals. The tower is reserved for special prisoners. I believe John himself was locked up here by King Richard for a time."

"Good grief," Kendra said beneath her breath. "His own brother."

"The Plantagenets have a very curious idea of what a family should be," Marian said as she walked around the room lighting thin tapers in metal sconces situated every two feet around the wall. The guards had waited on the stairs for lack of room. "They have spent most of their lives stabbing one another in the back, trying to steal what is not theirs or protect what is."

"How do you fit into this mess?" Kendra asked, sinking down on the bed, suddenly weary.

"Me?" Marian turned to face her, her pale face drawn, strained. "I am no one and nothing. I am a distant cousin of Richard's, taken in out of his kindness when my parents were killed. I was but six years old. Their lands and estates, of course, became Richard's, but I was much older before I realized my cousin's concern for me might not have been as great had I not had property. I try to remain as inconspicuous as possible.''

Kendra felt a wave of pity wash over her. Poor little girl, to lose her parents and then be made to feel she had been taken in only out of charity and for her meager wealth.

''Surely King Richard cares for you. And I can tell that Navarre does.''

A smile touched the girl's face as she blew out the lighted taper she held and crossed to the bed. ''Navarre is the kindest man in all the world.'' She sank down beside Kendra. ''He is the only one I truly consider my family, and he is not even my kin. He still treats me like a brainless child, but at least I know that he loves me.''

''And Richard?''

''Oh, I suppose Richard cares in his own way. But you must understand, I am but a woman and what I think or feel means less than nothing to anyone.''

''Except Navarre,'' Kendra prodded, anxious to hear her answer.

''Oh, perhaps. Even Navarre is, after all, still a man. If only he did not see me as such a child I might...'' she flushed and turned away. ''He is still the stubbornest man alive, I warrant, but he has been kind to me.''

Kendra hadn't missed the flush nor the words that preceded Marian's embarrassment. Marian loved Navarre. Oh, brother. If the girl ever found out just how intimate Kendra had been with Marian's hero, she could forget about gaining her help.

''I'm sure you'll find a nice man,'' Kendra said carefully. ''Won't King Richard find you a husband when the time is right?''

''A husband!'' Marian stood and flounced across the room, folding her arms over her chest. ''Richard is too busy to bother with me, and by the time he returns to England I may be too old to wed, or perhaps he will not return at all if Navarre and Garrick have their way.''

''You know they are against Richard and yet, you still lo—

like Navarre?'' Kendra watched the subtle play of emotion across the young woman's face.

"I am no fool. However, I do not know exactly what Navarre is plotting. I cling to the belief that Navarre is remaining true to Richard in his own way. The sheriff, however, is another story. Why Navarre has thrown his lot in with such a man . . .'' she shook her head. "I do not understand, and I have told Navarre if he will not confide in me I will no longer be able to believe in him.'' She sat back down with a sigh.

"What does he say to this?'' Kendra asked.

She smiled sadly. "Navarre has an answer for everything. The last time we spoke he promised to speak to John about finding me a husband next year, but I am so ugly that I doubt he will find anyone willing unless they are old or after what dowry is provided for me.''

"Ugly?'' Kendra said. "You are not ugly, Marian. You just need someone to help you bring out your better qualities.''

"Will you help me?'' Marian said, pouncing on her statement with the eagerness of a child. "You are so beautiful and if you will share some of your secrets with me, I promise I will be your friend and help you in any way I can.'' She looked shyly down at her hands. "Oh, I know I cannot look like you, but perhaps you could tell me how to make my hair shine like yours—or is that some special spell that only works on you?''

Kendra's mouth dropped open and she laughed aloud. "Marian—I am not a witch. But I do know some special beauty tricks that will help you. All you need is the right makeup and shampoo and . . .'' Kendra stopped in midsentence as the full import of Marian's words sank in. "What did you say, I mean, before. If I make you beautiful, did you say you would help me?''

"If you can make me beautiful,'' Marian said, her blue eyes serious, her lower lip trembling slightly, "I promise, Kendra O'Brien, I will do anything you ask.''

A slow smile graced Kendra's face. "I'll hold you to that, Maid Marian.'' She narrowed her eyes as she lifted one long, greasy strand of hair. "I'll tell you what, let's start with a nice shampoo.''

Chapter Eight

Kendra's luck was improving. Marian managed to sneak into Navarre's room and find her satchel. She always took a bag full of "emergency" paraphernalia on her trips abroad and so it contained makeup, shampoo, lotion, perfume, and a dozen other items that would help her make Marian beautiful. She hadn't dared to ask the girl to look for the item she was really worried about, the gun. Marian watched in fascination as Kendra dumped the bag on the bed and the two cameras tumbled out, along with a jumble of bottles and tubes. The girl pounced on the Polaroid camera and held it up reverently.

"What is this wondrous thing? Is this what you will use to transform me?" she asked, breathless.

"No." Kendra took the camera from her and tucked it firmly back into her satchel and Marian promptly picked up her 35mm camera. "Marian, please, give it back. That was a present from my Uncle Mac and he's . . . he's gone now."

"Oh, I am sorry, Kendra. Is that what this writing says here?" She turned over the camera and displayed the small metal plate on the back. Kendra reached down and took the equipment from her, running one finger across the plate. She'd forgotten Mac put that on there. It read: To Kendra, a good reporter, All my love, Uncle Mac. He had given it to her the day after her first big story broke. A "good" reporter. That was high praise coming from Arthur Mackenzie. Her throat tightened convulsively.

"Yes, here, let's put this away and start making you beautiful, all right?" she said briskly.

Marian beamed at her question and nodded enthusiastically as Kendra tucked the camera away inside the satchel.

All she needed now was for someone to accidentally take a picture with her instant camera. No doubt she'd be accused of capturing their souls in the little gray box.

"Do you have some other wondrous machine inside your bag with which to transform me?"

Kendra sighed. Teenagers. They were the same in any century it seemed, prone to the dramatic and wild imaginations. "I am not a witch, Marian. I will transform you with the use of makeup, surely you've heard of makeup?"

Marian bit her lower lip. "Do you mean like the carmine salve some women rub on their cheeks, or when they take burnt wood and rub it above their eyes?"

"Sort of," Kendra said, forcing herself not to roll her eyes.

The transformation took longer than expected. First she had to talk Marian into going to the bathhouse for a good scrubbing. Marian had shuddered, but when Kendra produced a sweet-smelling bar of soap from her bag, and coconut scented shampoo, the girl grabbed both and almost ran down the steps of the tower to comply with Kendra's commands. When she returned, free of grime, her hair clean and shining, Kendra was struck by the pure beauty of the girl that had been hidden by layers of dirt.

Two hours later Kendra sat back from her work with a sigh. Triumphantly she handed the little mirror from her purse to Marian.

"All right," she said, "now you can look."

Marian rose from the stool where she had patiently bided her time while Kendra worked her magic, and took the mirror from the other woman's hand.

"What manner of looking glass is this?" she asked in amazement, turning the mirror over in wonder. "I have never seen such a thing in all of my life. I—" Marian's mouth dropped open as she looked into the mirror and got her first real look at Kendra's handiwork. She lifted one hand to her face, her expression incredulous.

"What do you think?" Kendra asked softly.

Marian opened her mouth twice but no words emerged.

Kendra's smile widened. Marian's dirty brown hair had washed out to a lovely ash blonde, and now free from the heaviness of dirt and oil, the tresses had a natural curl. Marian's glorious mane waved in splendor down to her waist and the girl ran one hand through the soft curls as if to reassure herself they belonged to her.

Her pale eyes with their pale lashes were now enhanced by a subtle amount of mascara and eye shadow that brought attention to the beautiful blue of Marian's irises. A good liquid makeup base and faint rose blush at the cheekbones had taken away the girl's sallow complexion, while a softly natural rose lipstick completed the simple but lovely picture. The girl was a beauty, no doubt about it, and Kendra smiled with satisfaction as Marian sank down on the bed, a stunned look on her face.

"Truly you are a witch," she whispered.

"No," Kendra said, "I just know how to apply makeup. Lucky for you my kit comes with colors for autumns and summers. You can have that set of makeup. I'm an autumn so I don't need them."

Marian frowned. "Autumns? Summers? I do not understand." She raised the mirror again and gazed into it. "Will you teach me this sorcery so that I may perform it myself if you . . ." she hesitated then went on ". . . if you are not here?"

"You sat right here and watched everything I did, Marian. Did you hear me chant any spells or wave my magic wand?" Kendra said.

"You have a magic wand?" Marian asked in hushed wonder.

Kendra sighed and ran one hand through her hair. "No, I do not have a magic wand and that's my point. You are a beautiful young woman. I just cleaned you up so your natural beauty could shine through. That isn't magic, it's just know-how."

" 'Know-how'?" Marian tried the unfamiliar word aloud, then smiled. "Thank you, Kendra O'Brien. I care not if you are a witch or simply have this know-how. You have made me beautiful and I will be eternally grateful."

Kendra grinned back. "You should smile more, it really

brightens your face. Oh, and stop wearing this mousy color of brown.'' She touched the edge of Marian's sleeve. ''You're a summer and you should wear lots of pastels or clear reds and blues.''

''Again with these strange words. I am a summer? How may I be a season of the year?'' Marian frowned. ''What is a pastel? You speak so oddly, Kendra O'Brien. From whence did you say you came?''

''I didn't. Do you know why? Because not one soul has bothered to ask me. Just because I happened to be in Avebury—''

''There—you have done it again. Why do you call Abury, Avebury? And why do you speak so strangely? Where is your home, Kendra O'Brien?''

''It's just Kendra, if you don't mind.'' She rose from her position in front of the girl and crossed the room to the one window. She leaned one elbow on the stone sill and gazed out into the night. ''My home is very far away, across the ocean.''

''In Normandy?'' Marian asked in wonder. ''Are you Norman, then? But you speak the Saxon tongue. Navarre taught me. Did he teach you also?''

''No, he didn't. And no, I am not Norman, I . . . oh what's the use?'' Kendra turned away from the window in frustration. ''You wouldn't believe me if I told you. No one would.''

''I told you that if you would make me beautiful I would help you, that I would listen,'' Marian reminded her. ''You have kept your part of the bargain, now please''—she reached out one hand toward Kendra—''I wish to keep mine.''

Kendra stared at the young woman for a long moment. Making up her mind abruptly, she crossed to Marian, took her outstretched hand and sank down beside her.

''I must escape from the tower,'' Kendra said, squeezing the girl's hand she still held. ''I can't tell you everything, but I am here to help England, and if I remain locked away here, England—and others—will be in great danger.''

Marian squeezed Kendra's hand in return and leaned forward eagerly. ''Are you speaking of Richard? Do you seek to help him?'' When Kendra hesitated the girl rushed on. ''You need not fear me, Kendra O'Brien. Although I love Navarre dearly and wish to believe that everything he does is for a good reason, I do not wish for Richard to be harmed. Since Navarre will not take me into his confidence and explain his reasoning, I have decided I must help Richard in whatever way I can.''

Kendra smiled in relief, then sobered abruptly. ''But how can you betray Navarre if you care for him so much?''

One petulant lower lip thrust forward and Kendra almost laughed, reminding herself that after all she was dealing with a teenager, not an adult, and a neglected, lovestruck teenager at that.

''Has he not betrayed my loyalty by refusing to confide in me?'' she asked. ''I care not what happens to him.''

''I think you do not mean that,'' Kendra said with a smile.

Marian blushed and lowered her newly mascaraed lashes. ''You think rightly, Kendra O'Brien.'' She looked up, her face twisted with anxiety. ''I do not wish for Navarre to be harmed.''

''Trust me,'' Kendra said softly, ''I will do my best to see that Navarre isn't hurt.''

The expression on Marian's face shifted to one of confusion. ''Why does Navarre seek this treasonous course of action? Why does he seek to betray his king? They were once such dear friends.'' She shook her head. ''I do not understand. It seems there is so little that I understand.''

Kendra put her arm around the girl and gave her a quick hug. ''I know, love, it's hard for me to understand as well. But perhaps together we may be able to find the answer to Navarre's treachery.'' The corners of Marian's lips curved up slightly and Kendra could see how much being included meant to the lonely young woman. ''So how about it? Will you be my friend? Will you help me escape?''

''Aye, that I will, but there is more you wish to tell me, Kendra O'Brien. I sense it.''

Kendra stared at her a moment, amazed once again by the girl's astuteness.

''Yes, I want to tell you, but you mustn't tell anyone what I'm about to tell you, Marian,'' she said. ''If you do, they'll lock me away forever and ever, but I need your help to get back home.''

"I will help you in whatever way I can," Marian said with childlike solemnity. "And I give my word that I will tell no other living soul."

"Okay, well—"

"What is this 'okay,' " Marian interrupted. "You say it all of the time."

Kendra flushed. "Do I? Bad habit. It's slang."

"Slang?"

"Never mind, I'll explain later." She hesitated. "Are you sure you can handle this?"

"Handle?" Marian's pale blue eyes clouded with perplexity. "In faith, Kendra O'Brien, I do not understand."

Kendra hesitated. Marian was little more than a child who had grown up under Navarre's care. A medieval child. Why should she expect her to keep her secret? And yet, she needed to tell someone, needed someone to be on her side in this crazy century.

Reaching over to the girl she lifted a bottle of makeup from her hand, then the mascara, eyeshadow and blush. She watched Marian's face fall as the "magical" ingredients disappeared back into Kendra's bag.

"But, Kendra I thought—"

"Marian, do you think I'm a witch? Tell me the truth, because it's very important."

The girl started to speak, then closed her mouth and frowned, deep in thought. At last she ran her tongue across her lips and for the first time since Kendra had met her, spoke clearly and without a trace of her usual shyness.

"No. I do not know why, because surely you have worked magic on me, and you have very strange ways, but I do not really believe you are a witch." She leaned forward and impulsively laid one hand on Kendra's arm. "You see, I met a witch once," she said, and shivered delicately. "She was an evil old woman. Even if she had not admitted it to me, I would have known because I could feel the darkness in her soul."

"And what about my soul?" Kendra asked softly.

Marian's face lit up. "Your soul is kind and gentle. You are a good person, Kendra O'Brien."

"Thank you," Kendra said, feeling more than a little touched at the young woman's observation.

"What is it you wish to tell me, Kendra O'Brien?" Marian said, interrupting her thoughts.

"Marian, this is going to be hard to believe—even harder than believing I'm not a witch. You must promise me that what I'm about to tell you, you will not reveal to another living soul. I hate to put it this way but if you'll keep my secret, and help me," Kendra swallowed hard, feeling as if she were withholding candy from a child, "I'll give you the makeup."

Marian's chin lifted and Kendra saw the brief flash of anger in the girl's eyes. She felt her hopes fizzle.

"I'm sorry, Marian," Kendra began, only to be cut off by the girl, who raised her hand to stop her speech.

"I thought you were different," she said, her voice filled with pain. "I thought you would treat me as an adult, but here you are, thinking you must bribe me, like a child, so that I will keep your secret." Her newly mascaraed eyelashes fluttered downward. "I am so disappointed."

Kendra felt a warm flush of shame and reached over to take Marian's hand. "I'm sorry, Marian. I didn't mean it that way at all. You know, even adults make and take bribes." She smiled at the girl but received no response. Kendra stumbled on, trying to salvage the situation. "Marian, what I have to tell you is so incredible that the truth is, I'm just afraid."

Marian lifted her gaze and her pale blue eyes widened. "You are afraid? But you are so brave, Kendra O'Brien. You stood in front of John and the sheriff without crying or wailing as many other accused witches have done. I was very impressed."

"Thanks," Kendra said lightly, "but I was afraid and I still am. I don't want to end up in the nuthouse."

"The nuthouse? You mean where we store nutmeats?"

Kendra shook her head, feeling once again the chasm of culture widen between them. "No, I mean where they put people they think are crazy—or do they just assume they're all witches?"

"Ah, you mean you fear if you tell me this secret I will believe you are addled in your mind."

"Exactly."

"I promise I will not." Marian leaned toward her earnestly. "Do you not realize by now, Kendra O'Brien, that I am your friend?"

Kendra took a deep breath. "I hope so, Marian, I sincerely hope so."

It was hard to begin, but at last Kendra haltingly told the girl her story from the start to her presence in the tower, leaving out only the part about the gun. She didn't want Marian to worry even more about Navarre and Richard's feud. Marian said not a word through the entire tale and Kendra grew more anxious with every sentence she uttered. Would the girl tell the sheriff that not only was their captive a witch but a crazy witch? Kendra finished and sat back to watch Marian's face.

The girl sat as though carved of stone for a very long time, then she looked up at Kendra and smiled.

" 'Tis a wondrous tale," she said softly.

"It's the truth, not a fairytale."

"Of course it is the truth, and why did you fear I would not believe you?" Marian's now sculptured brows puckered above her eyes and Kendra could see the fear there once again that she thought her a child.

"Because it's a pretty strange story, wouldn't you say? For a woman to travel through time?"

"Perhaps. Tell me of your time." She clasped her hands together, her eyes bright with wonder. Kendra sighed and began to tell her about the future, too tired to care if she was altering the course of history or not. She told her about cars and planes and trains and movies. Marian was fascinated by the movies and wrung detail after detail out of Kendra. When at last Kendra couldn't think of another thing to tell her, the two lay back upon the small bed and stared at the ceiling, each lost in her own thoughts.

" 'Tis wondrous," Marian said again, her voice soft with awe. "I wish I could see a movie."

"You could be in a movie," Kendra said, smiling to herself.

"Really?" Marian sat up, her pale face flushed with color. "Oh, wouldn't that be—"

"Wondrous." Kendra finished for her, then laughed. "I wish we were in a movie right now and I'd write us out of this."

"How would you do that?"

"I'd have Arnold Schwarzenegger scale the castle wall, blast the sheriff and his men, then carry me off in his arms."

Marian giggled. "Oh Kendra, you are a wonderous storyteller. Tell me more of this Arnold."

Kendra stared at her. "I still don't understand why you believe me."

Marian looked away, then rose gracefully and crossed to warm herself at the fire. "Perhaps I think it depends upon your point of view."

"Your point of view?" Kendra blinked at Marian's calm acceptance, then moved to stand beside her. "Marian, traveling through time has nothing to do with a point of view."

"Ah, but whether or not I believe that you have traveled through time does. Did you not say you found this time portal near the mounds of Abury?" Kendra nodded. "Then there is no reason in the world I should not believe you. From the dawn of time the mounds have been known to hold great secrets. Strange occurrences happen there each year and it is a place revered by those who believe in magic and also those who believe in—" she broke off and turned to poke the fire to life with the small poker provided.

"Who believe in what?" Kendra prodded, captivated by this new side of her young friend. Marian poked the embers until a new flame rose to lick the bottom of the log resting there, then lifted solemn eyes to meet Kendra's own curious ones.

"Who believe in a kind of magic that has nothing to do with witchcraft," she whispered. "You have told me your secret, Kendra, and now I will trust you with mine. If you tell Navarre or the sheriff I could be burned as a witch, so you see, by telling you, perhaps you will trust me with your own fears."

"Good grief, Marian, what is it?" Kendra said, taking the

135

girl's cold hands between her own, feeling a sudden apprehension as she waited for her to speak.

"There is a man, a wise man who lives in the heart of a great, dark forest." She glanced up at Kendra. "He teaches me, and a few select others, about things that are beyond our ken."

Kendra felt a chill dance down her spine as Marian pulled away from her and crossed over to one of the two small, diamond-paned windows cut into the tower wall. "What do you mean?" she asked.

"He is so brilliant, Kendra," she said softly, gazing out the window, twisting one long strand of hair around her fingers. "He teaches such wondrous things, things no one else has even thought of before, I am sure. Magical things that he says are not magic, just the simple work of God in nature." She whirled around, her eyes bright. "Did you know there is power in lightning that can be harnessed and used to actually create a light inside a home? Did you know that everything in the world is made up of tiny, tiny little things called molecules and that in them lie many secrets? Did you know there are other, tiny things called germs and that is why men injured in battle die—because the germs in . . . infect," she stumbled over the word, "infect the wound?" She spun around in the center of the room while Kendra looked on, her mouth hanging open, her heart pounding. "Oh, Kendra, please do not think me mad—but the study of this science is too—"

"What?" Kendra cried. She crossed to the spinning nymph and grabbed her by one arm, stopping her joyous dance in midturn. "What did you say about science?"

"That's what he calls all of these discoveries—the study of science." Marian shrank back from the look on Kendra's face. "Oh, please, Kendra, I promised to keep your secret and I beg you to keep mine. If Navarre ever found out, he would kill Cennach."

"I won't tell Navarre," Kendra said, feeling relief flood through her like a warm rush of adrenalin. "But you must take me to Cennach, Marian, immediately."

"Why?" she asked, her eyes round. "Oh, of course, you think perhaps he can help you return to your own time." She frowned. "Oh, Kendra, I know not. He is a wise man, but surely what has happened to you lies more in the realm of magic than science."

"Marian," Kendra said calmly, "Cennach must be a time-traveler too."

Navarre was not drunk but if he had two more glasses of ale he likely would be. Getting thoroughly soused was not going to help, of that he was reasonably certain, but he lifted the tankard to his lips again. No, even if his mind were thoroughly befuddled with drink, the image of the auburn-haired witch would jerk him back to consciousness as it did night after night in his dreams. A chill shivered across the back of his neck.

It was Acre all over again, this haunting. For months after he had returned from the Crusade, Talam's face had been burned into his mind, never allowing him to sink into the sweet haze of pleasant dreams or forgetfulness, no matter how much he drank.

Your fault, her amber lips had whispered in his dreams, *your fault*. It had nearly driven him mad.

Navarre pushed the empty tankard away and lifted his tortured gaze to watch Garrick drain another. Now this woman—spy—witch—had shown him he had never truly faced madness. She had shown him an element of insanity he had never before encountered. It twisted inside of him, burning him, searing him with its heat.

Desire.

"So you think she is a witch," Garrick said, setting his mug down carefully on the rough tabletop of the tavern and raising one aristocratic eyebrow. The Black Crowe was the sheriff's favorite place to toss down a few draughts after a hard day's work, and tonight Navarre had thought it a good place to break his news about Abury and the witch.

The Crowe was not the worst tavern he'd ever seen, neither was it the best, but the ale was excellent, the wenches willing, and best of all, the sheriff and his peacekeeper were more than welcome there, since the owner was Norman. Navarre had been too weary this night to face the cutting glances of the

137

Saxon descendants of Edward. How he wished he could simply run away from it all. He sighed. Honor would not allow such a cowardly retreat.

"I know not what to think," Navarre growled, pushing the chair beside him away from the table with one booted foot. He had not wanted to tell Garrick about Kendra, but his behavior in the sheriff's chamber demanded that he do so. Still, he hesitated to tell him of the strange weapon the woman had brought with her. "I have told you of the prophecy, of this woman's strange and mystical appearance, the odd enchantments she utters, her attempts to seduce me, this unquenchable lust I have for the wench—what is your counsel?"

Garrick leaned forward, elbows propped on the table, his well-defined chin resting on his fists, smoldering gray eyes belying the calm expression on his handsome face.

"You fought me for her, old friend," Garrick reminded him. "You pulled your sword and I believe you would have killed me on the spot had I not been able to make you see reason."

"Nay," Navarre said quickly, "I would not have done so. I saw not the wench with her bruised face but . . ." he hesitated, curling his fingers around the handle of his tankard and bringing it to his lips, effectively stopping the flow of words.

"Talam?" Garrick asked.

Navarre's knuckles gleamed white around the pewter handle as he lowered it to the table. "You promised we would never speak of it," he said, his voice deceptively soft.

"I apologize, dear Navarre." Garrick leaned forward again, this time more fervently. " 'Twas not your fault the wench died, 'twas Richard's! Did he not give the order to murder all the inhabitants of Acre? Were you not ill with a grievous wound at the time and many miles away?"

"She should have been with me," Navarre said, staring with unseeing eyes across the tavern. "She wanted to go with me."

"And Richard would not allow it, do you not remember?" Garrick suddenly reached over and grasped him by the wrist. Navarre reflexively raised his other hand, clenched into a fist.

"Will you fight me again, old friend?" Garrick murmured,

the burning embers of his eyes softening as Navarre flushed and lowered his fist.

"I could have opposed Richard," he said, jerking away from Garrick's touch. "I should have. Then Talam would have been with me, where she belonged, instead of—" he broke off and buried his face in both hands, the memories sweeping over him like the hot desert winds of Outremer: Talam begging him to take her with him. Talam left behind to die with the rest of Richard's hostages, at Richard's command.

Garrick rose and moved around the table, draping his arm across the knight's back, his cloak, which he had not removed, enclosing the two. The sheriff pressed his lips close to his friend's left ear. Navarre could smell the ale on his breath and knew his friend was the worse for drink, still, his touch sent a wave of disgust through him. He shook the thought away. It was no more than a comradely gesture.

"It is well you remember," Garrick said, his fingers clutching the back of Navarre's collarless shirt, his mouth against his ear. "That is why we are here, why we seek justice, why Richard must be defeated. He cared not for you, or your love, or for the precious England he left behind."

"Enough." Navarre stood, feeling oddly relieved as Garrick's hand fell away from his back. He tossed two coins on the table and turned away, shrugging into his own dark cloak. Garrick was right. Richard was the reason his love had died. Richard was the reason England was slowly dying. He pressed his lips together as a new idea dawned upon him. Perhaps the weapon the woman had used against him could serve a better purpose in the future. How quickly and cleanly the metal lump had sliced through his mail. How quickly and cleanly it could slice through Richard's as well. It struck from a distance, albeit not silently. Still, a man could use it and likely escape before being spotted.

"There is more I must tell you, privately. Let us return to the castle. I am besotted enough to sleep now, and I confess, I am weary."

"Certainly," Garrick said with a smile, tossing two coins down as well. The two men moved across the room to the front door. Navarre ducked under the sill and took a deep, cleansing breath as the crisp night air whipped across his face. Garrick joined him and Navarre watched his friend's smooth face turn harsh in the shadows of the moonlight, cheekbones dark slashes across his skin, eyes almost silver. He looked like a wolf, Navarre thought, and he passed one hand across his eyes. He must be drunker than he had thought.

"What I have to tell you is hard to believe," Navarre said as they walked together down the narrow street that led from the tavern to the stable where their horses awaited. Their boots crunched on a light layer of snow that had fallen during their stay inside, and Navarre wondered suddenly if Kendra was warm enough in the tower. He shook the thought away.

"Whatever it is, I doubt I will be greatly shocked," said Garrick. "And I will believe you, because you have never lied to me, Navarre."

"And never will, I warrant," Navarre swore vehemently, then glanced up at his friend. "Then you do not believe the witch could be controlling what I say to you?"

Garrick shook his head. "Nay, a witch is not the Almighty. She can only do so much. Your thoughts are your own, it is another part of you that is under her spell, my friend." He laughed loudly at his joke and Navarre flushed. Even now, even as they walked and talked, in another part of his mind he was thinking of her, wanting her, burning for her.

"Aye," Navarre agreed. "Then here it is. The woman brought a weapon with her that can cause a fireball to burn through a man's armor." He paused and jerked his cloak aside, pushing his sleeve up to reveal the bandage on his upper arm. "She used it on me."

Garrick stopped dead in his tracks, his eyes focused on Navarre's arm. He slid the soft cloth of the wrapping upward and poked at the still healing wound.

"What did it feel like?" he said in amazement.

"Hurt like bloody hell," Navarre replied. "Felt like a hole was bored into my arm by something that pierced with the fury of a sword and burned like a red-hot poker."

"How far away was she from you?"

"A good bit—two furlongs perhaps."

"Could it have killed you, do you think?" Garrick ceased

his explorations of the wound and shifted his gray gaze to the knight. Navarre pulled his sleeve back down and nodded, his lips pressed tightly together.

"Aye," he said softly. "It could."

Garrick's face split into a beatific smile. "Perhaps we should return to the inn and drink some more, for surely we now have much to celebrate."

"Richard?" Navarre asked, knowing full well what the answer would be.

"Richard, indeed." Garrick rubbed his hands together and blew on them. "An assassin could use this weapon to kill King Richard from a distance, making his escape an easy matter."

"Aye," Navarre said, pushing away the prickling of conscience that he still dealt with from time to time. It was one thing to kill on a battlefield, quite another to contemplate cold-blooded murder.

"There's just one more little matter I believe we should settle, ere the night is over," Garrick said softly, taking a pair of leather gloves from his pocket and pulling them on.

"What matter?"

"The matter of the witch, of course, for indeed, I, too, believe her to be a sorceress." Garrick tugged at one earlobe, as though the realization distressed him. "The fact that the wench has such power over your emotions is proof enough for me. Unless, of course, you happen to be in love with her?"

"In love with her?" Navarre laughed sharply. "Are you mad?"

Garrick shrugged and pulled his cloak more tightly about him. "Look at your irrational attachment to Talam in Outremer," he said, gesturing with one hand. "I never really understood that, my friend. An infidel, little more than a whore and yet—"

Without warning, Navarre seized the sheriff by the back of the neck and slammed him up against a nearby building. The knight towered over Garrick by a head, but the man did not seem in the least rattled by his friend's sudden behavior.

"Did the witch tell you to kill me, my friend?" he asked, his voice hushed with concern. "Is that the reason for these strange, unprovoked attacks of late?"

Navarre immediately released him, stepping back, arms spread wide as he cursed himself and Kendra broadly under his breath. He turned away, running one hand through his hair, Garrick's words crashing through his mind.

"You said she could not control my mind," he reminded him, his breath coming hard.

"But she controls your emotions and that, my friend, can be much worse." Garrick cocked one brow at him. "Have you bedded her or no? For that is the way that a witch can place a man under her power, you know. She binds his body to her first, then his emotions. And if given enough time, I daresay perhaps your mind might be forfeit as well."

Navarre closed his eyes. Could it be true? Could this new, unreasonable fury he felt with Garrick be the woman's doing? But how? She had given him no orders, said no words concerning the sheriff.

That you understood, anyway.

Navarre felt the fear grip him by the throat. The woman had often spoken in a nonsensical manner as they traveled to Nottingham. He had tried hard to ignore her blathering. Could he have missed something? Or was she, even this very moment, chanting a spell, that because of his indiscretion with her in the crag and again in the bath, gave her power over him? It chilled him, the thought that someone could control him, control his actions. It must stop. It must stop now.

"Your pardon." Navarre turned back to face the sheriff. "I believe you are right. The woman has ensorcelled me. I suppose there is little question what must be done."

"Find out how to use the weapon, and then she must be killed," Garrick said, "but not by fire."

"No? But—"

"You must kill her with your own hands." Navarre shot him a startled look and Garrick rushed on. "Once you have been ensorcelled by a witch, there is only one way to break the evil bond—by taking her life yourself. You must take a dagger newly honed in the fire, no more than a day, and plunge it into the witch's heart." Garrick's hand came down on Navarre's shoulder as the man continued to stare at him, stunned. "Heed me," he said, his words hushed, "I am well versed in

142

the ways of black magic. 'Twas often used in my father's house after I came to bide there as a child.''

"What?" Navarre turned to his friend, unable to hide the horror that swept over him at the sheriff's words.

Garrick nodded, his gray eyes gleaming in the moonlight. Navarre shivered, once again finding the sight of his friend's silver-blond hair blowing in the night breeze, his silver eyes glazed with memory, vastly disturbing.

"Aye, my father's wife was a witch," Garrick said, turning and walking toward the stable again. Navarre hurried to match his strides. "It was a closely guarded secret but one my father was privy to and later, I as well. Shall we say that my step-mother enjoyed small children—enjoyed making them suffer, that is. She would often try her latest spells and incantations on me or the servants' children, as well as other, more earthly experiments." Navarre closed his eyes against the hollow sound of his voice and the mental picture of small children at the mercy of a wicked, demented woman.

"You never told me this," Navarre choked out, too furious to say more.

"It was before I knew you, and later, I feared your reaction." Garrick's mouth twisted into a wry grin. "It would seem my fears were not unfounded. Am I now less in your eyes, old friend—again?"

"Of course not!" Navarre stopped abruptly, laying one hand on the sheriff's shoulder. "We have always been brothers, Garrick, not by blood but by common bond. Nothing can change this. I swear it!"

"Nothing?"

Garrick's question was softly spoken and Navarre met his questioning gaze with his own resolute one.

"Nothing," he swore.

"Take this then." From beneath his cloak Garrick drew out a long object. He held it out to Navarre.

"A dagger? But I have my own."

" 'Tis newly honed just today," the sheriff said. "Take it." Navarre complied and Garrick smiled, clapping him on the back. "Go home, my friend, and sleep. Tomorrow will be soon enough."

Navarre drew the dagger from its sheath. It caught the silver shimmer of the moonlight and as the light danced across the long, sharp blade the knight swallowed hard, his throat tight with an emotion he could not define.

"Tomorrow," he whispered.

"Quickly!"

Marian held the candle higher and motioned for Kendra to follow her down the steep stairway. Marian had become nervous and fretful once they discovered the tower guards had disappeared. Kendra had reasoned that perhaps they were just sleeping on the job, holed up somewhere instead of doing their duty, but Marian had stared at her as if she had lost her mind.

"No soldier in Nottingham sleeps on duty," she whispered, "for fear the sheriff will have him drawn and quartered."

Kendra decided not to pursue the subject but suggested they use the situation to their advantage. Marian had agreed and led Kendra down the tower steps.

"I don't get it," Kendra said as they stopped at the bottom, Marian in front with the candle. "Why would Navarre and the sheriff leave the castle so unprotected—and at night? This is very—"

The rest of Kendra's sentence was lost as something grabbed her from behind. Her breath left her suddenly and before she could scream, a hand clamped down roughly over her mouth. Marian stood a few feet away, likewise held by a shadowy figure, the candle lying extinguished at her feet. Knowing it was up to her to save them, Kendra began to struggle, kicking backward, trying desperately to bite her abductor, but his hands were like iron, his grip unbreakable.

All at once Kendra remembered the last self-defense class she'd taken a few months before leaving for England. Without hesitation she sagged, letting her entire body weight go limp in the arms of the man who held her. The suddenness of her action, coupled with the dead weight, broke his hold. Kendra jerked away and scrambled to her feet, only to collide with another shadowy body who sent her tumbling headfirst into the dirt.

The blow wasn't serious but it stunned her momentarily,

and before she could regain her equilibrium Kendra found herself flat on her back, straddled by one of their assailants. Someone else came rushing up in the darkness with a candle, and a flame danced suddenly above her chest as the man sitting on top of her brought his face down to meet hers. Her vision cleared in time to look up into an attractive face, at least what she could see beneath the brown hood that half-hid his features.

"You are the one sent for Richard, are you not?" the man said, his lips scant inches from her own. "Answer me quickly if you value your life."

Kendra opened her mouth, shut it again, took a chance, and nodded. The man smiled and she stared up at him in amazement. His smile lit up his face, and now she could see his eyes fairly danced with life and intelligence. Who was this man?

"Excellent," he said, standing up and bending down to reach for her hand. "You must come with me, quickly, before we are discovered." He pulled Kendra to her feet, then swept her up easily into his arms.

"Wait a minute!" she cried finding her voice at last. She kicked out with both feet, thrashing about in his arms. "Who are you and what do you want with me?"

"We have no time for explanations, my lady," he said, grunting as he struggled to hold on to her. "You must come with me."

"I'm going nowhere until I know who you are and where we're going!" Kendra said fervently.

With an oath, the man dropped her in the dirt. Kendra grunted as her backside struck the ground, then stumbled to her feet and turned to confront the man.

"How dare you accost us in this manner!"

The man bowed, his hood falling back, momentarily displaying a rich chestnut brown mane of hair cropped just below his ears. He jerked it back into place. "I beg pardon, my lady. In what manner would you rather be accosted?"

Kendra couldn't resist the quip nor the good-natured sound of his voice, and her own lips curved up in amusement. "Who are you?" she repeated.

The man motioned to the candle-bearer and the flame

145

danced nearer once again as her attacker lifted one hand, hesitated, then pulled the hood back from his face. It dropped to his shoulders and the light of the candle illuminated his face. Kendra realized with a start that her first appraisal of his good looks had been less than accurate. He wasn't just attractive, he was absolutely gorgeous.

Eyes a deep sea-blue gazed back at her, openly appraising her features, apparently liking what he saw. His thick, brown hair was cropped an inch below his ears, making his face, with its high cheekbones, appear even more sculptured, more aristocratic. His full, sensuous lips were accented by a well-groomed goatee and his aquiline nose gave him such a regal air that for a moment Kendra wondered if perhaps Richard the Lionheart were not attempting to sneak back into his castle to foil Navarre and his friends. From behind her came the sound of a quick intake of breath, and Kendra turned to see Marian staring at the man in wonder.

"It is you," she whispered. "I wasn't sure—the darkness— but it is you."

"Who?" Kendra said, wondering if her intuition was correct and she stood before the King of England. "Who are you?"

The man swept her a low bow. "I am but milady's humble servant," he said, then straightened and tossed her a rakish grin. "Once I was called Robert of Locksley, but now I am known as—"

"Robin Hood," Kendra whispered.

His smile widened. "The very same. At your service, milady," he said moving to lift her hand to his lips. "And you are?"

"Kendra," she said, staring into his face, shocked at the reality of meeting a legend. For some reason meeting him eclipsed her encounter with "Prince" John or the Sheriff of Nottingham. Could it have something to do with his dashing, charismatic personality?

"My name is Kendra O'Brien."

"Irish. I am quite a fan of the Irish, though I must admit you are not at all what I expected. Forgive me for the impropriety of our introduction, but as you can see I am in somewhat of a hurry. We must leave before the guards are missed.''

"Robin? Do you not remember me?" Marian's voice echoed plaintively from behind.

Kendra's estimation of the legendary hero rose as he turned, hesitated, then with a smile, hurried to Marian's side.

"Marian, dear Marian, please forgive me. I did not realize it was you. I thought you to be a serving girl—" He stopped, no doubt realizing how poorly that sounded. "That is to say, when I last saw you, you were but a child. Now you have grown into a beautiful young woman." He kissed her hand and Kendra could almost see the girl's heart fluttering through her tunic.

"Now, we must away," Robin said. "I am sorry I am no longer welcome in your home, Marian. I would dearly love to speak with you. However . . ."

"Take me with you!" Marian said, her face radiant in the glow of the candlelight. "Oh, you must, Robin, for if you leave me here the sheriff will surely shut me into the tower for helping Kendra escape."

"Ah, so you were helping her." His smile was approving and Marian blushed gracefully. "Do not fear, my lady. He will not know you had any part of it if you return to your room. There is no need for you to journey with us."

"Robin." Marian moved to his side and Kendra watched in amazement as the shy little church mouse changed before her eyes into a bold little fox. She lay one hand on the outlaw's arm and gazed up into his eyes beseechingly. "I did not wish to reveal something so unseemly to you after so shortly renewing our acquaintance, however, I feel that I must." She lowered her gaze and her newly darkened lashes brushed her cheeks demurely.

"What is it, my child? But please do hurry in the telling." Robin glanced into the darkness and motioned to the large man holding the candle. He handed Robin the taper and slipped around the side of the tower.

"It is John," Marian said, twisting her hands together nervously. "He has been saying things to me lately that frighten me. He has told me that he wants me. He says in time, he will have me." Her lower lip trembled slightly. "In faith, Robin, I do fear for my virtue."

Robin's brows collided above stormy eyes. "He would not dare! He would not dare to touch Richard's ward!"

Her eyelashes swept upward, and round, light blue eyes gazed up at him. "He says that I am now his ward, along with everything else that belonged to Richard."

"Damn the man!" Robin struck his fist into the palm of his hand and whirled away from her, clasping his hands behind his back. "This is what we have to look forward to if John takes the throne!" He stopped his pacing and glanced back at the girl. "Surely, Navarre would not allow—"

"Navarre is not always in Nottingham, my lord."

"Aye, aye," he agreed, nodding. "And Navarre is not the man he once was, else he would not have taken the devil for his brother." He was silent for a moment, then nodded once, sharply. "Aye, you shall come with us."

"Robin, are you mad?" The large man he had sent presumably to scout ahead came striding up, his deep voice filled with disbelief. "You cannot abduct the king's ward!"

Robin grinned. "I am not abducting her. She has asked for my protection. As a knight of the realm, I am honor bound to give it."

"How do you know she speaks the truth about John?"

Robin dismissed the question with a wave of one hand. "She is the Lady Marian," he said, "that is enough for me."

Kendra shot Marian a questioning look across. Had John said such things to the girl or was it just a ploy to convince Robin to take her along? Marian met her gaze with unflinching resolve and Kendra shrugged, willing to give her new friend the benefit of the doubt. Besides, there was the slightly more important matter of finishing her escape to worry about.

"I hate to break up this little gabfest," Kendra said, "but didn't you say something about getting out of here before the guards are discovered?"

"My lady Kendra speaks rightly," Robin said. "Come, both of you, let us waste no more time, for surely if I am caught within the walls of Nottingham the sheriff will have my head."

Robin took her hand and to Kendra's surprise, tucked it into the crook of his arm and smiled down at her. She didn't miss the troubled look that suddenly crossed Marian's face as one of the other men offered his arm to her. Was this a trap? Could they really trust this outlaw?

"Where are we going?" Kendra demanded, snatching her hand away.

"Why, to Sherwood Forest, milady," Robin said, "where else?"

Chapter Nine

"Of all the incompetent, dull-witted—!"

The sheriff broke off his tirade and slammed himself back down on the rough-hewn bench. He leaned his forehead against one hand, his elbow propped on the table in front of him, long blond hair hiding the angry expression that had been there for the last half hour. Navarre de Galliard, peacekeeper, stood before Garrick Neushaw, hands clenched at his sides, his temper under a fragile control.

"Take care, Garrick," he said softly. "Your tongue will get you killed yet."

Garrick looked up at him, brushing the long hair back from his face. "Do you hear how you speak to me?" he asked, his eyes narrow. "It is the witch's curse and now she has escaped due to your neglect."

"I speak so to you not because of any witch but because you overstep the line between us." Navarre took a step toward him and lowered his voice. "I will tell you again that the face we present to John is but a facade. In private we are yet equals and I will be treated as such."

"I am still the Sheriff of Nottingham," Garrick said, drumming his nails on the rough tabletop. "You are still the peacekeeper. Am I to simply allow you to do whatever you wish? If so, then I must be willing to face John's displeasure."

"John is an ass and you know it," Navarre said evenly. "He will do whatever we tell him to do."

Garrick paused, lifting a goblet from the table, swirling the contents as he kept his gray eyes fixed on the knight's face.

Navarre stared back at him unflinchingly. At last the sheriff took a drink; then he set the goblet back down with an air of decision.

"Of course you are right, Navarre. I apologize for my ill temper. Please, seat yourself." The sheriff gestured to the bench on the other side of the long table where the servants usually met for their meals. "We shall break our fast together and decide what is to be done about the witch's escape."

Navarre tossed his leather gauntlets down on the bench and sat. He was silent as the servants brought bread, cheese, fruit, and wine to the table. Then he filled his plate and ate. Garrick had called him to the lesser hall early that morning and informed him of Kendra's escape. Neither of them had broken their fast and both were the worse for drink from the night before. Navarre glanced up and noted the dark shadows under the sheriff's eyes. His own face looked just as haggard and drawn, he knew.

"My lord! My lord!"

Navarre looked up, startled, as one of the castle's serving maids ran into the hall, her tear-streaked face contorted with panic.

"What is it, Sara?" Navarre asked, rising and taking two long strides to reach her side. "What is wrong?"

"My Lady Marian!" the girl cried, sinking to the floor in front of him.

Navarre leaned down and grabbed her by both arms, dragging her to her feet. "Marian? What of Marian?" He shook her. "Speak up, girl!"

"She is gone!" the maid said, almost swooning in his arms.

Navarre released her so abruptly that the girl almost fell to the floor once again. "Is that all? No doubt she arose early and is taking a morning walk, or is at her prayers in the chapel. Mayhap a turn in the kitchen will cure you of your hysterics." He sat back down and glanced over at Garrick, who was viewing the proceedings with amusement.

"No, no, my lord," the girl squealed, rushing to the knight and falling down on her knees at his side. "You do not understand. I have had the servants search the entire castle and she is not anywhere to be found."

151

Navarre frowned and broke off another piece of bread. "Then you must look again. She must be here—where else could she . . ." The words died in his throat as recent memories flashed across his mind. Memories of Marian telling him how she had sneaked out of the castle and followed him to the forest; memories of Marian telling him someday she would run away.

"But that is not all, my lord!" the servant wailed, taking a bundle from behind her back and thrusting it into his face.

"What is it then?" Navarre fairly shouted, pushing the bundle away. "Tell it and be done with it!"

The maid, trembling, unfolded the wadded up material and spread it on the table, beside his plate. Crimson stained the bundle of light blue silk and Navarre rose slowly, one hand moving to touch the edge of the cloth.

"Dear God," he whispered.

"Aye, sir, I have been tryin' to tell ye—'tis my Lady Marian's nightdress. Someone has murdered her!"

The wail rose from her throat again as Navarre's hand closed on the material and crushed it together, his eyes squeezed shut, his face distorted with pain.

"The witch," Garrick said softly, rising and reaching over to touch the silk himself, his eyes fixed on the bloodred stain. He stared down at it as if transfixed, then shifted his gaze to the girl crying on the floor.

"Your voice is quite distressing," he said with a frown. "Perhaps your tongue is in need of surgery, think you?" The girl closed her mouth abruptly and scurried away.

Navarre clutched the material between his hands as the pain pierced through him. Marian. Murdered by the witch. If only he had not brought the mysterious woman here. If only he had killed her the moment he saw her appear in Abury. What kind of atrocities had Marian suffered—might be suffering even now? The thought that he might still have time to save the king's ward propelled him into action.

"There may yet be time to save her. She may yet be alive."

Garrick lifted a golden goblet to his lips. "Aye, at least, what's left of her may yet be alive. 'Tis quite common for a

152

witch to desire the blood of royalty, you know. They drink it, thinking it increases their power.''

Navarre paled. ''Before God,'' he said raggedly, ''I swear that if the sorceress has harmed Marian, I will kill her.''

''Kill her anyway. Then the spell will be broken, and you will be free.''

''Aye,'' Navarre said, his voice hard. ''But Marian will still be dead.'' He stood for a moment, reining back the rage that threatened to send him crashing into the nearest wall in frustration. How could he have ever entertained the thought of trusting the witch? How could he have ever touched her, kissed her, wanted her?

Taking a deep breath, he picked up his heavy gauntlets from the bench and began pulling them on with quick, hard motions. ''I ride,'' he said softly.

''Good luck, Navarre.'' Garrick lifted his goblet in tribute to the knight. ''I would accompany you, but John requires my presence today.''

''I need not your help,'' Navarre said, turning on his heel and striding to the door.

''She could be anywhere by now.''

He stopped and looked back. ''No. She had help and I know exactly where to look. I will find her, and when I return, I will have a present for you.''

''A present?''

''Aye.'' He drew the dagger the sheriff had given him from the scabbard at his waist and looked down at it, the anger welling up inside of him like a living beast.

''The heart of a witch.''

Sherwood Forest. Kendra looked around in wonder at the enormous trees towering over her, looked around in awe at the lush, green undergrowth that provided such a wealth of camouflage for Robin Hood and his band of merry men. She smiled. Since her arrival in Robin's camp two days before, she had learned that many of the legends about the outlaw were far from true, while others were remarkably accurate.

His men were not particularly merry, in fact some had quite a predisposition toward complaining. However, ''Little'' John

153

was a huge bear of a man and completely satisfied her mental image of what Robin's right-hand man should be, while Alan-a-Dale, soft-voiced minstrel, was not the effeminate lazybones she'd thought at first glance, but a passionate womanizer who enjoyed walking around the camp without his shirt on to show off his muscles.

She felt oddly safe here, and were it not for one unfortunate fly in the ointment, Kendra O'Brien, girl reporter, might actually find a little peace in Sherwood. Kendra glanced over to where Marian sat on a fallen log, idly braiding her hair, listlessly watching the proceedings in which Kendra occupied center stage. Since they had arrived in Sherwood and Robin had shown Kendra so much attention, Marian had not spoken two words to her, nor would she discuss Cennach.

"The center of the target, Kendra!" Robin called.

Kendra nodded and tossed him a bright smile as the outlaw lifted his longbow, fit an arrow to its string, pulled it back and let it fly. Kendra watched in fascination as the arrow shot through the air, flying so fast it could scarcely be seen. It struck the center of the target and a cheer went up from the small crowd that had gathered to watch. Kendra clapped her hands loudly and, rising from her own vantage point, walked over to Robin's side to congratulate him.

"That's ten in a row," she teased, "and I believe I am quite impressed for one day, Sir Robin Hood."

"Are you now?" he said, removing the quiver of arrows from his back. "In that case, perhaps it is your turn to impress me." Kendra hesitated, then smiled as he placed the longbow in her hands. From the moment she had slid off Robin's horse after riding in front of him during their daring escape from Nottingham, he had not left her side for one moment. Even at night he slept outside the makeshift tent the outlaws had fashioned for her and Marian. Guarding them, he said.

It was soon obvious to all, and especially to poor Marian, that Robin was smitten with Richard's salvation, and determined to woo her. Kendra had wrestled with her worries over Marian's fragile ego, then finally gave up. Marian had been madly in love with Navarre only days ago and now she had a crush on Robin. No doubt if they spent enough time in Sherwood it would be Little John she set her sights on next. Kendra sighed and turned her attention back to Robin smiling down at her.

"It is important that even a lady be able to protect herself, should, God forbid, there not be a man to do it for her."

Kendra smiled, thinking of how she had wounded Garrick's pride, and other essentials, back in the castle.

"You must show Marian how as well," she said, turning to call to her young friend. The log was empty, Marian nowhere to be seen. Kendra sighed, resolving to speak to Marian as soon as possible. The girl had been staying inside their tent most of the time, sulking, Kendra supposed, though she had never seen Marian sulk. She seemed too sensible. A picture of Marian's petulant face when talking about Navarre sprang to mind and Kendra smiled to herself.

"Never mind," she said, smiling up at Robin. "Please, show me."

Robin placed the longbow in her hands, then wrapped his arms around her. Kendra was struck by the strength she felt emanating from this man, the sense of protection she felt every time she was near him. Unlike Navarre, this was a man she knew she could trust. He pressed his thigh against the back of hers and Kendra quickly reevaluated her analysis of the man.

"Place this hand here," he said, taking her hand and placing it on the curve of the bow, "and the other, so." Kendra wrapped the tips of her fingers around the bowstring and smiled up at her instructor.

"Nay, nay," he said, squeezing her around the middle with his left hand and laughing. "Do not cling to the bowstring or 'twill take the hide from your lovely fingers. Gloves—you must have a pair of gloves." He snapped his fingers and one of the grinning lackeys, who always seemed nearby when Robin was around, hurried off to do his bidding.

"I think I'm about ready for a break anyway," Kendra said as the people who had been watching drifted away to other interests. She tried very hard not to be alone with Robin any more than she could help, out of consideration for Marian, but today she was feeling depressed and his company was, she had to admit, quite comforting.

155

"You are ready to break?" Robin stared at her perplexed. "We broke our morning fast hours ago—or do you mean that I have fatigued you so mercilessly that you feel your bones are about to break? Forsooth, you do speak strangely, Kendra O'Brien."

Kendra laughed. "What I mean is I am ready to rest and perhaps take a walk, if you don't mind, Robin."

"Am I invited, milady?" he asked softly, bringing her hand to his lips, drawing her near. She gazed up at him, once again mesmerized by who and what he was. It would be very easy to fall prey to his magnetic personality. Very easy, indeed.

"No," she said abruptly, then smiled to soften the word. "I mean, I feel the need for a little privacy. Do you mind?"

His smile lit his face and he doffed the forest green cap he wore. "I always mind when I am deprived of the presence of such a lovely lady, however, as it happens I must be away from camp for several hours anyway."

As if by magic, Little John suddenly appeared at Robin's elbow. "Have you forgotten we plan to ride tonight, Robin?" Little John asked, glancing at Kendra and then back to Robin. "The barons are headed for Nottingham Castle."

"I have not forgotten, Little John, although with such a lovely distraction before me I scarcely think you could fault me if I did." His sea-blue eyes twinkled at Kendra as he brought her hand to his lips. "Do return to camp soon, milady. I shall leave word with the watch to expect you."

"Of course," she said, relieved she wouldn't have to deal with Robin's open advances just yet. It would give her more time to think, perhaps to talk to Marian. She turned and glanced at the fallen log, once again wondering where the girl could be. At the beginning of the longbow exhibition she had not realized Marian was anywhere around. The best archers in Robin's band had pitted themselves against him one by one until at last only he had been left. Kendra felt her admiration for the man growing hourly. Then she had noticed Marian sitting alone and the guilt had descended.

She bid Robin and Little John good-bye, listening with only half her mind to their admonitions not to wander far from camp. Now as she walked through the forest, head down, the depression swept over her again. Robin was wonderful, the perfect man, the perfect hero, but he wasn't . . .

No, he isn't Navarre, the small voice in her mind said bluntly.

"I don't want Navarre," she said aloud. "He's rude, overbearing, disloyal—"

And you love him.

Kendra stopped dead in her tracks. She tossed her unbound auburn hair back from her shoulders and felt something turn over deep inside of her. She loved Navarre de Galliard. She loved a knight in medieval England who was guilty of treason, who had tried to seduce her, accused her of being a witch, who even at this moment was probably hunting her down so he could drag her back to the castle and burn her at the stake.

"I do not love him," Kendra whispered. She began walking again, striding deliberately through the forest, toward the spring that lay hidden deep in a special part of Robin's lair. He had shown it to her the day before, hinting around that he would like nothing more than to spend some moonlit evening there with her when the days grew warm. Robin was handsome, sweet, heroic, sexy . . . so why didn't his touch set her blood on fire as Navarre's did? Why did the thought of kissing him seem only mildly interesting instead of the focus of her life? If she didn't know better she'd think that perhaps she was the one being bewitched.

She sighed. This part of the forest grew more tangled with growth as she neared the spring. It was a very private place, secluded, a perfect lover's trysting place. Today it was unusually warm and the sun was bright in spite of the cold, crisp air. She knew that when and if it came time for Robin to make his play, it would be here, in this isolated spot. He seemed smitten with her, or was that just an act? Should she let down her guard a little more, be a little more responsive? C'mon, O'Brien—she blushed as she faced the truth of her thoughts— what you're really wondering is should you make love to Robin Hood?

"What a story that would make," she said aloud. She stopped to get her bearings and realized she was only a few feet from the spring. The water bubbled up from beneath a

Tess Mallory

dense tangle of what in spring would be a lush array of green-
ery, but at present was brown and brittle. The spring splashed
down over smooth rocks and into a pool a few feet wide and
several feet deep, then flowed out from there to create a small
stream. The outlaw band used another spring for their drinking
water and it was an unspoken rule that this spring was reserved
for Robin and his special guests—even in the winter.

It was too cold to partake of the beautiful pool of water but
she couldn't help sitting down beside the stream and, discarding her shoes, plunking her feet into the cold water. How many
"guests" had seen this special place, she wondered. While
Robin seemed quite fond of the ladies, he didn't appear to be
the womanizer Alan was. He was more serious, she decided,
more intense. It must come from being the leader of a band
of outlaws.

With a sigh, Kendra lay back and stretched her arms above
her head, letting the peace of Sherwood and the spring soothe
her frazzled nerves. It was so nice here, she thought, lifting
her hair from beneath her and spreading it behind. It would
be so easy to stay here and help Robin Hood bring justice to
England. She raised up on both elbows, her mind suddenly
spinning.

Why not? If she had no way of returning to her own time,
could this be the answer to her future? If Robin fell in love
with her, she could stay with him and help him fight Navarre
and Garrick and John. She could be the woman behind the
man, so to speak; she could help Robin with her knowledge
of future events. It was an absolutely terrific idea—except for
one small problem. She didn't love Robin Hood.

"So what?" Kendra said aloud, sitting up and pulling her
knees to her chest. She stared down into the water, her mind
churning like the bits of dead leaves in the water.

So what if she didn't love Robin? Wouldn't it be worth it
to be with him if it meant she could survive in this time period,
and even have a fulfilling life, given the situation? Life was a
desperate gamble any way you looked at it, no matter what
path she chose. All of her life she had played it safe, until her
husband and child died so horribly. Then she had thrown cau-

tion aside and plunged into life, not caring about the consequences.

Her trip back in time had made her more cautious, and that was fine, but she realized now that she had begun to revert back to the old Kendra, the Kendra who never took a chance, never really thought for herself, never took control of her own life. James and Nicole's death had changed that, forced her to take chances, to think for herself, to plot her life's path alone. Even though Mac had been right about the risks she took, still, she didn't want to return to being that old, fearful Kendra. Kendra stood up suddenly, untied her cloak and tossed it aside. Quickly she jerked the blue overdress she wore up and over her head, threw it down and began struggling to remove the underdress as well. She managed at last, then stretched her arms skyward. The sun was fading on the distant horizon, blocked partially by the forest's thickness, and Kendra lowered her arms, wishing it were summer, wishing she could step down into the shallow pool, clad only in the thin shift she now wore.

What am I trying to prove, she wondered, shivering as the disappearing sunlight brought a colder chill to the air. That I'm brave enough to catch pneumonia? She laughed aloud and hugged herself tightly. The tips of her breasts hardened with the cold and suddenly Kendra remembered strong arms holding her tightly in warm, lavender-scented water; golden eyes that seemed to melt the very bones in her body as his hands caressed her skin. She closed her eyes and sank down on the ground. She spread her cloak and lay down on it, ignoring the cold, reveling in the feel of freedom that came from discarding her cumbersome clothing.

I should have asked Robin to come with me, she thought. I should make wild, passionate love to him and pledge myself to help him in his quest to free England from men like John and Garrick and Navarre. And this would be my life, to live safely, in freedom. Without Navarre de Galliard.

Kendra sat up and pulled the cloak up and over her shoulders. Enough braving the elements and proving that she was still a free spirit. Her hair streamed down over her shoulders as she leaned forward and covered her face with her hands.

Without Navarre. Life without Navarre should hold no fear for her, should hold no qualms, and yet, the thought of life without him sent a sharp pain through her heart.

"Oh, Navarre," she whispered.

"Missing me, mon cher?"

Kendra looked up and gasped. Navarre de Galliard stood on the opposite side of the pool, his dark hair dancing in the fast approaching dusk, his golden eyes burning. Before she could scream he had jumped to the other side and pulled her into his arms. Had she thought Robin's arms were strong? They were but reeds in the wind. Navarre's were iron, two steel rods that could hold her forever.

"Navarre." Kendra whispered his name, then without hesitation pulled his head down to hers, covering his mouth with her own. He stiffened, and to her surprise, thrust her away from him so forcefully that she fell backward, hitting the ground hard. She rolled to her back, her heart pounding as she stared up at the knight and saw that the fire burning in his eyes burned not with desire, but with hatred.

"Witch." He spat the word out as he stalked toward her. "Whore. Murdering sorceress." He stopped directly over her prone body, his legs braced on either side of her as he slowly pulled the leather gauntlets from his hands and threw them aside. He reached one hand to his waist and Kendra watched his deliberate movement, swallowing hard as he grasped the hilt of a long, thin dagger and pulled it from its scabbard. With the other he reached inside the folds of the dark gray cloak he wore and took out her Smith and Wesson.

"Navarre," she whispered again, this time because she could not find her voice. "What are you doing?"

"Your evil is over," he said harshly, kneeling and straddling her waist. "Or it will be in a moment. But first you will teach me how to use this sorcerous weapon. Do so, and you will die quickly, refuse and your screams will be heard as far as Nottingham."

Kendra's heart thudded dully in her ears and she was no longer cold. She couldn't feel, couldn't think. Navarre was going to kill her. Navarre didn't love her; he hated her. He was going to kill her.

With a cry, Kendra shoved him sideways and his slight movement in that direction allowed her to slide from beneath him. She scrambled backwards, pushing with both feet against the mossy ground in her mad attempt to escape. Navarre tossed the gun aside, reached out and grabbed her by one ankle, halting her frantic attempt. Slowly, he dragged her back to him, his fingers like steel around her legs as he straddled her once again, pinning her hands to her sides with his knees, holding the thin, razor-sharp blade to her throat.

Kendra stared up at him, lying as still as one already dead. It was no use trying to fight him. She could no more escape Navarre than she could stop loving him. The realization struck her with the force of a blow and she ran her tongue across her dry lips, searching for words that would not come.

"I could not believe it at first," he said, his voice dull and flat, his breath warm against her face, his strong thighs trapping her legs beneath them. "Would not believe. I wanted to think I was wrong, that Garrick was wrong. But when I saw the blood on Marian's gown I knew that all my worst fears had come true."

Kendra felt her heart quicken at the sight of the raw pain on his face.

"It is my fault again that an innocent has died." His eyes were glazed, hollow, and the sight frightened Kendra more than his words. "And I should kill you for that alone. As it is, I shall kill you to put an end to this enchantment, this evil you have spun around me, this fire you have ignited that cannot be quenched."

Navarre lifted the dagger with both hands high above her chest and Kendra felt the suffocation of fear choke her even as his words echoed in her mind. What had he said? There was blood on Marian's gown? An innocent had died? Oh my God! She willed herself to speak.

"Navarre, I did not kill Marian! I don't know what you're talking about. She's right here in the camp."

"I have watched the camp for days and I have not seen her," he said, the blade frozen above her breast. "You lie."

"No!" Kendra arched against his weight, tears burning in her eyes as she fought to keep her voice calm. "I swear to you that Marian is fine. I would never harm her, or anyone else!''

Navarre stared down at the woman, wanting to believe her words. It would be an easy matter to let her prove she spoke the truth but it mattered not. Whether Marian lived or no, the enchantment was stronger than ever. As his body pressed against hers, he had felt the fire engulfing him once again. The thin chemise she wore lay almost transparent against her skin, her peach-colored nipples hard beneath the cloth. He could feel his flesh responding even through the cloth of his leggings, the warmth spreading through his legs even as he held the dagger poised to end her life. A groan of despair escaped him. This was madness, insanity—witchery.

Her chest rose and fell rapidly, each breath pressing her creamy white skin against the chemise. Navarre closed his eyes to the sight and let the anguish rush over him. He lowered the dagger. How could he kill a woman? Even if she were a witch—how could he take her life in cold blood? He opened his eyes and saw the fear in her azure gaze, yet there was courage there as well. He had known from the first moment he saw Kendra O'Brien that not only was she trouble, she was different. She had strength, character, a sense of her own identity, intelligence, unlike any other woman he had ever known. Was it because she was a witch that she possessed these qualities? Was there any way around her death?

Navarre shivered with the cold realization that there was not. There was no other way. This enchantment would torture him as long as Kendra lived.

Kendra saw the glazed look return to his eyes, even as she saw the tears on his cheeks. Her knight had fought the battle within himself, and won. Navarre lifted the dagger. The blade in his hand began to tremble and Kendra braced herself to die, keeping her eyes open from the sheer force of her will, determined she would not make it easy for Navarre to take her life.

"Before I die," she said, her voice shaking only the slightest bit, "I want to tell you for the last time that I am not a witch. I have never even met King Richard, and while I believe in what Robin Hood is doing, I am not helping him.''

"So you have said," Navarre's own voice was laced with weariness. "It changes naught."

"And the last thing I have to say before you murder me is this—I love you, Navarre."

She expected the dagger to come plunging down at her words and steeled herself for the pain. Instead, he stared down at her, the expression on his face stunned, as though that was the last thing he had expected her to say. The weapon fell from his hand. His golden eyes were round, frozen like a predator's sighting his prey. Then, suddenly he was lying beside her and she was in his arms, his body hard and warm against her.

"God, forgive me," he whispered into her hair, then with a suddenness that startled her, covered her lips with his and thrust the hot warmth of his tongue into the depths of her mouth, claiming her, searing his passion into her, demanding hers in return. The intensity of his need frightened her and Kendra pulled away, struggling to be released. Navarre jerked away and sat back on his heels, one hand encircling her wrist as with the other he stripped himself of his dark leggings.

"No," she said, twisting her arm in his grasp. "Navarre—wait."

Kendra cried out as he flung her back to the forest floor, his half-naked body pressing hers to the ground, his mouth burning against hers once again. The shift had ridden to her waist and he pushed the material higher, slipping his hands beneath to touch the warmth of her skin. Kendra felt the shock of Navarre's hot flesh against hers as she twisted beneath him, inadvertently pressing herself more tightly against him.

Navarre's mouth touched her ear as he whispered fervently, his breath hot, his voice tense. "We want each other. This is what we have both dreamed of," he said. "You have won, Kendra—let the sorcery be complete. I can no longer fight it, I can no longer fight the way I feel."

His lips moved to the side of her neck and Kendra knew she was lost. His hands slid down both of her arms, sensation dancing in their wake as they skimmed over her skin and across the cloth clinging to her chest. Kendra gasped as Navarre's hands touched her breasts, caressing, kneading, bringing her nipples to aching pulsation. Then his lips closed around one burning bud, suckling it through the cloth with a roughness she should have feared, but suddenly did not.

Instead she threw back her head, arching her back as his mouth seared the flesh of first her right breast and then her left. He tried to lift the cloth but it was too tight. Impatiently he grabbed the lacy neck of her chemise and pulled, ripping it down the middle. Kendra felt his chest meet hers, the roughness of his hair colliding with the smoothness of her skin. He bent to caress her breasts again but she lifted his face, her lips suddenly against his lips, then the hollow of his throat. He smelled of faint lavender and sweat and something intangibly male and Kendra abandoned herself to the passion and threw caution to the wind.

Navarre groaned as the woman yielded to him. Nay, she did not yield—she gave, passion for passion, fire for fire. He shuddered with desire as her hands moved down his back in slow, sensuous circles, then again as she opened herself beneath him. Her warmth called to him, surrounded him even as she took his face between both hands and darted her small, wet tongue inside his mouth, the movement taunting him with its symbolic mating. Navarre squeezed his eyes shut as the insanity wrapped around his mind, and suddenly there was nothing left but Kendra's body against his. The universe had slowed to a single thought, a single focus: to ease the fire searing his blood, to partake of the sweet heat she so willingly offered.

Navarre sheathed himself in her warmth like a sword finding its scabbard, and suddenly he knew why he burned so relentlessly, why the enchantment was so strong. Because he belonged with her. Whether she be witch or no, he belonged with her, fit with her like a glove and a hand. Whatever powers had thrown them together must have known what he knew now—this was meant to be.

Kendra wept silently with joy as Navarre kissed her mouth, her eyes, her hair, caressing the side of her jaw with the tip of his tongue before plundering her mouth even as he continued to plunder the secrets below. This was not sex. This was not some carnal fulfillment of the flesh, she thought in some distant part of her mind. This was a joining, a union, a bonding as strong as the marriage vows she had taken with James so long ago. And she was giving herself to Navarre, emotionally, physically, in a way she never had with James.

Navarre possessed her mouth again. She tasted of honey and light and when she began to move beneath him, he no longer cared if he was enchanted or not; no longer cared whether his immortal soul was in danger, or if he survived the night, or if England survived at all. God help him, he cared not if Marian was alive or dead, for his soul was lost, as was his heart.

Kendra arched her back as Navarre filled her, matching her movements to his, stroke for stroke, feeling the ecstasy flood her veins as he joined his body to hers. Like a white-hot iron he burned his passion into her, his weight pressing her down against the forest floor. Tiny twigs scratched her bare skin, but she didn't notice. Gone were the birds, the trees, the spring, the forest. She and Navarre dwelt within a magic circle of their own creation; a circle wherein nothing else existed, save the fire between them.

White-hot he burned inside of her. White-hot she received him. They flamed in one accord, higher and higher, dancing the pagan, wordless litany of man and woman beneath the boughs of Sherwood. The world shifted into mindlessness and Kendra cried out in thankful wonder to the fates that had brought her to this time, this place, even as Navarre echoed his joy against her lips, as the inferno rose, and utterly consumed them.

Chapter Ten

Kendra awoke shivering in the strong, safe circle of Navarre's arms. He lay against her back, one arm around her waist, the other beneath her head, cushioning her from the roughness of the forest floor. They were both turned toward the small fire he had built sometime during the night, and she had never felt so safe, so protected, so completely content in her life.

I never knew it could be like this, she thought. Never. Not when I sowed my wild oats in college, not when I married James. No man has ever moved me like this. No man has ever touched my soul, until now.

She felt the guilt and disloyalty to her dead husband begin to sweep over her and she pushed the emotion firmly away. In this time and place James had not yet even existed. It was pointless to feel guilty in such an unreal situation.

"You are like warm silk," Navarre whispered into her ear.

"You are like hot iron," she whispered back, smiling as she remembered the first time she'd made the mental comparison. His chest shook with a deep chuckle and the curly hair there tickled her back. She laughed aloud.

"Hot iron, is it?" he said. "And I only tickle you? We shall see about that."

Much, much later, Kendra snuggled against Navarre and closed her eyes. The moon in the dark night sky was beginning to set, and she knew dawn was not far behind. She should be thinking of what this day would hold for her—for both of them—but she could not. She could not shatter the bubble of happiness surrounding them with anything as mundane as reality.

"Tell me you are not a witch," Navarre said suddenly, his deep voice soft, almost trembling.

Kendra sighed. Reality had a way of making itself heard, it seemed, no matter how hard you fought against it.

"Why would you believe me now?" she asked, unable to lift her gaze to his. "Actually, I expected to wake up and find you gone—or else—not to wake up at all." Kendra pressed her lips together, ashamed of the lie. The thought had never crossed her mind.

"I am sorry," he whispered, tightening his arms around her. "I never wanted to kill you, indeed, I have wanted nothing more than to join with you since that first moment at Abury. It was the fire you created inside of me that I took to be enchantment. I thought only of you day and night. I could not sleep, could not eat. Garrick said the only way to be free of you was to take your life with my own hands."

"How long have you known the sheriff?" Kendra asked, glancing up at him hesitantly.

"Many years. We knew one another in Normandy when we were both just boys. We were both the bastards of English noblemen and were brought to our father's houses at a young age. Their estates joined at one side and we grew up together. When we were grown we became mercenaries and traveled around the world. We returned to England after hearing of Richard's plan to auction off titles and estates to fund his next journey to Outremer."

"I don't trust him and I don't think you should either," Kendra said impetuously. Navarre looked down at her, one dark brow arched in question. "You forget how he treated me." Navarre laughed and with a sharp cry, Kendra pulled away and struck his chest with one tight fist. "He almost raped me and you can laugh?"

"I laugh not at his violence, for I know Garrick's ruthlessness quite well."

"Then why do you laugh?" Kendra fumed, struggling as he pulled her more tightly against him once again.

"Because you think it odd that any man could resist your

charms for long, especially a man of Garrick's station who is used to taking what he wants.''

Kendra was silent for a moment. "I know the ways here are different from the ways back . . . back where I come from, but Navarre, it is still wrong for a man to force a woman."

"Aye," he said softly, running one hand lightly down the side of her bare thigh, "I agree. But what if he can convince her instead?"

"Oh, no you don't." Kendra said with a laugh, her anger dissipating as the now familiar heat ran between them once again. "We are talking, Sir Galliard, for the first time, and I for one am learning a great deal." She leaned against him and felt his sharp intake of breath as her bare breasts grazed his chest.

"Do that again and you will find this lesson at an end." He bent his head to her throat and bit her skin delicately. "But I may teach you something else."

"Why do you believe me now?" Kendra whispered, her eyes closed as Navarre's teeth traced a sensuous path down the side of her neck. "All this time . . .''

Navarre lips stilled against her skin. He lifted his face to hers and Kendra was startled by the deep pain she saw mirrored in his eyes. "All of this time," he said, "I thought this fire between us some kind of magic—sorcery. I could not bear to face the truth."

"What is the truth?" She said, reaching up and brushing a long strand of dark hair back from his jaw. His eyes, now dark as amber, flamelike, with golden flecks in the center, bored into hers.

He lifted his hand to her face and smoothed her lower lip with his thumb. Kendra felt the electricity shoot down her throat, across her breasts, to pool at the apex of her thighs. She gasped and Navarre covered her lips with his own almost savagely as he pulled her to him. Kendra met his passion and was disappointed when he broke the embrace, his breathing heavy, his hand still caressing her face.

"The truth is that I love you," he said, moving his fingers slowly across her jawline. "And I vowed that I would never love again. Everything I love, withers. Everything I touch, dies.''

"That isn't true," Kendra said, taking his face between her hands and speaking fervently. "Why do you think I threw myself at you that first day—just because you were tall, dark, and handsome?''

Navarre frowned, the corner of his mouth lifting slightly. "You do speak most strangely," he said.

"Well, okay, it was partly because you were tall, dark, and handsome." She caressed his inner thigh lightly with her fingers, enjoying the way the gold flecks in his eyes darkened as she did. "But it was more. I didn't realize it then, but I know it now. Your heart called to mine, Navarre, across time and space, your heart called to mine.''

He shook his head. "You have witnessed the violence inside of me, were almost its victim. I cannot take the chance that someone else I love will die because of me.''

"Tell me about her," she said, rubbing her head against his chin, her legs tucked beneath her, "Tell me about the woman you think died because of you.''

With a sigh, Navarre smoothed her hair, then ran one hand through his own. It was late and the moon had risen. In its light, Kendra studied his features, amazed to see the vulnerability there, softly etched in the usually harsh lines around his mouth and eyes. Gently she brushed the back of one hand across his check. Without turning he took her hand and brought it to his lips.

"It is a long story," he said after kissing each of her fingers. "One only Garrick knows, and Richard. It reveals my hidden shame.''

"Do you mean, your treason against Richard?''

He dropped her hand and nodded. "Aye. The reason that I turned my back on the man who was my friend and my king.''

The sound of a twig snapping behind them made Kendra whirl around. The leaves on small bushes moved slightly with the cold breeze that chilled them. Navarre, too, had turned, his golden eyes searching the forest.

Kendra realized, with a sudden jolt, that she had been missing from camp almost the whole night and no one had come looking for her, not Robin, not Marian, not the guards, no one. Tiny prickles of uneasiness crept up the back of her neck as she gazed around at the darkened glade. If any of Robin's men came upon them now, Navarre would become their prisoner. In spite of her own feelings about what he was attempting to do, Kendra knew with all of her heart she didn't want Navarre to be captured.

"I think we should go," she said. "It isn't safe here and—"

"No." Navarre stilled her movements, taking both her hands in his, drawing her close to him once again. "This I must tell you first. There must no longer be secrets between us."

Kendra inhaled sharply. No secrets between them. Could she—dare she tell Navarre the truth now?

"It was in Outremer, during the Crusades."

"Outremer, that's the holy lands, right?"

Navarre nodded. "They are called that as well." He bent his left knee and balanced his arm across it, his gaze fixed on the midnight forest. "I was Richard's friend, his bodyguard, in fact. I always rode at his side, ready to protect him from danger. Garrick was one of his trusted advisors and the three of us were as close as brothers." He glanced over at Kendra. She placed one hand on his forearm.

"What happened?" she asked softly.

"There was a woman called Talam." One jaw muscle tightened in the moonlight. "She was the daughter of an obscure merchant who bought and sold merchandise to us without his sultan's knowledge. She was no one." Navarre's throat trembled as he swallowed hard, then lowered his gaze. "I loved her."

Kendra waited for him to continue and when he didn't she squeezed his arm softly. He looked away, his eyes fixed on some distant point in time.

"Richard hated her. She was an infidel and he could not understand how one of his men, his knights, could fall in love with such a one. Bed her, yes, that he understood, but not love. Garrick tried to intercede for me, but he came back from a long talk with Richard and told me that the king had said if I took her back to England and married her, he would strip me of my knighthood and my titles. I would lose everything I worked so hard to obtain.''

He moved away from Kendra's gentle touch and sprang to his feet. Muttering an oath, he stalked a few feet away, and clad only in his leggings, stood glowering out at the silent trees. Kendra sensed that she must give him time to deal with the emotions of his tale, and she sat quietly, waiting for him to speak.

''We came to Acre,'' he said at last, ''a great fortified city that took many days to conquer. I was sorely wounded in the battle and taken with many others to Crete to recuperate. Unconscious, feverish, I didn't even know where I was for many weeks. When Garrick came to get me he told me I almost died.'' He turned back toward her, his dark hair almost silver in the moonlight. ''I wished I had. For he also told me that Talam was dead.'' Navarre shook his head, as if the thought of the news once again bewildered him. ''At first, I thought she had been killed in the battle, and I blamed myself that I had not protected her.''

Kendra stood at his words, feeling his pain as though it were her own. Moving to his side, she stood motionless until, with a suddenness that surprised and moved her, Navarre jerked her into his arms and buried his face against her hair.

''But she didn't die in the battle,'' he said, his arms holding her like a vise, pressing her body into his, his voice muffled. ''Richard gave Saladin, the leader of the Saracens, an ultimatum—surrender, or watch the people of Acre die, every man, woman and child. He took them and—''

''Don't.'' Kendra pushed away from his embrace and placed one hand softly against his lips. ''Don't torture yourself. I remember reading about it. Richard massacred them.''

Navarre stared down at her. ''You read about it? Where? Wait, you say can read? Oh, yes, you are a scribe, I had forgotten.''

''Yes, I—never mind—I know how the story goes. Talam was one of those killed?''

''Richard made sure of it,'' he said bitterly, turning away from her. ''Even now I see her face, at night, in the daytime, when I tried to kill you—'' He spun back around. ''Perhaps

171

God allowed her to stop me. Don't you see? She is dead because of my love—because I was unable to protect her. And what if I had listened to my own superstitions or to Garrick? What if I had—''

''But you didn't.''

His eyes narrowed. ''I could have, more easily than you imagine. Never forget, Kendra, that I am a soldier.'' He moved toward her and Kendra shivered as his voice caressed her name for the first time. She stood, conscious all at once that she was naked except for his cloak draped around her shoulders. ''I am not a soft-voiced gentleman who knows how to woo and court,'' he said, walking toward her slowly. ''And I, like Garrick, am used to taking what I want. I am no nobleman. I am Navarre de Galliard, bastard, nothing more.''

Kendra saw the raw need in his eyes, the almost savage need to wipe the past from his mind, to exorcise the pain of what he had just revealed.

''I am not afraid, Navarre,'' Kendra whispered.

He took a step toward her, and involuntarily she took a step back. He laughed, but the laughter did not reach his eyes.

''Are you not?'' he asked.

Kendra swallowed hard as the knight continued to move toward her, one slow step at a time. Like a lion stalking his prey, she thought, wondering why she continued to back away when she longed to take him in her arms and once and for all dispel the demons. It was his eyes, she decided, as her back met the smooth bark of a tree. She stopped abruptly, unable to move farther.

His eyes were no longer those of Navarre but a predator; he was no longer her lover, but a man haunted by ghosts and driven by revenge. He stopped inches away from her and Kendra's heart began to pound, her breath growing shallow as he slid one hand down the center of her chest and with the other tilted her face upward.

''Will you love the Black Lion as you have loved the man, Navarre?'' he said, his voice low and harsh.

''Yes,'' she whispered.

Kendra gasped as Navarre pressed her back against the hard, smooth wood of the tree behind her, his mouth coming down roughly on hers, bruising her skin. His kiss was demanding, powerful, and completely barbaric. She tasted her own blood but made no sound. He did not ask for her response, he took it, ravaging her mouth, his hands moving with the same roughness as his tongue over her bare skin. Kendra cried out in fear even as she felt the passion he commanded rising inside of her.

She closed her eyes against the sight of his feral countenance as she struggled against dual monsters, fear and passion, Navarre and the Black Lion. He wanted her to blame him, to agree with him that he was evil, at fault because of Talam's death, that he could easily have been the instrument of her death as well. Yet, at the same time, he wanted her to absolve him, and wipe away the pain with her body. And she would. She was no longer afraid.

Navarre tore his mouth from hers and grasped her chin between rough fingers. "Open your eyes." She obeyed. "Now do you fear me?" he demanded. "Now do you know that all I touch must be forever spoiled, forever scarred?"

"No," Kendra whispered, threading her hands through his dark hair and pulling his mouth close to hers. "No. Your touch gives me joy and your love gives me life. I love the Black Lion as I love the man, Navarre."

With a groan, Navarre pressed her back against the tree and sheathed himself in her warmth once again. Kendra felt the wave hit her as roughly as had Navarre's first savage kiss, picking her up and throwing her without mercy into the churning sea of her own desire. Mounting the wave, the passion pushed her upward even as she saw, through half-closed lashes, Navarre's face still twisted as if in pain.

"Say that you love me," he whispered.

"With all of my soul."

With a roar, Navarre carried Kendra out of her body, out of her senses, sending her to ride passion's crest, sending her spinning into a place only Navarre could create, only she could enter, a place to which they journeyed together, in the wake of Navarre de Galliard's tears.

* * *

Tess Mallory

Kendra awoke much later. She blinked, then sat up, startled, unsure for a moment where she was. The forest came slowly into focus along with the sight of Navarre standing a few feet away wearing only his leggings, his back to her. She smiled but the gesture quickly faded as she remembered the decision she had made after the last passionate ride Navarre had taken her on just before dawn.

"Navarre," she called softly. "There is something I must tell you."

"I believe you are not a witch." His voice was oddly strained and Kendra pulled her shift on, then stood and crossed quickly to his side. "But I must have an answer," he said. "I must know the truth." He turned. Both of her cameras dangled from one hand, her bag from the other, his dark brows troubled, knit together. "I have shared my secrets with you. Now it is your turn."

"Yes." Kendra bent to retrieve the rest of her clothing from the ground, keeping her eyes downcast, feeling suddenly awkward. "That's what I want to tell you—my secret. How I came to be here, and why you cannot use my gun—" he frowned at the unfamiliar word and Kendra hurried on "—the weapon I injured you with, to keep Richard from the throne of England."

She glanced up at him. Navarre handed her the cameras and folded both arms across his broad chest, his golden eyes warm, yet filled with caution.

"I am listening," he said.

Navarre sat in stunned amazement as Kendra began to weave a strange and fanciful tale of a magical wind that had swept her from the year 1997 to the year 1194. As her story progressed, his emotions ran the gamut from anger to incredulity to fascination, and at last, to astonishment.

A woman from the future. A woman caught in the forces of God and nature flung backward in time. She told him of a world where men could fly, even to touch the moon and the stars. It was impossible. It was insane. He had told her so and she had picked up one of the small gray boxes, pointed it at him, and before he could move, pushed a button. Thinking it

174

another weapon, he expected another searing pain and jumped in reaction as a strange, soft sound, almost like a cat purring, emanated from the box, just before a square of paper shot out from the bottom of it.

Kendra handed him a hard square of paper and on its surface was a perfect likeness of him. He had dropped it as though his skin had been seared and rose with a roar from the tree stump where he sat.

She had calmed him and then shown him the other box, telling him it made similar ''photographs,'' but of a higher quality. She pointed it at him too, after moving a round circle on the front of it back and forth. The box made an odd ''click'' and he gazed with interest at the bottom of the box to watch his image appear again. Nothing appeared, however, and she told him those kind of pictures had to be ''developed'' with something called chemicals. He found himself growing more fascinated with each word she spoke and, with her instruction, peered through the camera as she told him about ''settings'' and ''composition'' and something called a ''flash.'' Navarre caught himself, realizing he was swallowing her tale without so much as a question.

''Cease!'' He stood, slicing the air with the edge of his hand. ''I cannot listen further. My God, have I fallen in love with a madwoman? Kendra, this box that paints my picture—'' he stood staring down at her, the question he would not ask in his eyes.

''I swear, Navarre, I am not a witch, and I am not mad,'' Kendra stamped one leather-clad foot in frustration. She gathered the two squares from the ground and shook them in his face. ''I'm telling you the truth. How else would you explain it?'' She held up both hands to stop him from speaking. ''I know, I know—witchcraft.'' She sighed, pushing back her tangled auburn hair.

Navarre groaned silently to himself, following the gesture of her hand with his gaze, remembering the perfume of her red-gold tresses, and the way he had wound the cascading length around his hand while they made love, drawing her lips to his. Crossing to her side he grasped her by both arms, shaking her slightly.

"Do you not think I wish to believe you?" he demanded. "How can I? Your tale is beyond sensibility."

"What about your druid lady's prophecy?" she asked, jerking away from him, blue eyes flashing. "Was that sensible? Was it intelligent for you to wait at Avebury for Richard's salvation to appear simply because some old woman said it would happen?"

Navarre stiffened. "At first, I did not believe it was prophecy. I believed it was a clever way for the woman to relay a message to Locksley from Richard. But what I witnessed in Abury had to be a type of magic. It would be foolish to deny it."

"In my world there is a kind of magic, called science. Men study how the universe was created, how it works, what it does. But that kind of magic is simply knowledge, Navarre, the kind of knowledge I'm trying to share with you." She held out both hands to him imploringly.

Navarre pressed his lips together, then released his breath explosively. "Knowledge and magic are not the same. One is of God, the other of the devil."

Kendra turned away, her shoulders slumping with dejection. "What can I say," she murmured, "what can I do to prove that I'm telling the truth? Would you believe me if I told you what happens to Richard? To John? To the whole Plantagenat family?" She turned to face him, a few wisps of hair dancing across the pallor of her face.

"If I told you that Richard will die a few years from now, killed by an archer's last arrow, would that convince you? If I told you John will eventually rule, would that stop you from murdering Richard?" She smoothed the linen of her tunic-like dress with one hand, her eyes lowered. "The camera that made your photograph. Could even a witch do that? What about the gun? Is it like any weapon you've ever seen or heard of? Navarre," she said, wetting her lips, "you must believe me. I am from another time, another place—I am from the future. I lived in a place called New York City, I was married and had a little girl but they were both killed before I traveled back in time. I was a reporter for a newspaper, a kind of scribe. Please, Navarre, please believe me."

Her gaze burned into his and Navarre very nearly looked away, but instead, looked deeper, trying to see into the heart of this woman he loved. There was no evil in her, of that he was certain, but was there madness?

She moved to stand beside him, wrapping her arms around his waist, gazing up at him. "Do you believe my words of love were false as well? I would never lie to you. Will you believe me?"

" 'Tis a wondrous story to believe, were it but true."

Kendra jumped at the sound of the harsh voice cutting through the stillness of the forest behind them. Navarre moved to put his arm protectively around her, then his golden eyes narrowed and he dropped his arm from her shoulder.

Robin Hood stood in the clearing, a longbow in one hand, the other clenched at his waist, his eyes dancing with anger. Twenty men flanked him on either side. Navarre could see Marian timidly poking her head from behind the outlaw.

"Good morrow, fair maid—or does the term no longer apply?" Robin said with a brief bow in Kendra's direction.

Navarre thought quickly. He knew not how much the outlaw had overheard of her insane tale, but he did know that if Locksley thought Kendra had been persuaded to Navarre's side of things, he would take her prisoner. Better for them both if he thought her affections toward him only a ruse to help Richard. Breathing a silent prayer that she would understand and go along with his ploy, the knight turned on her, his hands clenched into fists.

"So this is why you seduced me, wench! You lure me into Sherwood, leaving me open to an attack from Locksley and his cutthroats."

Kendra stared at him, her mouth open, her blue eyes registering first shock, then fury. Navarre felt his spirit sink. She thought he meant it, that he did not really trust her. In faith, he must tell her the truth later. He could make her understand.

"I did not!" Kendra exploded. "If you don't believe me ask Robin—ask Marian! There was no plan."

"As if I would believe them. At least you were telling the truth when you said you did not harm Marian." He darted a glance at the girl. "Did she? Tell me truly, Marian, and mayhap I will forgive you for your own treachery. The blood on your gown—whose blood was it really? Did you leave it to lead us to the witch or was it to make me grieve and lament your passing—or was it the witch's idea?''

"Kendra knew nothing about it," Marian said softly, hanging her head. "I—I was angry with you for ignoring me, for leaving me at the mercy of John and Garrick. I stole chicken's blood from the kitchen. I suppose I thought if you cared, you would follow." She glanced over at Kendra. "I am sorry, Kendra."

"You should not be asking her forgiveness but mine," Navarre said harshly. "You repay my kindness with wickedness!"

"Do not speak to Lady Marian about treachery and wickedness," Robin said, casually slipping an arrow from the quiver on his back and fitting it into the longbow he held. "For that is a crime you know too well yourself. As for this encounter, I am quite willing to take credit for that which is mine, old friend, however, in this I must plead innocent. Nevertheless, I do thank the lady if indeed her plan was to deliver you into my hands. However, I do not understand the meaning of the story she was spinning unless it was meant to delay you until we arrived."

"I did not plan this," Kendra said emphatically, "and my story is true. I was sitting by the spring—"

"Sitting very enticingly, I might add," Navarre said.

Suddenly Kendra had had enough. She whirled on Navarre, her hand flying to connect with his solid face in a resounding whack. He flinched and she spun away from him, resolutely stalking over to Robin Hood where she stood, arms folded across her chest, her expression furious.

"I do think that—" Robin began, only to be cut off by Kendra's angry voice.

"Shut up! I've had enough! I've had enough from all of you! You're going to listen to me!" She punched her finger into the astonished outlaw's chest as he and his men looked on, open-mouthed. "You heard me tell Navarre my story. I am from the future! I don't know why I was brought back here but here I am! Now if you want to lock me up, kill me,

burn me at the stake, go ahead and do it! But there's one thing
you should know. Since I'm from the future I *know* the future
and I could be a great asset to your plans to save England!
Moreover, Navarre and Garrick have a weapon that could easily kill Richard from a great distance. So I suggest everyone
be a little nicer to me, if you want my help.''

She sank to her knees and covered her face with her hands,
too exhausted to go on.

Robin stared down at her for a long moment, letting the
longbow sag, the arrow between his fingers.

"Your words ring true," he said, "and it would explain
much. Yet, there is only one way to find out where you speak
the truth or lie.''

Kendra looked up at him, her face streaked with tears, her
voice calm. "What do I have to do?" she asked. "Just tell me
what to do.''

The corner of Robin's mouth lifted in a half smile. "You,
milady? Why you do not have to do a thing. Little John!"

The big man strode forward at the command. "Aye,
Robin?''

"Go into the forest. Find Magda and bring her here."

"Magda?" Kendra's eyes widened at the sound of the
name. "Is she the druid priestess, the one who prophesied I
would come?''

"The one who prophesied that Richard's salvation would
come to Abury," Robin said. "Aye. She will come and tell
us if your words be false or true.''

"What about him?" Little John asked, jerking his head toward Navarre.

Robin lifted the longbow once again and pulled the string
taut, the shaft of the arrow balanced straight between his fingers and the bow. He turned the point toward Navarre de Galliard and let the arrow fly. Kendra cried out as the shaft darted
through the air toward the knight.

"Navarre!"

Navarre didn't move as the arrow winged toward him, even
as the two men holding him dropped his arms and fled. Navarre de Galliard stood straight and unyielding, staring at
Robin Hood, his golden eyes burning with suppressed anger.

The arrow swept past him and buried itself with a resounding plunk in a round knot in the tree.

Robin smiled with a curious kind of satisfaction, then turned back to Little John. "Tie him up," he ordered. "Tie them both up and set a guard over them. We shall hear what Magda says about the woman, whether she be Richard's salvation"— the smile disappeared as suddenly as it had come—"or his destruction."

The woman called Magda sat at the fire's edge, her eyes closed, her hands clasped together in front of her, her throat quivering with the low-voiced keening she had begun the moment she first saw Kendra. Little John had brought the druid priestess into the camp a few minutes before sundown and now he, Robin, Alan-a-Dale, Kendra, and Navarre all sat watching the old woman rock back and forth performing her strange ritual. A handful of Robin's men stood guarding them. Marian sat in the shadows, her eyes round with wonder. Kendra and Navarre sat on the ground with their backs touching, their hands tied together behind them.

"What is she doing?" Kendra asked, craning her head back toward Navarre.

"She is communing with the gods," Navarre said, his voice low. "In a moment she will cast the runes to the ground and read them. Your fate rests in her hands."

Kendra closed her eyes. "I thought you believed me when I said I wasn't a witch," she whispered. "Did all of last night mean so little to you? I gave myself to you, body and soul. You said you loved me. Did you think to revenge yourself on me by making me think it was true?"

Navarre opened his mouth to tell her it was only a ruse to protect her, when out of the corner of his eyes he caught sight of Alan-a-Dale sitting behind the copse of bushes at their backs, listening very attentively to their conversation.

"Aye," he said roughly. "You had tortured me with your seductress ways for so long, that I decided to make you burn with the same fire you had lit inside of me. Now that I have satisfied myself, I am free of you."

He grimaced as he felt Kendra's sharp intake of breath and

felt the tremble in her body at his words. Cautiously he felt for her hands behind his back, hoping to press them and communicate to her his pretense. He was surprised when she complacently curled her fingers inside of his. Turning around toward her as far as the ropes would allow, he saw one eyelid slide into what could have been a wink before she glared back at him.

"Do not speak to me," she said, averting her face. "For you have sorely wounded me with your hateful words. I knew you were evil and that Robin was good! May God forgive me for ever believing your words of love."

Magda stopped singing abruptly, then slowly turned and looked directly at Kendra. Their gazes locked for a long moment and Navarre saw Kendra shiver as the old woman's eyes narrowed.

"Bring her to me," she said.

Robin cut Kendra's bonds and jerked her to her feet, propelling her toward the old woman, his face grim.

The forest had grown dark again and Navarre wondered how soon he dared try to escape. If Magda declared Kendra to be Richard's salvation, Robin would grant her freedom and in return, she would help him as soon as she could, of that he was certain. He frowned. Or rather, he was reasonably certain. Surely she had realized his ploy, else she would not have winked at him. Unless that was mayhap an accident, not intended as a signal. No, of course it was. Of course she knew he had not truly betrayed her.

Robin stopped at the old woman's side and, dropping Kendra's arm, bowed from the waist, one hand sweeping down toward Magda.

"Milady," he said politely, "this is Magda, the last druid priestess in all of England. Do not fear. Even if Magda's words speak against you, I promise no harm will come to you." His white teeth flashed evenly in the moonlight. "Unlike my friend, Navarre, I do not mind that your beauty has ensorcelled me, and I welcome any fire you may wish to ignite within me."

Navarre felt the jealousy dart through him, then smiled

grimly to himself. Locksley would burn in hell before he would touch Kendra.

"Come here, child," Magda said, motioning with one gnarled hand. Kendra sank down beside her, her eyes suddenly round and fearful. Magda lifted one hand to her face, touching her cheek lightly, staring deeply once again into the woman's eyes, her own pale ones hawk-like in the moonlight. Kendra stared back at her as one transfixed, and Navarre shifted uneasily on the ground.

He had heard many tales of Magda. Magda the Good, she was called, but nevertheless, the thought of Kendra's fate resting in the hands of a pagan priestess who still worshiped trees and a whole plethora of gods made him suddenly quite nervous. He leaned forward as Magda picked up Kendra's hand, turning it over and smoothing the palm with her own. She then cupped Kendra's face between her withered fingers and gazed for another long moment into the woman's eyes.

"Your palm speaks of great destiny," Magda said at last, "and your eyes have revealed your secrets. Robin has told me naught of you, neither where you came from, nor whom you are." She chuckled, the sound deep and surprisingly pleasant. "In spite of himself, Robin is, in fact, quite the Christian. The only way he believes poor Magda anymore is if I tell him all, without his giving me so much as a hint."

"Enough, Magda," Robin said quietly. "Read the runes and tell me of this woman—who she is, where she is from, what her purpose is in England."

Magda nodded, wisps of thin gray hair falling forward as she dropped Kendra's hand and picked up a jumble of small, stone-like tablets from her lap.

Magda was keening again, soft and low, and Navarre felt a prickle of apprehension dance up his spine. Kendra glanced back at him and he saw fear in her eyes, then carefully, almost imperceptibly, she once again lowered her left eyelid. He hadn't realized he'd been holding his breath and now expelled it in a sigh of relief. She understood. Relieved, yet impatient to be rid of his bonds, Navarre tested the ropes that held him. He froze as Magda's voice drifted back to him.

"Do not struggle so against your destiny, Navarre de Galliard," she said in her singsong voice. "You must allow the salvation to touch you as well."

Navarre saw Robin glance his way, and responded with a shrug.

"Tell me of Kendra O'Brien," Robin said.

The priestess dropped Kendra's hand and stood. "She is not what she appears to be. Her home is in a far and distant place, and yet, it does not yet exist. She lives where men fly and people live to great ages, where people speak to one another from far distances through small boxes, and where other, powerful boxes control almost everything. Their powerful, mighty weapons destroy everything in their path and warfare has become so fearful they dare not wage it for fear of destroying the earth itself. She is from the far and distant future, my lord."

Robin flung the drink he held into the fire, his face wreathed with anger. "Again this nonsense! I care not of men flying or small boxes. Is she the one sent to save Richard?"

Magda paused, the moment long and pregnant. Navarre tensed as he watched Kendra's back grow rigid with apprehension.

"Aye," Magda said, nodding her gray head. "She is Richard's salvation, but she also brings his destruction with her."

"The gun," Kendra whispered under her breath.

"She spoke of a weapon," Robin said quickly, "a weapon that Navarre and Garrick can use to kill Richard."

Magda nodded, continuing to stare at the runes. "Aye, I see it now. She is Richard's salvation, though perhaps not as we supposed." She turned and looked directly at Navarre. "Perhaps this would be a good time to inform Sir de Galliard about the barons journeying to Nottingham, eh, Sir Robin?"

Navarre shot the outlaw a suspicious look. "What does the crone mean?"

Robin crossed the short expanse between them, coming to a stop in front of his prisoner, legs spread, hands on his hips. He stared down at Navarre, his sharp-featured face shadowed in the firelight, his gaze searching that of his old friend. Navarre returned his stare, trying not to remember the carefree days before the crusade when he and Robin had been friends.

Apparently the same thoughts were crossing the outlaw's mind, for suddenly he squatted beside his prisoner, his face earnest, his voice low.

"Why, Navarre?" he asked. "Why have you turned against Richard and England? I know you are too intelligent not to realize the destruction that will come if John sits upon the throne. Or perhaps you hope to be one of those who will pull his hapless strings and in this way rule England?"

"You know better than that, Robin," Navarre said, finding it hard suddenly to maintain his anger as his old friend spoke to him so frankly.

Robin shrugged. "I know nothing about you now. The Navarre I knew would not have thrown his lot in with such men as Garrick Neushaw, nor Richard's ruthless brother. The Navarre I knew would have been at my side, helping me fight the men who are bleeding England dry, not fighting with them."

"It is Richard who has bled England dry, my friend," Navarre said solemnly. "He sold her lands and titles to the highest bidder—I am proof of that—so that he might journey to other lands and wage war against the innocent."

Robin lifted one tawny brow in surprise. "Surely you do not consider infidels innocent?"

"I consider any woman or child an innocent, regardless of their religion."

"Ah." Robin sat down beside the knight, linking his hands together. "You speak of Acre."

Navarre glanced over at Kendra and Magda. The two sat silently, their gazes fixed on the two men. The knight nodded.

"Aye. If you've heard of the atrocities there then you know why I have turned my back upon Richard."

"War is not pretty, Navarre. You know that better than I. Soldiers kill and oftentimes it is the helpless and innocent who must pay."

Navarre twisted his arms suddenly against the ropes holding him. "War does not justify murder," he said, his voice deceptively soft. "Not even for a king."

Robin nodded. "I have heard tales of a great knight whose heart was stolen by an infidel maid. When she died, at Richard's command, they say the knight turned his back on his king and vowed to one day murder him.''

Navarre saw Kendra struggling to keep from looking at him, felt Magda's eyes upon him, and fought against the rage bubbling up inside of him.

"Children's fables," he said, when he could govern his words. "What is this of the barons?"

"Ah, yes, another interesting twist to the story. I and my men began a journey to Nottingham last eve, which is why the fair Kendra's absence went unnoticed. I had taken most of my men, leaving only some younger louts as guards, none of which had yet met our beautiful guest." He nodded in Kendra's direction. "Along our journey we chanced to bed at an inn—Alan-a-Dale and Little John and I—whilst the rest of the men continued toward Nottingham." He stood and paced a few steps toward the fire, his hands clasped behind him. "Can you guess whom we met at the inn?"

"I am not a child to play at guessing games," Navarre growled.

Robin spun around, the cocksure grin back in place. "A large group of men entered as we sat drinking our ale, several of whom I recognized—Warwick, Suffolk, and others—" Navarre stiffened and Robin's smile widened. "What do you suppose could have moved those worthies to journey together?"

Navarre stared back at him stonily. He and Garrick had arranged for a meeting with the barons, but it was not to be for another fortnight. Had Garrick taken advantage of his absence and called for the barons to meet without him?

"Rather a foolish proposition, wouldn't you say," Robin went on, "for all of the most powerful men in England to gather together in one place? 'Twould make them an easy target for their enemies."

"What is your point?" Navarre demanded.

Robin crossed back to him. "My point is this—join me, Navarre. I know not what treachery you are about, but there is still time to pledge yourself anew to your sovereign." He waved one hand as Navarre opened his mouth to speak. "I do not say Richard is perfect, far from it. He has abandoned England, entrusting it to such as I, yet without granting me any authority or pardon.'' He bent down beside Navarre and the knight saw the fervency in his old friend's eyes. ''I do not hold England for Richard, I hold it for England. And yet, Richard is her king, right or wrong, and I will not see him usurped by one such as John.''

''And if there were another?'' The words were out of Navarre's mouth before he could stop them. The old feelings of camaraderie were still strong between the two men, making Locksley an even more dangerous foe than he had supposed.

''Another?'' Robin shook his head. ''While Richard lives there is no other.''

''Therein lies your ignorance,'' Navarre said, the anger surging inside of him at Robin's words. ''For I do not hold with the belief that God has ordained Richard as king, to do as he pleases, responsible to no one, to take England down into the ocean if it suits his fancy! If he is to be king then let him act as a king! How many days has he spent on these shores since being made our sovereign? How much interest has he shown in our affairs? Nay—'' he shook his head vehemently ''—he has sold England to those who may bid the highest.''

''Of whom you are one.''

''Aye, which is my point exactly. When a bastard such as I can buy his place in nobility then something is wrong, Robin.''

''Your father was noble. I see no conflict.''

''That is not the issue!'' Navarre stumbled to his feet and two men ran up to him, swords drawn. Robin motioned them back.

''And what is the issue, my friend?''

''The issue is this: England must no longer be held hostage by the whims of idiotic or selfish kings who seek their own pleasures whether those pleasures be wine, wenching or wars! England must govern herself, using the minds of men who have a vested interest in her government, her lands, her laws!''

Navarre stood trembling with emotion, aware he had said too much, yet he was too angry to care. Locksley wielded great power in this part of England. If he could be persuaded, other barons would follow. His mindless following of Richard filled

Navarre with frustration, especially since Robin acknowledged Richard's failures.

Robin stared back at him, stroking his goatee thoughtfully. "This does not sound to me the voice of a man who seeks to place John upon the throne. Will you speak frankly to me, Navarre? Will you tell me what your true quest involves, and why the barons are gathering at Nottingham? I sent men ahead to watch the proceedings and hurried back here in hopes you would confide in me as you used to, long ago."

"What of the woman?" Navarre asked, glancing over to where Kendra silently sat beside Magda.

"She will remain under my protection." Robin motioned to Little John. "Take her to my tent. I will speak with her further there."

"And does your protection include your bed?" Navarre asked, his voice carefully controlled.

Robin smiled. "If it pleases the lady."

"She is not for you," Magda said suddenly, rising from her hunched-over position in front of the fire. Her thin shoulders were stooped, yet Navarre could feel the power emanating from her as she turned and pointed a shaky finger at Locksley.

"She must fulfill her destiny and then return from whence she has come."

"I still don't know where that is, old woman," Robin said impatiently. "So far all I've heard is a lot of nonsense about the future and a broad indication that perhaps she will aid Richard in some unknown way. I have no time for this." He turned back to Navarre. "Will you tell me your true intent for England?"

"Would it make any difference to you if it did not include Richard upon the throne?"

The two knights' gazes locked in a silent struggle. At last Robin shook his head.

"Nay," he said with a sigh. "I am bound to my king and I shall not betray him."

"Then I have nothing else to say."

"But I do."

Navarre and Robin both turned and stared at Kendra. From the moment she had taken her place beside Magda she had not uttered a word. Now she stood in front of the fire, auburn hair cascading around her in unbound glory, the firelight from behind turning it into a shimmering flame. Both men drew in a sudden breath of wonder, then frowned at one another as Kendra moved toward them.

"I don't know Navarre's plans," she said, "but I know he is a good man. He loves England as much as you do, Robin. Why is it so impossible for the two of you to join forces?"

"Because he bids me betray my king," Robin said. "Which I will never do."

Kendra turned to Navarre and he felt his heart flip over as the firelight illuminated her face. Her lips were still swollen from his kisses and he longed to reach for her and begin their lovemaking anew.

"Navarre," she said, her eyes boring into his, her lips trembling, "I must say something to you that you will not wish to hear, but please, listen to me."

He frowned. What was she up to now?

"I am listening," he said.

"Whether Robin believes me or not, you have said you believe my strange story." She pointed to Magda. "Magda believes and has affirmed that I am from the future, so hear me!" Her pink tongue darted across her lips and Navarre felt a wave of premonition sweep over him. When she spoke again it was slowly and distinctly, as though she spoke to someone who was addled, or dim-witted.

"Richard is meant to be king," she said. "I know the future—I have read the history books. Richard lives until the year 1199 and there is nothing you can do about it. John will succeed him and in spite of him, England will become a world power."

"Even if you know the future," Navarre said harshly, "that future could be changed. If Richard dies—"

"Treason!" The cry rang out from the men gathered around the fire until Robin held up his hand to silence them.

"Hear the bastard out," he said, his eyes like shards of ice.

"If Richard dies, the future will be changed," Navarre said. "And you have given us the means to do so."

"Exactly why I must now convince you not to kill him!"

Kendra said, picking up the skirt of her gown and moving toward the two of them. "I don't even know if you can change history, but if it's possible, then Richard's death would set into motion a series of events that would ultimately change the outcome of English history."

"The girl speaks the truth," Magda said, rising and standing beside her. "There is more concerning her own welfare if you would hear it. She must return to her world soon or not return at all. Heed me. You must listen to the words she will speak to you and do not cast her aside in your anger. She speaks the truth."

"So you do conspire with my enemies," Navarre said, feeling the old suspicions seeping back into his mind. "You side with Locksley and their murdering king."

Little John took a step forward, his hand on his sword. Robin stopped him with a gesture, his eyes fixed on Navarre and Kendra.

"I side with history!" Kendra said fervently. "Look, Navarre, I don't know why I was sent here but I do know what is supposed to happen to Richard if the course of time is to continue as it was meant to continue. Besides, if you want John on the throne, can't you take heart in knowing that when Richard dies in 1199, his brother will finally ascend the throne?"

"It is not John I wish to see on the throne of England!" Navarre spat out the words, then whirled to face Robin. "There! I have said the truth, Locksley. My goal is not to place John upon the throne."

"Then who?" Robin demanded. "Yourself? Garrick?"

"Nay." Navarre shook his head slowly. "One whose claim to the throne is undisputed."

"And whom might that be?"

"The barons of England."

Robin blinked, then smiled, then laughed out loud.

"Do you mean to tell me that you want England to be ruled by a handful of men who cannot even govern themselves?"

"They would not hold all the power," Navarre said. "It would be a system wherein there were checks and balances, where no one man could rape England or her people at his whim!'' The bitterness overwhelmed him as he spoke the words and suddenly he wanted very much to convince Robin to join his quest.

"And there would be no king?" Robin asked, amused.

"Perhaps a queen," he said enigmatically.

"Eleanor? Aye, she has more sense than all of her sons I grant you, but if you think she will let the barons tell her what to do you are insane."

"She will do what is best for England, of this I am confident."

Robin walked around the circle, his fingers smoothing his short beard thoughtfully. "So this is why the barons are gathering at Nottingham—to overthrow Richard and place themselves in control."

"What of the barons?" Navarre asked apprehensively.

Robin stopped with his back to the knight, then spun around, his blue eyes intense. "Join me, Navarre. Tell me your plans and together we will save England from such as the sheriff of Nottingham."

"Oh, do allow me."

The men whirled, and Navarre stumbled to his feet at the sound of Garrick's voice. The small circle had been surrounded by the sheriff's men, who were armed with spears, swords, and bows. Garrick walked toward the firelight, his black cloak whipping about his thighs, his smooth face filled with triumph.

"Good evening, Sir Robin," the sheriff said as he strode forward, sword in hand. "I do hope I am not interrupting anything of importance."

Robin's sword was in his hand in an instant. "Welcome, dear Sheriff, to my humble home." He bowed and gestured around the circle with one hand. "But, please, let me welcome you properly."

He swung his sword in a high arc and Garrick blocked the move with his own steel, his laughter ringing out across the clearing. With Robin's shout, the battle began.

Navarre struggled against his bonds as a host of men descended on the outlaws and the sound of metal clashing and men shouting filled his ears.

"Kendra!" he shouted against the growing din, dodging first an outlaw's sword and then one of the sheriff's men brandishing a dagger. He butted his head into one's stomach and slammed one boot-clad foot into the other's crotch, wincing himself as the man went down. The light was dim and he had no doubt that Garrick's men might accidentally kill him in the fray.

"Kendra!" he roared again, then felt a small hand on his arm. He looked down into azure eyes and lips curved into a loving smile. How could he have ever thought her evil?

"Be still," she said, turning him away from her. He could feel something slicing into the ropes tying him and in a matter of moments he was free. Without a word he swept her into his arms and carried her out of the clearing.

"Stay here," Navarre commanded as he deposited her behind a thick clump of bushes. "I'll be back for you." Leaving her sputtering her protest, he headed back for the fight. Picking up a discarded sword, Navarre threw himself into the fray, cutting, parrying, lunging. Men were everywhere, fighting in the dim moonlight. It reminded him of when they took Acre and had fought long into the night against the Saracens. He stumbled to a stop, his sword sagging.

Acre. He had vowed after Acre he would never take a man's life again. In the years since that time, even as *custodis pacis*, he had not broken that vow. Even though he knew Garrick thought he planned to murder Richard, his true intent was only to incarcerate him. He searched for Garrick through the melee, hoping to put an end to the battle, and could see, across the clearing, that he was still fighting Robin, the outlaw fighting valiantly in spite of the fact that his blood-soaked left arm hung uselessly at his side.

Navarre watched the fight, and suddenly he knew that he could not let the sheriff kill his old friend. Robin might have misguided loyalties but he was a good man, a man who wanted the best for England. He strode forward, dodging falling bodies and flying arrows.

Navarre turned with a roar as the searing pain of a blade sliced into his shoulder from behind. The man still holding the bloody dagger was not an outlaw as he'd supposed, but one of his own men from Nottingham.

"Be you mad, man?" Navarre cried, letting his sword arm drop as his left hand pressed against his right shoulder where the blood flowed freely. "Is it so dark that your eyes cannot see I am your captain?"

The man's black eyes wavered slightly, then his mouth split into a leering grin, exposing ugly, discolored teeth.

"Don't smile at me, man!" Navarre lifted his sword. "Answer me or defend yourself!" The man continued to leer, his sword at his side.

Navarre's breath left him suddenly as a searing pain plunged through his back. He fell to his knees, feeling the steel rammed into his flesh, the blood coursing down his side, soaking through his tunic.

Kendra. She would weep for him, he thought, as dark spots danced before his eyes. His vision blurred, the dark spots surged suddenly together, blinding him, pulling him down into a dark, silent void.

Thrill to the most sensual, adventure-filled Historical Romances on the market today...

FROM  *LEISURE BOOKS*

As a home subscriber to Leisure Romance Book Club, you'll enjoy the best in today's BRAND-NEW Historical Romance fiction. For over twenty-five years, Leisure Books has brought you the award-winning, high-quality authors you know and love to read. Each Leisure Historical Romance will sweep you away to a world of high adventure...and intimate romance. Discover for yourself all the passion and excitement millions of readers thrill to each and every month.

Save $5.⁰⁰ Each Time You Buy!

Each month, the Leisure Romance Book Club brings you four brand-new titles from Leisure Books, America's foremost publisher of Historical Romances. EACH PACKAGE WILL SAVE YOU $5.00 FROM THE BOOKSTORE PRICE! And you'll never miss a new title with our convenient home delivery service.

Here's how we do it. Each package will carry a FREE 10-DAY EXAMINATION privilege. At the end of that time, if you decide to keep your books, simply pay the low invoice price of $16.96, no shipping or handling charges added. HOME DELIVERY IS ALWAYS FREE. With today's top Historical Romance novels selling for $5.99 and higher, our price SAVES YOU $5.00 with each shipment.

AND YOUR FIRST FOUR-BOOK SHIPMENT IS TOTALLY FREE!
IT'S A BARGAIN YOU CAN'T BEAT! A Super $21.96 Value!

LEISURE BOOKS *A Division of Dorchester Publishing Co., Inc.*

Get Four Books Totally FREE – A $21.96 Value!

▼ Tear Here and Mail Your FREE Book Card Today! ▼

PLEASE RUSH
MY FOUR FREE
BOOKS TO ME
RIGHT AWAY!

Leisure Romance Book Club
P.O. Box 6613
Edison, NJ 08818-6613

AFFIX
STAMP
HERE

Chapter Eleven

Kendra held Navarre, his blood spilling over her gown, crimson soaking into green. Tears coursed down her cheeks and she cried out in anger and frustration. She hadn't obeyed his instructions to stay hidden but had found a good, hard tree branch to use as a club and had jumped into the fight, swinging with the best of them. She had just cracked one of their assailants across the back of the head when she saw one of the sheriff's men stab Navarre in the back. Now she tried desperately to stanch the flow of blood from his wound with a wadded up piece of cloth torn from her dress.

"Navarre," she whispered, moving to press her lips against his dark hair, her heart aching. "Don't die, Navarre. I promise I'll find some way to help you in your quest if you just won't die."

"Excellent."

Kendra froze at the sound of the sheriff's voice, then slowly turned to face him. He stood, crimson tunic brilliant in the pale light of morning, black cloak whipping around his legs, fists on his hips, triumph in his cold, gray eyes.

"I shall hold you to your promise," he said softly.

Dawn was breaking above the tops of the trees and Kendra saw that the fighting had almost stopped. Robin's men lay scattered across the clearing, into the forest, some of them dead, others moaning from their wounds. She didn't see Little John or Alan or Magda and she hoped against hope that they had escaped.

"Where is Robin?" she asked suddenly, "and Marian?"

"Sir Locksley is alive, never fear," Garrick assured her. "I have bigger plans for him. And Lady Marian is quite well. I promised John that not a hair on her lovely head would be harmed. You, however, are another matter entirely."

Kendra's arms tightened around Navarre as the sheriff took a step toward her. Four men ran up to him just then, their dirty faces looking to him for instruction. He jerked his blond head toward her.

"Take them to Nottingham," he ordered, then smiled as two of the men seized her roughly by the arms and pulled her to her feet. Navarre rolled from her lap to sprawl on the ground.

"Navarre is seriously injured," she cried. "I have medical knowledge, let me help him."

"No doubt," Garrick said, "since you come from an era far removed from our humble time."

Kendra couldn't stop the gasp of fear that escaped her.

"Oh, yes," the sheriff went on, "I overheard the entire story from beginning to end. Quite remarkable."

"You believe me?" Kendra asked, astonished.

Garrick cocked one tawny brow. "Ah, I see. You think me a superstitious barbarian like the rest of these idiots. I may play the part, but never doubt my intelligence. I was reared in Normandy, not England, my dear."

"Then you don't believe in witches?"

His face darkened. "On the contrary, I believe them to be quite real, and quite dangerous. However, I do not believe that you are a witch—believe me, I know the difference—nor do I think a mere woman capable of inventing a story of such incredible proportions." Kendra glared at him and his smile widened. "I was particularly entranced by Magda's words concerning the mighty weapons of your time. But we shall discuss that later. I'm sure you will be very happy to cooperate with me and tell me just how a person goes about journeying through time."

Kendra thought quickly. Apparently Garrick was under the impression that she could teach him how to time travel. If she could use that premise to buy Navarre and herself some time . . .

"If Navarre dies," Kendra said, tossing her long hair back from her shoulder, "the only thing we'll be discussing is how you plan to kill me, for I'll never help you then."

Garrick's eyes widened. "Ah, so you do care for dear Navarre. I am so glad. He thought you were only toying with him for your own amusement."

"I can't wait to tell Navarre that his dear friend is the one who authorized this slaughter," Kendra said.

"I care not what you tell the bastard," he lifted the hood of his cloak to cover his fair hair against a sudden gust of wind. "De Galliard is no longer vital to my plans. I'm quite happy to leave him here to rot, or hang him from the highest turret of Nottingham Castle."

Kendra blinked. "You mean—" she shook her head. "Why am I surprised? Of course you aren't interested in helping England. You're only interested in helping Garrick."

"Of course," he acknowledged. "And you, too, shall help Garrick."

"Only if you spare Navarre," she said, lifting her chin determinedly. Their gazes locked for a long moment, then Garrick nodded.

"Release her. Let her accompany de Galliard in the cart. When we get to Nottingham, throw them both into the dungeon."

"The tower would be better," she dared to interject as the men untied her ropes and Garrick turned to leave. "It's cleaner, less risk of infection."

The sheriff turned back slowly, his gray eyes boring into her. "Take them to the dungeon," he repeated, "and throw them in." He lifted one finger and shook it under Kendra's nose. "Do not try my patience."

"And don't try mine," she said, clenching her fists at her sides, her heart pounding with suppressed fear. "I have nothing to lose, you know."

"You have everything to lose, and everyone," he said. Reaching out he seized her face suddenly between strong fingers, tilting her chin upward. "I have watched this camp for days. I know you love de Galliard and that you also have

195

affection for Locksley and his men as well. And do not forget Marian.''

''You wouldn't dare harm the king's ward.''

He chuckled softly, the sound sending a chill through Kendra's blood.

''Wouldn't I?'' He relaxed his fingers and slid them down the length of her throat, into the valley between her breasts. Kendra stiffened at his intimate touch, her face flaming red. He laughed again. ''Do not think you can buy Navarre's life so cheaply. You will tell me your secret of time travel, aye, but do not think I have forgotten the business that lies unfinished between us.'' He caressed the top of her left breast, then dropped his hand back to his side, his gaze never leaving her face. Kendra shivered as the sheriff gestured to one of his men and stepped back, his thin lips twisted in a satisfied smile.

''Take her.''

Navarre awoke flat on his stomach to darkness and the sound of men moaning. He blinked, unsure if his dimness of vision was because there was no light or because he could not see. After a moment, relief surged through him as he began to make out images around him. A dozen or more men from the outlaw's camp sat in various stages of prostration and pain. He squinted around, his fingers digging into cold stone and something that smelled suspiciously like dung. With a start, he realized where he was—in the dungeon of Nottingham.

He pushed himself up, then cried out as an excruciating pain sent him back to the hard floor. The sound of quick footsteps hurrying to his side alarmed him and with effort he opened his eyes.

''Don't move,'' a soft voice said.

Kendra. He smiled and tried to answer, but it was too much effort. He closed his eyes and let the comforting blackness take him away. When Navarre awoke again he had no idea how much time had passed. The pain in his back had eased and his mind felt clearer. Lifting himself warily, he eased to a sitting position, ignoring the sudden stab of fire accompanying his movements.

He looked up and saw her moving toward him, her auburn

hair unbound and tangled, her blue eyes wide with a tenderness that pierced him more thoroughly than any dagger ever could. He felt shaky with relief. She had not been taken from him. Garrick had not killed her.

"Navarre," she whispered, sinking down beside him. "You're awake. I thought—" Kendra suddenly burst into tears and threw herself against him, her arms wound around him.

Navarre held her tightly, stroking her hair, confused and disoriented, but still coherent enough to recognize her relief.

"I will not die, my love," he said.

Kendra lifted her face from his chest and touched his lips with one tremulous hand. "I was afraid—oh, Navarre—when you didn't wake up . . ." she broke off, then pressed herself against his uninjured side. "Please, just hold me."

He gathered her closer with his left arm. "What have you heard? Obviously, I was betrayed by own men."

"Yes," Kendra said. "Led by Garrick."

He nodded and leaned his head back wearily against the stone wall behind them. "Aye. But I confess, I do not understand."

"He doesn't want the barons to rule England as you do, Navarre," she said, shifting his weight, providing herself as a pillow against the roughness of the dungeon wall. "I believe he wants to rule England himself."

Navarre laughed shortly. "Even Garrick would not be so foolish as to think he could become king. It takes power, the kind of power Garrick doesn't have." He glanced back at her. Kendra bit her lower lip and he saw the turmoil in her eyes. "What is it?"

"Time travel could give him the power he needs," she said.

He turned and faced her, his befuddled brain unable to make sense of her words. Shaking his head slightly he sagged against the wall. "How long was I unconscious?" he asked.

"Three days."

"Three days!" He sat up abruptly. Then he gave in weakly as her fingers tightened around his shoulders, drawing him back against her. "What havoc may Garrick have wrought in this time? Have you spoken with the knave?"

"Navarre, please," Kendra begged. "You'll break your stitches open and believe me, pulling a needle and thread through your skin is something I do not want to do again."

Navarre gazed down into her flushed face, aware that she was suddenly keeping her eyes averted from his.

"I asked you a question," he said gently. "Have you spoken with the sheriff?" She hesitated, then nodded. "What did he say?"

Kendra opened her mouth, then closed it. Turning her face away from him, she stared fiercely into the dimness of the cell.

"Kendra," he said softly, "what is it?"

She seized his hand and brought it to her lips with a ragged cry. He could feel the warmth of her small tongue on his flesh and he gathered her back to him, covering her mouth with his, feeling the need to burn his claim upon her, to remind her of what they had discovered in Sherwood. She returned his kiss passionately, then with another cry, broke their embrace and lowered her face into her hands.

Navarre felt a cold anguish wash over him. "Tell me," he said, lifting a finger to trace the edge of her shoulder blade softly outlined beneath her gown. "Is it because I failed to protect you from Garrick, or because I would not listen to your warning? Or have you had time to realize that a union with a bastard such as I—"

"Stop it!" Kendra broke in with a sob, her azure eyes filled with tears. "I love you! But Garrick has already told me that tonight I will warm his bed. And this time there is nothing you can do about it."

"Tell me truly, has he sent for you already?" he asked, his throat tightening.

She shook her head vigorously. "No, I think he wants you to know when—when it's happening. Why does he hate you, Navarre? I thought you were friends."

"I know not." A sudden surge of dizziness swept over him and he leaned back against the wall as he pounded his fist against the stone in frustration. "This weakness consumes me."

"You lost a lot of blood," Kendra said. "Here, drink this." She held out a crude wooden cup filled with water and he took it from her, gulping the liquid down thankfully. "Your strength will return, but you mustn't push yourself too quickly."

Navarre drew one sleeve across his wet lips and glanced down at her, really seeing her for the first time since he had awakened. Torches ensconced around the wall provided a dim illumination. Her face was dirty, her hair matted and tangled. She'd lost weight in the three days they'd been incarcerated. And yet she was beautiful. He raised his left hand to her face and stroked his fingers across her cheekbone.

"Think you that I will allow Garrick to defile your body or soul?" he asked, his voice low.

She glanced down at her hands, dark lashes brushing against her pale skin. "What can you do?" she whispered.

"Mayhap more than you think. Where is Locksley? Does he live?"

Kendra looked up at him, her eyes questioning. "Yes, if you can call it living. They take him out every day and torture him."

"Locksley will survive. Now, come here to me." Kendra turned herself to face him and he pulled her toward him, drawing her head down to rest upon his broad chest. "What did you say before, about Garrick and time travel?" She began to tremble, and he could feel the depth of the fear consuming her.

"He wants me to show him how to travel forward in time, to the future, where there are weapons of incredible power that can wipe out whole continents, let alone an army. Then he'll bring them back here and rule the world."

Navarre did not move, allowing her words to sink into his mind. When Kendra had told him her unbelievable story he had not wanted to believe. But he had. Perhaps if he had not seen her appear at Abury in such a magical way, perhaps if he had not seen with his own eyes the strange box called "camera," or felt the sting of the "gun," perhaps if her speech had not been so nonsensical, perhaps then he would not have believed her.

No, even then he would have believed, for he had known from the moment he first saw Kendra O'Brien that she was not of his world. Suddenly he realized he was going to lose her. Perhaps he had known it from the beginning. Perhaps that was why he had fought so hard against loving her.

"And can you show him how to travel to your world, your time?" Navarre asked, the words heavy in his throat. Kendra shook her head. His relief was so intense the blood rushed away from his head and he felt dizzy, but he smoothed her hair back from her face and spoke casually. "Then we have nothing to worry about."

"I told him I could," she said, her voice muffled against his chest.

Navarre lifted her carefully away from him as he fought the anger welling up inside of him.

"Don't look at me like that," Kendra said sharply. "You always make me feel as though you're about to pounce on me and devour me. If you want to yell, then yell, but don't glare."

"Indeed, you need not 'yelling' but a sound thrashing," he shouted into her face. "Why in the name of—" he broke off his tirade and stared at her for a long moment, then slowly nodded his head. "Aye, I understand now why he let me live at all. You have promised him much power and your body."

"You were seriously hurt!" she said, jerking out of his grasp, her blue eyes dancing with fury. "I didn't know if you would even live, much less be in any shape to defend yourself. He started talking about hanging you, but promised he would let you live if I told him about time travel."

"And you offered to share his bed as well."

"That was his idea, not mine."

Navarre shifted away from her, his heart aching more sharply than the wound in his back at the thought of her being subjected to what Garrick called lovemaking. She had done it to save him and now he was virtually helpless to rescue her. Garrick would treat her as he had the women in Outremer, then he would kill her. Rage filled Navarre and he longed to lash out with his fists, yet he was as weak as a babe, and about as useful.

Keys rattled in the door to their prison and Navarre recognized the sound of Garrick's laughter echoing down the hall. Kendra shrank back against him as the door swung open and a man was shoved through. He hit the floor with a thud and Kendra cried out. It was Locksley, his aristocratic face battered almost beyond recognition. Kendra jumped to her feet and ran to the outlaw, kneeling beside him, lifting his head gently into her lap.

"Robin, can you hear me?" Kendra asked softly. Locksley didn't reply. Her only answer was the sound of his raspy breathing. She glared over at Garrick where he stood leaning inside the cell door. Wearing a hauberk of mail over a leather gambeson, he held a thin but lethal dagger, covered with blood. He sauntered inside, sliding the dagger back into the scabbard at his waist, then began stripping the leather gauntlets from his hands, his gaze fixed on Kendra's slim form.

"How dare you treat him this way?" she cried. "How dare you! What can he tell you that you don't already know? What information must you torture from him?"

Navarre marveled, not for the first time, at the woman's courage—at least when defending someone she cared for, like Locksley. He pushed away the fleeting stab of jealousy as she clucked over the outlaw, wiping his face with the hem of her tattered gown. Kendra loved him, not Robin Hood, of that he had no doubt. Now, if only Locksley would revive, perhaps the two of them could rush Garrick. There must be some men left in Nottingham Castle loyal to their captain. With those, and Robin's men, it might be possible at least to escape.

"Your time has not yet come," Garrick said to Kendra, his thin lips harsh in the dim torchlight. "I am here to speak with my old friend, Navarre. However, it is possible to change my mind and partake of your sweetness now if you so desire." Kendra stared up at him, trying bravely to hide the terror on her face. Garrick laughed. "No? Then hold your tongue, woman."

His gray gaze flitted over to Navarre, lighting on him as casually as though he were an old hound whose paw had been injured. Steeling himself not to groan, Navarre pulled his feet under him, and using the wall for support, stood. He was rewarded by the look of surprise that sprang into the sheriff's eyes, along with a certain wariness.

"Good evening, old friend," Navarre said, biting off the

words and pushing himself away from the wall. "Or is it morn, for you see it is difficult to tell in this hellhole."

Garrick laughed, the sound more chilling than the stone upon which Navarre had leaned. "You did not think it hellish when you were the one flinging the outlaws into its belly."

"And what law have I broken, Garrick, that I should be flung here to rot?"

One tawny brow lifted as Garrick gazed back at him complacently. "Why, Sir Knight, I have heard a dreadful rumor that you seek to kill our king and place another on the throne." He shook his finger, making a disparaging sound. "I confess I am shocked that a man whom I have treated as a brother should be filled with such treachery."

"Aye," Navarre said, his voice like iron, "I too, am shocked."

"Are you really?" Garrick dropped the feigned civility and smiled wickedly, crossing the room to Kendra's side. Leaning down he grabbed her by the arm, hoisting her to her feet, leaving Robin's limp body to roll to one side. The sheriff pulled her against him and she stood stiffly in his arms.

"I fear I have only just begun to astound you." He turned Kendra's face to his and kissed her, his mouth closing over hers in a cruel gesture that sent Navarre two steps forward before she jerked away and cried out.

"Navarre, no!"

Navarre pressed down his rage and tried to think rationally. He was too weak to overcome the sheriff. Attacking him now would only result in his own death and leave Kendra completely without protection. He must remain calm.

"You will not fight for her? A pity, but then perhaps the wench is not as important to you as I had supposed," the sheriff said. "I did wonder if you loved her as much as that wretched infidel in Acre." With one hard shove he pushed Kendra away from him. She sprawled at Navarre's feet but he could not look at her. His gaze was frozen on the baleful grin of the man he had once called friend.

"I had the devil of a time convincing Richard the woman was dangerous," Garrick said as Navarre stared at him in stunned silence. "He scoffed at me, you know. Said it was your life and if you wanted to bed the wench or marry her it mattered not to him. He was quite uncooperative about the matter.''

''You told me he would take my knighthood from me if I married her,'' Navarre said, closing his eyes against the rush of memories. ''You said he would cast me from him.''

''Aye, I told you that, and more,'' Garrick said with a laugh. ''I needed you, old friend, to fight with me against Richard. You loved him as though he were your bastard father—as though he were truly worthy of your adoration. I was your first friend, your brother, of a sort, and yet, once he befriended you, you preferred his company. And then the woman. Your fawning attention to her disgusted me and soon it was as though I did not exist.''

''That isn't true,'' Navarre said, frowning with confusion. ''I have always been your friend. We never had a cross word between us until Outremer, and then only because I saw a cruelty in you I had never seen before.''

''Cruel? I?'' He gestured to himself in feigned abhorrence. ''Oh, you speak of the whores on which I eased myself.'' He shrugged, sliding his hand down to cup Kendra's bottom, smiling as she glared up at him defiantly, her fists clenched.

''They were not whores but innocent women who had been abducted by drunken soldiers.'' Navarre began walking slowly across the room toward the sheriff. ''It was the first time I had ever seen you act in such a way.''

''I did nothing more to them than likely had been done before,'' he said, the smile fading from his full lips.

''You left them bleeding, babbling incoherently,'' Navarre said softly.

''You will not speak of this!'' Garrick pulled the dagger from its scabbard, his eyes glittering dangerously. ''It is I who have the story to tell, Navarre, not you, and so I bid you to listen and learn. When you were injured during the battle for Acre, I saw my perfect opportunity. I would not only rid myself of another who sought your time, your affections, but I would plant the seeds which would blossom into the ripe fruit of bitter revenge.''

''You ramble, Garrick,'' Navarre said smoothly, taking a

tentative step toward him, "like an old woman who has lost her senses."

"I killed your precious Talam, not Richard!" Garrick said triumphantly. "When he ordered the death of the citizens of Acre I saw my chance. First I tasted her. She was quite delectable, her skin all browns and creams."

He paused, his gaze raking over Navarre's face. The knight felt as though the breath had been knocked from him, as though a hard fist had been thrust into his belly. He could not disguise his hollow-eyed disbelief, and Garrick laughed in satisfaction at his obvious distress.

"I can see why you wanted to bed her," he went on. "I dragged her out of your tent and took her inside the walls of Acre, where I shoved her into the frenzy. The soldiers inside knew her not and she was quickly cut down with the others."

"Why?" Navarre said, hardly able to choke out the single word.

"Because I needed you. I came to you on Crete where you were recovering and told you my story of Richard's cruelty. You were quite easily manipulated, and in my brave Navarre I found the perfect foil to help me with my plan. Oh, I had to throw in some noble words and lies concerning what our goals for England were,'tis true, but now, all of that is at an end."

Navarre felt the blood leave his face again, his fists clenched so tightly at his side his nails drew blood.

"Damn you," Navarre said quietly, pushing down the trembling deep inside of him, the rage threatening to break free. How could Garrick have kept this evil side from him so completely? As boys they had laughed and played together, as men they had fought at one another's side, saving each other's lives more times than they could count. It wasn't until Outremer that Navarre realized his friend's cool demeanor might hide something darker beneath, and then only because of his ruthless using of the women there. But this betrayal—he never would have dreamed it possible.

"Damn you to hell," he whispered.

"Navarre . . ." Kendra said in warning. She rose to stand beside him, laying one small hand upon his arm.

Garrick resheathed the dagger, his eyes guileless and wide

as they raked over her once again even as he addressed Navarre. "Oh, and that isn't all, old friend. The barons are mine—oh yes, I met with them whilst you were bedding her in the forest—and they have agreed to place someone more worthy than Richard upon the throne."

"You've convinced them to crown Eleanor?"

"They do not care for the king's mother, she is much too willful and after all, is a woman. No, I convinced them otherwise." His thin lips drew back in a gleeful smile.

"Not John?"

"Nay, Lackland shall be dealt the same fate as his brother. 'Tis another, nobler fellow I am thinking of."

Navarre blinked in disbelief as Garrick's meaning struck home. "You? That is impossible. The barons would never agree to place a bastard on the throne of England."

Garrick lifted one blond brow. "If that bastard promised them land and titles, I daresay they would. Besides, you forget William the Bastard, the mighty conqueror who was our hero when we as boys were despised by others?" He leaned toward Navarre. "I knew then that my illegitimacy would not prevent me from achieving my destiny. If Duke William could rule England, then why not I?"

"William was a wise man, interested in bringing unity to England." Navarre gave him an appraising look. "What do you bring to England, Garrick?"

"The question is, what does England bring to me?" He threw his head back and laughed, loud and long. "And my ambition does not begin and end with England," Garrick continued. "With the help of this young woman's amazing ability to travel through time—if indeed, her tale be true—I shall gather weapons that will assure me not only of holding England, but of expanding her provinces to include, shall we say, the world?"

"You are mad," Kendra said.

"Am I?" Garrick shrugged. "Perhaps. Oh, yes, I need the weapon you brought with you, the—what did you call it, Navarre? The gun. Where is it, in your chamber?" Navarre remained silent and the sheriff smiled again. "Do not concern yourself, my friend, I shall find it."

Crossing the short distance between them, he took Kendra's hand, raising it to his lips. She shrank back as at the last moment he turned her hand over and drew his tongue down the center of her palm.

"Milady. I bid you adieu until this evening."

"I will kill you, Garrick," Navarre promised as Kendra's free hand dug into his arm, warning him not to react even as she shuddered inwardly at the man's touch. "If you try to take her from me I swear I will kill you with my bare hands."

"Ever the gallant hero, eh, Navarre?" He grinned at the knight. "But do not fret, for you see, the plans I have for Kendra include you as well. We shall share the lovely lady. Will that not be an evening fit for a king?" Snickering he released Kendra's hand at last. "Until tonight." He turned and swept out of the cell, leaving Navarre standing rigidly in the center.

He was helpless. Helpless to stop Garrick from hurting Kendra, just as he'd been helpless to prevent him from killing Talam. The fire inside of him, the rage, burned like an inferno, like a volcano about to erupt. He would go mad, go mad and beat his brains out against the wall.

"Navarre, I'm here. I'm here for you." Kendra's soft words swept suddenly like a soothing balm across the ragged wound Garrick had just carved into his soul, and with a groan he turned to her. Her azure eyes met his, filled with love and understanding as she opened her arms to him.

He entered that circle of comfort and felt the raging fire ebb. Burying his face in the warmth of her hair he let her hold him and he shook. He did not cry. He could not utter a sound. He simply stood there shaking, while Kendra's face pressed against his, her tears offered up in place of those he could not yield.

Chapter Twelve

Kendra looked up to see Robin Hood staring down at them, his face almost unrecognizable beneath the blood and bruises. He knelt beside them, his blue eyes serious as he swept Kendra and Navarre with an evaluating look. Navarre had slept for a time after his exhausting experience, and now sat looking vacantly into space. Kendra saw his hollow eyes quicken, however, as the outlaw stood over him.

"It is time we joined forces," Robin said haltingly, through swollen lips. "It is the only chance we have to escape the sheriff's wrath."

"Agreed," Navarre said, pushing himself to a more erect sitting position. Robin's hand came down on his shoulder, halting his movement, and the knight winced then glanced up at him warily. "Save your strength, old friend," Robin said. "You shall need it 'ere this battle is won." Robin sank to the floor and groaned aloud, then tossed the other man a grim smile. "As I shall need mine own strength. 'Gad, I feel as though all of my skin has been slowly peeled from my back."

"I'll bathe it for you," Kendra offered, starting to rise. Robin stopped her with a hand on her arm.

"It can wait."

"What is your plan, Locksley?" Navarre asked in a weak voice. Kendra looked up at him anxiously, the paleness of his face frightening her.

"Plan?" Some of the old humor returned to the outlaw's eyes at the subtle byplay between the two. " 'Twas my hope that you, Navarre, brilliant soldier that you are, would have one.''

"How many men are in this cell?" Navarre asked abruptly.

"There are twelve in here, counting myself. The others have been taken to other cells.''

"Did any of your men escape?"

"Little John, Alan-a-Dale, and Magda escaped along with about ten of my men. Marian was taken by Garrick and is once again ensconced in the castle, unharmed. At least, that is the information I gleaned from the guards' conversation when they thought I was unconscious.''

"Then it's possible your men could rescue us." Kendra's imagination kicked into high gear. "They could storm the castle, defeat the guards—''

"Not bloody likely," Robin interrupted dryly. "Little John could never take the castle with the few men left—as if we ever could.''

"But you sneaked in here before, when you helped me and Marian escape," Kendra reminded him.

"Aye. We had a friend on the inside, and it is possible Little John may try it again, though I hope he will not. The guards have no doubt been doubled at the gates and everyone will be on the alert. Am I correct, monsieur constable?''

Navarre nodded, the gesture filled with exhaustion. Kendra laid her hand upon his arm and squeezed it, alarmed at the defeat she saw written on his face.

"There would be no chance at all of someone sneaking into the castle this night," Navarre said. "Our only chance as I see it is to overpower Garrick when he returns to the cell, hold him hostage, and force the guards to release us.''

"A risky gambit at best," Robin murmured, stroking his short goatee thoughtfully, then looked up as the sound of a woman's voice echoed through the cell.

"I do not care what your orders are, I have brought food for the prisoners. In the name of King Richard I command you to open the door!''

Kendra rose at the sound of Marian's voice, hope springing up inside of her. She'd not seen the woman since longbow lesson in Sherwood and was relieved that Garrick had apparently not harmed her.

"Marian!" Kendra rushed to the door as the heavy wooden structure was pushed open a crack and Richard's ward slipped inside the cell, her heart-shaped face wreathed with concern, a bulky bag knit in both hands. The two women stared at each other for a moment, then fell into one another's arms.

"Are you all right?" Kendra whispered, breaking the embrace, then cupping Marian's face between her hands. She searched the young woman's pale blue eyes fearfully. "Did Garrick or John hurt you, Marian? Please, tell me the truth."

Marian shook her head, glancing at Robin and an unsteady Navarre as they silently approached the women. "Nay," she said. "John and I have talked." Her voice was hesitant, her eyes shifting first to Navarre and then to Robin. "I think I have planted some doubts in his mind about the sheriff and his goals."

"You must have 'talked' most convincingly," Navarre said harshly, "to gain entrance here. You are but a child, Marian— I will not have you playing the whore, even if it means my life!"

"Be silent," Robin commanded, his blue eyes suddenly dark with anger. Navarre closed his mouth abruptly. "Your lack of understanding, Sir Knight, where women are concerned is quite surprising." Robin took Marian's hand and bowed over it, his lips gently grazing her white skin before he straightened. "Lady Marian is not a child, but a beautiful young woman who would never play the whore for any man, do I speak truly, Marian?"

Marian looked up at the bruised Robin, mouth open, then cried out. "Robin, your face! What has that madman done to your beautiful face?" She lifted her hand to touch the deep gash running down the side of his jaw and he caught her fingers in his.

"I would not have you soil yourself with my blood," he said softly.

"Nonsense. Kendra, is there water?"

Kendra pointed to the water bucket and the young woman hurried over, wetting the cloth Kendra handed her, then hurrying back to Robin's side. She pulled him away from the other two, clucking over him like an irate hen, then ordered him to sit on the floor. She knelt beside him to tenderly cleanse his battered face. When she accidentally touched his back and he winced, she made him strip off his shirt. Kendra watched with admiration as Marian didn't blink an eye at the mass of welts and cuts, but simply began to cleanse them.

" 'Twould seem my little Marian has grown up," Navarre said to Kendra, his voice low and filled with amazement.

Kendra shook her hair back from her shoulders in exasperation. "It's about time you realized that. You know she's in love with you, don't you?"

Navarre lifted one dark brow, nodding toward Marian. She sat smiling adoringly at the outlaw. He gazed back at her, his eyes warm with feeling.

"With me, my love?" He inclined his head toward Robin. "I think not."

"Well, maybe you were just her first crush."

"Crush?" He shook his head, capturing her hand and bringing it to his lips. "You do speak most strangely, wench from the future."

"Aye," she said, moving to rub her cheek against his, uncaring about the stubble that bit into her skin. She turned his face to hers and kissed him deeply, feeling the sudden, desperate need to reclaim his love. He returned her passion, then slowly slid to the floor, his back against the wall, taking her with him. He broke the embrace and gazed deeply into her eyes, the hollowness in his own gone.

"I'm all right," he said softly. Kendra sighed and wrapped her arm around his waist, nestling against his side as he kept talking. His next words startled her. "You heard what Magda said about your return to your own time." It was a statement, not a question, and Kendra looked up into the intensity of his gaze. "The matter will not go away by ignoring it."

"Won't it?" Kendra asked, lowering her eyes to a torn place in his tunic where a few curling black chest hairs nested.

"Nay." Navarre lifted her chin with one finger, bringing her eyes level with his once again. "Kendra, do you wish to return to your own time?"

Her own time. Kendra stared at him, her mouth open. Civilization. Hot and cold running water, toilets, supermarkets, automobiles, clean clothes, air-conditioning, central heat. Hamburgers and french fries and a big chocolate malt. All the amenities of the life she'd left behind came rushing forward in her mind. Mac. Dear, dear Mac. The Chronicle and her career as a top-notch journalist.

"I . . . I don't know," she said, her fingers twisting in the front of his tunic. His chest rose and fell laboriously beneath the tattered cloth and impulsively she leaned down, her lips touching the smooth skin displayed under the torn material. His flesh was warm, alive. Navarre. Go home? Leave Navarre? Tears burned against her eyelids at the very thought.

She couldn't leave him, no matter what comforts she had to do without. She loved him, and she couldn't bear to lose someone else she loved. And yet, stay here? Put aside the fact most women didn't live past thirty-five and that the man she loved was an outlaw. Her biggest fear was that if she remained in the past, she would change history. The thought had plagued her more and more since Magda's pronouncement by the fire.

What if she couldn't find her way back? What would it mean to history if she stayed? Even if she were very careful, never rocked the boat politically, lived in isolation, her very presence in 1194 would change something about history—wouldn't it? Or was her life insignificant enough to not matter? But wasn't she even now changing history? Yes, she had accidentally brought the gun back and that was already changing the way things were going. If Garrick figured out how to use the weapon and discovered how to travel through time, who knew what the final result would be. She lifted her face from his chest to find Navarre's golden eyes dark with despair.

"Kendra," he whispered, "you must not go. Stay here with me. I will build a life for us, somehow, some way."

She stared at him, dazed, as his hands caressed the length of her hair. "I want to," she said, the words sounding dead to her own ears, "but I can't, Navarre. I can't."

Navarre lifted both hands to cup her face, bringing her lips almost angrily to his. He kissed her thoroughly, fiercely, then released her, his brows colliding like two thunderclouds above stormy eyes.

"You will not leave me," he said.

"Navarre," she whispered, even as his lips moved to caress her neck and coherent thought faltered, "I—I can't stay here. If I do, I'll be changing history. What if—what if we had a child together?" He raised his face from her neck and Kendra wished she'd thought of some other example. His eyes were soft and glowing, his lips curved up in a smile.

"Think you that is likely?"

Kendra blushed and shrugged, looking away from his intense gaze. "Who knows? I'm a healthy woman, why not? But that's not the point. If we have a child, then that's bringing another person into existence back in this time who didn't live before. That starts an entirely new generation of de Galliards that would never otherwise have existed."

"Perhaps I would have had children anyway," he said. "That proves nothing."

"Look at how much damage my being here has done already. If it wasn't for my bringing the gun back, you might have given up on this stupid plot against Richard."

Navarre shook his head. "Nay, it would have changed nothing."

"All right," Kendra conceded, "but if you or someone else uses the gun and succeeds in killing Richard, then it will change history and it will be my fault."

"This has naught to do with whether you stay or go."

"Yes it does, it—" she broke off as a new thought came to her. "You could come back with me," she ventured, knowing even as she said the words it would never work. Navarre in the twentieth century? Navarre with his wonderful code of honor and fierce dedication to justice? The modern world would swallow him whole.

"Nay," he said, echoing her silent thoughts. "This is my world. This is where I belong. If there were no danger of altering history, would you stay?"

Kendra felt suddenly panicky as his golden eyes bored into hers. "I don't know. Navarre, I don't know if I belong here."

"You belong with me," he said, his voice husky with feeling. "You belong in my arms."

"I know," she whispered, wrapping her arms around his neck and leaning her head against his shoulder. "Maybe I won't even be able to leave. We really don't know if there's any way for me to return to my own time."

"But if you can?"

Kendra opened her mouth to speak, to say she would never leave him, but could not. The lines around his lips tightened and he nodded, then let his head fall back against the wall, his eyes sliding shut.

"Lady Marian!"

A guard's dirty face peered through the small window of the cell door, his nose pressed between the bars.

"You must leave the prisoners, milady," he said gruffly, "or else the sheriff will have my head."

"One moment."

Marian rose from Robin's side and crossed to Kendra, a cloth-wrapped bundle in her hands. She shoved it at Kendra, her pale blue eyes wide and frightened. "Friar Tuck says prayers for your souls," she whispered.

"Lady Marian! Leave the prisoners now or I shall be forced to come in after you."

Marian rose quickly and gave Robin one last, anguished look. "Robin, I—"

"Yes, Marian?"

She bit her lower lip then drew a harried breath. "I shall pray for you."

Navarre chuckled as she turned and practically flew across the room to the door.

"She's still a shy little girl if you ask me," Navarre said.

"Shy, yes," Robin agreed. "But no little girl."

Kendra moved away from the two men who commenced to argue. She tore the bread Marian had brought them into pieces, distributing it to the other prisoners, then bringing the remainder back to Navarre and Robin. They devoured their small portions then settled down against the wall to plot how they would take Garrick the next time he came into the cell.

Kendra turned away, unable to choke down her own piece

of bread. Her stomach ached with hunger, another ache to add to the growing list which included shivering cold and agonizing despair. Idly she watched a tiny spider near her head spinning its web from one protruding stone to another. It reminded her of an old story she'd heard once about Robert the Bruce, a hero of Scotland. He'd been defeated by the British three times and had gone into a cave to brood and think. There he'd watched a spider fail three times to form its web, yet succeed on the fourth time. Deeming it a sign from God, he'd returned to the battle and on his fourth try, won the day.

Kendra watched the little spider intently, praying silently for some miraculous idea, some symbolism to strike her as it laboriously spun its thin silk and created its tiny work of art. But there were no answers in its web, though she watched until her eyes ached and the little creature scurried away into a crack. Perhaps there were no answers at all. Navarre wanted an answer from her. If she could go back to her own time, would she? She leaned against the cold stone, hugging her arms about herself. The answer didn't matter. The questions didn't matter. Garrick would not honor his agreement with her. He would kill Navarre and as soon as he tired of torturing her, she would die too.

Why? She squeezed her eyes shut. Why had she come across time and space to find her one true love if this was to be their end?

She didn't realize she was crying until the tear had trickled to the edge of her chin. Reaching up to wipe the moisture away, a much larger hand suddenly imprisoned hers. She looked up into the golden eyes of Navarre. With a sob, Kendra threw herself against him, her arms around his neck. He gathered her to him as her sudden cry rent the silence around them. One of the guards peered into the cell, then laughed and passed on. Robin and the other prisoners moved tactfully away, leaving Navarre to comfort her in relative privacy.

Kendra clung to her knight. Her tears seemed never ending, as though a dam deep inside of her had broken, as pain, submerged for years, poured out of her, drenching both of them with the truth of their predicament, drowning them in its sadness. At last, her stomach twisted one last time and she stopped crying, as suddenly as she had begun. Feeling empty and bereft, she stood within the protection of Navarre's arms and leaned her head against his chest, silent and spent.

"I'm sorry," she whispered, "I'm not usually such a baby. It's just that—" she broke off as the tears threatened to return. She brought herself back under a tenuous control, her lashes brushing her cheeks as she kept her gaze on her clasped hands. "I'm so afraid, Navarre."

"Garrick will not harm you," he promised. "I failed Talam, I will not fail you." He raked his fingers through her tangled hair, gathering the mass over one shoulder and using it to draw her nearer. "Talam was the first woman I truly loved, and my love for her was deep, but it was nothing compared to the love I bear you, Kendra. Do you know why I thought you a witch?" She shook her head wordlessly. "Because I had never felt such desire for a woman in all of my life, had never known a burning fire that possessed me night and day, and so I thought that I must be enchanted." He hesitated. "Do you know now what I believe?" he asked.

Kendra shook her head again, azure eyes locked with golden.

He leaned toward her, his lips close to hers as he spoke softly. "I do believe you have enchanted me, Kendra O'Brien," he said, laying one finger across her lips as she started to protest. "But not with magic. You have enchanted me with your courage, your sense of honor, your love of life, your good humor, and aye, if I be honest, your beauty. But most of all, you have enchanted me with your love. Think you that I will lose you easily? To Garrick? Even to time itself?" He shook his head. "Nay. We shall find a way, you and I, a way to circumvent the very powers of heaven if need be."

"And what about hell, my love?" Kendra whispered.

"Aye," his voice buried itself in her hair, along with his kiss, "if I have to fight the devil himself."

"Talking about me again behind my back, eh, Navarre?"

The two looked up and Kendra sagged against Navarre as the door to their cell swung open and they stared into the laughing eyes of the Sheriff of Nottingham.

Heart pounding, Kendra clung to Navarre, protesting audibly when the knight gently but firmly pushed her away from him, facing the sheriff in a warrior's stance. Robin moved to stand beside him. She glanced from Garrick to the eight guards behind him and paled.

"No, Navarre," she whispered, moving to his side. "There are too many of them." Navarre stiffened and shoved her again, more roughly this time.

"Stay back, Kendra."

Garrick laughed, hands behind his back, his black cape whipping about him as he and his entourage entered the dirty room. "Do you challenge me and my men, Navarre?" His even teeth flashed as his gray eyes darkened to charcoal. "How noble, how brave, how . . ." his smile disappeared ". . . stupid."

Navarre went for the sheriff's throat at the same instant that Garrick jerked his hand from behind his back. To Kendra it all happened in slow motion, the knight's desperate lunge forward just as Garrick's hand appeared, the gun in his clutches. Kendra heard herself scream as two shots rang out and Navarre went down, Robin beside him. Then everything went back to real time as one of the guards grabbed her from behind, the injured men of Sherwood rose to attack the guards, and all hell broke loose.

Kendra kicked and screamed against her assailant but he stood as unmoved as a statue to her batterings, his hands like twin vises around her wrists. Kendra could hear the shouts and cries of the men as the soldiers moved in and began flailing the prisoners with their fists as well as their feet. Suddenly the man who held Kendra hoisted her up onto his shoulders. Continuing to scream at the top of her lungs, she craned her neck around, fighting desperately to find Navarre. At last, she saw him, lying motionless on his side near the door, Robin beside him.

"Navarre! Robin!" Neither man answered and Kendra began to thrash in earnest. "Let me go you rotten bastard! Let me go!"

Garrick swept her a languid look, then nodded at two of his men. They crossed to the fallen men and pulled them to the center of the room. To Kendra's relief, they both began to moan and struggle against the guards, proving they were at least alive. They slumped against one another. Robin's shoulder was bloody and a rivulet of crimson ran down the side of Navarre's face. But it looked to her like neither had been directly hit.

"Navarre!" Kendra cried, struggling so violently that her guard lost his grip and she went crashing to the floor. Her elbow hit first and she was blinded by the pain for a moment. When her vision cleared, Garrick towered over her, his leering smile sending a wave of nausea through her before he turned to Robin.

"Locksley, old fellow, you must be the first to hear the good news. Richard's ransom has been paid and he journeys even as we speak, hurrying home to England."

" 'Tis the best news you could give me," Robin said, his voice laced with pain as he clutched his shoulder. "Though why you yourself would call it good I know not."

Garrick feigned astonishment. "My dear sir, I would have you know that Prince John and I are so anxious to see dear Richard again that we have sent an entourage to meet him, to accompany him on the long journey back to England. Why, who knows what might befall the king if he were not properly protected? Alas," his eyes grew sad, his mouth clownishly pulled down at the corner, "in spite of our efforts, I would not be surprised to hear that King Richard never returns to England." His voice fell to a stage whisper. "He has many enemies, you know."

"Aye, one who is Satan's spawn," Robin said, trying to stand. He collapsed back to the floor as Garrick's laughter swept through the dank cell.

"Hardly that, my friend, though I do thank you for the compliment. My dear stepmother would have been proud. And now, if you will excuse me, my friends, I would like to retire." He reached down and grabbed Kendra, pulling her up and into his arms. His hand closed over her breast and she cried out as he tightened his fingers. Kendra reacted immediately, trying to kick him in the shin, but Garrick only dodged her blows, laughed, and squeezed harder. Hot tears of frustration and shame burned down her cheeks as he lowered his head and drew his tongue down the crevice between her breasts.

"No!" The ragged cry sent the sheriff back a step from her as Navarre shot up from the floor and buried his fist in Garrick's face. Kendra went down, sobbing, as eight guards converged on the knight and dragged him to his feet. Garrick pulled himself up from the floor, wiping a thin trickle of blood from his mouth, his gray eyes like shards of glass as he faced his attacker.

"I swear upon my mother's grave," Navarre said harshly, struggling against the men holding him, "if you take her now, I shall hunt you down like the dog you are and slowly torture you to death!"

"That will be difficult to accomplish, I wager, while hanging from the gallows," Garrick said. "You have lost, Navarre. Robin has lost. Richard has lost. But I at last, have won! And now, I shall celebrate my victory." He moved toward Kendra.

Navarre went suddenly still between the men holding him. "Let her go," he said. The desperation in his voice brought fresh tears to Kendra's eyes as she slumped against the guard restraining her. "In the name of our friendship, I beg you, let her go, Garrick."

"In the name of our friendship?" Garrick smiled and took a step toward him. Kendra stiffened as he stopped inches away from Navarre, then she stared in confusion as the sheriff lifted his hand and drew his fingers gently down the length of the knight's face, an expression of tenderness in his eyes.

"I think not, dear Navarre," he whispered, letting his fingers curl inward. "Our friendship is officially . . . over. Or will be as soon as the execution takes place tomorrow morning."

"No!" Kendra shouted, straining forward. "You promised."

"Oh, I didn't tell you? So sorry, so remiss of me. Yes, I've decided to entertain Nottingham tomorrow by hanging all of these scurvy outlaws."

"You promised you wouldn't hurt him!" Kendra screamed helplessly, feeling almost beyond sanity as the sheriff raised his fist. "You promised!"

Garrick's laughter filled the cell, echoed off the stone walls and pierced her throat, her eyes, her ears. She watched, suddenly silent, frozen, as the sheriff buried his fist in Navarre's stomach. That first blow doubled him over. The second brought him to his knees. Kendra felt her legs collapsing beneath her even as the guard held her erect.

"Stop it! Stop it!" she cried, as Garrick's fists cut into the man she loved. "I won't tell you the secret if you kill him. Do you hear me? I won't tell you!"

Navarre lay in a heap on the floor and Garrick stepped back from him, cradling his fist in his hand.

"Bring her."

Kendra couldn't seem to stop screaming. She screamed as she was dragged back and hefted once again onto the guard's back; she screamed as he headed for the cell door, Garrick behind him; she screamed as the door slammed behind them and the sheriff bolted it shut. Then she stopped screaming, for someone else was screaming. Kendra's breath caught in her throat. She began to sob silently, closing her eyes against Navarre's ragged cry of despair.

As the guard carried her away, and Navarre's desperation followed her, a strange calm settled over Kendra. It was up to her now, and panicking would only make things worse. She had to remain cool. She had to think. She stopped struggling as they journeyed through the dim corridor and ransacked her brain for an idea, an answer, a way out. She was coming up empty for the fifth time as suddenly her transportation slowed, then came to a complete halt. A strong, unfamiliar voice rang out.

"Put her down. Release that woman at once!"

Lifting herself up on her captor's shoulder and twisting around so she could see who had spoken, Kendra stared in amazement at the challenger. A man stood in the hallway in front of them, his form silhouetted against the torchlight, legs braced firmly apart, his girth almost as wide as his height, which was little more than five feet. How this tiny butterball of a man thought he could defy the sheriff and his guard was a puzzlement. Who was her diminutive defender?

"Father Tucker." Garrick's voice sounded hushed, strained. He gestured to the soldier beside him and Kendra slid to the floor in a startled heap.

Kendra stared up at the man who had so easily commanded the sheriff. His bald head gleamed in the dim light as he bowed it toward her. His brown robes were a trifle grubby, but a large golden crucifix hung from the rosary beads around his thick waist. His face gleamed with ruddiness, while a circle of curly gray hair made a ring about his head, giving him an almost angelic look. That gentle comparison stopped abruptly with the man's eyes, which were a dark, steely blue. They were eyes that seemed to see to the core of a man's soul, eyes that now had the effrontery to cast a look of condemnation toward the Sheriff of Nottingham.

Kendra glanced at Garrick, who stood frozen, practically hugging the stone walls of the corridor. Fear, stark and real, glistened in the sheriff's eyes, and with dawning comprehension, Kendra made the connection. *Father Tucker*. Friar Tuck. *Friar Tuck*. Robin Hood's Friar Tuck? How many could there be? But what was he doing living in Nottingham Castle instead of taking care of the souls of the merry outlaws living in Sherwood? Perhaps he hadn't yet gone over to Robin's side. Perhaps he didn't even know what was going on. In any case, his next words brought a glimmer of hope to her heart.

"What evil are you about this night, my son?"

The words were soft, concerned, but his stern gaze belied their gentleness.

"Father," Garrick whispered, "I thought you had left the castle."

"You hoped I had left," the priest said tersely. "You hoped I would not see the new depths of degradation to which you have descended." He shook his head. "I had such hopes for you, Garrick. You were doing so well."

"You do not understand. This woman—"

"This woman is now under the protection of Holy Mother Church. Give her to me. Now."

The sheriff nodded and Kendra didn't waste time asking stupid questions. She jumped to her feet and hurried to the ample protection of the priest's body. Friar Tuck shook his finger at Garrick. "And while I attend to this lost lamb, you will ask God to have mercy on your immortal soul. I will assign penance for you directly. This way."

The sheriff dismissed the guard. Kendra glanced back over her shoulder fearfully as Garrick followed the priest meekly down the corridor. They arrived in front of a wooden door so small Garrick had to duck to fit himself through the opening. Inside was a room about half the size of the cell she and the other prisoners had occupied. Plain to the point of being ugly, there were no tapestries, no stained glass windows, no statues, save for one of Mary. A table was crowded with candles of various sizes and heights and the light lent a ghostly aura to the chamber. A giant crucifix hung on the wall behind a crude altar, and hard benches lined either side of the room, forming an aisle down the middle. Tuck led Kendra toward a small booth built to one side, draped with red velvet curtains.

"I shall hear this child's confession first," the priest told Garrick, "and then yours. Prepare yourself."

Once behind the curtains, Friar Tuck took Kendra's hand and squeezed it sympathetically. "Poor child," he whispered. "From the looks of you, you have already endured much."

"Don't worry about me," she said, "it's Robin Hood who is in danger—and Navarre de Galliard." Kendra searched his face as he didn't respond to her words. "Are you Robin's friend? Do you know he is in the dungeon? Are you Friar Tuck?"

"Shhh," he cautioned, peeking out between the curtains. Garrick knelt obediently before the altar. Tuck turned back to her, one side of his mouth quirked up in quiet amusement. "I am Friar Tuck and I am indeed Robin's friend. I have worked hard to maintain my place within these walls, child, in order to help not only Robin, but others in Nottingham, so please, keep your voice down. Marian has told me of your plight and there is no need to worry."

"I'm sorry," Kendra whispered. "How will you help them?"

"There is no way tonight," the priest said softly, "but do not despair."

"But he's going to hang them in the morning!"

Tuck patted her hand. "Robin is my friend and I will not leave him here to die. Navarre de Galliard is another matter, but, because of his kindness to Marian, he shall be freed as well.''

''Thank you, Father,'' Kendra said sincerely, breathing a sigh of relief. ''You're as terrific as your legend.''

The priest blinked at her, then chuckled again. ''My legend? Faith, I did not know I had one.''

Kendra parted the curtains slightly and watched Garrick kneeling before the altar. She let the curtians fall back together. ''Why is the sheriff obeying you?''

''That is a long story. Suffice it to say that I am the one man who helps hold the demons haunting him at bay.''

The curtains of the booth were suddenly jerked apart as the Sheriff of Nottingham thrust his face into the private sanctuary, his lips twisted in a leering smile, his gray eyes dancing with depravity.

''I have asked God for a favor,'' Garrick said with a short laugh, ''and He, in His infinite wisdom, has granted it. Step aside, dear Father, for God Himself has ordained that the woman is mine to do with as I see fit.''

Kendra shivered and shrank into the corner of the booth.

''Nonsense,'' Tuck snorted, placing one hand against Garrick's chest and shoving him back from the curtains. He stepped out of the confessional and glared at the sheriff. ''God has done no such thing. The woman stays here, with me.''

The gray eyes darkened and Kendra began to fear for the little priest. Whatever power he wielded over Garrick seemed to be waning fast.

''Who the hell are you to tell me what I can or cannot do?''

''You know who I am,'' Friar Tuck said, his hands folded in front of him, ''and Whom I represent. Your disrespect will not go unpunished. Take care you do not push me too far.''

''I am the Sheriff of Nottingham.'' Garrick's mouth twitched, then spread into a mocking smile. ''And in my city, I do the punishing. Take care you do not push me too far.'' He lunged for Kendra. Using the heavy crucifix dangling from his belt, Tuck popped him on the forehead much as he might have an unruly dog. Garrick sat down unceremoniously at the foot of the steps, one hand to his head, his gaze unfocused, disoriented.

"You will not take her," the priest said. "You must fight your darker side, Garrick. We have spoken of this often and you can have the victory if you only have faith."

Garrick rose to his knees, his fair face drawn up in a dark scowl. He crept toward the priest like an uncaged animal. "This night will see you out of Nottingham Castle—forever."

"Then who will protect your soul from the minions of hell, my son?" Tuck asked softly. The sheriff stopped in his predatorial approach, his face suddenly stricken. "From the demons your stepmother called forth to possess you when you were but a child?"

Garrick's eyes widened, like a wild animal trapped, then went dull and hollow. Slowly he turned back and faced the crucifix on the wall. Kendra stifled a sob as his childlike, bewildered voice echoed around them. "She is not here. Say she is not here, Father."

"Do not fear, Garrick," Tuck said, and Kendra felt tears again at the sound of the true compassion in the priest's voice. "Your stepmother is dead. She can no longer harm you. It is your own wickedness that harms you now, and others."

A pounding at the door drove the bewilderment from Garrick's eyes as the wooden barrier slammed open. The soldier outside cursed as he bent almost double through the opening, then stood at attention in front of the sheriff. Garrick blinked, as though awakening from a sleep, and with sinking heart, Kendra saw the sharpness return to his eyes like the edge of a steely blade.

"Jenkins, what are you doing here? I told you to take de Galliard's place with the men."

"Nottingham is under attack," the big man reported. "Those cursed outlaws have infiltrated the walls and are setting fires all over the city."

"Good. At last, they have made a fatal mistake." Garrick paused and looked back at Kendra. "Do wait up for me my dear, for I will be back to celebrate my victory with you, whether dear Father Tucker likes it or not."

His laughter rang out again as he left the chapel, pulling the door shut behind him.

"He's crazy," Kendra whispered, her voice echoing in the silence of the room.

Tuck shot her a sharp look. "You didn't know?" She shook her head and he shrugged. "Aye, and has been since he was just a wee lad, though it has only recently come to the forefront of his personality. His mind is double-sided, changes from moment to moment. At times he is the child he was before his stepmother—" he shook his head and fell silent.

"What?" Kendra prompted.

"There are horrors even a man of God fears to speak aloud. Rest assured, Garrick did not become the monster he is by himself."

"It doesn't matter." Kendra sank to a bench, her legs suddenly too weak to hold her. "He is a monster and he intends to kill Navarre, Robin, and all of his men, at dawn."

Tuck sighed and sat down beside her, taking her hand in his. "Have faith, my dear. Remember how God sent an angel to open the cell where the apostle Paul was imprisoned?"

Kendra leaned her face into the palms of her hands. "Somehow I'd feel better if I knew they had something a little more definite to count on, Father. Do you have a plan? Is this attack on the castle part of it?"

The priest didn't answer and in irritation she lifted her face to his, only to find his blue eyes twinkling as he patted her shoulder.

"God works in mysterious ways, my child, and many have entertained angels unawares. Now, wait here and I will fetch you a softer pallet."

Kendra tried to return his optimistic smile as he walked away, but she felt her emotional strength crumbling. Blinking back tears, she stretched out on the bench, her hands trembling beneath her head.

"Angels," she whispered. "Dear God, let them bring swords." She fell asleep with Navarre's name on her lips.

Chapter Thirteen

The servants came for Kendra in the chapel the next morning and after an initial protest, Friar Tuck changed his mind and encouraged her to go with them.

"On the tourney field my dear, you will be better able to flee when all hell breaks loose."

Kendra frowned at him, confused by his less than priest-like statement. "Is all hell going to break loose?"

His only answer was an enigmatic smile. Kendra followed the servants as they led her to a luxurious chamber. There they dressed her in a long, beautiful emerald green gown made from a velvety material that seemed to caress her skin. The sleeves fit her arms perfectly and ended in dramatic points extending over her hand. Over this gorgeous dress another was added, made from a glorious fabric of shimmering gold. This gown's sleeves were form-fitting to the elbow, then widened and hung beneath her arms almost to the floor. It was edged with wide, emerald green trim, the girdle a twisted belt of green and gold with long gold tassels hanging almost to her feet.

As the servants pulled her closer to the fireplace to dry her hair, Kendra found herself wishing Navarre could see her in this beautiful ensemble. So far, he had seen her primarily clad in dirt and muck. It would be nice for him to see her looking halfway decent for a change. She sobered as she realized he would be seeing her—dressed like a queen, standing at Garrick's side to watch her brave knight die. Resolutely, she pushed the thought away. Navarre was not going to die.

By the time Kendra's hair had been dressed, part of it

braided and drawn back with a golden thong, the rest of it left to hang in rich waves down her back, she was shifting her feet impatiently. When would this be over? she wondered in exasperation as one of the women wove ribbons of green and gold into her hair.

Kendra was relieved to see her bag draped over her chair's ornate back, and she determinedly swung the satchel over her shoulder as she stood. Marian had brought it to her in the chapel, bless her thoughtful heart. Today she wasn't taking any chances. When the opportunity came to run she was taking it, and she wouldn't leave anything behind that might change history. She pushed away the thought of the gun. They would retrieve the weapon. Somehow, she and Navarre would rid the medieval world of the violence she had unwittingly unleashed upon it.

During the slow walk back to the castle, Kendra watched for any opportunity for escape, but there was none. The guards flanked her, three on either side, as though Garrick had warned them to expect some kind of attempt from her. She was ushered back into Garrick's chamber and the servants left her, at last, to await their lord's pleasure.

Turning her thoughts desperately away from her fears, Kendra took her mirror out to get a look at herself in the elaborate dress. Examining the trim on the loose overdress more closely, she realized it had been embroidered with intricate Celtic circles. Circles. How fitting. They were, after all, the root of all of her problems. If she hadn't been standing out in the field near Avebury when that crop circle started forming, she wouldn't be in this mess.

A knock came at the door and she looked up, suddenly apprehensive. Was it time? Was Navarre being marched even now to the gallows or the block or whatever they called it? She bit her lower lip hard and drew blood. If Friar Tuck didn't save them—she refused to finish the thought. Of course he would save them. Of course he would. The door swung open.

Magda entered the room, her gray hair streaming over one shoulder in a long braid. She was dressed in a plain, brown gown, carrying a bowl of fruit. Apparently the guards had taken her for what she appeared to be, a servant.

"Quickly," the woman said, shutting the door behind her, "I must speak with you."

"Magda, did the priest send you?"

The old woman looked at her in confusion. "The priest? He will not even set foot in the same room with me, much less speak to me. Nay, I have come of my own accord, to help you." Magda moved to stand beside her and rested one hand on the woman's shoulder. "You must learn the secret of time, and soon."

Kendra turned and stared down at the woman. She was surprised to find the priestess only came up to her shoulder. She hadn't noticed that in Sherwood.

"Can you tell me?"

"No," Magda admitted, "but there is one who can. You must come with me and journey to meet Cennach."

Kendra frowned. The name sounded vaguely familiar. "Who's Cennach?"

"A wiseman, a sorcerer." Her pale eyes grew large and her hands waved expressively. "He knows the secrets of time. Cennach will help you."

"Thank you so much for the information." The sound of Garrick's complacent voice sent Kendra spinning around to face him, her fists clenched at her sides, angry at herself for her foolish lack of caution.

He laughed as Magda glowered at him from behind Kendra. "Come, my two little witches. We shall attend the tourney fields where a most amusing spectacle awaits us, then we shall journey to the home of this most incredible wiseman. What did you call him? Ah yes, Cennach."

"And if we refuse to take you?" Kendra's voice quavered.

"Refuse?" He brushed one long lock of blond hair back from his face. "If you refuse, I will kill Marian."

"Marian has already fled the castle, for all I know."

Garrick waved one hand dismissively. "It matters not. You will do as I say or I will kill someone else—Magda, a child from the street—anyone will do." His gray eyes gleamed down at her and Kendra felt suddenly cold at the ruthlessness she saw mirrored there. "I have observed you most carefully and while you would rather die than reveal something you

227

think detrimental to England, I do not believe you would allow another to die to protect the same knowledge.''

Kendra licked her lips, unable to speak for a moment. He was right, of course.

''If you interfere with time,'' Magda said, breaking the silence, ''you risk destroying all, even that to which you aspire.''

''Shut up, old woman,'' he ordered, opening the heavy door and bowing to Kendra. ''Come along, ladies. The festivities are beginning and it would not do to have the guests of honor absent, now would it?'' The amusement faded from his silver eyes as Kendra didn't move. ''I grow weary of your rebellion, my dear. Will you be good or no?''

Kendra stared up at him defiantly and Garrick's gaze shifted to a servant girl down on her knees across the hall, scrubbing the stone floor. He reached inside the loose folds of his tunic and withdrew the Smith and Wesson. Kendra sped across the room to grip his hand fiercely, her body blocking his.

''I will be good,'' she said, her voice choked, her heart pounding with the realization that another human being had almost died simply because she didn't have the good sense to know when to give in.

The sheriff stared down at her and slowly lowered the gun. He didn't touch her, but bent his head until his mouth was almost brushing hers.

''You will not simply be good, my dear,'' he whispered. ''You will be absolutely delicious.'' He began to laugh, the sound starting softly and growing as he shoved her and Magda into the hallway; it followed them like a disembodied being out of the castle and into the tourney field where Navarre and Robin, and the hand of death, awaited.

They led the prisoners out of the dungeon and into the bright morning sunlight. Navarre squinted up at the yellow orb, then lowered his gaze to the ground. He and Robin had agreed to present themselves as beaten prisoners, and secretly he wondered who was fooling whom. His hands were still bound behind him, the ropes still sawing into the raw flesh. He trudged along behind Robin, forcing his feet to move one step in front of the other, needles of pain shooting through his limbs. It was almost laughable, he realized, to think there was any possibility of escape. They had learned the attack on the castle the night before had been easily put down, the remaining outlaws scattered back into Sherwood.

Robin stopped abruptly and Navarre ran into the outlaw, stumbling to a halt, jerking his head up to see what was happening. They were lined up in the center of the tourney field, where once a year combatants met for sport, or to settle old grievances. A long platform had been built, with ten nooses hanging across the beam spanning the length. It stood like a hulking shadow behind them.

Navarre hardly glanced at it before he narrowed his eyes against the sunlight and scoured the tented pavilion only ten yards in front of them where the nobles always sat. There was Garrick, dressed like a peacock in his favorite red and black and gold, a beautiful black cape with a red lining adorning his shoulders.

It was a crisp, cold day and Navarre shivered in his torn, ragged garb. Then he willed himself to stop. To show any kind of weakness was to lose honor on this day of all days. Flags waved above the bright pavilion. Cloth, in Garrick's colors of black and red, had been hung down the sides of the wood frame to create a tent-like structure, which protected the nobles from the glare of the sun. The seats in the pavilion were full, crowded with barons and friends of John and the sheriff, while a great throng of people, Saxon peasants for the most part, pressed against the barrier erected around the tourney field. As the men were marched out, the peasants had given a resounding cheer, whether for the men themselves or the spectacle about to take place, Navarre wasn't certain.

He didn't see Kendra at first, then the sheriff moved and she came into view. She wore gold and green, her hair like a cascade of fire over one shoulder. Sweet, beautiful Kendra. Woman from another world, another time. How different he had hoped their fates would be. If only he had not wasted the time in which they had been together. Her face looked haggard, drawn, and he closed his eyes against the sight. When he opened them again, she was seated beside the sheriff. The furrows between his brows grew even deeper when Marian entered the pavilion from the other side, Friar Tuck guiding her elbow.

Cursing under his breath, Navarre willed himself to stay strong. If he were going to die, he didn't want those he cared for most in the world to be subjected to the pain of watching his death. He had hoped Garrick would at least have the decency to shield the women from this horror. He should have known he would not.

"Courage," Robin said at his elbow.

"Courage," Navarre replied, lifting his chin to meet whatever came next.

Garrick stood and the boisterous crowd immediately fell silent. "Good people of Nottingham," he began, "I stand before you to make two announcements: first to tell you that at long last Sherwood Forest has been made safe for free men to pass through on their way to London, for at long last, the outlaw Robin Hood has been captured and even now awaits his sentence."

A few in the crowd cheered his words, but the majority began murmuring angrily. Navarre glanced at Robin. The outlaw stood as straight as the arrows he wielded, a grim smile on his face.

"I did not realize so many of the people were loyal to you," Navarre said, his gaze searching the mass of people frowning and milling outside the field.

"Aye, I warrant Garrick did not realize it either, until now." As if he heard their muttered conversation across the field, the sheriff raised his hands to quiet the crowd. "Secondly, I wish to announce that Prince John, in the absence of his dear brother, King Richard, has decided to lower your taxes. When the collector next visits your door, he will ask for only half of what you usually pay."

A rousing cheer at that rose from the people gathered. Trumpeters stationed at either side of the pavilion sounded their instruments triumphantly.

"Now he's using his head," Robin said. "That will gain him the favor of the people more than any other single thing he could do—if he really does it."

"That was my bloody idea," Navarre fumed, glaring up at the sheriff. Garrick turned at that moment and his gaze locked with that of the knight. Was it his imagination or did Navarre see the slightest glimmer of regret in the eyes of his onetime friend? If there was, it vanished without a trace as Garrick turned and crossed to John, whose head was bent next to Marian's.

Navarre saw Robin staring at the two, then the outlaw turned toward him, his eyes steady.

"I would like to tell you before they separate us that I understand now what you have been trying to do for England." His mouth tightened beneath the mustache, then he hurried on. "You are a good man, Navarre. I hope we may die as friends."

Navarre nodded, "I, too, have grown in my understanding of things. However, I feel differently about our dying as friends." Robin's lips twitched at his words and Navarre grinned. "I wish we might both live as friends, that I might join you and rid England forever of the true pestilence."

Robin's features relaxed and an answering smile lit his face. "I shall hold you to that," he said softly.

They turned toward one another then, gazes locking, eyes speaking silently the respect and admiration they could not put into words. At last, Navarre nodded and Robin inclined his head. Navarre looked up at the pavilion, feeling strangely unburdened.

John, clad in black and gold, stood and moved to the front of the pavilion, a short, thin man wearing scribe's robes beside him. The little man unfurled a long parchment scroll, then stood waiting as if for the prince's command. Banners of gold emblazoned with John's standard flew at each corner of the pavilion, and the king's brother looked up at them proudly, as if to draw the crowd's attention to the fluttering cloth. The people quieted again and John began to speak.

"It has been my singular honor," John began pompously, "to be here as a support, a guide if you will, to England and her people, through the shaky times since Richard's imprisonment in Austria. Everything possible is being done to bring the king home where he belongs, but until that time—if, please

231

God, it ever comes—it falls to men like the Sheriff of Nottingham, and myself, to make sure outlaws like those before you today do not steal what is rightfully England's.''

"Or what John thinks is rightfully his," Robin said out of the side of his mouth. "I understand your efforts, Navarre. What I cannot comprehend is your choice of comrades.''

"At the moment, I would have to agree with you. I do not understand myself.''

"This judgment," John was saying, gesturing to the scribe, "was made by the Sheriff of Nottingham with my full endorsement, and shall now be read.''

The scrawny scribe stepped up, the unfurled scroll held in front of him.

"Be it known that on this day the outlaw Robert of Locksley, also known as Robin Hood, by order of the Sheriff of Nottingham, has been found guilty of numerous crimes listed below, including but not limited to murder, theft, treason, skullduggery and arson.''

"Skullduggery, is it?" Robin said loudly from the field. " 'Tis hard to recall but I do not remember ever digging a skull in my life.''

The crowd laughed and the scribe frowned disapprovingly at the outlaw. He cleared his throat and continued. "The following men have also been found guilty of these crimes, as they have attached themselves to the outlaw and followed his command." He read off a long list of names, ending with Navarre de Galliard.

A collective gasp rose from the assembled people. Navarre's name was one they had long associated with the sheriff and with the peace of Nottingham. The knight stood a little straighter as the scribe continued.

"All of these men, found guilty of crimes against England, shall be taken this morn and hanged by the neck until dead.''

Navarre saw Kendra's hand at her throat and for a moment their eyes met. Filled with pain and worry, her gaze hit him with an impact he did not expect. He tried to convey, through his own expressive eyes in that brief moment suspended between them, how much he loved her, how much he regretted what had been done to her. Her lips curved up tremulously.

A shout went up and Navarre turned to find the long row of men being shoved toward the gallows. Not unexpectedly, the guards jerked Robin out of the line, then Navarre, and hustled them to the wooden platform before the rest.

Navarre sent a wide, wild look about the field. If help was coming, 'twould be now. But no help came as he and Robin were led up the steps of the hastily erected structure and stopped beneath the first two nooses. Garrick had risen to stand beside John and now moved forward, taking center stage.

"Let the leader of the outlaws be hanged first. And let my former friend, Navarre, join him, to show all of Nottingham that no one is above the law. If you have committed a crime and you call me friend, do not expect me to save you from your justly deserved fate."

Navarre stared at the man he once prided himself on knowing so well and could not help the words that sprang to his lips.

"And do not think that by calling him friend you protect yourself from his betrayal, either," he said loudly from the gallows. His gaze fell on a few of the barons who had attended, now shifting uneasily in their seats as he looked at them. "My lords, do not think that you will be immune once the sheriff gains enough power. Once you have served your purpose you will be dispatched as easily as I."

"Silence!" Garrick roared from the stand. "Guard, if you allow that criminal to speak again, you will join him on the platform!"

The guard rushed forward and stuffed a foul-smelling cloth in Navarre's mouth, but the knight didn't care. He'd said his piece, for what it was worth. A drumroll began in the distance and the noose was lifted and slipped over his head, then tightened around his neck. Navarre swallowed hard as he felt the rope burn into his throat, the painful reality no longer avoidable. With effort he pushed the dirty rag from his mouth with his tongue and took a deep, shuddering breath.

There would be no escape. Today he was going to die.

Chapter Fourteen

The king's brother continued to talk, praising himself and Garrick. Navarre could see Kendra's stricken face, white against the burgundy cushioned chair she sat upon. He closed his eyes, wishing it were over.

"Robin."

Navarre felt hope rise anew in his heart at the sound of the roughly spoken word. He'd only heard Little John's voice a few times but could never forget the deep, resonating sound, even obscured by a hangman's hood and a whisper.

"Aye," Robin replied to the man standing behind them, his own tone calm and unsurprised.

Little John moved behind the outlaw and Navarre heard the wonderfully soft sound of a rope being cut in two.

"Keep your hands behind you," he cautioned, then moved to Navarre. "What about him?"

The knight tensed, unaware he was holding his breath until Robin nodded, and Little John sliced his bonds as well. He released his breath slowly, thankfully, and readied himself for whatever came next.

"Why in God's name did you attack the castle?" Robin whispered, keeping perfectly still. "You knew you could not win."

"Aye, but now they will think we tried and failed, will they not? They will not expect another attempt," Little John said softly. "We have horses ready. I will leave the nooses slightly loose around your necks. When I kick the boxes from beneath your feet, pull the rope from your neck and use it to swing off the gallows backward. Roll under the platform. Help will be there. Ride like hell for Sherwood and we'll join you after we take care of the sheriff and his men.''

"What of Marian and Kendra?" Robin whispered, hardly moving his lips.

"No time," Little John shook his head. "We shall have to get them out later."

"Nay," Navarre said hoarsely, "I shall not leave without them."

"Nor I."

Their hangman sighed as if he'd expected their words. "Stubborn bastards, ain't you?"

"Aye," Navarre whispered again, "Though Robin's parents were married. I am the only bastard."

"But I confess to the stubbornness," Robin agreed, daring to wink in Navarre's direction, his good nature returning now that the odds were more evenly divided.

"Whist," Little John said, "the banty rooster and the strutting cock have finished. Be ready, lads, and we shall get you out of this yet."

Navarre nodded, and squinting against the mid-morning sun, searched the pavilion once again for Kendra. He found her, green and gold like a fragile morning flower. Suddenly he wondered if she knew of the escape plan, or did she think she was about to watch him die?

Kendra twisted her hands together in her lap, glad for the heavy cloak Garrick had thrown about her shoulders before leaving the chamber. The cold she felt had nothing to do with the weather. Ice seemed to harden in her chest as she watched Navarre and Robin Hood being led up the steps to the gallows.

She gripped the arms of the chair in which she sat, feeling helpless and filled with angry frustration. She was next to Garrick, whose place of honor was just to the right of John's huge throne-like chair. Marian and Friar Tuck sat to John's left, both looking self-conscious and nervous. Magda had been left behind at the castle and Kendra had no idea what was happening to her.

As Garrick and John stood and addressed the people, Kendra leaned across Garrick's empty chair, hoping to catch Friar Tuck's attention. The priest glanced her way and for an instant she saw the worry in his eyes. It disappeared as he shook his head the slightest bit and returned his now complacent gaze to the field. Marian stared down at her hands, but with Kendra's movement she looked up and in her eyes Kendra saw an echo of her own pain. She smiled reassuringly at the girl and felt the kinship between them renew itself.

It was obvious that Friar Tuck couldn't, or wouldn't, give her a sign or a clue of what was about to happen. The scribe was reading the charges now and she listened intently to his voice drone on, a terrible coldness twisting in the pit of her stomach as the words "hanged until dead" pierced the air.

Her gaze searched the field and the throng of people outside the barrier. Surely Robin's men were here. Surely they had not all been captured. Surely they would not let their leader die. But would they let Navarre die? Her throat tightened convulsively. If Little John managed to save the outlaw would he still let Navarre hang? Robin's men knew nothing of the new burgeoning friendship between the two. Why would they not simply shoot Robin's rope in half, throw him on a horse, and leave Navarre to hang? She closed her eyes against the sickening thought.

The sheriff and John returned to their places, the prince settling himself back in his "throne," Garrick standing beside him, his haughty face wreathed in satisfaction.

Kendra perched on the edge of her chair, the twisted knot in her stomach making her feel nauseous and shaky. She refused to look at Garrick, instead keeping her eyes fixed resolutely on Navarre. Straight and tall he stood, his head held proudly high, his shoulders unbowed. Kendra studied his noble face and wondered how she had ever doubted he was a hero. If only he could live, he would help England by the mere fact of his existence.

He is not going to die, she told herself fervently. Friar Tuck promised he would help him and couldn't possibly be sitting here calmly if he were about to die. She glanced over at the priest again and saw the tension in his face. The doubt crept in again quickly. What if his plan failed? He must not be too sure of the outcome or he wouldn't have that harried look, or be wiping away perspiration from his shiny brow.

Garrick whirled around just then, his black cape billowing from his shoulders, his triumphant smile widening as his gaze fell on Kendra. She could see he rightly judged the despair in her eyes and swept her a low, mocking bow.

"I do apologize for subjecting you to this tragedy," he said. "However, I find it quite an effective deterrent to those who contemplate rebelling against me. You do know how it works, do you not? The rope either breaks his neck, or leaves him to strangle slowly. A good hangman tries to position the knot in such a way that the death is a quick, painless one." His eyes gleamed down at her. "Unless he has been otherwise instructed."

Kendra couldn't speak, couldn't think. Her fingers curled tense around the arms of the chair on which she sat.

Garrick took his place, sweeping his cape from beneath him. He propped his elbows on the arms of the chair, steepling his hands together in front of his chest as he slanted a calculating gaze toward Kendra, as if waiting for her to speak.

Her heart in her throat, Kendra laid one hand on the sheriff's arm and looked up at him boldly, her voice a silken purr. "Please, my Lord Sheriff, put an end to this, and I will do whatever you ask. I will grant your every desire." She lowered her voice. "I will give you the secret to time travel and more. Name your price and I will pay it. Last night—"

Garrick cut her off with a downward gesture of his hand.

"Aye, last night the good father saved you, but do not believe that will happen again. I have plans for that meddlesome fool as well." Kendra shivered as she saw the promise in his cool gray eyes. "You will make good on your promise to me."

"Not unless you free Navarre," Kendra said, the palms of her hands suddenly clammy. "If you hang him, I'll die before I give you the secret of time travel—or my body."

The sheriff leaned back against the high-backed chair, a miniature of John's. He lifted one shoulder eloquently as he turned his attention back to the tourney field.

"Will you let Marian die too? And Magda? I think not. No, Navarre will die—he is too dangerous to let live—and your body will be mine, along with your mysterious secret."

"You can't do this," Kendra breathed, her fingers moving to grip the man's arm. "You can't let him die. He's your friend!"

"Was my friend." Garrick carefully unpried her hand and placed it back in her lap, giving it a proprietary pat. "You will find in life, my dear, that a friend is very much like a good horse. As long as he serves you well and faithfully, he is well treated. However, when he is no longer of any use to you, the most merciful thing you can do is put him out of his misery."

Kendra sat up suddenly straight, Garrick forgotten. A man dressed entirely in black, his face covered with a hood, had positioned Navarre and Robin in front of the first two nooses and now was dropping the knotted ropes over their heads. Her limbs moved of their own volition as she slowly stood, her heart thundering in her chest, seeming to keep time with the drums pounding the death knell across the tourney field.

"No," she whispered.

The hangman prodded the two men to step up on wooden boxes a foot high, then readjusted the ropes and glanced toward the pavilion.

"Are you ready, my lord?" Garrick said to John.

"You are sure there can be no fear of reprisal?" John said, leaning toward the sheriff, his words low. He watched the gallows anxiously and Kendra saw, in that moment, how weak this would-be king really was.

"A goodly portion of his men await the gallows, my lord," Garrick assured the pretender to the throne. "The rest ran scampering into the forest like the cowards they are. Rest assured, there is nothing to fear."

"Very well, then," John said, sitting back and straightening his shoulders, "let it begin."

With an oily smile in Kendra's direction, Garrick raised his hand and brought it down savagely. In a matter of seconds, the boxes had been kicked from beneath the feet of the condemned men, leaving them to swing from the gallows pole.

"No!"

The cry was wrenched from Kendra as she stood, frozen, watching Navarre's body dangle from the rope. She screamed again and started down the steps to the field just as the chaos ensued. Suddenly the air was rent with shouts and curses as the crowd of Saxons outside the fence surged across the barrier and flooded the tourney field. The sound of swords clashing and arrows whizzing by rose up around Kendra, along with the tide of men, armed with daggers and clubs, wooden pitchforks and lit torches, swarming around the base of the pavilion, kept at bay only by the soldiers positioned there.

Kendra swayed, disoriented by the mob, feeling the precious moments tick by as she tried to push her way into the crushing throng. She couldn't see Navarre, so frenzied was the fighting. Looking desperately for help, she turned, then gasped and stumbled against one of the poles holding up the pavilion roof. With a cry, she tried to run into the crowd, but the sheriff grabbed her by the arm and jerked her back.

She fought him, knowing every second she spent struggling was a second of breath denied Navarre. Had anyone helped him? He was dying and she had to reach him. The sheriff slapped her savagely across the face and, like a wildcat protecting her young, Kendra attacked, clawing his face, kicking and biting as she tried desperately to get away, to reach Navarre. But Garrick's hands were like steel bands as he continued to hold her against him, parrying her blows. At last she stopped fighting and began to sob incoherently.

It was too late. Garrick lifted his fist above her and she waited for the blow to come, hoping it would kill her, hoping when she next opened her eyes it would be to find that at last she and Navarre would be where time was no longer a hindrance to their love. She prayed for the darkness to come quickly.

"Come, lovey," the old woman crooned, the long, tapered fingers gently combing through the auburn hair. "Ye must eat something."

Kendra ignored Magda's words and after a moment the priestess sighed and left her beside the stream alone. She stared idly down at the tiny floating leaves being swept away by the slow-moving current of the brook, wishing her thoughts could be as easily swept away. It was sunset, the daylight fading quickly behind the trees of the forest. It didn't matter. Nothing mattered anymore. Navarre was dead, and she wished she had died with him.

She didn't know what had happened back on the tourney field. Apparently there had been some kind of attempt to free Robin and his men, but it had failed. What had happened to Marian or Friar Tuck, she didn't know. She only knew that Navarre was dead, and Robin too, for she had seen him kicking at the end of his rope before the melee began. Navarre, Robin, dead, because of one man's evil. The hatred in her heart quickened and she touched the bruise at her temple, vowing silently once again to kill Garrick. She would find the right time and the right place and she would destroy his life as surely as he had destroyed Navarre's . . . and hers. The possibility of revenge was all that kept her alive these days.

"Ah, there you are, my dear. Daydreaming again, are we?"

Kendra looked up at Garrick, keeping the expression on her face carefully vacant, her eyes hollow. She had not spoken nor eaten since she had been knocked unconscious by Garrick, then awakened to find herself in a camp of sorts in the middle of a forest. Vaguely she recalled Garrick telling her that after the execution—her heart constricted at the thought—they would journey to find the wiseman, Cennach. Apparently, they were on their way.

"Come, come, do you intend to starve yourself to death?" Garrick said. He was his usual impeccable self, even when roughing it, she saw. His surcoat this time was a deep burgundy, trimmed with a wide geometric pattern in black, his under tunic also black, matching his ever-present black cloak.

Kendra shivered and pulled her own cloak more tightly around her, dreading the coming of the night and its freezing temperatures. She scrubbed absently at a spot on her gown, then realized how foolish her efforts were. Garrick had given her a more durable traveling dress of heather-gray wool, but it was already filthy. Her hand stopped moving against the gown and she sighed. What difference did it make?

Garrick knelt down beside her and distractedly, Kendra watched the disappearing sunlight play across his blond hair. Curious how some strands were white-blond and others honey-gold, she thought absently. Like the burnished colors on the back of a rattlesnake or a cobra, lovely and lethal.

Taking a deep breath, Kendra tried to refocus her attention on what the sheriff was saying. She found herself more and more slipping away to some inner world, away from the sharp pain of reality, a reality without Navarre.

"You will eat," Garrick ordered, "or I will make you wish you had. I have no desire to bed a scrawny wretch. Eat, or I promise Magda will suffer for your insolence."

He handed her a wooden bowl containing some kind of stew, along with a trencher, a sort of bread rather shaped like a spoon. With a sigh, Kendra took the bowl and dipped the crust of bread into the liquid, bringing the lukewarm food to her mouth. Garrick watched her chew for a moment, then cursing beneath his breath, turned and stomped to the other side of the campfire.

The mouthful of stew was difficult to chew, simply because it took too much energy. She was tired. Tired of living, she realized. What use was it, anyway, if everyone you ever loved was always taken away from you? What point in existing? She had found herself enshrouded in a depression so dark, so deep, that everything appeared gray. It felt as if she were encased in a tinted bubble, wrapped in a cotton haze, in full view of life's happenings, yet unable to reach out and touch the reality around her. Food had no flavor, color no beauty, life no joy. Navarre was dead. How could she go on without him?

Magda slipped up beside her just as she was setting aside the rest of her stew. Kendra drew her knees up and wrapped her arms around them, staring down at her leather boots as she waited for the woman to speak. She was unprepared for what Magda had to say.

"If there is a way, you must return to your own time," the old woman said softly.

Kendra sighed, wishing she would leave her alone. She wanted to lie down and sleep. The sun was setting and another long night lay ahead. So far, Garrick had kept his distance. But she knew that wouldn't last.

"Yes," she said wearily, "yes, I know."

"Nay, you do not know. The sorrow you feel over Navarre

241

de Galliard's death is sharp, but whether he lives or no, you must needs return to your own time to prevent your own sorrowful death.''

Kendra glanced back at her, her breath caught in her throat for a moment. "Have you seen something? Heard something? Is there any chance Navarre isn't . . ." her words faded away and she shook her head. "I saw him. I saw him hang. This is pointless. Garrick plans to kill me soon.''

Magda sighed. "I fear the sheriff plans to keep ye quite alive.'' She stretched out one gnarly hand in front of her and opened the clenched fist. A rune lay there, the curious symbol catching the firelight. "And yet, death awaits ye if ye stay here.''

"Without Navarre, what does it matter?" Kendra whispered.

"Does his babe that grows within ye matter?" Magda opened her other hand under Kendra's nose. Another rune lay there. Kendra jerked her head up, her eyes wide with disbelief. "Aye," the old woman said, her voice a mere whisper, "this rune says you bear his son. The other that you will both die in childbirth.''

"No," Kendra said, her throat dry, her breath constricted there.

"Aye, yet there is still a chance. You must return to your own time.''

Kendra couldn't speak for a moment. She spread one hand over her belly. Could it be true? Or was Magda using this ploy to give her a reason to live? She closed her eyes. Oh, but it would give her a reason to live. To bear Navarre's child, to have a part of him to keep, to be a part of her life forever. Mac would love him as much as she, and she would never let anything happen to him or let him forget what a wonderful man his father had been. She would watch him grow to be a strong young man with dark hair and golden eyes.

Kendra's throat closed convulsively as the grief rolled over her. Gasping, she fought down the bitter emotion, determined not to fall apart in front of the sheriff. She must remain cool and calm if there was any hope of escaping him. Kendra glanced toward the man furtively, hoping he had not seen her bout with anguish.

Garrick looked up just then, and caught her gaze upon him. He turned and she saw he had the gun in his hand. A squirrel twittered in a tree nearby and the sheriff turned and lifted the pistol, took aim, and fired. The little animal dropped to the ground. A bird was also dispatched before Garrick laughed and tucked the weapon away. Then he gave Kendra a long, meaningful look as he resumed his place beside the fire.

Kendra turned back to Magda, her grief now replaced by panic, her heart pounding with new fear as she pressed her fingers against her abdomen.

"Help me go back," she whispered. Reaching out, she took the runes from the woman's hand, her fingers curling around the ancient stone.

Navarre sat beside Robin of Locksley, feeling old and tired. With the help of Little John they had made it out of Nottingham and into a secret hiding place in Sherwood Forest. Once there, Locksley would not allow his right-hand man to tarry, or lend him aid. He sent him straightaway to find King Richard and warn him of Garrick's treachery and the assassin—or assassins—stalking him.

Navarre leaned his head in his hands and shivered as the memories of the morning flooded into his mind. There had been a moment after he felt the noose tighten around his neck that a sheer, suffocating panic had seized him and he had known with a certainty that he was going to die. As the rope bit into his throat, shutting off his air, his feet kicking wildly beneath him, he had reached up with his freed hands to save himself—but the knot stayed tight around his throat. As he struggled to loosen himself, he had thought of Kendra. How unfair that after all of his years of wandering, of loneliness, he had found his heart mate, only to have her snatched from him by his own death.

He had thrashed like a fish on a hook, raging silently against God and man, dying, when suddenly he felt Robin lifting him back to the fallen box and ripping the knot open that bound the noose around his neck. What followed next was a blur. He remembered Robin shouting, pushing him down, then he saw the outlaw fall, pierced by an arrow. He reached him somehow and managed to wrest his dead weight onto his back, then Little John had appeared and spirited them both away.

Once hidden away, Navarre had removed the arrow from Robin's shoulder and bandaged the wound. Now the outlaw lay sleeping as one dead for the past four hours as Navarre impatiently waited for him to awaken. Kendra and Marian were still in Nottingham and who knew what their fate had been after the condemned men escaped? He could only pray they were all right.

Navarre flexed his fists then knotted them again. Every fiber of his being commanded him to leave Robin, to hie himself back to Nottingham, but he could not. The wound was severe, and if left unattended, Locksley could die. Even if his own conscience would let him leave, which he doubted, his love for Kendra would not. She would hate him for letting Robin die. Robin had saved his life. He was bound to stay with him, trapped in Sherwood, while Kendra could be at Garrick's mercy.

By midnight Robin was burning with fever. Navarre had cleansed the festering wound in his shoulder and bound it, but the outlaw had soon after succumbed to a sweating delirium. Now he lay shivering convulsively and Navarre knew not what else to do. The knight had covered him with everything available, which wasn't much—a cloak Little John had brought, a change of clothing—then moved him as close to the fire as was safely possible. He feared every moment the fire would lead Garrick's men to them, even though he'd built it with green wood, cutting down on the smoke.

Navarre's own wound was beginning to pain him again, as well as the burn around his neck from the hangman's noose, but he ignored both, intent on saving Robin and controlling the mad urge he felt at every moment to fly back to Nottingham to find Kendra. Now, as Robin grew worse, he sighed, and, kneeling beside the outlaw, hesitantly did something he had done only once in the last two years. Crossing himself, he began to pray. The sudden sound of hoofbeats sent the murmured prayers for help from his lips as he peered out of the thicket, drawing the dagger he'd used for Robin's surgery.

Two horses skidded to a stop nearby and, to his astonishment, he saw Marian and Friar Tuck tumble off the backs of the mounts, looking frantically into the thicket.

"Robin!" Marian cried softly, taking a tentative step toward their hiding place. "Navarre! Are you there?"

Navarre sheathed his weapon and parted the thick bushes in front of him, rising to his full height, flexing his back as he did so. He'd not realized how cramped he had been inside the leafy cave.

"What in the name of Christendom are you doing here?" he said, his voice rough but his lips smiling in welcome relief.

"Navarre!" Marian threw herself against him. "Are you all right? Alan-a-Dale told us of this place. He thought Little John might have hidden you here. Is Robin all right? Where is he?"

"Calm down, little one." Navarre hugged her tightly, then pushed her away from him, bending slightly to meet her eyes, his hands on her shoulders. "Where is Kendra?"

Marian's blue eyes clouded. "The sheriff has taken her and Magda to find the wiseman, Cennach. He wants Kendra's power of traveling through time!"

Navarre straightened. "Yes, I know. Thank God the two of you are here. I dared not leave Robin in the condition he is in but—"

With a cry, Marian dove through the bushes behind him and Navarre was left facing the priest, who smiled at him wearily.

"Will he live?" he asked, his hands folded across his tattered brown robe.

"I know not," Navarre confessed. "But now that Marian is here he will have a better chance. She is very skilled in the healing arts. I must go, immediately. Which way did Garrick go?"

"South. But wait, my son. There is something you must know. Little John did not reach the king to warn him. I have brought you his sword."

Navarre stopped in his striding toward the horses and spun back, his gaze flashing down to the weapon in the Friar's hands. "He did not? What happened?"

Tuck's voice rose, his wide brow furrowed with worry.

"Word has come to us that not ten miles from here he was thrown from his horse. He has broken his leg and cannot make the journey. Robin must be told."

"He is in no condition to be told anything."

"Navarre!" The cry came from the thicket, ragged and hoarse.

Navarre and the priest exchanged glances, then headed into the thicket. The knight would not kneel next to Robin as Tuck was doing, but stood over him, his arms crossed firmly over his chest.

"You heard?"

Robin nodded. "Navarre—"

The knight lifted one hand to stop his words. "I know what you ask and I cannot. You know I must ride after Kendra. Marian says she has been taken from Nottingham by the sheriff. Her life is in danger." He started to turn but was stopped by the sheer desperation he saw on Robin's face.

"Navarre, you must."

With a sigh, Navarre dropped to one knee, meeting the man on his level. "Listen to me," he said softly, "you are asking me to risk the life of the woman I love."

"Aye." The outlaw nodded weakly. "But has it not been her quest to make sure Richard lives? This is what Marian has told me. And I will send men after the sheriff and Kendra." He reached one hand out weakly and encircled Navarre's wrist. "You must save Richard—and England."

"If the sheriff learns the secret of time travel there will be no England to save," Navarre argued. "Stopping him must take priority. Besides, do you not remember that I am the man who wants to stop Richard? I fear you are delirious."

"You were wrong about Richard, at least insofar as he did not order Talam's death. You turned your back on your king, your friend, without ever giving him even a chance to defend himself. You plotted treason and murder against him."

Navarre swallowed hard as a lump formed in his throat and the outlaw covered one of his rough hands with his own and squeezed, his fevered gaze burning up at him.

"But in the dungeon I saw that you are still Navarre de Galliard, knight of the realm. I am giving you this chance to restore your honor. Save Richard, swear your fealty anew to him, and all will be well."

Navarre hesitated, then shook his head. "I do not know if I can."

"I will make sure Kendra is not harmed," Robin said, his fingers biting into Navarre's arm once again.

"She must return to her own time soon and I must be there when she does."

"I will make certain she delays her leaving until you return," Robin promised.

Navarre ran one hand through his hair in frustration. "Magda said the transference between our times must happen soon. I cannot journey to Normandy and beyond and return in time."

"Richard will die if you do not go."

Navarre rose, feeling the knowledge of his duty to the man who had saved his life tighten around his chest. "Send Alan instead," he said, turning away from Robin, his shoulders tense. "Or the friar."

"Does your honor truly mean so little?" Robin pushed himself up on his elbows and began to cough, grimacing as the pain shook him. Then he lay back, spent. "Alan is a minstrel, not a warrior. Tuck is too old and fat. Sorry, Father."

"You only speak the truth my son," Tuck said with a smile.

"I need you, Navarre, your strength, your ability, your sword."

"I doubt I can even lift a sword," Navarre said quietly.

Robin did not answer and the silence stretched tautly between them.

Navarre could not refuse and keep what little honor he had left. Robin knew it, and Navarre cursed the man silently for using that sense of duty against him.

"Very well," he said at last. He turned and saw Marian shrink back from the fire in his gaze, knew the mask of anger now settled there frightened her as it once had frightened Kendra. He did not care. "I shall journey to find Richard and I shall save him. Then my debt to you is paid, Locksley, and our bond, brief as it has been, will once again be broken."

He stalked out of the thicket, toward the horses Marian and

Tuck had ridden. With a start, he recognized his own horse, Kamir, outfitted in his familiar black saddle and bridle. Marian must have somehow managed to steal him back from the sheriff. He rushed to the stallion, ashamed at the leap of pure joy he experienced as he smoothed his old friend's mane. Pulling himself weakly into the saddle, he leaned down and patted the horse's neck, then straightened, tossing his hair back from his face, feeling his own strength return as he drew from the strength of the horse beneath him.

"We shall ride, Kamir," he said, staring with unseeing eyes into the forest. "We shall ride like the winds in the deserts of Outremer, and God willing, we shall save the king. But I will not leave her in the hands of Garrick, not for Locksley, not for Richard, not for honor, not for England herself."

Chapter Fifteen

The sheriff and his entourage crossed yet another river. Each mile covered seemed like a hundred to Kendra. Her horse had been equipped with a sidesaddle at first, but she had protested so violently that Garrick had finally ordered a different saddle placed on the mount. Now she wondered if riding sidesaddle would have been any easier on her posterior. Riding with her skirts hiked up was no picnic either. Goosebumps stood up on her legs like tiny mountains and she shivered constantly both from the cold and from the leering grins the sheriff gave her exposed flesh. She soon resolved that as soon as possible she would beg, borrow or steal a pair of leggings to cover her bareness.

Wearily she tried to endure what seemed sometimes to be an endless pace as they rode, often four or five hours at a time without a break. There was too much time in which to think and Navarre's death rose up before her, sending a tight hand to constrict her heart and undermine her strength. The only thing that kept her going was Magda's prophecy about the baby. The priestess, whether her prediction was true or not, had given her a new reason to live and a strong incentive to find a way back to the twentieth century.

She would return to her own time, find her life there again with her baby. This time she wouldn't be so foolish, she wouldn't risk her life on newspaper stories, she would use her time wisely, make more friends, raise her son. She would relegate this strange and mystical episode in her life to a closed chamber of her heart and mind and never think on it again.

249

But when their son was older, she would tell him, somehow, of his father, though she wondered how she could make him understand. It would be like telling him a fairy tale and saying it was true.

Now she not only wanted to return to her own time, she was anxious to do so. She had no desire to give birth in the twelfth century and if Magda's prophecies were to be believed, to do so would mean her death. There was still enough of the skeptic in Kendra to doubt the validity of the old woman's words, but if she did that would mean she might not be pregnant either, and that would mean she had lost every part of Navarre forever. It was another week before her cycle was due. Then she would know. Until then, she had to believe Magda spoke the truth. She had to.

According to Magda, during one of their cautiously whispered conferences late at night, Cennach had spent his life studying the strange circles that appeared from time to time in England. He lived secluded in a cavelike dwelling deep within a wooded valley, which the priestess had assured a tired and grumpy Garrick, they would reach that day.

When Kendra had pressed Magda about Cennach, who he was, where he came from, she had grown uncomfortable and would only say that all would be revealed when they arrived at the wiseman's home. Now, as Kendra rubbed the ache at the base of her spine, she wished it could all be over, whatever lay ahead. Weariness seemed to be settling into her bones like a living entity. She was sick of dirt and filth, sick of dodging arrows and swords, sick of leaping from one harrowing experience to another.

One corner of her mouth curved up ruefully. Wouldn't Uncle Mac love to hear that, she thought. It had taken a trip back in time where she had been thrown in a dungeon, accused of being a witch, almost killed numerous times by crazy knights and sheriffs, to bring her around. She had no greater desire in life now than to live in peace and raise Navarre's child. Her hand crept to her belly as Garrick called out for the caravan to start moving again.

Suppose she couldn't return to her own time, and suppose Magda was wrong and she and her son didn't die in childbirth?

She couldn't imagine letting her child grow up in this backward, archaic time. Not without Navarre. It was one thing to visit medieval England, quite another to raise a family there. True, she had entertained the thought of having a baby with Navarre and staying in the past with him, but now that the fantasy had become a cold reality, she knew she couldn't, certainly not without Navarre. But she might not have a choice. If Cennach couldn't help her return to the twentieth century she was stuck here, doomed to give birth in these primitive conditions. Her throat constricted and Kendra shut her eyes, willing the tears not to flow.

"Old woman!"

Garrick's voice came from in front of them. Magda pulled back on her horse's reins and Kendra followed suit, halting the golden gelding she'd been given to ride. The gold had reminded her of Navarre's eyes and she had wept the first day over its mane when Garrick wasn't looking. She patted the horse's neck, murmuring quiet encouragement as the sheriff thundered back to them and drew his white stallion up a scant few inches away from them.

"How much farther?" he demanded, his blond hair lying flat and oily upon his brow. "Where is this Cennach? I begin to doubt that he even exists. And if I find that he does not—"

"Just over this rise in the valley," Magda said. "But I must go ahead and warn Cennach, so that our welcome may be assured."

"One of the guards will go with you," Garrick said, his horse prancing beneath him, as though he sensed his master's impatience.

Magda shook her head. "If Cennach sees soldiers he will simply disappear, melt away, and we will never find him. I give you my word that I will return. Do you think I would leave Kendra in jeopardy?"

Garrick's gaze swept over the woman, hesitant, evaluating, then at last he waved her on. "Very well. I will allow you a quarter hour's lead and then we will follow. You will return to meet us and show us the way to his dwelling, or I will kill her."

Magda inclined her head, then shot Kendra a look of encouragement before turning her horse in the direction of the rise, and kicking it into a gallop. She disappeared over the top of the hill and Kendra felt a sinking sensation in the pit of her stomach. What if the woman didn't come back? What if she simply escaped into the forest, never to be seen again? She swallowed hard, willing the bile in her throat to subside. The caravan moved on, and Kendra's heart began to pound painfully.

The next few moments would decide her fate. Would Magda lead them to Cennach, who could help her return to her own time? And if she did, would the sheriff really allow her to make that journey? Worst of all, would Garrick be able to travel through time to the future, then bring back advanced weapons of war that would make him not simply England's king, but the world's?

Navarre, Navarre! her heart cried, the sorrow piercing her anew. If only you were here you wouldn't let this happen. You would stop Garrick.

After fifteen minutes Garrick gave the signal and they thundered across the English countryside, heath and gorse kicked up beneath the hooves of the horses. In the distance Kendra could see what had, in her time, been waving fields of wheat and barley like those at Avebury, and was struck with a sudden sense of déjà vu, as well as a wave of despair. How could she ever hope to return to her own time? Crop circles were anomalies—there was no way anyone could know where one would form next. It was impossible. She was doomed to die giving birth in medieval England.

Cut it out, O'Brien, her stronger, inner voice commanded. *Granted, you haven't been in a situation like this before, but you've been in some tough ones. You know about hygiene, things that could result in a safer childbirth. You'll make it, somehow, and don't forget, Marian is still your friend. If she's okay, she'll help you if you can't get back. Richard will return to England and he'll be so grateful that you helped his ward he'll want to reward you.*

The thought of King Richard being grateful to someone like her brought an amused smile to Kendra's face. It faded quickly as a shout suddenly rang out. Ahead, Garrick held up one hand for the group to stop and Kendra sighed with relief when she saw the approaching rider was Magda. She pressed her knees into the gelding's side and moved quickly through the entourage of guards and supply wagons to Garrick's side.

"He is here," the old woman said breathlessly, "and he is quite anxious to speak with both of you. He makes one condition—the guards must remain here."

Kendra glanced at Garrick, expecting an angry protest, and was surprised when the sheriff smiled, then threw his head back and laughed, the fine tendrils of short blond hair dancing in the breeze.

"Of course, I am quite capable of protecting myself." He patted his side and Kendra saw the bulge there that meant he still had the gun. There had to be some way to get the pistol away from Garrick, some way to stop his evil plan. Before she could think further, Garrick reached over and grabbed the bit of her horse's bridle, pulling her abruptly after him. They hurried over the last few yards of open country and went into the twisted forest that lay before them.

Chapter Sixteen

Navarre crossed the river Trent riding hard. He pushed himself for several days, hardly stopping to allow himself or Kamir a draught of water. He could find Kendra on his way to Normandy, he reasoned, save her from Garrick, and still keep his word to Robin. The thought possessed him as he raced across England, pausing at every inn and tavern to inquire if anyone had seen the sheriff and his entourage. Few had, but occasionally a word would come—the tale of a glimpse of a woman's auburn hair, or the sighting of an old crone—that would send him in a different direction.

The trail twisted farther and farther south toward Northampton, which led him also toward London and a ship that would take him to Normandy and Richard. By the fourth day he had lost the trail. He'd heard nothing about an auburn-haired woman in the last day's ride, and he was exhausted. At last Navarre succumbed to his body's needs and sought out the nearest inn. He took a room and tossed the innkeeper a whole crown in return for fresh clothing and a hot bath. The bath turned out to be tepid, the clothing worn, but when the knight finished his ablutions and had eaten a meal of hot mutton and potatoes that wasn't half bad, he felt almost himself again. He headed downstairs to the tavern for an ale, and hopefully, conversation that would lead him to Kendra.

He pulled up the hood of the brown cloak he had taken from Robin in the forest, letting it partially conceal his face. It was an odd garment, edged with green Celtic knots, delicately embroidered. He'd never seen the like and thought absently that it must have cost Robin quite a penny. He looked covertly around, wondering whom he should approach and casually bring the talk around to any strangers who might have passed that way.

The customers were a dirty lot, but better than the usual grade of filth found in a place like this, he acknowledged. His gaze roamed over them—a smithy, his hands black, his well-muscled arms stretching the fabric of his shirt; a number of serfs, grubby, toothless; two whores plying their trade; and a drunken priest snoring in the corner.

Besides these, there were farmers and the general riffraff a tavern attracted. Navarre had just about decided to approach the blacksmith when the innkeeper set a large mug of ale down in front of him and bent down with a conspiratorial wink.

"Didn't recognize ye at first, guv'nor," he whispered. Navarre stiffened and his right hand went to the sword he had laid on the bench within easy reach. "Then I saw yer cloak. 'Tis only one who wears that cloak. Sir Robin, how may I assist ye?"

Navarre stared up at the man blankly, then his face split into a welcoming smile. The knight leaned away from the fetid breath of the man and studied his eager companion, marveling at how the mere presence of Robin's cloak could inspire such enthusiasm. When he went upstairs later, it was to sleep his first real sleep in a week. Kendra and the sheriff had been sighted. They had stopped at this very inn to water their horses just the day before and a servant boy had overheard that they were on their way to Coventry. Now as he lay on the thin mattress the innkeeper had provided, he smiled at the thought of the loyalty shown him purely on the basis of Robin Hood's cloak. How Locksley would love hearing this story. His smile faded as he remembered that his newfound friendship with the outlaw was over, destroyed by his demands on Navarre's honor. His mouth hardened. He was breaking that word of honor even now as he pursued Kendra instead of heading directly for Normandy.

If Richard died, would Kendra hate him for not stopping the assassin in order to save her? It seemed to mean so much to her, this "preserving of history," and perhaps she was right.

It did not take a man of knowledge to know that even a small thing changed must have repercussions upon those things around it. And the death of the king of England was not a small thing. He closed his eyes. Neither was his love for Kendra O'Brien. He would find her tomorrow, he vowed, then he would save Richard.

Kendra dismounted thankfully, pulling her long skirt free of the saddle horn, ignoring the tearing sound as it caught. They had arrived at the dwelling place of Cennach, the wise. Magda had met them as promised, and led them deep into the forest until they came to a hill rising unexpectedly out of a clearing. Cennach's home blended so smoothly into the surrounding terrain that Kendra had been amazed to see the hillside they approached broken by the presence of a brown wooden door, a window, and a chimney. Upon closer inspection she realized that a round, sod-type house had been built into the side of a small hill. Part of the living space appeared to be within the hill itself and, as Kendra stared at the dwelling, she knew, with a start of amazement, that she was looking at a medieval underground house.

A box filled with bright red flowers made a splash of color beneath the window, and across the 'roofline' was a profusion of English ivy, disguising where the entryway left off and the hill began. The home was nicely camouflaged and were it not for the window box and its bright companions, it would indeed be difficult to find the place, were you not looking for it. But the oddest thing about Cennach's home was the circle of large, neolithic rocks surrounding it. Kendra recognized them as being similar to the one she had hidden behind in Wiltshire so long ago as she waited to photograph a crop circle.

Now she stepped around one of the huge stones, gazing up at it in awe, half afraid to get too close to it. There was something about this place that made her feel uneasy. She glanced around, trying to put her finger on what it was, and could not. There was an aura, a feeling permeating this place, as though fairies watched them from beneath tiny toadstools, and invisible forces waited to see if the intruders meant to do good or evil. She shivered and drew her cloak more firmly about her.

Magda walked ahead of them and paused beside one of the circle stones, then motioned for them to come forward, her gray hair rising to waft about her face in a soft wind that suddenly swept across the sheltered glen.

Kendra licked her lips and took a deep breath. She didn't believe in magic or voodoo, at least, she hadn't before a sorcerous storm had sent her back in time. Now she prepared herself for anything, for she was not certain that whoever, or whatever, they were about to encounter, was even of this world.

Magda stepped up to the door in the side of the structure and knocked loudly. "Cennach, *Fad saol agat*. Long life to you."

Garrick stood silently next to Kendra as the door slowly opened. A tall, broad-shouldered man walked out, clad in a rough brown woolen shift, a heather-gray blanket thrown around his shoulders for a cloak. White hair swept his shoulders and keen green eyes looked out of a face lined with years and wisdom. His gaze fell on Kendra and his mouth dropped open.

"*D'ar m'anam*," he said softly. "By my soul."

"You," Kendra took a tentative step forward. "It's you— Professor." Her lips parted in a relieved smile, then she frowned. "But this is impossible," she said, "you were only in your fifties when you disappeared."

"You know one another?" Garrick asked, watching her carefully.

Kendra caught herself, realizing what a foolish blunder she had made. "No," she said in what she hoped was a convincing voice. "Of course not. I beg your pardon, sir, I mistook you for someone else."

Garrick looked at her suspiciously for a moment then turned and bowed low before the older man, spreading his hands apart respectfully. "We thank you, wise Cennach, for allowing us to come and seek your counsel."

Cennach had composed himself as soon as Kendra denied knowing him, and now gave his full attention to the impatient sheriff. His dark green eyes swept over Garrick. Kendra could see him evaluating the man, weighing him, discerning his character and drawing the right, dreadful conclusion.

"Come in," he said at last, with a small bow in a general direction. "You have come a great distance."

Kendra followed Garrick, Magda, and Cennach into the house, her mind whirling. Professor Ian McKay had been one of her favorite teachers in college, a master physicist whose class she had taken by accident. He had convinced her not to drop out, promising to help her through the necessary math, and she had found the experience riveting and mind-broadening.

Now, as she watched the elderly man lead them into the interior of the sod house to a cheerful kitchen, well lit by some sort of skylight in the ceiling, she wondered how it could possibly be the same person. Ian MacKay had been in his late forties or early fifties when he disappeared. This man had to be seventy. Was it just a coincidence? A look-alike from the past? No, he had recognized her just as she had recognized him, of that she was certain.

Cennach moved around the kitchen quite gracefully for such a large man, she noted, handing out curious wooden cups and bowls, pouring out wine and spooning up stew. A crude, rectangular table sat on the dirt floor, with benches on either side. He gestured for everyone to sit and eat. Kendra suddenly realized she'd not eaten since early morning and it was now the middle of the afternoon. Kendra and Magda took seats on either side of where Cennach sat at the head of the small table and ate their stew silently. Garrick took his bowl and stood near the doorway, consuming his meal quickly as he glanced furtively out the opening from time to time.

Kendra frowned at him. Was he worried someone would find them? If so, why hadn't he brought the guards along? And who was left to even rescue them, she thought sorrowfully. Marian, perhaps? Her stomach twisted and suddenly the smell of the stew made her feel queasy. Kendra pushed the bowl away as grief, sharp and unbidden, stabbed through her. Cennach fastidiously cleaned the last of his stew with a hunk of bread, then set the bowl aside and steepled his hands together in front of him.

"Now, how may I be of assistance?" he said softly.

Kendra opened her mouth, then closed it. There was no mistaking that soft, slightly Scottish voice. It was Ian McKay!

"Magda has told me a little about your situation, milady," he said, in the same calm tones she remembered from college, his eyes warning her to play along.

"Magda tells us you know the secret of traveling to other times," Garrick said, striding over from the doorway and standing beside Cennach. "I will pay you well to share that information with me."

Cennach barely granted the sheriff the courtesy of an upward glance before turning back to Kendra. "That is yet another discussion," he said. "First I must hear the lady's request."

"I'm afraid it's really the same as the sheriff's," she said, shifting uncomfortably on the bench, "although for quite different motives," she added, darting an angry look toward Garrick. "I went to England to find a man named Ian McKay who had disappeared while doing an experiment concerning crop circles. I went to investigate. While I waited at the site of the crop circle, a terrible storm arose. I was caught in it and knocked unconscious. When I awoke, I was here, in the past. That's the short version, if you catch my drift."

Cennach had begun nodding his head and she saw that a subdued excitement had him in its grip. "Aye, your story is similar to—" he broke off, then smiled and continued "—to others I have heard."

"You mean it is possible?" Garrick said, leaning forward, his gray eyes feverishly bright. "She is telling the truth? How do you know?"

Cennach rose and moved away from the table, his brown robe flowing freely behind him. He stood with his back to them for a moment, then turned, and Kendra flashed back to her college days when McKay had taken center stage, then paused before telling some fascinating fact of science to his class. She felt the same familiar awe now as he began to speak.

"I know because I am a seer, a man of knowledge." The lines around his mouth deepened slightly as his lips curved up.

"But not a witch," Garrick said hastily. "Magda said you were not a witch or a sorcerer."

"No, I am not a practitioner of witchcraft or druidism. I have, however, seen strange things, my Lord Sheriff, things you cannot possibly comprehend. There is such a thing as time travel. Now, you may believe me, or not."

"Aye," Garrick nodded thoughtfully, "but you must admit,'tis a fanciful story."

"Fancy is sometimes confused with reality, I agree, but at times reality is not granted enough possibility of fancy."

"Cennach," Kendra began, not wanting to talk in front of the sheriff but seeing no other choice, "is there any way for me to return home?"

"Perhaps."

"I told her that if anyone could help her, it would be you," Magda said, patting Kendra's hand.

"And what of me?" Garrick broke in, jumping to his feet. "I must know the secret! All of England depends upon it!"

Cennach swept him a disdainful look. "I doubt that, my lord. As a matter of fact, I daresay England would be destroyed if men begin jumping through time, pursuing their own objectives."

The animation left Garrick's face and his hand closed around the sword at his side. Kendra heard the now all too familiar sound of metal against metal, as the sheriff drew a dagger from a short scabbard at his waist, next to his sword. He held the tip of the weapon just beneath Cennach's chin.

"I am willing to pay well for the information," Garrick said, his fingers tense around the hilt. "However, I am also willing to mete out punishment if you should refuse."

"Your threats do not frighten me," Cennach said, his face stoically composed. "I am an old man. Death holds no terror for me."

"I wonder if this young woman shares your sentiment?" Garrick asked, his handsome face wrinkling into a mocking smile. "Despite the death of her lover, I fear she desires to continue her life, in her own time. A pity." He dropped the sword from Cennach's throat then reached out and grabbed Kendra by the nape of the neck and pulled her from her seat.

She cried out as the wooden chair toppled sideways, scraping her leg, then gasped as the sheriff jerked her against him and lifted the blade to her throat.

"It would, indeed, be a pity for her life to be ended," Cennach said. Kendra swallowed hard as she saw the regret in her teacher's eyes. He wouldn't give this evil man the secret of time travel, she knew it with a certainty. Not even if it meant both their lives. Her eyelids fluttered shut as his next words confirmed her thoughts. "But I cannot tell you."

"Such a pity, especially since she carries a child." Magda gasped and the sheriff turned Kendra toward her, one arm around her waist, the other still holding the dagger. "Ah yes, my dear witch, there is little I do not know. Since I was a child, surrounded by fear and intrigue, I found I could more nearly predict the actions of my dear stepmother if I watched what she said to other people when she thought I wasn't around. Your private conversations were not always as private as you thought, my dear. Nor has your ailing stomach gone unnoticed."

"Your stepmother was an evil woman," Magda said, moving to his side, one gnarled hand on his sleeve. "She practiced the black arts and was well known to those of us who did not. Can you not see, my Lord Sheriff, that her wickedness has warped your outlook, given you a distorted sense of right and wrong?"

"Aye, you may be correct," Garrick said, "and who better to know than a fellow witch?" He turned, and without warning, plunged the dagger into Magda's chest, then wrenched it free as she sank to the floor, the front of her gown quickly turning crimson.

Kendra screamed and struggled futilely against the sheriff. The pumping blood was a sure sign a major artery had been pierced.

"Let me help her!" she cried. "In the name of God, let me help her!"

"Ah, but that would defeat the purpose, would it not?" Garrick said. "And God has very little to do with it."

Cennach hurried to kneel at the old woman's side. He pressed his hand against the wound, but even before he looked up at Kendra and shook his head she knew it was too late. He held Magda in his arms as the last of her life's blood ebbed away.

"Bastard!" Kendra screamed. "Heartless, wicked bastard!" Garrick brought the dagger back to her throat and she choked back further words, sobbing brokenly.

"Interesting, do you not think, that the great prophetess could not see her own death approaching." He chuckled, then gestured toward her broken body. "Take her outside," Garrick commanded. "I cannot bear the stench of death."

"Amazing, since it follows you like an obedient hound," Cennach said harshly. With a sigh, he picked Magda's lifeless body up in his arms and carried her outside. In a moment he was back, his green eyes flashing with anger.

"I would never help you now," Cennach said, his voice tight with control. "Do you think I would give a monster like you such power?"

"But you do not understand," Garrick said, and Kendra was chilled by the sincerity she heard in his voice. "The only way to kill a witch is to plunge a newly honed blade into her heart. I told Navarre this, but he would not yield to me. He would not yield. These two are the evil ones, not I. These two!"

"You are insane."

Kendra wracked her brain frantically for some possible means of escape. This couldn't be the way her life ended, not now, not when she was carrying Navarre's baby. Wasn't it enough Navarre had been taken from her? Wasn't it enough that she was probably trapped here in the past forever?

"Please God," she whispered aloud, "please help us."

"You do not seem to understand," the sheriff said, his voice strained. Kendra gasped as he pressed the sharp point of the dagger into the soft skin beneath her collarbone, pricking her slightly. She began to tremble as a thin stream of blood trickled down her chest. "I am the Sheriff of Nottingham," he said, his words growing more fervent, more intense, "and you must do as I command or I will kill this witch as I did the other."

"Then you must destroy us both," Cennach replied calmly, "for I will not let you kill her without a fight, and I will not tell you the secret."

"I will kill her and I will make you long for death. In the end you will tell me what I want to know."

Garrick's laughter broke against Kendra's ear and she shuddered. Her mind was blank, her ability to move, gone. In all of her adventures as a reporter she now realized she had really never worried about making it out of whatever danger she had placed herself. She had always weathered it through, using her survival skills when and if she could. If she lived, fine, if she didn't, at least she'd be with James and Nicole. Perhaps she would feel the same now, would rush headlong toward death in order to be with Navarre again, if it were not for the little life inside of her. Now she wanted more than anything to live, to have one more chance to do it right.

Kendra saw something flicker in Cennach's eyes and he walked slowly to the left, causing Garrick to turn with him until his back was squarely toward the open door. "Be still, old man. I know many ways of torture, which, I assure you would soon have you begging for death."

It was the distant sound of a horse's neigh that alerted him. Garrick turned just as a blade came crashing down, knocking the dagger from his hand. The sheriff thrust Kendra away from him and drew his sword, bringing it up barely in time to block the next sweep of his attacker's sword as metal rang out against metal like the triumphant peal of a bell in a cathedral. Kendra had fallen to the floor during the melee, and she lay there with her hands over her head, her legs beneath her, afraid to move lest she be caught in the middle of the swordplay.

Now, the sword was struck as well from Garrick's hand and it clattered to the floor. With a loud cry, the sheriff threw himself across the room, toward Kendra's crumpled figure, one hand closing around her arm as he stumbled back to his feet and pulled Kendra to hers. His bruised fingers darted to encircle her throat as he thrust her in front of him and she clawed at his hands. She froze when she got her first look at Garrick's assailant.

He stood silhouetted in front of the doorway, the sunlight behind him reverberating like a halo around him, his shoulders filling the space, his dark hair flying freely about his rugged face, his bloodied sword gripped tightly in his hand. Wordlessly he untied the cloak about his neck and flung it to one side as he stepped into the light streaming down through the skylight.

Navarre. She tried to speak his name, but Garrick's fingers bit too tightly into her neck. Navarre. How could it be? How could he be alive? Relief, painfully sweet, flooded through her as the knight, now clad only in a loose linen shirt and leggings, took a step toward her, his golden eyes burning as he stood, sword in hand, like some dark avenging angel about to deal Satan a crushing blow. Tears flooded down her cheeks.

Garrick didn't seem startled at all, and Kendra knew, as she stood trembling with reaction, that the sheriff had known all along Navarre was alive; had known, and had enjoyed torturing her by keeping the knowledge from her.

"And now the celebration is complete," Garrick said. "My old friend Navarre has arrived to be reunited with his ladylove in death. How quaint, how heroic. The kind of thing bards will sing about, no doubt."

"Surrender, Garrick," Navarre ordered, and the sound of his deep voice sent a thrill coursing through Kendra's veins. "Let Kendra go and let us put an end to this."

"And let you skewer me in cold blood? I think not, old friend. However, if you are willing to give me a more sporting chance I will be happy to release the lady."

Navarre smiled, his golden eyes narrow with hatred, and Kendra thought it was the most frightening sight she had ever seen. "Very well. Let her go and pick up your sword. But let us step outside where there is room to swing a blade."

Garrick shoved Kendra toward Navarre and he caught her. She threw her arms around his neck and pressed herself against him, kissing his chest through the V of the shirt he wore, weeping over the ragged burn encircling his neck. She ran her hands over his chest and arms, as if to reassure herself that he was real. He was alive. Navarre was alive.

The knight pulled his gaze from the sheriff long enough to bend his lips to hers. Kendra kissed his mouth, his chin, his cheekbones, his nose, laughing and crying at the same time. Cennach circled around the sheriff, never getting within arm's length as he moved to stand beside the couple.

"I thought you were dead," she whispered, "Oh, Navarre, I thought you were dead." He touched his lips to her hair briefly and Kendra felt a surge of warmth course through her.

"Nay, sweet love, I am very much alive."

"But only for a time." Garrick brandished his sword in front of him, back and forth, watching the blade, his eyes glazed. "Remember all the times we dueled together, Navarre? Testing our strength, testing one another?" He looked up and smiled. "Have you ever bested me? I think not. Why do you think you can best me now when you are ragged and weary and wounded?"

Navarre did not answer him, and instead bowed toward the door. Garrick laughed and swept out of the room with Cennach and Kendra following quickly after. The two men faced one another in the clearing, like animals—predators—Kendra thought, each waiting for the other to make his move. At last, Navarre's sword rose and the now familiar metallic sound rang out as Garrick raised his own to block the sweeping blade. As though someone had rung a bell, they began to fight in earnest.

Garrick was a good swordsman, swift and agile. Kendra watched anxiously as Navarre bore down upon the man, again and again, silver metal flashing between them, the sound of their swords echoing across the valley. She took heart, for if Garrick was a good fighter, her knight was nothing short of incredible. Kendra watched Navarre fight with a kind of awe. He was like a machine, a terminator in action, but as the fight wore on, her hope faltered. Navarre was weakening, his sword arm drooping a little more with each blow he fielded from Garrick.

"Are you ready to surrender and place yourself once again at my mercy, oh mighty Navarre, bastard friend of the great Richard?"

"I shall be happy to accept your surrender at any time, old friend."

Watching them fight was like watching an old movie, Kendra thought, as the two men squared off again and began their vicious strokes anew. Navarre was slower than Garrick but stronger. In spite of his wounds, their different strengths made them about equally matched. Metal rang out against metal and

Kendra cried out as Garrick lunged, his sword's point nicking the side of Navarre's arm. The knight recovered quickly and brought his weapon upward, knocking the blade aside.

They circled each other, then fought. Circled, then fought. Kendra felt Navarre's weariness, could see it on the sheriff's face as well. It wouldn't be long before one of the men would drop from sheer exhaustion and the other be the victor. As they circled each other again for what seemed like the hundredth time, Garrick suddenly went down in front of Kendra. She stepped back, but it was too late. Garrick rolled, sprang to his feet and grabbed her, thrusting her in front of him, his sword across her middle.

"You would hide behind a woman's skirt, Garrick?" Navarre said, approaching him cautiously, sweat dripping from his face, his breath labored. "Is there no honor left in you? I thought in spite of everything you were still a man. But perhaps I am mistaken."

The long, wide blade was instantly beneath her chin and Navarre froze in his tracks. Kendra stiffened as well, afraid to breathe, let alone move.

"I would not say such things if I were you, my friend," Garrick whispered. "I fear it would cause great consternation for you if your ladylove's head were to roll at your feet. Put down your sword."

"Aye," Navarre said, dropping his sword to the ground and spreading his hands apart. "Very well, Garrick. Kill me if you must, but let her go. Let her go back to where she belongs."

"She shall, indeed, return." Garrick raised one blond brow. "And do not fear for her, dear Navarre, for I shall be at her side."

Kendra's mouth went suddenly dry as she shot Cennach a desperate look. She'd rather die here and now, with her baby, than risk this madman having access to Navarre's child, as well as the rest of her time's weapons and evils. The wiseman nodded imperceptibly and she knew he wouldn't tell Garrick the secret. Wouldn't willingly tell, she thought frantically, but what if Garrick tortured him? How much could a man bear before he broke and confessed all?

"Let her go, Garrick, and I swear I will do whatever you ask."

"Would you really?" Garrick lowered the sword and gazed at Navarre thoughtfully. "Of course, I think you know what I shall require of you, my dear, dear friend. Hmm, interesting. I will think upon your offer, but first things first. You will kneel before me, Navarre de Galliard."

Navarre hesitated, then moved in front of the man and knelt. Garrick began to laugh, the sound chilling Kendra as she choked back an angry protest.

"At last, old friend, you are in the right position—at my feet, begging for my mercy. Stay there a moment and let me look at you, let me grow used to the adulation of my people."

"Of course, my Lord Sheriff," Navarre said, bowing his head respectfully. Kendra stared down at him, wide-eyed. What was he up to?

"Soon you will call me 'Sire,' " Garrick said, the crazed light returning to his eyes. "So begin now, please. 'Of course, Sire'."

"Of course, Sire," Navarre said. "I bow humbly before you and offer up my fealty to you."

Kendra felt Garrick release her abruptly, and startled, she ran to Cennach's side, clutching his arm as she wondered what in the world Navarre was up to. The sheriff stepped toward the kneeling figure, his mouth open, his eyes glazed.

"Will you truly, Navarre?" His voice was breathless, his chin-length blond hair falling over his forehead like a child's. " 'Tis more than I hoped for. But if you are willing, we may join together once again." His face was flushed, his smile too bright. "If you will, I promise that together we shall rule England."

Kendra watched the insanity sparkle in the man's eyes and glanced at Navarre kneeling on the ground before him. Garrick still held his sword and Kendra's heart began to flutter like a dove within her chest as the sheriff stopped directly in front of Navarre, the blade in his hand.

Suddenly Garrick lifted his chin, and Kendra marveled not for the first time at the beauty of the man's face. In that moment the sheriff looked quite regal, quite kingly in his craziness, and she felt a sudden pity for him. She quickly dismissed the emotion as he lifted the sword and balanced the flat of the blade on Navarre's shoulder.

"Navarre de Gaillard, I, Garrick, King of England, am about to dub thee a true knight of the realm. Do you swear fealty to me as your king from this day forth?"

He's completely insane, Kendra thought fearfully. *What if Navarre doesn't respond the way he expects him to?* She couldn't imagine Navarre swearing fealty to him, not even to save her.

"Aye, Garrick," Navarre said. "I promise I will swear fealty to you as my king," he looked up solemnly, his golden eyes steady. "On the day we meet in hell."

With a roar of outrage, Garrick lifted the sword above his head and brought it down. Navarre rolled away, the blade missing him by inches. His foot shot out, striking the sheriff in the knee with a loud crack. As the man went down, Navarre wrenched the sword from his hand, then rolled to his feet and stood panting, his golden eyes flashing his victory.

"I yield, I yield," Garrick said, his voice muffled. "I am beaten." His body was curled up almost in a ball as he began rocking back and forth, his hands stuffed inside the open edges of his tunic.

"Stand up," Navarre commanded.

As the man on the floor slowly uncurled, Kendra went cold. The gun. Garrick still had the gun.

"Navarre, the gun!" she screamed just as Garrick sprang to his feet and whirled, the Smith and Wesson in both hands.

"No," she said, shaking her head as the despair came crashing down on her. "No."

"Ah, yes, my sweet Kendra. Yes, yes, yes. Now I hold the power, and I shall have the unique privilege of letting my dear friend Navarre watch you die, a little piece at a time. I see you remember this little instrument of power, eh Sir Knight?" His features hardened. "Put up your sword."

Navarre glared at him, shaking with anger and frustration, then with an oath, resheathed his sword. "Why are you doing this, Garrick?" he asked savagely. "We were friends once. Why do you hate me so now?"

Garrick's face twisted, his thin lips curling back from his teeth, his eyes narrowing. "Why do I hate you, dear Navarre? Perhaps because it is my lot in life to hate. Perhaps because in spite of the fact that your upbringing was very nearly as horrible as mine, you rose above those dreadful memories in a way that I never could. Perhaps I hate you because you never respected me the way you respected Richard."

Kendra looked up at Navarre, and saw sadness mirrored in the eyes of the man she loved.

Kendra trembled in Navarre's arms as Garrick's eyes grew wilder, his voice more strained.

You reject me, just like her—like that witch who was my mother." The gun in his hand dipped as he wiped the moisture from his face. "I killed her you know," he said, the maniacal grin faltering for a moment, then returning full force. "Yes, I killed her with my own hands, with a newly honed dagger in the heart. 'Twas the only way I could be free of her incantations, of her spells."

The smile faded and suddenly Kendra had a fearful glance at the little boy who had endured a demented woman's torture. His gray eyes clouded and he looked down at the gun he held as though he had never seen it before. His lower lip began to tremble.

"She would sing to me, sometimes," he said softly, "after she had—had done things. And the songs were so sweet it almost made the pain worth enduring."

Navarre carefully moved Kendra away from him, his body tensed like a lion about to spring. The sheriff saw the motion and snapped the gun back level between them, his gaze clearing and his smile returning.

"Pain can be so sweet, can it not, Navarre? At least, to the one inflicting it. I shall greatly enjoy inflicting many kinds of sweet, sweet pain on your lady, and letting you watch. Now, how shall we begin? I think that first I must at least partially disable you in order to fully enjoy this lovely lady at my leisure. After all, I do not want to be interrupted by a mad knight's quest for vengeance."

"Stop now and I will not kill you," Navarre said, his voice dangerously low as he placed Kendra firmly behind him.

"I cannot stop, dear Navarre," the sheriff said, cocking the gun and squinting one eye as he aimed the barrel at Navarre's belly. "Have you ever had a gut wound, old friend? No? Ever seen a man die from a gut wound? Ah, yes, in the Crusade. Then you know it takes quite a long time and is very painful. I think such an injury would give me the time I need in which to relish your lady, and would protect me from any heroic tendencies you might feel compelled to exercise."

Kendra's heart pounded so loudly she felt sure everyone else could hear it. If Garrick shot Navarre in the stomach at this distance it wouldn't make him die slowly but would instantly kill him. Forgotten was the baby, the chance to travel back to her own time. She couldn't bear to lose him again. She couldn't.

"Let us begin," Garrick said.

"No!" Kendra ran the short distance separating them and threw her entire body weight against Garrick, managing to wrench his arm up slightly just as she felt the pistol recoil and heard the shot resound across the glen. They fell to the ground together, rolling across the rough terrain as each fought for possession of the weapon. The sheriff twisted her arm savagely and Kendra screamed as Garrick wrenched the gun away from her and sprang to his feet, pointing the gun directly at Navarre's heart.

"I grow weary of battling your wenches, Navarre," Garrick shouted, "and so I must dispense with allowing you a lingering death." A drop of spittle trickled from the corner of his mouth and his eyes became unfocused, clouded. "Now it is ended, my friend," he said sorrowfully. "Now it is over."

Kendra jumped to her feet and ran to Navarre just as she heard the fatal click of the trigger and . . . nothing happened. She spun around to see the sheriff staring down into the muzzle of the gun, his brows knit together.

Out of bullets! she thought gleefully. And not another one to be found in the entire twelfth century! A new thought seized her. Had the gun merely misfired?

Before she could warn Navarre, he let out a ferocious roar of rage and shoved her out of the way, drawing his sword once again. Garrick took one look at the furious knight and fled, stumbling backward over the rocky ground. Halfway to his horse he turned at last and ran, flinging himself on the back of the white stallion, and pulling himself barely erect before digging his heels into the startled horse's side, sending it leaping into action. Kendra felt her knees give way with relief, and she crumpled to the ground. She cried out as Navarre tore after the man and threw himself on the back of Kamir, his face dark with rage.

"Navarre, wait!" she cried, stumbling to her feet and running to block the way of his prancing black stallion. Kamir reared back on his hind legs as her arms began flailing in front of him and she screamed as one hoof came perilously close to her face.

"Kendra!" Navarre jerked Kamir's head to one side and the horse's hooves came down only inches away from where she stood. Undaunted but breathless, she grabbed the reins of the steed and glared up at the knight.

"You aren't going after him, Navarre!" Kendra shouted. "You don't understand—there may still be another bullet in the gun. It may have misfired!"

"All the more reason I must follow him. Where do you think he is headed?" He shouted back. "You heard his tirade—do you think he will stop now? He is going after Richard!"

"Then let someone else stop him!"

"Nay, you are safe now and I must honor my promise! Let go of the bridle, Kendra, and get out of the way!"

Kendra stepped back from the horse, feeling as though she'd been kicked in the stomach as Navarre's horse plunged forward, carrying the Black Lion back into battle.

Chapter Seventeen

Kendra stared after Navarre, feeling stunned as she watched him disappear into the forest. Then she felt anger, red hot and furious. All this time she'd been talking herself blue trying to convince him not to kill Richard and now that she needed him, was about to leave his life forever, now he had to be a hero and save the king! Shaking her fist after him impotently she turned to face Cennach, feeling her old investigative reporting adrenaline starting to flow—only this time she would use it for a much more personal goal.

"He isn't leaving me behind," she said, in a tone meant to brook no opposition. "I need your help. Please pack food for me and let me borrow some of your clothing."

"Kendra," he said, walking slowly toward her, his white brows pressed together disapprovingly, "I feel I should warn you that if you interfere in Navarre's quest, King Richard could truly be killed and all of history changed."

"I don't care!" she said petulantly, even though she felt a warm flush of embarrassment wash over her. "He's not going to leave me like this." Tears brimmed in her eyes and she brushed the moisture away brusquely. "I'm sorry. Of course I care, but I'm not going to stop him. I'm going to help him. Now will you help me or not?"

Cennach shook his head. "No, my dear. Navarre is an excellent horseman and you would never catch up with him. You would be making yourself vulnerable to every piece of highway riffraff in England. Besides, you have no way of knowing where he's gone."

Kendra turned away from the man, arms folded tightly across her chest. "I know exactly where he's gone—to save King Richard. Well, that's just fine but he's not doing it without me. If he can find him, so can I."

The old professor crossed and placed his arm around her shoulders, which smelled faintly of lavender and herbs. Kendra steeled herself against the rational tone of his voice. "A frantic ride on horseback day and night to catch up with Navarre would be most ill-advised. Remember, you carry Navarre's child. Don't you owe it to him and to yourself to protect that child? On top of everything else, you could miss your opportunity to return to your own time."

He squeezed her shoulder comfortingly and Kendra couldn't help but feel his calm seeping into her frazzled nerves, but she shook her head anyway, furious at herself for being unable to stop the cascading tears. Damn Navarre for his blasted honor, and damn Cennach for being an old man who couldn't ride with her to catch the wretched knight!

Kendra pushed a lock of wavy auburn hair back from her face, feeling immediately ashamed. If Navarre didn't have his damnable code of honor he wouldn't be Navarre. And of course, Cennach was right. She couldn't take off on her own, it was too dangerous. If it was just herself, she wouldn't hesitate, but she had to think of her baby. Already the events of the day had taken their toll on her strength. She felt dizzy and sick to her stomach and her hands were shaking. The weakness of her own flesh, now, when she needed her strength, made her even angrier.

"I know, I know," she cried in frustration, shaking off his comforting arm and pacing back and forth, waving her fists in the air. "But you don't understand. I'm never going to see him again!"

"How do you know?"

She stopped in her tirade and looked back at him. "What did you say?"

"I said, how do you know you'll never see him again? Kendra, I have traveled back and forth between our two times. There's no reason to think that you may not be able to do the same."

273

Tess Mallory

Kendra stared at him. "Sort of like a commuter marriage, you mean? I live on the east coast and he lives on the west and we visit from time to time." She laughed bitterly, pressing her palm against her head. "From time to time—that would be funny if it wasn't so awful. Besides, I can't come back and see him if he's dead, can I?"

"Your logic is indisputable," he said gently.

"Besides, I . . ." she hesitated, averting her eyes ". . . I don't want to travel back and forth through time." She looked up and met the professor's compassionate gaze, cursing herself inwardly for her cowardice. "I've faced a lot of things in my life, Professor, but this is one experience I don't want to repeat if I can help it. He—" she broke off as the sound of hoofbeats thundered suddenly across the valley.

Kendra whirled in the direction of the noise, terrified that more of the sheriff's men had followed them. With relief she saw there were only three horses, slowing to a walk as they approached. To her astonishment, riding the first was Marian, of all people, followed by an obviously wilting Robin Hood, and Friar Tuck, quite uncomfortable on his bony steed, which looked none too happy at hauling his hefty load.

"Marian!" Kendra cried, running to her friend's side and helping her dismount. "Whatever are you doing here? How did you find us?"

"Robin can track anyone, anywhere," she said, laughing and shaking out her hair. "But where is Navarre?" Marian asked, peering around. "Robin said he recognized his horse's tracks."

"Yes, he was here, but he's gone." Kendra turned and saw Robin limping up to her, his face set in lines of exhaustion, one arm held across his middle. "He's—"

"A moment, Kendra. Sit down, love," Marian crooned to Robin. "Is there any fresh water? He would insist on coming as soon as he could even sit up without falling over, though I ordered him not to." She peered at Kendra. "You do not look well yourself. You are pale beyond belief."

"I will get water," Cennach said, and moved quickly into the house as Robin eased himself down on a broad, flat rock.

Friar Tuck came puffing up behind them, his usually jolly

274

face set in dark lines of fatigue. "Looks like a battle was fought here," he said, glancing around at the dark stain of blood still evident on the ground. "Was the sheriff—"

"He was here, but he got away." Tiny black spots were dancing in Kendra's line of vision and she willed them mentally to stop.

The outlaw stood slowly, the steel in his eyes matching his voice. "Where is Navarre?"

Kendra tried to clear her thoughts as the weakness she had felt earlier swept over her again. Slowly she formed the words, pushing back the encroaching blackness.

"He fought Garrick, but he escaped, and now Navarre has gone to find Richard." A sudden surge of strength sent her a moment's clarity. The bullets. There had been six to start with. She had fired one at Navarre. The sheriff had fired how many? Two? Four? She wasn't sure. The wave of blackness shimmered in front of her. If Navarre were killed, if Garrick used the gun on him—she took a deep breath and when she spoke her voice was limp with fear. "He has the gun, Robin, and he's gone after the king."

Robin's face paled and Kendra saw a dart of pain enter his eyes. She swayed and he took her arm, guiding her to the flat rock. "I must leave at once," he said softly.

"Oh, no, you won't," Marian said, her stern tones causing Kendra to rally a bit and raise both brows in surprise at the change in the maid once meek and mild. "You are too weak to do anything of the sort."

Robin sighed with exaggerated patience. "Marian, do not think I will allow my love for you to make me into a coddled egg," he snapped. "My king needs me and I will leave as soon as I rest a few moments and water my horse."

Marian fumed, then spoke again, in a petulant voice. "And how long do you suppose you will last on a long journey to Normandy, in your condition?"

"He will not have to travel to Normandy," Friar Tuck said. "Word has come to Prince John from Phillip of France that, as he put it, ''the devil has been loosed.'' Richard has been ransomed and is due to arrive in England any day. Once here he will be crowned in a new coronation ceremony in Canterbury."

Cennach handed Robin a dipper of water and the outlaw took it gratefully.

"Prof—I mean, Cennach, this is Robin of Locksley," Kendra said. The older man bowed to Robin, who inclined his own head respectfully.

"Magda spoke well of you," Robin said. "I wish there were time for pleasantries, and I do not wish to be rude, but have you anything to eat, my friend? I must leave at once but we have not eaten since early this morning."

"Yes, of course, I will prepare something." The professor turned and went into the house.

"Where is Magda?" Robin asked abruptly.

Kendra felt the pain anew as she told Robin the terrible news of the old woman's death. When she finished, the outlaw's lips were pressed tightly together and fire flashed in his blue eyes. Marian moved to stand beside him, her arm linked through his, offering support, as Friar Tuck stood nearby looking helplessly dazed.

"Magda, dead?" he whispered.

"Damn the man!" Robin swore, slicing the air with his fists. "I will cut out his black heart when I find him!" He cursed again, roundly, then sighed and ran one hand through his hair in frustration. "Cennach!" he called out. "I must be on my way!"

Kendra crossed to Robin and laid one hand upon his arm, her eyes flashing with determination. "I'm going with you."

The professor appeared at the doorway of his home, holding a cloth sack, his face wreathed in concern. "Kendra, I beg you to think of your baby."

"Baby?" Robin opened his mouth, shut it, then opened it again as he stared wordlessly at Kendra. Marian stared as well, her lips forming an oval, her blue eyes blank with shock. Kendra sighed, then started to tell them about Magda's final prophecy, when Friar Tuck spoke up, his voice filled with grief.

"Where is Magda's grave?" he asked. "We must pay our respects."

"Aye," Robin agreed, finding his voice, "she helped us so

often in Sherwood that I often jested and told her she must begin wearing Lincoln green.''

"We have not even had time to bury her," Cennach said apologetically.

"I will bury her," Friar Tuck said, fingering the cross hanging from the chain around his waist. "Please, take me to her."

"Forgive me, Father, for not helping you," Robin said, patting the priest on the shoulder, "but I must go, I must stop him." The sorrow in his eyes shifted to steel. "We are not so very far from Canterbury." Robin took the sack of food from Cennach and walked back to his horse as Marian followed, arguing a blue streak. At last he turned and placed both hands on her shoulders, gazing down into her eyes, effectively silencing her.

"I will go," he said. "Now stop this childishness and be silent as becomes a maid. Come, kiss me good-bye and I'll bring you something pretty from Canterbury."

Kendra stifled a laugh as Marian's mouth dropped open. The young woman recovered quickly however and stamped her foot as she glared up at the smiling man.

"Something pretty from Canterbury? Think you that I am a child? That you can wave a pretty ribbon in my face and I shall leap for joy and clap my hands and do your bidding? Get you gone, Robin of Locksley, and I care not if you ever come back."

She turned away from him, arms folded decisively across her chest. Robin laughed and pulled her back around and into his arms, planting a kiss firmly on her unyielding lips. She glared up at him, then squealed indignantly as he slapped her bottom before turning to mount his horse.

"You—you—you outlaw!" she spluttered, and lifting her dainty foot, slammed it into his own posterior.

Robin spun around, his eyes wide with shock. He burst into laughter and kissed her again. "Ah, Marian, I knew there was spirit in you. I shall be back before you know it."

"Wait, I'm going with you," Kendra said. "It will only take a moment to change my clothes." Robin shot her a startled look and Marian turned to her in alarm.

"Kendra, you mustn't," Marian said in horror. "You might lose the babe!"

"I have been telling her that very thing." Cennach crossed to her side.

"Poppycock," Kendra scoffed. "Women in the twentieth century ride horses, swim, do aerobicize, all the way to term." Just thinking about her modern counterparts filled her with a new sense of her own ability and Kendra stood, relieved to find the bout of weakness had passed. She was a strong woman and must stay strong, not allowing the antiquated beliefs of these backward people to influence her actions.

"Aerobicize?" Marian said, rolling the word over her tongue.

"All right, Kendra," Cennach conceded, "but what about returning to your own time? We have not yet discussed this and there is much you must know. For one thing, there may not be a lot of time left to you."

"What do you mean?"

"It will take time to explain."

"Time! This may sound funny coming from a time traveler, but I don't have time for this right now," Kendra said, exasperated.

"Kendra," Marian interrupted, "you have told me much about where you came from and you will be much better off giving birth there. Do you know how many babes never see their first birthday here?" A sob caught in her throat. "Oh, Kendra, if I could have my child in a place as clean as you have described to me, I would not let anything stop me."

"Your child? Marian, you aren't—"

"No, no," she said hastily. She glanced up at Robin. "But we hope to have children, one day." The outlaw leaned down and took Marian's hand.

"Aye, my love, that we will, and every one of them will be strong and fair." He turned back to Kendra. "Now, young lady, will you be good?"

Kendra sighed and nodded. "All right. But I don't like it. Thank you, Robin," she added. "Please, will you give Navarre a message for me?" She looked down at her stomach, cradled beneath her hand. "Tell him that I love him."

A shadow crossed Robin's face. "Aye," he said softly, "if I have the chance."

Kendra frowned at his words, wondering if perhaps Robin had had a premonition of some kind that he wouldn't return, that he would be killed. She'd read of men going into battle having clear visions of their own deaths. But that seemed unlike the practical Robin Hood. She continued to ponder his words as the outlaw leaned down again and kissed a somewhat appeased Marian on the lips.

"I am sure Marian will want to see you off on your journey," he said, "and so will I, if possible. Where will the departure take place?"

"Wiltshire," Cennach said from behind them. They turned and he lifted both brows, his green eyes curiously gentle. "You have come full circle, Kendra. Your destiny lies once again upon the Abury plains."

Robin nodded, then reached for Kendra's hand. She glanced up at him, perplexed at the gentle way he lifted her fingers to his lips, and the stark pain she saw reflected in his eyes.

"I am sorry, Kendra. Perhaps you may take comfort in the fact that what I do, I do for England. I will spare him if I can." He dropped her hand and shot Marian a loving look, then spurred his mount forward and disappeared into the forest.

Kendra stared after him, his words sending a paralyzing fear coursing through her body. What had he said? He would spare him? He would spare whom? Not Garrick, certainly, for why would Robin think his life or death would concern her? Not Richard. Icy fingers gripped her throat and her eyes fluttered shut. She heard Marian cry out and Cennach as well, then strong hands were guiding her back to the house. She sank down on the front step and began to tremble.

"He thinks Navarre has the gun," she whispered. "He thinks it is Navarre who is going to kill the king."

The blackness overtook her after all.

After she regained consciousness, it took both Cennach and Marian to keep Kendra from jumping on her horse then and there and following Robin. At last she could see that her struggles were in vain and she allowed them to take her into the house and tuck her, still protesting, into bed. The professor gave her a glass of wine to help her "brace up." Then he went out to help Friar Tuck in the grisly duty of burying Magda. Marian sat perched on the bed beside a pale Kendra.

"I must go after him," Kendra told her, taking her hand and pressing it fervently. "You don't understand. I was rambling when Robin first arrived and said something about Navarre going to find Richard. I was thinking about Garrick and how he had the gun and I blurted out, 'He has the gun'! Now Robin thinks Navarre is going to kill the king! Don't you understand what I'm saying?"

"Oh, I do not think he misunderstood you," Marian said in a soothing voice. "He told me that he and Navarre became quite close during their time together in the dungeon. I assure you, they are good friends now. Navarre even promised that he would ride to stop an assassin from killing Richard, although he knew it meant leaving you at the mercy of the sheriff."

"But don't you see—" Kendra seized the cool cloth Marian had placed on her brow and threw it across the room "—that's exactly why Robin may have doubts. Navarre didn't go directly to save Richard. He rescued me instead!"

Marian bit her lower lip and looked more anxious at that, then shook her head. "Robin would never hurt Navarre. He knows how much he means to me."

Kendra closed her eyes and leaned back against the pillow. It was no use. She would simply have to wait until everyone was asleep and then make her move. It was close to sunset already. She opened her eyes to tell Marian that she wanted to be alone for a while, only to find the young woman staring at her, her own eyes filled with pain.

"Kendra, are you sure you are with child?" Her voice was hushed and Kendra looked away from her stricken face, hoping she wasn't going to have to endure a lecture from a teenager on the evils of giving birth to an illegitimate child.

"I honestly don't know, Marian. All I know is that Magda said I was, and I am beginning to suspect she spoke the truth." She brushed one hand wearily over her forehead. "Cennach says Magda was hardly ever wrong in her predictions.''

"Magda always spoke the truth," the young woman said.

Kendra turned back at the strained sound of her voice. Marian's lower lip trembled and she looked as though tears were imminent.

"Marian," Kendra said, "what in the world is wrong with you? It's a baby, not the plague. Things could be worse."

"Robin seemed concerned," Marian whispered.

"Robin? I don't know why he should be."

"Then it is not . . . he is not . . ."

Come the dawn. Kendra groaned mentally. "Of course not, Marian."

Marian looked down at her hands, her lower lip still quivering. "I saw the way Robin looked at you while we were at his camp, and—and the two of you did walk together, unchaperoned in the forest quite often."

"I swear to you," Kendra said, squeezing Marian's hand tightly. "I never, ever had a thing with Robin. No way, not at all. He's a nice guy, but he's all yours. This is Navarre's baby."

The relief flooded across the young woman's face. "Oh, Kendra, I am so very glad. Does Navarre know?"

"No," she sighed. "I didn't have a chance to tell him."

"When will you be married?" Marian asked, now swelling with excitement. "You must let me help you plan everything. I have a lovely dress I've never worn. You are welcome to it, it is the color of violets and would look so well with your hair, and the girdle is gold. The surcoat is of a deep purple and—" she broke off, then frowned at Kendra. "What is so amusing?"

Kendra burst out laughing, fighting to keep from dissolving into hysterical tears. "You are, you sweet girl. Planning all of these wonderful things, but it's impossible."

"Why?" She studied Kendra's face and nodded. "I see, you think he will not return, but I say that he will. Robin will not kill him, and Navarre loves you more than anything. I have seen it in his eyes and when he returns I know he will marry you."

"Even if he comes back, I'm going home, Marian." Ken-

Tess Mallory

dra's voice was tight with anguish. "I've asked him to go with me but he refuses." She stopped and covered her face with both hands. Going home. Leaving Navarre. How could one thought bring such joy and the other such grief?

"I brought you your bag," Marian said, her eyes soft with sympathy. She went outside and after a few minutes came back carrying the familiar leather satchel. "You left it behind and I thought you might need your things."

Kendra opened the bag and was surprised and pleased to find both of her cameras. "Thank you, Marian."

"Do you feel like coming outside?" Cennach said, poking his head in suddenly at the doorway. "We are going to have a brief ceremony for Magda."

"Of course," Kendra said, throwing the light coverlet off of her. She stood and took Marian's hand. "Come, Marian, let's tell her good-bye."

The forest did not lend itself well to digging graves since the ground was covered with bracken, bramble, tree roots, and rocks, but Friar Tuck and Cennach had managed to carve a shallow grave for Magda. As the brief service came to an end and the sun set behind the hills, the two men shoveled what dirt there was into the grave, then the four of them worked quickly to cover the grave with rocks to keep animals from desecrating the makeshift tomb.

"I'm afraid we have yet another task left to us," Friar Tuck said abruptly as he stood from his task and eased his back with one hand. "As we approached the forest, in yon glen we saw some of Garrick's men. Navarre must have killed them before he arrived here."

"That duty must wait until morning, my friend," Cennach said. "The night is not safe. Predators abound."

"Aye," said the priest, nodding. "I confess I feel no great compunction to make sure their souls reach a safe haven, wicked as that may sound. I will to bed. These bones grow wearier by the minute."

"The women will sleep in the small bedroom and I have coverlets on the floor in the larger room for us," Cennach said. "I will be in shortly." The priest said his good nights, then he rose and disappeared into the house, his shoulders still slumped dejectedly.

"I, too, am ready to sleep." Marian stifled a yawn. "Kendra, are you coming?"

Kendra turned toward Cennach, feeling infinitely tired and all too aware of how much farther she had to go before this night was over.

"Cennach, I know you are as weary as I am, but we can't put this off any longer." She moved toward the old man and laid one hand gently across his arm. "Tell me how I can get back home."

Chapter Eighteen

Marian's eyes widened. "Suddenly I am not sleepy at all." She sat back down beside Kendra, her hands clasped around her knees, her expression expectant.

Cennach smiled at the eager look on her face, then turned to Kendra. "It is quite a tale. Are you sure you don't want to wait until tomorrow to hear it?"

Kendra nodded, fighting the impatience she felt even as she knew she must hear Cennach's words. Right that moment she wanted nothing so much as to ride after Robin and stop him, to warn Navarre, but for the sake of her child she had to sit here and listen to Cennach's story.

The professor was silent for a very long time, and Kendra had to control herself to keep from jumping up and shaking the words from the man. At last, he began to speak.

"Marian does not know I am from another time." He glanced over at her and she smiled.

"After meeting Kendra," she said, "I began to suspect perhaps that was why you knew such wondrous things you taught me about, things she seemed to be aware of also."

Cennach nodded. "Very astute of you, my dear. Magda always said you were my best student."

"The professor is the man who was teaching you about science," Kendra said thoughtfully, shivering against the cold night air. She turned back to Cennach. "Did Magda know, I mean that you were from another time?"

"Yes. She sought me out when she heard of the "madman" living in the forest." He gestured to Marian. "You see, Marian, in my own time I was a university professor, a teacher, and I taught my students exactly what I've been teaching you for the last few years. I had been studying the relationship between phenomena—those are unusual and unexplainable occurrences—and physics for many years, always from a skeptic's point of view. One of those phenomena was that of the mysterious crop circles. I had read a great deal about the circles and when I heard a contest was to be held in England, offering a prize to the person able to duplicate a crop circle, I decided to come over.''

''I remember reading about that,'' Kendra interjected. ''It was said that the man-made crop circle was exactly the same as the 'real' crop circles.''

''Wait, what is a 'crop circle'?'' Marian asked, her pale brows pressed together.

Quickly Kendra explained the mysterious circles that had led her to England in the first place. Marian smiled and Kendra couldn't help but notice the difference in the attractive young woman sitting beside her and the mousy teenager she had first met in Nottingham.

''Oh, you mean the fairy circles. I've always known they were magical. Do you mean they have something to do with your travels through time?'' Her eyes widened again and her hand slipped through the crook of Kendra's arm, like a child at a horror movie who needs reassurance. Kendra laughed softly and squeezed her hand.

''I am getting to that,'' Cennach said, frowning at her with what Kendra recognized as a dearly familiar gesture. ''I went to England to make my own decision regarding the 'contest' and found that something amazing had happened. While one crop circle was being manufactured—and it literally took six to seven hours—a so-called 'real' crop circle appeared in a nearby field in what locals report was less than an hour's time. I observed both the fabricated circle and the one which appeared so quickly, prepared to find no differences.'' He paused dramatically and Kendra leaned toward him.

''And?'' she prodded.

''There were striking differences in the way the stalks were pressed down, at least, differences that could be seen under the microscope. I also observed something rather extraordinary."

"Little green men?" Kendra asked flippantly, then smiled as the professor frowned down at her.

"A blue light, accompanied by a popping sound, appeared as I walked through the 'real' circle."

"Did you say a blue light? I saw blue lights!"

"Did you, now?" His green eyes twinkled with the good humor she remembered from his class. "Well, I began to do more research on the subject, studying the work of other physicists. I began to be fascinated with the possibility that some power was actually creating the circles, or was generated by the circles, and as I studied more, I began to feel there was an intelligence behind the creations."

"Intelligence? Do you mean like aliens from another planet?" Kendra frowned at the old man.

Cennach shook his head. "I don't know for certain what I mean, but tell me, when you crossed through the portal, before you passed out, did you feel anything unusual?"

Kendra considered the question. "Well, I'm not sure," she said. "It felt as if a magnet were pulling me into the center of the circle, and there was a buzzing feeling under my skin—but, yes, now that I think about it, before I was pulled into the circle, I felt like someone was there, watching me, or following me."

"Yes." Cennach nodded. "I had the same experience."

"Wait a minute." Kendra sat up straighter, her mind whirling with Cennach's words. "You said portals. Do you mean the circles themselves are portals of time?"

"It isn't the circles themselves that are the portals I speak of, but the force which forms the circles. That power creates a portal—an entryway if you will—to other times. It is in the midst of its creation that the time portal opens."

He drew his knees up to his chest and gazed up at the stars beginning to appear before going on. "I've spent the last twenty years trying to figure out the mathematics as well as the physics, but simply put, when a circle is being formed, intensely powerful magnetic waves are harnessed into a kind of 'whirlpool' or 'tornado' effect that pushes the grain in the field down into the intricate patterns. Some people believe there are certain places in the world where these magnetic waves are more powerful, more concentrated. My theory is that these waves also possess a heretofore undiscovered quality that disrupts the time-space continuum.''

"Wow," Kendra said.

"Wow," Marian echoed, then tried the new word again under her breath a few times until Kendra poked her with her elbow.

The two women were silent for a long moment, then Kendra lifted her own gaze to the star-studded sky. "But what creates the magnetic waves?"

Cennach frowned. "Therein lies the mystery. Is it the work of extraterrestrials playing god with lowly humans? Is it God Himself? Is it a natural phenomenon that has unnatural consequences? All were possibilities I had to consider. As to why the portal opened into this particular time period, I do not know."

"But if they opened to the same time, why are you so old?" Kendra blurted, asking the question that had been on her mind since the beginning of their conversation. "You were a young man when you disappeared."

Cennach laughed and rose stiffly to his feet. "Thank you my dear. I was actually a middle-aged man of fifty-one illustrious years. One night I was sitting in a field of wheat that had been known to be frequented by crop circles and a forming one took me away. I was transported back in time also, but to the year 1171, not 1194. Why my circle took me to a different year, again, I do not know." He spread his hands apart. "I have been living here for the last twenty-three years."

"Did you ever try to return?" Marian asked.

"Yes, I did. That is how I learned the secret of time travel. Tell me, Kendra," he said abruptly. "How long have you been in the past?"

She shrugged. "When I arrived it was the middle of February, so almost two months, I guess." Apprehension gripped Kendra's chest. "What's wrong? There isn't some kind of time limit, is there?"

Cennach shook his head. "I have no idea if the portals will

open indefinitely for a traveler, or if there are time constraints, but I suggest we do not delay. You must seek out your circle.''

"Seek out my—Cennach, this is all very confusing,'' she said. Marian nodded silently. The sun was gone and the night air chilling. Kendra's cloak had been used to wrap Magda's broken body and she rubbed her arms vigorously, refusing to allow herself to think about the priestess. "So, cut to the chase, Professor, please, and tell me how do I get home?''

"Be patient, my dear. I am getting to that. After a couple of months of observing medievalism, I felt I should try to find a way to return to my own time. As a scientist it seemed imperative to return and write about my experiences—one experience in particular.''

"One experience?''

He sighed. "Before I stumbled into the time portal in England, I had just learned that I had terminal cancer.''

Kendra laid one hand on the professor's arm, her eyebrows knit together in concern. "Oh, Professor, no.''

"Can-cer—what is that?'' Marian asked.

"A terrible disease in our time,'' Kendra said softly. "It's often fatal.'' Her fingers tightened around Cennach's arm and he patted her hand reassuringly.

"It's all right, my dear, for you see, after I had been in this century for a few days, I realized something extremely odd—I no longer felt ill. I began to gain weight as I found my appetite again. My pain was gone.''

"That's marvelous! But how?''

"I don't know, but I have a theory. I traveled backward to the past, to a time before I was ever born.'' His bushy brows lifted and he smiled. "How could I have cancer when I have never yet existed?''

"Wow,'' Marian said, and Kendra smiled involuntarily.

"Go on,'' she urged.

"I felt even more compelled to return then, to show my colleagues that here was possibly a way to cure mankind of its most deathly disease.'' He laughed at the amazed look on her face. "Oh, I know, it sounds crazy, but having experienced the ravages of the disease, I knew people would risk anything on the chance it would cure them. The scientific community had to know!'' His fist came down into his palm with a resounding thud. Kendra reached over and covered his hands with one of her own.

"They didn't believe you, did they?"

He shook his head, his eyes downcast. "No, and who could blame them? Not only was my story of time travel ridiculous, but as soon as I reached my own time, my cancer returned. When my doctor gave me the news, I headed back to my apartment, packed a bag with equipment and supplies and headed back to England."

"And you found another forming crop circle?" Kendra asked, astonished. "Aren't the odds against that happening phenomenal?"

"Yes, in fact, I did the math and they are over a trillion to one. That was when I began to believe the circles were not just aberrations of nature, but works of a higher intelligence." He spread his hands apart. "How else can you explain the fact that when I returned to the field where I was first taken back in time, the circle reappeared and for the second time swept me back to the same year, 1171? Once here, my cancer disappeared again and I have been as healthy as a horse ever since. Unfortunately, the aging process is one that seems to be a factor for me whether I have literally been born yet or not."

Cennach chuckled, smoothing the rough brown material of his robe with both hands, his brows knit thoughtfully together.

"Once I had chosen to stay here, I began to see that my knowledge and my experience were needed here for various things—medicine for one. You see, I had always wanted to be a doctor but my life took another path. In this time, however, just knowing how to clean a wound properly can mean the difference between life and death. I began to see I could make a difference. I took on a few students, eventually Magda and Marian, as well as a youth or two who have promising potential—"

"But Professor," Kendra interrupted, "aren't you afraid of damaging the balance of history, of changing things by being here?"

"Now that is a very good question," he said, staring up at the stars. "There is no easy way to explain something so complex," he said, his green eyes flickering across the heavens. "I have worked very hard on the calculations involved, and it would seem that unless I introduced some vastly unknown quantity—for instance produced a mechanical engine or a gun—" He lowered his gaze to hers and smiled as Kendra grimaced "—before its proper time in history, or unless I caused the death of some historic person of consequence, then there is little danger. We have come so far back in time as to make the changes our normal, everyday existence would cause to be inconsequential."

"I see." Kendra kept her gaze on the heavens too, her mind whirling. She could stay in the past and not worry about hurting anything. The problem was, she didn't want to stay, not if her baby was at risk.

"Now, my dear, let us talk about your return."

"Yes." She turned and faced him. "How do I get back?"

"I believe if you return to the field of Avebury, your circle will come for you."

Kendra shivered at the thought of some paranormal entity "coming" for her. "It must have been hard on you, staying here all that time, alone."

"Oh, I wasn't alone. I had Magda as a friend." His voice softened. "I will mourn her passing once this is all over." He brightened. "And I have enjoyed my students like Marian and others." He glanced over at the young woman half asleep beside him and his lips curved up gently. "And I have helped people here. All in all, my life has been most rewarding."

"Professor." Kendra gripped his arm as a sudden, terrible thought struck her. "If I return to my own time, will I still be pregnant, or will it have been taken away because this happened in the past?"

Ceannch frowned. "I have considered that question already and I believe you will still be pregnant. Your trip through time will not be erased. It happened, and anything which took place here, will still have happened."

"But your cancer—"

"The cancer was a condition I had before I came here. It was not a result of my being in this time. If I had, for instance, lost a leg in this time, then returned to my own time, I would still be legless. Does that help you, my dear?''

Kendra sighed. ''Yes, but it is terribly confusing.''

''I agree.'' He turned and faced her, taking one of her hands in his. ''Kendra, either the circle will take you home or it won't. Either you will be pregnant when you return or you will not. It is up to you to decide if you are willing to take these chances.''

''But how do you know the circle won't take me back to some other time—a more ancient time?''

''All I can tell you is what my experience has been. I was brought back to my own time, only days after I left.''

''And you think there is an intelligent force governing these portals?'' She shook her head. ''It's frightening to think about putting your life in the hands of some otherworldly beings, although maybe that's preferable to simply jumping into some crazy phenomenon! But what if they don't like me?''

Cennach laughed and dropped his hands from her shoulders. ''Remember, there is a possibility that a higher power is at work, not necessarily an alien one. Perhaps I was needed here. Perhaps you were. Who knows? But you don't have to leave, my dear. You are quite welcome to stay here. I'm sure Navarre would be thrilled if you chose not to go.''

Kendra moved away from the professor. ''I can't. Magda saw in the runes that if I remained in the past I would die in childbirth, along with my baby. Of course, it's possible Magda is wrong about everything. I might not even be pregnant. I have no proof, at least not yet.''

The older man's smile disappeared and he shook his head, a solemn look on his face. ''Magda was seldom wrong in her prophecies. By all means, then, you must return to your own time. It was a full moon moon when you arrived. In a fortnight the moon will once again be full. We will try then.''

''I want Navarre to come back with me,'' she said softly. ''Is that possible, do you think? Would it change something? Hurt history?''

Cennach shook his head. ''I do not know. I have never gauged the outcome of such a scenario. We have traveled to the past. Navarre would be traveling to the future.''

Kendra paced impatiently toward the house, then spun

around, her forehead creased with worry. "So all I have to do is return to Avebury and hope my circle will appear and take me home?"

"That is correct."

"And me without my ruby red slippers," Kendra quipped.

Cennach laughed and put one arm comfortingly around her shoulder. " 'The Wizard of Oz.' Ah, movies. I do miss them."

Kendra's gaze softened. "I wish you could come back with me."

"It's all right, Kendra." He squeezed her shoulder. "My life is here and I am satisfied. Now, let us get some sleep, for tomorrow we must begin our journey. Wiltshire is quite some distance from here." He glanced over where Marian was sound asleep on the ground, curled up in her blanket. "I see once again I've bored one of my students into slumber. Marian." He reached down and shook her gently. "Marian, wake up."

"Huh? Wha—" Marian sat bolt upright and began apologizing profusely. "Oh, Cennach, I do ask your pardon. What did I miss?"

Cennach stood, then leaned down and helped her to her feet. "Come, my dear, and I will give you a very brief synopsis on our way inside. I believe Kendra needs a few moments alone."

"Professor."

He glanced back, his kind face poised in a familiar yes-what-is-your-question attitude. Kendra smiled.

"Thank you," she said. "Thank you for everything."

"You are most welcome, my dear. Don't stay out in the cold too long. Good night."

"Good night." Kendra murmured the farewell, pushing away her guilt for making him think she had so easily given in to his request not to follow Navarre and Robin. She stood and began to pace in a small circle. She would leave to follow Robin before dawn, since even she wasn't foolhardy enough to travel alone at night. Once she made sure Navarre and the king were all right, she would return to Avebury and see if the circle would reappear and take her home again.

Home. Where was that now, exactly? Her life with Mac and the Chronicle didn't even seem real anymore, but strange and far away, so very far away. Kendra lifted her gaze to the sky, to the stars shining like finely cut diamonds upon a velvet cloth. She picked out one of the brightest and, closing her eyes, made a wish that turned into a whispered prayer.

"I wish . . . I wish . . . oh dear God, let him be all right. Protect him. I can't bear to lose him again."

Kendra wasn't Catholic but she didn't think God would mind that she made the sign of the cross, then hurried inside to prepare for her journey and wait for dawn.

Navarre rode through the night as though every demon in hell were nipping at his heels. As he fought to cover the miles between Cennach's home and the coast of England, his thoughts fluctuated wildly between the knowledge that Garrick held a deadly power in his grasp and the fact that he had abandoned the woman he loved without explanation. As the miles flew by, his thoughts flew just as quickly.

If Kendra traveled back to her own time before he returned, could he survive the loss? She wanted him to go with her to the future, to a time where he would be a burden weighing down her life. The things she had told him were wondrous, amazing, and, if he were honest with himself—frightening. He would be an ignorant barbarian next to the people in her century. How could he do as she asked? And yet, how could he ask her to stay? How could he leave his world, the only life he had ever known? How could he ask her to give up hers? If only he had more time.

Time. How ironic, he thought, as he slowed Kamir to a walk, giving them both a chance to catch their breaths. *The very element that I need more of, is that which will take Kendra away from me.*

Navarre ignored the sudden constriction around his heart as he kicked Kamir back into action, pressing onward, onward, toward the coast. He kept to the byways, stopping only to sleep for a few hours each night, then rising again to take to the road. Garrick did not have that much of a headstart, yet there was no sign of him along the road. Outside of London, the knight stopped in a tavern and overheard several nobles talking excitedly about the king. He was able to make out from their conversation that Richard had already arrived in England and was even now on his way to Canterbury where he would be newly crowned as England's king.

Feeling the time growing shorter, Navarre drove himself harder. He circled around London, crossed the Thames, and headed farther south for the coast and Canterbury. As his objective grew closer he began to plan how he would get close enough to Richard to protect him from Garrick. Perhaps a disguise that would get him past the guards. A tinker or a blind beggar, hobbling up to see the king? Nay.

He dismissed first one idea and then another, and in the end decided the best course of action was to find Garrick first. If he couldn't find the sheriff, he would find a way to get as close to the king as possible and add his guard to those he knew would be surrounding Richard. If Garrick used the gun there would be no way to protect the king. He could fire from a distance and never be caught, for who would believe that a small object could send death from so far away? He must find the sheriff and put an end to the threat against the Lionheart without revealing himself to the king, if at all possible. He had no doubt that Richard had received full reports about Navarre's traitorous activities since their days together in Outremer.

Navarre made it to Canterbury on a chilly April evening, just before sunset. As crowded as London, an aura of celebration permeated the city and its streets. Wearily he searched for a place to rest, to prepare himself for what was to come. As evening faded into night, his weariness became more pronounced and his temper more frayed as one inn after another turned him away. Boarding establishments were filled to overflowing as dignitaries and nobles rushed to find a place to stay for the festivities that would begin the next day and continue for the rest of the week, culminating in the crowning of the king.

Frustrated, hungry and exhausted, Navarre finally rode Kamir to the outskirts of the city and found a quiet glen where he rolled himself in his cloak and tried to sleep. But sleep would not come to him. He stared up at the stars. Would Kendra hate him for abandoning her? He would not blame her if she did, and yet, she herself had urged him almost from the moment they first met to save Richard. He tossed restlessly on the hard ground as other probing questions pressed against his brain until at last he sat up, and allowed the thoughts and questions free rein.

Kendra was right, of course, about returning to her own time. She did not belong here and would find life extremely difficult. If they had children together, she would no doubt watch at least one or two of them die, from disease or complications at birth. His chest tightened. She could die herself. It was a hard life, no doubt about it. The events of Richard's coronation day would, perhaps, make it even harder. He knew that it was possible he would be killed, either by Garrick or Richard's men.

How would Kendra live if he were not there to protect her? Would she end up in the streets, some toothless wench plying her trade? He shuddered and shook the thought away. No, Kendra was right, but dear God how hard it was! How he wanted to share his life with her, have children with her, grow old with her.

He raked one hand across the stubbly beard he'd not taken time to scrape away during his frantic journey across England. Another man would do these things, he thought, feeling suddenly empty. Kendra was young, beautiful. She would have no trouble finding a husband. Navarre closed his eyes against the image. Someone else marrying Kendra, his Kendra, combing her auburn hair, kissing her peach-colored lips. Someone else siring her babies.

His eyes flew open and with an oath he flung his cloak away from him and stood, wishing impotently for something to fight against besides this terrible sense of loss plaguing him. He clasped his hands behind his back and began to pace back and forth. There had to be a way. She wanted him to go with her to her own time. He had been thinking of it, during the days and nights of his journey, had considered it long and hard and had come to the conclusion that, after all, Navarre de Galliard was a coward. The thought of traveling through time, of journeying to a far and distant future, frightened him more than any battle he had ever faced, any foe he had ever fought.

Somehow he must convince her to stay with him. Kendra

was his. He would not give her up. If they lost children——He felt a quick thrust of unfamiliar pain in his heart and he squeezed his eyes shut for a moment, fighting the emotions assailing him. Regaining control, he opened his eyes and lifted his chin. If she lost any children, there would be others. He would give her as many as she could bear.

And if she died giving birth? A voice echoed in his mind. *Then what?* He brushed the thought away. It would not happen. He would not let it happen. If, however, he did not return in time to stop her from leaving, he would lose her forever. He must fulfill his promise to Robin and hurry back to convince Kendra she must stay in the past with him. Resolutely he lay back down on the ground, and pulling the thick cloak up to his neck, he willed himself to sleep.

Chapter Nineteen

While Marian snored softly in the bedroom they shared, Kendra raided Cennach's chest and found some old clothing that must have belonged to the man when he was younger and thinner. She slipped a pair of brown leggings and a matching tunic on and, after rummaging a little further, found a short, muddy-colored cloak and hood such as she had seen common people wear. She donned those, too along with a belt made from a kind of twine. Pausing in the next room only long enough to snatch a loaf of bread from Cennach's cupboard, tiptoed between the sleeping friar and professor and made her way silently out the door.

Rosy with dawn, the promise of the rising sun warmed the tops of the trees and belied the chill clinging to the ground. Kendra shivered as she found her horse. The gelding had been unsaddled by someone—Friar Tuck most likely—and now had to be resaddled. Kendra surveyed the animal through narrowed eyes. She had done a little riding in college and when she was a kid in Texas, but it had been a long time since she had saddled a horse. Still, there was no alternative. She couldn't ride such a long distance bareback.

After several false starts, Kendra managed to get the leather and wooden apparatus on her horse's back and fastened it under its belly, tightening it as much as possible, though the way the animal puffed and blew, it was hard to tell if the girth was right or not. Finally, Kendra gave up and left it as it was. Tying the supplies she'd gathered securely behind the saddle, she swung her leather satchel over her shoulder and, untying the reins, guided the golden horse into the forest. There she found a fallen tree and used it to pull herself up into the saddle.

It shifted with her weight and she eased herself back the other direction, wondering if she should get off and try to re-cinch the thing. The sun made up her mind as it pierced suddenly through the treetops and darted into her eyes. There was no time left. If she were going after Navarre, she'd better be on her way.

Aware that by leaving she might also be giving up her chance to return to her own time, Kendra gazed back over her shoulder at Cennach's home, took a deep breath, and turned the horse toward Canterbury, and Navarre.

The baby was perfect. His hair was soft and fuzzy, dark like Navarre's, his eyes the blue of the English sky. Marian handed the child to her, wrapped in a soft blanket, and Kendra cradled the tiny infant to her breast. His mouth opened and closed like a baby bird's and minute, porcelain fingers curled around her index one as she gazed down at the precious gift she held.

The pain struck unexpectedly, piercing her in the lower abdomen. She doubled over and someone snatched the baby from her arms. She couldn't see for some reason and the pain struck again, bringing more darkness.

"My baby!" she cried, clutching her belly with one hand and reaching out with the other. "Give me back my baby!"

"Your baby is dead," a strange voice murmured next to her. "You killed it."

"No!" Kendra tried to get up but the pain brought her back down. Rough hands encircled her arms and shook her savagely. At last she could see. Someone in a dark cloak was taking her baby away. He turned and smiled back at her. Garrick. Garrick had her baby. Where was Navarre? Navarre would stop him! Kendra groped in the darkness that came crashing down over her once again. Navarre was gone. Navarre had gone to save the king. Navarre had left her and their baby to die.

"Navarre!" The scream was torn from her throat and someone shoved her backward. She couldn't move. Her limbs were numb. She was dying and her baby was gone.

298

Kendra awoke, cold sweat beaded above her lips and trickling down between her breasts. Her breath felt frozen in her lungs, caught by the vivid vision of losing her child. She had ridden hard for three days after leaving Cennach's, sleeping wherever she could find a place at night, driving herself onward during the day until she could go no farther without falling off the saddle in sheer exhaustion.

This night she had searched for somewhere safe to lie down and sleep, but the forest had thinned and there was no usual hedgerow or dell where she could hide herself from the human and animal marauders that roamed about when the sun went down. Dozing on her horse's back, her mount must have smelled water, for she had awakened suddenly to find that they had stopped beside a clear stream within a wooded glen, a perfect place to camp for the night.

Kendra had wrapped her cloak around her aching body and as was her usual custom, climbed the nearest tree and cradled herself between the twisted tree branches, hoping her baby wouldn't be born with "rockabye baby in a treetop" as his favorite lullaby. She'd fallen into a deep sleep until the dream, and the pain, had jerked her back to consciousness. Now she slid down from her perch above the ground, the pain in her lower abdomen doubling her over. Shivering uncontrollably, Kendra checked herself for the telltale symptom of blood and, finding none, gulped back the sobs threatening to overpower her.

Was she losing her child? Had she endangered her baby by her breakneck trip across country? Of course she had—she was a fool! But her heart jumped to her defense. How could she have done otherwise? She couldn't have simply let Robin go after Navarre thinking he meant to kill Richard. But now what if she couldn't find Navarre? What if Robin found him first? And what if she missed the portal of time and was trapped in this century where she was destined to die in childbirth, and Navarre's child with her?

The eruption of pain burst forth from her in great gulping sobs as her hands protectively pressed against her belly, the helplessness of her situation encompassing her.

"Don't do this," she whispered to herself between the racking cries shaking her. "Don't give in. Be strong. Navarre's life depends on it, your life—"

"And Richard's life?"

The deep voice came at her from behind. Kendra froze, then slowly turned her head to search the darkness, her heart pounding. Garrick? She could see no one. The trees grew thickly here but still the moonlight danced in spots across the glen. Kendra couldn't stand, but she managed to pull herself to a sitting position to face her adversary, fists clenched, hair streaming down her back, unbound by the hard journey.

"I knew I should've gone straight to grandma's house," she muttered under her breath, then gasped as another pain ripped through her.

"Kendra, it is you, is it not?"

Kendra's breath left her in a sudden surge of relief as she recognized the second sound of the voice and a tall man stepped out from behind a tree. "Robin? Robin, is that you? Oh, thank God, thank God." She began to cry again as the outlaw crossed to her side, kneeling beside her. A stray beam of moonlight illuminated his bruised face and Kendra reached up instinctively to touch him, then curled her fingers into the front of his tunic for support. She felt suddenly faint.

"Are you mad?" he demanded. "Do you risk the life of your child in this reckless manner? What say you?"

"I had to come," she said brokenly, clinging to him and hating the weakness in her that required it. "Thank goodness I found you in time. You misunderstood me, Navarre is not going to kill Richard with the weapon I brought back from the future." Robin didn't respond and her hands slid up to his shoulders. She shook him as hard as she could. "Do you hear me?" she shouted, forcing him to look at her. "Navarre is not going to kill the king. Garrick has the gun and Navarre has gone to stop him!" She collapsed against the outlaw and felt the long shuddering breath of relief escape his lungs.

"Aye," he said softly, smoothing her hair and patting her on the back, "I hear you. I am relieved to hear you say so, for I had no desire to kill Navarre."

"Or be killed by him," Kendra mumbled against his chest. He chuckled. "So sure are you that your hero would best me?'' He shrugged. ''Aye, well perhaps you're right. I should not have dashed away so hastily without speaking with you further. No damage done, thank God, so rest now, and tomorrow we will find Navarre—and Richard.''

''What about Garrick?''

''Garrick as well. Now rest you.''

''Robin, I . . .'' she shivered again and he leaned toward her, concern wreathed on his face.

''Are you all right, Kendra? Are you ill?''

''It's the baby,'' Kendra said, a catch in her voice, ''I'm afraid I'm losing the baby. But I couldn't let Navarre die. I couldn't.''

''Shh,'' he whispered, shifting to lean against a large tree trunk nearby and pulling her against him. She hesitated only momentarily before gratefully accepting his offer. ''Here now, of course you could not. Tell me, do you bleed?''

She shook her head wordlessly.

''Then worry not. Likely you are just exhausted and saddleweary. After a good night's sleep you will be yourself once again.''

Kendra looked up at him suspiciously. ''How do you know so much about pregnant women?''

Robin blinked, taken aback for a moment by the implications of her tone of voice, then he laughed. ''I was raised in a household consisting of ten older sisters, milady. Believe me, I am quite knowledgeable when it comes to the anatomy of a woman.''

Kendra smiled up at him. ''I bet you are. Thank you, Robin.''

''Good night, Kendra.''

Sighing, Kendra relaxed against the outlaw, hoping she wasn't offending Marian by allowing herself the comfort of Robin's arms. The pain was subsiding a bit now and she could only pray Robin was right.

Soon, she promised silently, her hand sliding across her still flat stomach. Soon everything will be all right. Tears filled her eyes again and she blinked them away.

Navarre.

She sent out the message silently.

Tess Mallory

I need you.

Kendra moved restlessly against Robin's chest, then glanced up at him. He was staring off across the stream, toward Canterbury, his blue eyes hooded.

"Robin?" she whispered.

"Aye?"

"If you knew Marian would die having your baby, and you knew that you could save her by letting her escape to another time and you'd never see her again, would you?"

" 'Tis an answer you know already, milady," Robin said.

"Aye. But what if you could go too? Would you?"

There was a long moment of silence, then Kendra felt Robin's hand slide around her waist and give her a comforting squeeze.

"You forget, Kendra, Navarre knows not of the child. Sleep now, and save your questions for the man who can answer them, for I am not Navarre and whether I would go or not is of no consequence."

Kendra sighed and let one final tear slip down her cheek before hardening her resolve. Robin was right. Only Navarre could answer her questions and only she could guard the child within her. The best way to start was by getting the rest she desperately needed.

"Good night, Robin," she said. "Thank you for being such a good friend, to both of us."

He patted her again. "Sleep, little mother, all will be well on the morrow."

"I hope so, dear outlaw." Kendra's eyes slid shut as another pain rippled through her. "I hope so."

The morning of Richard's coronation dawned clear and bright, but clouds of apprehension followed Navarre de Galliard as he pushed his way through the crowd already gathering in the streets of Canterbury, his broad shoulders demanding passage when other, lesser men would have been turned back by the sheer crush of people.

Although he had feared for the king during the week in which he had searched for him to no avail, Navarre felt fairly sure that Garrick would choose to kill the king in a more public

302

way than by murdering him in his bed. Garrick would take great delight in allowing the king to make his grand promenade in front of his cheering subjects, the conquering hero home after having survived war and incarceration, only to be struck down moments before the crown descended upon his head. Aye, such a scene would give the sheriff a pleasure he would not easily forgo.

Navarre shoved through the crowd, heading for the tall stone wall that directly paralleled the steps of the cathedral. Once there, he scaled the seven-foot rock surface easily, settling himself atop the three-foot-wide vantage point as his mind continued to ponder the sheriff's strategy. He had been in league with a madman, he realized now, as he sat in feigned nonchalance, one knee crooked, one hand dangling casually near his sword; Garrick was a madman whose savage thinking and actions he had seldom questioned. And he should have, aye, he should have.

Navarre ran one hand through his tousled hair and sighed. So compelled had he been to seek revenge upon Richard, he had somehow managed to turn a blind eye and deaf ear to Garrick's excesses. Was he, then, less guilty than the sheriff? He tried to push his guilty thoughts aside as he searched the crowd for a glimpse of the king or Garrick.

He had camped in his now familiar glen again last night, but had not slept. All he could think about was Kendra. Had she already left his world or had she perhaps missed her circle of time? He found himself hoping she had, then dismissed the selfish thought. If she stayed, it must be because she wanted to stay. He would not force her, and he knew, in his heart of hearts, that she would leave him.

Navarre turned his attention back to the crowd. Garrick would be hard to spot, but it was reasonable to assume he would strive to place himself where he would be able to aim his weapon most effectively. If there was only one of the bullet things left in the weapon, Garrick would want to make sure he struck Richard and did not waste his last cylinder of death on some spectator. Navarre could only hope that from his lofty perch there was a chance he could spot the sheriff before the sheriff spotted him. He wore a cloak with a hood pulled over his face, but of course, Garrick would likely do the same.

A huge tree grew behind the wall on which he sat and Navarre moved so that he could lean his back against the broad trunk which butted up barely an inch away from the stone. The wound in his back pierced him suddenly, sharply, but he ignored the pain. As Navarre's gaze scoured the crowd in the street and the places he suspected Garrick might choose for his attempt, he fought to keep his thoughts on Richard and away from Kendra. Suddenly a cheer went up from far down the street and Navarre pulled himself to his feet, one hand on a protruding branch of the tree that spread out over the top of the wall. Gazing down the thoroughfare he could see in the distance the first banner of the king, held high above the crowd, moving toward the cathedral. Instinctively, Navarre knew Garrick would wait until the king reached the steps of the church.

Before he dismounts, Navarre decided, that's when Garrick will strike. He looked around, feeling the minutes ticking away with a dreadful finality. Feeling a moment of sheer panic, he spun around searching the crowd. Where was Garrick? Why had he thought he could find the man in this press of people? Better he had tried to confront the king and warn him directly instead. Nay, he had searched for Richard as well in the days he had been here, to no avail. The king had been kept sequestered away. Now he must do whatever it took, even if it meant delivering himself for arrest in order to warn Richard. But would his warning come in time?

Kendra, Kendra! his mind cried out. *I should have listened to you sooner. Now Richard is lost, and my grand sacrifice of leaving you is for naught.*

He allowed himself the brief luxury of imagining what it would have been like to spend the rest of his life with her. They could have run away to Ireland or Scotland. He had a little money saved. He could have rented a cottage and a little land and . . . and what? What would he do in this idyllic new world? Grow turnips? Raise sheep? What?

The cheers intensified and Navarre pulled his thoughts back to the present. Idiot. Fool. He had no future, no life to look forward to. He had thrown away his life, his honor, his allegiance to his king—for good reasons, he still believed—but he had gambled and lost. And he had thrown away Kendra in the name of that same honor he had already destroyed. Mad. He was quite, quite mad. The procession came closer now and Navarre found himself craning his neck to see the approach of the king.

Suddenly, the monarch came into view: Richard on the back of a prancing white horse, clad in the costume of the Crusade, chain mail armor covered with a split-sided tunic, a crimson cross slashing the front of it. The king smiled and waved at the crowd, his golden-brown beard neatly trimmed, his head covered only with his own natural crown of golden curls, his white teeth flashing down at the peasants cheering him. Navarre felt the thrill pass through the people below him and was amazed that he still felt it himself. This was the Richard he had known, that he remembered so well—Richard the conquerer, the smiling warrior, the hero.

Just then Richard threw his head back and laughed, loud and long. The sound was achingly familiar, and painful to the knight. How, Navarre wondered, did England's absent king find anything to laugh about when his country was on the edge of chaos? Thinking back to all of the long nights around campfires when he and Richard had grown so close, the king had laughed away Navarre's concerns for England, always turning the conversation to his interests in Normandy or the Aquitaine.

Suddenly, as he watched the smiling king waving and laughing, Navarre understood. To Richard, England was a second thought, like a bastard child. His first love had always been for Normandy and the Aquitaine, his legitimate heir. England had never been a priority to the king. The thought was sobering, distressing, but at least it helped Navarre understand the man a little better. And yet, was his real first love for any country or just for his own ambition?

Richard's progress was slow, hindered as he was by the crush of the crowd, but the horse he rode managed to prance forward a little farther until he was even with the wall on which Navarre stood. In the center of a wide street, the king was still a good twenty yards away, but from where Navarre stood, if he'd had the magical gun, he could have sent a bullet straight through the heart so lauded for its courage.

"A perfect target," he murmured aloud.

"I quite agree," a cheerful voice above him said.

Navarre spun around. Sitting comfortably, straddling two branches four feet above his head, the Sheriff of Nottingham grinned down at him, his eyes dancing with barely contained delight, Kendra's gun in his hand.

"Wonderful view from up here," he said, "and so private. Pity the leaves weren't a little fuller, but for this time of year you really can't expect more."

Navarre slowly drew his sword from its scabbard, the noise hushed amidst the tumult of the crowd below him. "Come down here, Garrick."

"I think not, old friend. For while you may think the king is a perfect target at this particular time, I prefer to wait for a more, shall we say, dramatic moment in this grand pageant."

Navarre took note of the unnatural brilliance of the man's eyes and his flushed features. Perhaps if Garrick were on the edge of out-and-out madness, as it appeared, he could talk him out of the deed. In spite of himself, in spite of all that had happened, Navarre realized he did not want to kill Garrick.

"Garrick, I can put this blade through your heart before you can draw your sword in time to stop me." The sheriff's smile widened as he turned the barrel of the gun toward Navarre. "That does not frighten me," the knight said. "I know you only have one bullet left and I doubt you want to waste it on me."

"Is that what they are called, bullets? How clever. Your bluff is clever as well. I doubt you are really sure just how many of these magical arrows of death are left to me."

Navarre frowned. Garrick was right. Kendra had tried to recall exactly how many bullets had been fired, but of course, there was no real way to know.

"You cannot hope to get away with this," Navarre said softly, glancing down at the street, trying to keep track of where Richard's procession was. Still a good way from the steps of the cathedral. It was there the sheriff would kill him, he knew, just before he entered the cathedral.

"Of course I shall get away with it," Garrick said, his tone amused. "No one will see me and even if they did, it would only appear that I was watching the return of our majestic Lionheart with the rest of the anxious people of England."

"If you kill him you will be caught," Navarre said, gauging the distance between them, wondering if he could kill the man before he could fire the gun.

"He will still be dead." Garrick squinted one eye and peered down the gun barrel at Navarre. "Besides, I have arranged a surprise for you. You are the one destined to be blamed. I have it all arranged."

"The barons will listen to me," Navarre said, his voice sounding unconvincing even to himself.

Garrick laughed, the sound swallowed up by the sudden increase of the noise in the crowd below. "What will you tell them, old friend? That a woman from the future brought a weapon back with her and I used it to murder Richard while sitting idlely in the top of a tree, a good twenty yards away from him?" His pale eyes narrowed. "I encourage you to do so."

"I will tell them you plotted against him," Navarre said,

"Save your breath," Garrick said softly. "As soon as I kill the king I will shimmy down this tree and grab the first person I find, asking frantically what happened to Richard. Thus I will establish the fact that I was nowhere near the king when he was killed."

Slowly the sheriff used his thumb to pull a movable part of the metal on the weapon backward. Cocking it, Kendra had called it, the thing which had to be done before the gun would fire. Navarre had grilled her thoroughly about the weapon during their grim stay in the dungeon.

Garrick's once handsome face seemed pale and puffy in the bright sunlight and it seemed new lines had been etched into his usually flawless skin almost overnight. For a moment, Navarre saw something shift behind the man's eyes and when he spoke, it was almost with the old camaraderie from their days in Outremer.

"It is not your death I want, Navarre," he said softly, and the knight noted the man's hand was trembling. "It is his. He

307

who has wronged us both. Now, put away your sword. Let me do what must be done.''

Kendra clutched the edges of her crude cloak together and shifted her bag to a more comfortable spot on her shoulder as she tried to see over the heads of the people pressing against her and Robin. She had awakened to find the pain completely gone. After a hearty breakfast that Robin had prepared, she had felt once again like her old self. She was grateful that her panic of the night before had been a false alarm. She had been afraid her episode would slow them down in their pursuit of Navarre, but she had been able to ride with no further problems. Now she and Robin stood in the heart of Canterbury waiting for the king to arrive for his coronation, and it seemed that all of Richard's tallest subjects in the kingdom had chosen to stand in the area directly in front of her.

"Do you see any sign of Navarre?" she said to Robin who, even at six feet, was having obvious difficulty.

"I cannot see anything except this reeking tide of unwashed humanity," he said with a grimace. "This is hopeless, we— look out!" he jerked her backward just in time to keep her from being stepped on by a horse whose master had mistakenly thought to use the beast in order to get closer to the king. They had left their own horses in a public livery, both a little nervous at the thought of their only means of escape being so far away from their immediate positions.

"I'm all right," Kendra reassured him. "I know, boost me up so I can see above the crowd." After a couple of false starts, and against Robin's better judgment, at last the outlaw bent down and allowed her to straddle his shoulders. He stood, balancing her around his neck, his fingers biting into her knees, grunting as she struggled for a toehold against his ribs.

"This is not right," he said between clenched teeth. "A lady should not—"

"Haven't you discovered yet that I'm not a lady, Robin, dear?" Kendra said, unable to keep from teasing him. "Since when do ladies dress like serfs, ride a horse like a man and climb on outlaws' backs so they can get a better view of the king?"

"Since never," Robin grumbled beneath her, "and why do
I continue to be surprised by your—Watch your feet will
you?" He shifted her foot out of his face. "Just be careful.
Remember last night."

Kendra didn't answer. Across the street, Navarre stood atop
the stone wall, staring up into the branches of a tall tree growing behind the wall, sword in hand. He stood like a man frozen, and even from this distance, Kendra could tell something
was terribly wrong. He was gazing up into the branches of the
tree, his face pale and drawn, then she saw his lips move and
realized he was speaking to someone in the tree. Suddenly he
swore—she could tell by the all too familiar way he ducked
his head and spat a word out angrily, though she couldn't hear
him over the throng between them. He sheathed his sword and
all at once she knew with a surety what was happening.

"Let me down!" she cried, her shout absorbed by the teeming voices around them. Robin knelt down, gratefully, and she
slipped from her perch to the ground. "It's him!" She grabbed
the outlaw's arm and pointed in the direction of the wall. "It's
Navarre! You can't see but Navarre is on top of that wall and
Garrick is in the tree above him."

"I can cut a path to him," Robin said, reaching for his
sword. Kendra stopped him, one hand over his.

"No, you mustn't. It looks as though perhaps Navarre is
stalling him, or else the sheriff is waiting until Richard reaches
a more prominent position. If we draw Garrick's attention he
may not wait any longer, or he could turn the gun on Navarre."

" 'Tis true," Robin said, his hand falling back to his side,
his handsome face twisted with frustration.

Kendra's gaze scanned the crowd. Richard had paused now,
not too far from the wall. This would be an ideal time for
Garrick to make his move. She had to do something, but what?

Think, O'Brien, think!

What could she do? How could she reach Navarre and help
him and how could she help him if she couldn't reach him?
She gazed up at the sky, searching for divine guidance or
messages from Mars, wishing the intelligence that had brought
her to the past would deign to give her an idea, a plan, any-

thing that would help her save Navarre and the king. Nothing came. No brainwave from outer space, no sudden burst of genius. There was nothing above but the blue sky and the graceful arched branches of the huge trees on either side of the road with the sunlight bursting through them in sporadic flashes of warmth.

Kendra smiled. "Listen," she said, turning to Robin, "you try and reach the king. Pull him off his horse, do whatever it takes to make him less of a target." She patted him on the shoulder and started moving away from him.

"What are you going to do?"

"Never mind." Robin didn't budge and she widened her eyes in exasperation. "Have you got a better suggestion?"

The outlaw shook his head. "All right, but I have a feeling Navarre and Marian are both going to have my head this time."

Chapter Twenty

With one last hesitant glance in her direction, Robin stepped into the crowd and disappeared. Kendra continued to inch her way down the street, her back pressed against buildings lining the roadway. At last she reached her destination: the foot of a huge oak tree. Its branches stretched up almost as high as the spectacular monument to God called Canterbury Cathedral. There were several of the trees that grew straight and tall, then three-fourths of the way up, near the top, began to bow. Through some quirk of nature, the top branches had grown together with the branches of the tree across the road to form a leafy archway. Directly across from where Kendra was now standing was the tree in which Garrick was hiding. She could conceivably climb up her tree to the top, then use the enter-twined branches to reach the other side, and, using the strategy of surprise, stop Garrick.

Would she have time? She didn't know, only knew she had to try. Looking up at the huge tree, Kendra almost lost her nerve. The branches at the top seemed thin and narrow from where she stood, and extremely far away. As a kid, she had been an ace tree climber, and in the last few days, she had climbed quite a few in an effort to stay alive. But scaling the brown monolith before her was quite another matter. And what about the baby? If she fell . . . she shuddered. Still, she could see no alternative. If Richard died all of history would be changed and who knew what havoc she might find when she returned to her own time?

Grateful she had worn leggings and not a gown, happy to

find a low branch to start her perilous assent, Kendra swung herself back and forth on the limb. Then, with a grunt, she swung her legs up and over, hanging upside down for a moment to the amusement of the people standing nearby. As she pulled herself up, scraping her palms and one leg as she did, she soon realized why no one else was taking advantage of this lofty view of the proceedings. The bark of this particular tree, which she was unfamiliar with, seemed to be of wood that splintered if you so much as touched it. She pulled one from the palm of her hand, then looked up and took a deep breath.

All right, O'Brien, here's where you live up to your reckless reputation. She patted her stomach shakily. *Baby girl or boy, hang on.*

Carefully Kendra climbed from limb to limb, making the assent as quickly as she could, feeling fortunate that the branches were close together, making it fairly easy to advance rapidly. Her shoes were of soft leather and gave her an added advantage as she mounted the branches. The bag hung heavily from her neck and she tried to ignore the ache it was creating between her shoulderblades.

"Don't look down, don't look down," she told herself aloud.

Kendra reached the place in the tree where the branches began to bow over the roadway, creating a natural arch. Ahead of her, by just a few feet, more branches interconnected with branches from the tree bowing in identical fashion on the other side—Garrick's tree. Gritting her teeth, Kendra slid across the limb, inching her way forward, wincing as bark and smaller branches protruding out of the limb bit into her legs and hands. All at once, she stopped, breathless and dismayed, as the branches ahead of her suddenly thinned dramatically.

Trying to fill her lungs again and succeeding only partially, Kendra saw that while the branches from the two trees were indeed, woven together, the connecting limbs were too thin to support her weight. Trying not to panic, she saw there was a short space between the sturdy branches on her side and the sturdy ones on the other tree. If she held on to the tree limb to which she was clinging and swung out, she could probably reach the branch on the other side that would support her.

Probably.

Trying not to think about what she was doing, Kendra inched forward a little farther, then swung her legs off the limb to dangle in midair. That was when the paralysis hit her. She couldn't move. She couldn't swing forward, she couldn't go back. The nausea rose up to consume her and a terrible hysteria slid around her neck and grabbed her by the throat.

She was up so high, so high! She was going to fall. She was going to fall and she would die and her baby would die and Navarre would die! Her dream came back to her along with the accusing voice—"You killed your baby!" echoed through her brain. Is this what it meant? Had the dream been a premonition? Had Kendra O'Brien once again rushed in impetuously and risked her life—and this time, the life of her child—in a foolhardy attempt to play Superwoman? She was going to die, and her baby would die with her and Garrick would kill Richard and then Navarre.

The ground swayed beneath her and she closed her eyes. For some reason she kept hearing the voice of her Uncle Mac, on the last day she had ever seen him.

"You have a death wish, Kendra O'Brien. You have a death wish."

Kendra opened her eyes. Below her the cheering throng of people danced and drank and shouted in celebration of Richard's return. Richard, mounted on his white steed, was almost at the steps of the cathedral. In another few moments, Garrick would kill Richard, and then perhaps, Navarre. The Sheriff of Nottingham would win.

"No," she whispered aloud, then again, stronger, as she pulled herself back up on the limb from which she hung. "No! I do not have a death wish, Uncle Mac. I have a baby inside of me who needs a father."

Pushing away her fear, Kendra calculated the distance between the branches, then quickly, methodically, untied the rope-like belt she had donned along with the rest of Cennach's clothing. Tying it around the limb securely in a loop, she slipped both hands inside the circle of rope and without further hesitation, jumped off the limb, swinging her legs toward the other side. Back and forth she swung, moving across the narrow space between the trees, her arms aching, her momentum increasing every time her weight carried her back, her voice gaining strength as well with every sweep through the air.

"I—

want—

to—

live!"

Kendra let go. As she had calculated, the power of her last swing tossed her directly against a branch strong enough to bear her weight. She gasped as she hit it, then grabbed the limb and clung to it, sweat pouring from her face, her hands bleeding and raw, her heart pounding. She was trembling. She was about to throw up. She was on the other side, in the other tree, the tree that held the Sheriff of Nottingham, and the weapon of death she had brought to the past. Now if only Garrick hadn't spotted her.

"Garrick, give this up," Navarre demanded, his fingers still clenched around the hilt of his sword in its sheath so tightly he could feel his bones beneath the skin. "I am leaving for Scotland as soon as I am able," he said desperately. "Forget all of this and come with me. We shall begin anew, together."

Garrick lowered the gun he had leveled at Navarre's head. "After all I have done to you, old friend?" he said, cocking his blond head, his voice soft with a singsong quality to it. "You would do that for me?"

"We have known each other since we were children," the knight said, just as softly. "You are ill, Garrick. I will help you."

The sheriff seemed to consider his proposition. "And what of your lovely lady? Will she be coming with us?"

"Nay," he said sharply. "She will not be coming."

"Of course not." Garrick turned the gun back to the procession below. "She will return to her brave, new world, and I shall accompany her."

"Do you doubt I will kill you?" Navarre's voice was brusque, hushed with contained emotion.

Garrick smiled down at him. "I doubt that you will sacrifice your own life for that of a king you no longer respect.''

"Will you shoot me then?'' Navarre asked. ''I tell you, Garrick, it will come to that for I will not let you kill Richard. There is more at stake here this day than one man's life. I believe there is only one bullet in that gun. Either use it on me or give up this mad quest.''

"Will you trust your life to Kendra's words—about the bullets, I mean?''

Navarre felt the sweat running down his side now as Richard and his group of soldiers started up again at last, slowly moving toward the cathedral.

"I would trust my life to her words, aye,'' Navarre said. ''But my life will be willingly forfeited, if need be.''

"You believe your noble sacrifice would enable you to regain your lost honor, no doubt.'' Garrick's thin lips curved up in a smirk. ''What a fool, but then, you always were a conscientious bastard, even as a child.''

Navarre dared not look away from the man but he could see from the corner of one eye that Richard's entourage was moving steadily now, soldiers having been dispatched to hold back the crowd enough to let the king pass without further molestation by his adoring subjects. Navarre felt his time running out. He was about to die. He would be able to kill Garrick from here with his sword, but probably not before the man could shoot him. Too well he remembered the speed with which the fiery dart had struck him when Kendra shot him on that long ago day at Abury. How very long ago that all seemed now.

Kendra! his heart cried out. *If I could but hold you one more time.*

The king had reached the steps and turned in the saddle, lifting his hand in a benevolent gesture of appreciation. Garrick took careful aim.

"Say good-bye to your king, Navarre.''

The Black Lion roared, his sword slicing out of the sheath and upward. A flash of light, brighter than the sun itself, first startled, then blinded Navarre even as he felt his blade sink deeply into Garrick's chest and heard the sheriff's cry of anguish. Navarre stumbled backward from the dazzling light which flashed again and again, his eyes filled with the visual echoes of glowing round orbs. He fell to his knees atop the wall and almost slipped off, but caught himself and gained his balance. The blindness was clearing now a little and the knight could make out the sight of Garrick dangling from the tree branch on which he had lain, his eyes rolling back in his head as blood poured from the wound, staining the brown tunic he had worn to disguise himself. The sheriff lifted himself up briefly, then collapsed back to the limb, his body sliding sideways into Navarre's arms.

Choking back his grief, Navarre helped ease Garrick down to lie flat on the top of the wall, his life's blood pumping out of him with every rasping breath he took. The knight held him in his arms, remembering not the sheriff who was dying, but the boy inside of Garrick, who had already died so many years ago at the hands of an evil woman who had dared call herself his mother.

"Navarre," Garrick spoke through lips frothy with blood as he lifted one hand to the other man's face. "Is it you?"

"Aye," Navarre whispered, oblivious to the shouts of the crowd surging toward the wall. " 'Tis me, Garrick, rest easy now, all will be well soon."

The man coughed, then shook as an agonizing paroxysm of pain seized him. Blood spilled from the corner of his mouth as he fought for breath, his fingers twisted in the front of Navarre's tunic.

"Mother, Mother please don't hurt me . . ." he whispered. The sob broke free from Navarre, unbidden, as Garrick's eyes rolled back in his head and his last breath left him in a shuddering sigh.

"She won't hurt you anymore, Garrick," Navarre said, sliding one hand across the dead man's face, forcing the eyelids down to hide the gaze of death. His voice was a whisper. "May God have mercy on your soul."

"Navarre."

Numbly, Navarre looked up. Kendra stood next to the tree, Garrick's gun in one hand, another object in the other that he recognized to be one of her magic boxes that captured images—what had she called it? A camera. Kendra! Kendra was here! She had not disappeared into time but had chosen to stay with him. Her face looked stricken with horror as she gazed toward the cathedral and not at Navarre at all. Was she horrified by the brutal act of violence she had just witnessed?

"Kendra," he choked out, lowering Garrick's body to the wall and standing. She didn't answer but turned a terrified gaze on him, her finger pointing wordlessly toward the steps of the cathedral, where Richard was dismounting. Navarre crossed to her side, his own gaze questioning.

"Didn't Garrick say he was sending an assassin?" she cried.

"Aye, but that was before he—" Navarre stopped, his blood suddenly cold. The fight wasn't over. He saw him, a big man with long dark hair, shoving his way toward the king, a shining dagger in his hand. There was no way to reach him in time. Suddenly he remembered Garrick's words: "I have arranged to have you blamed for the king's death." The sheriff had planned for someone resembling Navarre to stab the king, then slip away during the melee that would no doubt follow the sound of the gunfire. Navarre saw Robin Hood, still a good five yards away from the king, struggling to make it through the masses to warn Richard.

All at once, Navarre was back on the battlefield in Outremer. They were attacking Jerusalem and somehow Richard had managed to ride several yards away before Navarre could defeat the soldiers attacking him and redirect his attention to protecting the king. Two men on foot had grabbed Richard's horse by the bridle and the king had just decapitated one and was battling the other. What he had not seen was a third man about to run him through from behind.

Navarre shook the memory away and went into action. Moving away from the shelter of the tree, he reached an open space on the wall. His hood thrown back to expose his face as he bellowed, with all of his strength, with all of his voice, the same words he had shouted on that faraway field in the Holy Lands.

"Richard, you fool! Watch your back!"

Providentially the crowd had quieted in hopes the king would speak before entering the cathedral, and Navarre's words carried across the expanse of people to the ears of the

Lionheart. Like the well-trained soldier he was, Richard spun around, his arm half raised in defense, just as Garrick's man lifted his dagger to plunge it into the king's back. Richard knocked the blade from the assassin's hand, and in a matter of moments, the king's guards had wrestled the would-be killer to the ground.

"Detain that man and bring him to me!" one of the king's men commanded, pointing at Navarre. The knight thought he saw recognition dart across Richard's face, then just as quickly disappear. Six armored guards moved in double time across the avenue, scattering people in their wake. Navarre swung down from the wall, then turned to Kendra. "Get away from here, now."

Kendra laughed as she tucked the gun and the odd little box she held back into her bag. "I don't think so." She swung down from the wall and landed beside him. "I believe we're in this together, Sir Navarre."

He glared at her as the soldiers thundered up next to them, then shrugged and offered her his arm, warning the guards back with a fierce look as they raised their swords. "There is no need. We will not fight you."

"You never told me that the women in your century could fly," he murmured to her as they walked side by side to meet the king, "nor that they could wield weapons fashioned from the light of the sun."

"You never asked," Kendra said lightly, and gave him a brilliant smile that pierced his heart with the love he saw there. She had stayed and now what had he done? Jeopardized their chances together by revealing himself to Richard. He was an outlaw. The price on his head was death.

Their escort stopped at the steps of the cathedral and Navarre found himself looking up into the eyes of Richard the Lionheart.

"Navarre," the king said, the name oddly gentle on his lips.

"Aye." Navarre lifted his chin, meeting the king eye for eye, wondering if Richard expected him to throw himself at his feet and beg forgiveness. If so, he would have to think again.

"Only one man ever dared call his king a fool," Richard

said, speaking his native French and staring at the man sternly.

"And you were the only king who ever dared allow it," Navarre said, feeling the old respect and love for his sovereign in spite of himself. "Hello, Richard."

"You do not kneel before your king?"

Navarre continued to meet his steady gaze but did not reply. The arched, tawny brows of the king collided. Then the firm, full lips curved up beneath the man's beard in amusement. Somehow the gesture was not reflected in Richard's eyes. Navarre felt something poke him in the side and looked down into Kendra's admonishing blue gaze. With a sigh, the knight sank down before the king, but his head remained unbowed.

"Still the same Navarre, eh? As stubborn as hell. But I must confess I am surprised to find you also still watching my back. I had heard otherwise." His gaze moved to Kendra, then back to the knight. "Were the gossipmongers wrong?"

"No," Navarre said shortly. "I did plot against you, Richard, but"—he glanced over at Kendra—"I was convinced by others that without you, England—indeed the world—would never be the same."

"I see." Richard frowned and lifted one finger to brush his mustache. Navarre knew that gesture, it meant the king was displeased. "You admit to treasonous activities? Garrick said as much."

"Garrick is dead," Navarre said, impatient with this civility. He had expected to be condemned by Richard and this fairly genial conversation was making him uneasy. "The sheriff came here to kill you," he said flatly. "I stopped him. Unfortunately, I did not realize he had sent another assassin until it was almost too late. He planned to blame me for your death."

The king lifted both brows, then beckoned to one of his soldiers, who hurried over to turn his ear to his sovereign's whisper.

"Navarre." Kendra had stayed back out of the way while this ceremony proceeded, but moved beside the knight and sank to her knees beside him, keeping her eyes lowered. "I don't speak French, remember—*mon cher*? What's going on?"

"And who is this pretty woman?"

Kendra must have recognized the words *belle femme*. She looked up, startled, into the eyes of the Lionheart. He was smiling down at her, his hand extended to her. She placed her hand in his, awestruck at the thought of being presented to King Richard the Lionheart. "Kendra O'Brien, Your Majesty," she whispered.

"Lovely. Navarre, you must let me taste of her delicacies when you have tired of her."

"What did he say?" Kendra asked.

The edge of Navarre's mouth quirked up in a half smile. "He said you remind him of his sister."

"Oh."

"Where is Garrick?" Richard asked.

"On yonder wall."

"You killed him?"

"Aye." Navarre bowed his head, unable to hide the pain he felt with the speaking of the words.

The king jerked his own head toward one of his soldiers and the man hurried away. "You and Garrick were friends for a long time," Richard said, his voice quiet, thoughtful.

"Aye. It was with deep regret that I ended his life."

"The problem is, Navarre, I have only your word for this." Richard lowered his voice so that his words would not reach the murmuring multitude gazing on with unabashed interest, though it was unlikely many spoke or understood the Norman tongue. "You have admitted to treason," he whispered, "you have admitted to killing the Sheriff of Nottingham."

"You have my word as well."

Navarre turned. Robin Hood, Earl of Locksley, outlaw, knight of the realm dropped to one knee and drew his sword, holding it out, hilt first to the king.

"Welcome home, sire," he said simply. "My sword is yours."

"Robin," Richard said, openly delighted. He took the sword and drew the man to his feet, clasping him to his chest in a tremendous bear hug. "Robin, you old rascal! It is so good to see you! From what I hear you have not been idle while I was away."

"No, sire," Robin said as the king ended the impromptu

embrace and the outlaw stood respectfully in front of him. "I have had much trouble in Nottingham, from the sheriff and . . . others."

"Come now, Robin, you do not have to dance around it. It is common knowledge my brother John has been working his usual mischief. But what of this man? What of Navarre?"

Robin turned and gave the knight an even look, the expression in his blue eyes, for once, solemn and serious.

"This man has hounded me in Sherwood for the last year as he and Garrick plotted to unite the barons into a body of men who would help the new king make decisions. The new king was to be a man of the council's choosing."

"John?" Richard asked, his voice strangely calm, Navarre thought.

"Garrick wanted John because he knew he could control him. Navarre sincerely desired what was best for England and in fact, had another man in mind." Robin suddenly went down on one knee again. "I beg you for Navarre's life, sire."

Richard's face reflected his surprise and the noise of the crowd increased. "But why? You yourself have borne witness to his treachery."

"Not treachery," Robin said. "Perhaps bad judgment and the wrong allies, but not real treachery. Garrick believed you responsible for the death of the woman he loved."

"Woman?" Richard frowned. "What woman?"

"Talam," Navarre said softly. Kendra glanced at him sharply, obviously recognizing the name. "Do you remember her?"

The king stroked his beard thoughtfully as he gazed down at the man kneeling before him. "Aye, I remember. And you thought that I—but why?"

"Garrick convinced me you had her slaughtered along with the rest of Acre."

"Once Navarre learned that his quest for vengeance against you was undeserved by Your Majesty," Robin interjected, "he moved heaven and earth to stop Garrick, and to save your life. He saved mine as well."

"Stop, Robin." Navarre rested one hand on the man's shoulder. " 'Tis enough. I shall plead my own case."

Lifting his gaze, Navarre found it suddenly hard to meet Richard's eyes. The Lionheart. His king. Once his friend, now looking at him with suspicion, yet something more—hope, perhaps.

"May I rise, sire?" Richard nodded and Navarre stood, his shoulders stiff, his back straight. "I would beg your pardon, Your Majesty, if I could."

"You cannot?"

Navarre shook his head slowly.

Richard's face darkened, his jaw tightening. "Why not?"

"Because of Acre. Whether Talam was killed upon your orders or simply killed because of the massacre, it does not change what you did to those innocent women and children." He squeezed his eyes shut. "My God, Richard, I would never have believed it of you."

The king drew in a sharp breath and for an instant, Navarre felt the people around them, the trumpeters and the crowd and his own friends, fade, leaving only himself and the king in a protected bubble of mutual pain.

"Navarre, think you that I have not regretted that action a thousand times?" Richard whispered. "I am the king of England, but I am still a man." He lowered his gaze and Navarre had to fight the urge to reach out and touch him. "Do you think I have not wakened many nights since that day, stricken by the haunting cries of children dying?"

"I know not what to think, nor have I since that day. It is why I joined forces with Garrick and John," Navarre said.

Richard lifted his chin then, his blue eyes snapping with the courage he was known for as he faced Navarre's quiet accusation.

"What I have done I have done in the best interests of my men, my country, and my God."

Their gazes locked and a great silence stretched between them until Navarre broke it, shaking his head. "No man has the right to slaughter innocents, not in the name of war, certainly not in the name of God."

"I am Richard," the man said softly, "King of all England, ordained by God Himself. I have every right."

Navarre felt the pain of his loss all over, recognizing once again that he could no longer follow this man, this king. But he still had to make sure Kendra was spared whatever punishment would be meted out to him. Navarre dropped back to one knee.

"Richard, I have done much to wrong you, this I acknowledge, but this day I have saved your life, as Robin of Locksley has testified in my behalf. In return, I ask only that you allow this woman to go free, unharmed in any way." He gestured toward Kendra.

"What? What are you saying?" Kendra said, her blue eyes dark with suspicion.

"I am telling him that you desire him greatly and want to warm his bed this night."

"Navarre!"

The king silenced her outburst with a single penetrating look and Kendra bowed her head, even as she continued to shoot the knight beside her looks that promised retribution.

"I have already granted much simply by allowing you to live," Richard said. "The moment I returned to England you became an outlaw."

"I know."

"However . . ." Richard paused and turned to Kendra, taking her hand. "Milady, your life is cheerfully granted, though it was never in danger."

Kendra returned his smile cautiously, darting a glare at Navarre. Richard returned his attention to the knight kneeling at his feet. "You ask nothing for yourself, Navarre de Galliard? No pardon? You do not beg for your own life?"

Navarre hesitated, then looked up at the king. "I once pledged my loyalty and my allegiance to you. By breaking that pledge I felt I lost my honor. In my heart, Richard, I feel I have now repaid my debt to you, but I will not beg for my life. I am ready to die for what I believe I had to do. If allowed to live I would take myself from these shores and never return, on that you have my oath."

"Either scenario would be a great loss to England, my friend," Richard said softly, "either your death or your exile. However, rise, Sir Navarre de Galliard."

Navarre stood, pulling a confused Kendra to her feet. Seeing the fear in her eyes, he put one arm around her.

Richard paused and the crowd grew deathly quiet, straining to hear the king's next words. At last, he spoke.

"By merit of what you have done this day, I pardon you, Navarre de Galliard, from the sentence of death, reducing your punishment to exile. I am sorry, my friend," he said in a lower voice, "but who is to say when your sorrow may rise again and seek revenge? You will be escorted to the border tomorrow." He turned then to Robin. "And you, Earl of Locksley, are pardoned for any crimes against England." Richard lifted his gaze and turned his dazzling smile on the crowd that was watching this dramatic pageantry with breathless anticipation. "And from this day forth," the king said loudly, "may the people of England, and her king, be reunited in mind, in soul, and in their hearts. My people, I have returned!"

"Lionheart! Lionheart!" The chant began quietly, then gained strength as one person after another picked it up and the endearment surged like a wave through the crowd, growing louder and louder until the voices dissolved into a mighty cheer.

Navarre stepped back, pulling Kendra with him, leaving the king to stand at the top of the steps alone. Richard's head was lifted in regal splendor and for a moment, Navarre felt the old pull, the old adoration, tug at his heart before it faded, leaving only a hollow echo of what had been.

As the crowd went wild, the sound deafening in its thunder, Navarre drew Kendra more tightly against him. It was over. Richard the Lionheart, King of all England, had come home alive.

Chapter Twenty-one

"Exile? How dare that man exile you from England after you saved his life!" Kendra paced across the glen where they had camped, her arms folded across her chest, her red hair blowing as she walked.

"It matters not," Navarre said, squatting beside the camp-fire and tossing in small pieces of wood. "I had already made the decision to leave England if the king granted my life, even if he had not exiled me. Scotland, or Ireland perhaps will have use of a mercenary."

Kendra stopped in her pacing and spun around. The after-math of the day and her own heroics were just beginning to catch up with her, as well as the realization that if she planned to make it to Avebury field by the full moon she'd have to leave almost immediately. Navarre had said nothing of his plans, until now. She'd hoped that when the king exiled Navarre, he would see it as a sign that he was meant to return with her to her own time. What was left for him in the past now? Apparently more than she had understood.

"Scotland? Ireland? Is that your plan?"

"Aye." Navarre stood and brushed off his hands. " 'Tis said that Ireland is a beautiful place and much in need of men to fight—"

"To fight!" Kendra threw both hands up in the air. "I would think you'd had enough fighting to last you a lifetime."

Navarre gave her a steady look, hands on his hips as they squared off at each other. "And so I have, but it is what I am, what I do."

She crossed to him, laying both hands on his chest, knowing her heart was in her eyes, and all her hopes as well. "But there's so much more you could do, Navarre. In my time you—"

"*Your* time?" He took a step back from her. "Then you did not intend—you—" He closed his eyes and nodded. "You still plan to return."

Kendra's eyes widened. "Have I said anything to make you believe differently?"

Navarre shook his head. "Nay,'tis my own foolish thinking that led me to think—well,'tis no matter." He walked around the fire, hands clasped behind his back. Kendra watched him, feeling his pain, echoing it inside with her own. His dark hair danced in the slight breeze as he paced. Finally he stopped and faced her. "When?"

"I must leave tomorrow, Robin says, if I'm to make it back to Avebury in time. He's sent a message to Cennach and Marian to meet us there."

Navarre nodded again. "Aye. I must leave tomorrow as well. I am to be escorted to the border."

"Navarre." The word was a whisper filled with every ounce of longing and pain within her breast. She took a deep breath and the scent of rosemary touched her throat even as the softness of the night and the sorrow of the moment touched her heart. They gazed into one another's eyes, and Kendra saw her own anguish reflected back to her in the Black Lion's golden eyes.

"Will you walk with me?" he said softly. She nodded and he smiled. Picking up his cloak, he tossed it around his shoulders, then drew her within its warm cocoon as well, sealing them together as they walked in silence. He led her away from the camp and after a time, Kendra saw they were approaching a thick copse of woods. Glancing up at Navarre, she realized he was not simply taking her on a casual walk, but leading her to a definite location.

"What's going on?" she said, coming to a halt. "Where are we going?"

"You will see." Navarre's voice was like dark velvet and

Kendra felt a tremor of anticipation slip through her veins. "It is a surprise."

She allowed him to lead her into the moonlit woods. It seemed so long ago since they had touched, had melded their bodies together in mutual abandonment. If he had brought her here to the privacy of these woods for one last night together, she would give herself to him unashamedly, whether he agreed to return with her or not. She was leaving him, and she had not yet told him she carried his child.

Navarre led her into the shadowed place, helping her step over fallen branches and catching her when she stumbled over hidden rocks, until at last they arrived at a clearing, divided by a bubbling spring flowing through the center.

"This is lovely," Kendra said, gazing around at the picture-postcard scene.

"I found it one day quite by accident." Navarre guided her to the stream and knelt down. He looked up at her, her hand in his. "Come, kneel beside me."

Kendra frowned at the request, but something in his eyes compelled her to do as he asked. They knelt, and Navarre gazed down into her face, smoothing her hair back with tender fingers as soft tendrils drifted softly between them. His simple touch against her skin sent desire coursing through her and Kendra drew her breath in sharply, feeling the magic between them, knowing he felt it too.

"Are you determined to leave me?" he asked.

Kendra looked away, wishing she could turn her emotions away as easily. "Yes," she said, running her tongue across her lips as Navarre's fingertips began to trace a smooth path down the side of her jaw.

"Are you sure?" Navarre replaced the fingertips with his lips, touching her skin lightly with his tongue.

"Yes." Kendra shuddered at his touch. "But you can come with me, Navarre. Please, please come with me."

Abruptly his warmth fled as he stood and moved away from her. "Do you want to know the truth?" She nodded, apprehensively. He paced back and forth for a moment, then spun to face her. "I am a coward. I will not journey to your time because I am afraid."

"Afraid?" Kendra looked up at him, completely taken aback. She kept her voice light, however, almost teasing as she replied. "Navarre de Galliard afraid? I don't believe it."

"Believe it, for it is true." He walked around the clearing, hands behind his back, his face in shadow.

Kendra watched the moonlight glimmer on the blackness of his hair and as he lifted his golden eyes skyward, she was reminded again of the name Richard had given him, the Black Lion, and she remembered another night, when she had promised Navarre she was not afraid of the darkness inside of him. But she was afraid to live in his world, and did not blame him in the least if he felt the same about hers.

"How would your people ever accept me?" he said, almost to himself. "What would I do? How would we live? I have been a soldier all of my life but you were right—I am weary of the fight." He stopped and stared at her. "Does your time even have soldiers?"

"Unfortunately, yes, but Navarre, that isn't your only option." She jumped to her feet and hurried across the clearing to his side. "There are a hundred things you could do, that you'd be wonderful at and—"

"What things?" he asked suddenly, placing his hands on his hips and looking down at her with that demanding expression she had come to know so well. "Name one."

"You could . . ." Kendra stopped and stared at the man facing her, then looked—really looked at him—for the first time in a long time: long dark hair whipping across a face that could have been chiseled from stone. Golden eyes that saw the slightest injustice and demanded it be made right. A jaw meant to take on the world. Shoulders broad enough to carry that burden. Arms strong enough to fight for it. The man in front of her was a warrior. This was a man who needed a cause, a war, an enemy to battle. How could he ever be happy in her world? "You could be an American Gladiator," she finished, her heart sinking with the flippant words. "Or a romance cover model."

"I could be a what?" Navarre frowned down at her and shook his head. "You see? In your heart you know it is true.

I would never fit into your world and I would be an embarrassment, a burden to you."

"Is that what I've been to you?" Kendra asked softly.

"What? Of course not," he retorted, acting as though her question confused him. "You have adapted wonderfully well, do you not realize that? Kendra, you fit into my world, do you not feel it? You belong here, with me."

Kendra flew to his side, her arms encircling his neck. She pulled his face down to hers, their lips almost touching as she considered her words carefully before she spoke. "Are you saying, Navarre de Galliard, knight of the realm, defender of the soil, et cetera, that a mere woman has more courage than you? If I can brave your world, can't you do the same for me?"

Navarre stiffened and pulled her arms from around his neck. "It is not the same," he said, turning away from her.

Kendra stamped her foot, wishing she dared kick him in the shin. "Of course it's the same." She stomped over to him and jerked him around to face her. "I love you, do you understand that? I love you and if I have to be separated from you for the rest of my life, I don't know if I can bear it!"

Navarre held her away from him for a moment, then kissed her, with an aching gentleness that was almost frightening in its intensity. He led her back beside the stream and knelt down, pulling her with him. The expression on his face was unreadable. Reaching inside his tunic, he pulled out a long, beautiful scarf of gold and black—the Black Lion's colors—and, lifting her hand in his, wrapped the material around both their right hands, binding them together.

"Kendra O'Brien," he said softly, "will you marry me?"

Kendra's mouth dropped open but she couldn't speak for a moment. She moistened her lips. The silence of the forest echoed around them and finally she found her voice.

"But I'm leaving . . ." she whispered.

"Will you marry me?" Navarre repeated, his fingers tightening over hers.

Kendra lifted solemn eyes to meet Navarre's golden ones. If she went through with this, could she leave him? Could she become his wife and then return to her own time to have their baby without him? Tell him! her inner voice commanded. Tell him about the baby and about Magda's prophecy. He wouldn't want you to stay if he knew you would die in childbirth, and he might return with you if he knew you were pregnant! She opened her mouth to tell him, but nothing came out.

Twisting her hands together, Kendra continued to gaze at Navarre as she searched her feelings. Was she afraid for him to go back with her? Was that why she wasn't even giving him the chance by telling him about the baby? Or could it be she was jealous of her own child—if he couldn't come with her because he loved her, she didn't want him to come because of a child? That was ridiculous, of course she didn't feel that way. Or was it because if he knew about the baby, she feared he wouldn't believe Magda's prophecy and he would keep her from returning to Avebury? Even with Robin helping her, she doubted they could best Navarre, and she wasn't all that sure Robin would help her. Would Navarre be so selfish?

Can you be so selfish? she asked herself. *Tell him.*

"Navarre," she began.

"Kendra, there is so little time," he said, and for the first time since she had met him, Kendra saw real fear in his eyes. "Please, let me at least have this, before you leave me forever."

Kendra choked back the sob pushing up in her throat and nodded. "Aye, Navarre de Galliard, I will marry you."

The smile he gave her was unexpected and brilliant in its sweet intensity. He wet his own lips several times before speaking again and when he spoke, the words were more unexpected than his smile.

"Then before God I do say that this handfasting binds us together in holy matrimony."

Handfasting. Kendra recalled the term from her days in British Lit. When a couple could not reach a priest for a time because of extenuating circumstances, they would have a handfasting ceremony in which they would give vows to one another, binding them in marriage until such time as they could have a legal wedding. A wedding. Kendra closed her eyes, feeling a wave of panic sweep over her. This wasn't fair to either of them. This further binding of their hearts and souls would only make it that much worse when it came time to go. But somehow, she couldn't make him stop. She couldn't open her mouth to tell him so to save her life. Navarre covered their bound hands with his free one, and as if in a trance, she placed hers over his.

He smiled at her then, and all her fears seemed to dissolve into nothingness as he said the words she had dreamed he would someday say.

"I take thee, Kendra O'Brien, as my wife, to honor, to cherish, to love, to protect, as long as we both shall live. May God bless our union."

Kendra took a deep breath, then wondered at the calm voice she heard that was her own. "I take thee, Navarre de Galliard, as my husband, to honor, to cherish, to love, to protect, as long as we both shall live. May God bless our union."

"You did not say 'obey,'" Navarre said, bringing her bound hand to his lips again.

Kendra lifted both auburn brows and grinned. "Neither did you."

"Wife," he said softly, "I want you."

Kendra gazed up at him, knowing her love shone from her eyes, knowing that she was sinking further under his spell. That was funny, his spell, when he had suspected her for so long of enchanting him.

"Kiss me," Navarre said, taking her in his arms, one hand in her hair, the other around her waist. "Kiss me as though it is the last time you ever will."

Kendra felt the wave of love and pain crash over her like a wave breaking on the shore, as she kissed her husband, her love, her life, kissed him as though she would never again touch his lips with hers, as though she would never again feel the passion of his love. He gathered her to him then, and lifting her into his arms like a groom carrying his bride over the threshold, crossed the small stream and entered the woods at the edge. There was a dim light ahead as they approached, and when Navarre ducked down into a natural thicket, Kendra saw a thick blanket had been laid over the bed of leaves within, a basket with a bottle of wine and goblets placed at the side, and over a dozen candles set around the blanket's edge.

Tess Mallory

"Oh, Navarre," she whispered, pressing the palms of her hands together and lifting her fingers to her lips, "it's beautiful."

Navarre gently, almost reverently, touched his lips to hers. His kiss deepened and Kendra clung to him, feeling a sudden grief threaten to tear her soul from her.

This is the last time. The words echoed silently around them and through Kendra's mind like grains of sand bouncing against an hourglass. *This is the last time.* It ticked through her brain like a clock.

With fingers of velvet, Navarre removed her soiled clothing of the day and then his own. Wordlessly she took his hand and let him cover her with his cloak, then lead her back to the stream where they slipped into the shallow water and washed the grime from the days on the road from their bodies. Silently they touched one another, exploring one another, tasting, yet, always with an undercurrent of gentle resignation.

Tick, tick, tick. Kendra heard time running out for them as Navarre's hands soothed away the pain of her fears, and kissed away the shadows of her tears. She heard the grains of sand pouring through the hourglass, faster now, at the end, more quickly now that the grains were almost gone.

As Navarre captured her mouth, delving into the warmth so sweetly she could not help but cry out against his lips, for the loss that was coming, for the centuries of lovers parted by fortune and fate. Then she was pressing herself against him, burning her own brand into his flesh, as if to guarantee that he would never forget her, never forget their love. They rose from the stream and walked unhurriedly back to the blanket. There Navarre dried her with a large towel from the wine basket and Kendra let him, lying back against the soft material, feeling oddly drunk. Everything had a strange haziness to it, as though this was a dream, as though nothing was real.

Is it happening already, she wondered? Is this what I will remember when I return? Is this what it will feel like—a dream? As though it never was? Then she remembered the child inside of her and knew that she would always have the sweetest kind of proof. *Tell him!* the voice inside insisted. Still she resisted. Afterward, she promised. After their passions

332

were spent. She could not risk anything spoiling this moment, not even such blessed news.

Navarre dried her body as though it were a valuable piece of porcelain and when he was finished, he pulled her into his arms. Kendra parted her lips, welcoming the burning flame that was Navarre.

Tick, tick, tick. The last time. The words thumped through her heart, building in intensity.

"How can I leave you?" Kendra said huskily against the side of his jaw, breaking their embrace to caress his bristled face. "Please, come with me."

Navarre groaned aloud. "Let us not speak of this now." He covered her body with his own and Kendra stopped talking, stopped thinking, conscious only of the heat between them, the aching longing waiting to be fulfilled. His hands moved over her skin as though he sought to etch the memory of each part of her body. Lightly he caressed her breasts, her waist, her belly, her thighs outside and in, and the secrets they guarded as well. Kendra responded in kind, gazing up into her husband's face as she touched him, kneading his hard back muscles down to the apex of his taut buttocks, running her hands boldly down his thighs, crying out as he at last found the center of her fire and began stoking the smoldering embers.

Tick, tick, tick. The thundering roared between them even as Navarre possessed her body, giving his own for her to cherish, sealing himself to her, burning his memory into her mind, her flesh, for all time. His lips tasted of salt, and opening her eyes Kendra saw he was crying silently, tears dripping onto her breasts as he paid homage to each. She clasped him to her, letting her own tears flow, as he gently brought her to a tender release.

As Kendra arched against him, in some rational part of her mind, she realized he was not only making love to her—he was saying good-bye.

Tick, tick, tick. She clung to him as his tongue burned into her, no longer gentle. As though his good-byes were said and now he would speak his pain, silently, eloquently. His body thundered into hers, the rhythm between them beating in her ears like Thor's hammer. She rose to meet it, praying the roar

333

would increase, the storm would explode and the tick, tick, tick of time would be blotted out once and for all.

The power of their love came crashing down, outshining the fire of the candles, swirling the cacophony of passion and pride, pain and love, into a well-forged bolt of lightning that struck them both, seared them, burned them both forever with the eternal blue flame of their love. Kendra cried out, then cried in earnest as Navarre's seed surged inside of her.

Tick, tick, tick.

"Navarre, hold me, hold me," she whispered against his chest. "Don't ever let me go."

"Never," he whispered back to her, pressing his face into her hair and gathering her more tightly into his embrace. "Never," he promised.

Navarre woke from a brief slumber with the sensation of cool, soft skin being pressed back against his chest and thighs. The blanket over the two lovers had slipped down and he covered them again, then sighed with satisfaction and wrapped his arms around Kendra's waist, drawing her more solidly against him. He did not wish in any way to mar the sweetness of their lovemaking, but there was much that needed to be said. He knew she was determined to leave him, to go back to her own time, but he had confidence now that he could convince her otherwise.

Deciding upon the handfasting had been a last-minute decision, brought about by his desperation, but he did not regret it. It was not that he was trying to trap her, he told himself, either by the vows they had just repeated to one another, nor the love they had just exchanged, but he had thought perhaps if she knew how serious he was, how committed to loving her, to always being there for her, perhaps she would change her mind. He would give her the chance to make up her own mind, at least, before changing it for her.

She was awake. He knew by the way she flexed the muscle in her thigh, as though inviting him to begin their passion anew. He would, but not quite yet. Navarre pressed his lips against her hair, feeling his desire quickly rising as her own sweet scent lingering there filled his senses.

"Kendra," he began softly, "stay here with me." He felt her stiffen against him and he hurried on. "I have plans for us. I won't fight anymore. We'll go anywhere you like: Scotland, Ireland, perhaps Rome. I promise I will make a good life for us, somehow."

"Oh, Navarre," she whispered, her back still to him. She shivered a little as her body moved fractionally away from his and his heart constricted with apprehension. "The place I want to live doesn't exist yet, and won't for another eight hundred years."

He lifted himself up on one elbow, feeling the challenge ahead course through his blood the way it did before battle. There was no mistaking that this, too, was a battle, perhaps the hardest he would ever fight. "I thought you loved me."

He felt the sigh slip through her. "Of course I love me, but there are reasons I have to return. I've already almost changed the course of history with that stupid gun."

Navarre ran his hand smoothly up her side, covering her breast, kneading it lightly between his fingers. She moaned softly and leaned her head back to touch his. He felt ashamed to use her own body against her this way, but he was ready to use anything and everything if she would but stay.

"That was not your fault," he said softly.

Her voice was hushed with passion as she spoke. "We were lucky, Navarre. It could have gone the other way so easily. I just can't take any more chances of messing up the past."

He began to kiss her neck as he continued to caress her, reveling in the feel of the soft, peach-tipped globes that fit so perfectly in his large hands. His tongue touched her ear even as his whispered words did. "We could live somewhere isolated, where you would not affect other lives."

Her foot moved languidly up and down his shin and he knew she was considering his words. His hand slipped lower, across her taut belly and downward. Kendra drew in a quick breath, yet she did not tell him to stop, and he felt as though they played some unspoken game of rationale and arousal, talking so calmly even as she responded to his seduction.

"I'm not sure I could be happy living like that." She gasped out loud as Navarre dispensed with further enticements, and

easily fitted himself to her. "I love people," she whispered as
he began a gentle stroking inside of her, his lips tracing a path
across her shoulders, his hands encircling both breasts. "I—I
love being involved," she sighed, her body moving against
him, her back arched, "making a difference in the world. I
can't make a difference here, except in a bad way."

"Then your mind is made up," he murmured against her
hair, rocking a steady rhythm between them.

"Yes," she said, and he could tell she was near tears. For
a moment he despised himself, but did not cease his gentle
inducements. "You knew that before we did this. I tried to tell
you it wouldn't make any difference." Her voice almost faded
away, heavy with desire.

"No difference." Navarre stopped his movement and, pulling away from her, flipped Kendra to her back. "I will show
you what a difference it has made."

He crushed her to him, covering her body with his, filling
her, melding his body into hers, claiming her once and for all
as his own. Kendra cried out at the suddenness of his assault,
then tangled her fingers in his hair as his mouth descended
savagely on hers. He tasted the honey of her lips and could
no longer hold back the love, the rage, and the fear, that
swirled together inside of him in confused torment. He ravaged
her lips, possessing her mouth, calling into being once again
the molten lava that had lain dormant in both of them for too
long.

"I will not let you go," Navarre said, tangling his hands in
the lushness of her hair, forcing her head back slightly. He
gazed down into her azure eyes and knew he saw the same
conflicting emotions mirrored there. "You belong here with
me, Kendra, and here you will stay." His mouth took hers
again, his tongue mimicking the movement of the heated steel
he wielded below. She did not protest as he had half expected
but instead drew him closer, lifting her hips, welcoming the
almost punishing thrust of his body as he bound them together
in a way that words and promises never could.

"At night when I am alone," he said, his movement never
slowing, never changing, "I ask myself, how can she love me
if she is going to leave me?"

"Come with me!" she cried out, and Navarre kissed the tears streaming down her face, tasting the saltiness with satisfaction, feeling a strength from the fact that she loved him enough to cry, hating himself for pulling such a heady emotion from her.

"Stay with me."

"Navarre, stop," she breathed, "I can't stand this, please stop."

"You will stay with me," he said, beginning the rhythm between them again. It beat between them with the constancy of his heart, pulsing like his heart, pumping like his heart; and that was just as it should be because she was his heart, his life, his reason for being, and he would not let her go. "Say it," he commanded her gently, his lips against hers, his body within her. "Say you will stay."

"Yes," she said, her fingernails biting into his back, her mouth moving to his shoulder, her teeth ravaging him none too gently in return. "Yes, only—" she moved beneath him in wordless entreaty and with a cry of triumph, Navarre took her there, to the undiscovered country that lies between love and passion, to the place where only lovers dwell. He carried her there, soaring on a magic carpet of light and wind, and he felt her carrying him, opening her heart and her soul to the man she had married, to the man who had promised he would never let her go. They soared, they reached for the brightest star together, then exploded in a million fragments of light before drifting slowly, slowly, back to earth.

As Navarre fell asleep, he thought he heard Kendra crying. He started to ask what was wrong, but the lethargy seizing him was too heavy. He slept, secure in the knowledge that she was his, and would be until the end of time.

Talam looked up at him, her chocolate-brown, almond-shaped eyes reflecting the conflicting emotions she obviously felt.

"I think that it would be better if I return to my family," *she said softly, curling her hands together in her lap. Navarre chuckled, placing two fingers under her chin and raising her face to his. He stood above the slim, dark-haired woman, left*

foot braced against the stool on which she sat, left arm propped on his knee. One hand was covered with his metal-ringed gauntlet, the other reached down for hers.

"Nay, I think not," he said firmly, lifting her fingers to graze them with his lips. "You will stay right here in the camp and wait for my return."

She looked away, trying to hide her fear but not quite succeeding. "Your king, he does not like me, nor does your friend, the one with the pale hair. I am afraid to stay here without you."

"Nonsense," he scoffed. "I am sorry to leave you here but the battle will only take a day at the most. We are assured of victory. Then I will return and we will go to your family together. I must speak with your father."

Talam shook her head. "No, Navarre, you must not do so. I do not belong in your world, your England."

Navarre felt a quickening of fear around his heart and, abandoning his carefree position, sat down beside her, turning her to face him.

"What are you saying?"

"I am saying that I must return," she said, leaning toward him, her eyes fervent with pleading. "I love you, my dearest Navarre, but our love cannot be. I do not belong in your world, nor you in mine."

"You said you would marry me."

She shook her head again. "Our union can only bring grief to all concerned. You are a Christian and in the eyes of your friends, I am—and always would be—an infidel." He could not respond to her words for he knew she spoke the truth. She patted his hand. "You have a wonderful future ahead of you, my Navarre. King Richard values your advice, your friendship. Shall I carry the burden of knowing it is because of me that you would no longer enjoy that special bond?"

"I do not care," Navarre replied stonily. "Richard's prejudices are his own problem—and Garrick's as well. I love you and that is all that matters. If you love me, Talam," he said, his golden eyes deepening into amber, "you will stay here and wait for me."

"You will not release me to go home, knowing that I love you, knowing this can only lead to disaster?"

Navarre lifted his chin stubbornly. *"If you leave me now I will know our words of love meant nothing. I will not let you go!"*

Talam nodded. *"Very well, then,"* she whispered, *"I will stay, and may Allah have mercy on us both."* She lifted her lips to his, then her face began to blur and fade, to twist until it disappeared altogether. He reached out for her but there was nothing there. Then he heard a scream and turning, he saw her, fifty yards away from him, surrounded by laughing soldiers, swords drawn. He tried to run to her but could not lift his feet. He was frozen, paralyzed, and could only watch as the men lifted their swords above her. She looked up calmly then, and her eyes met Navarre's. This is your fault, *they seemed to say.* Because of you. *The swords came down and—*

Navarre awoke, the sound of Talam's screams still echoing in his ears, sweat pouring from every pore in his body. He was gasping, trembling, and reached out to assure himself Kendra was beside him. She was, sleeping deeply like a child. She was here. His stubbornness had not killed her as it had Talam. Not yet. He had been lucky so far. Not even Garrick's treachery had harmed her. But if he insisted she stay, what was to stop history from repeating itself, somehow, in some way? Garrick was dead, Richard had granted pardon, and yet, some ominous misgiving hung over him. He felt it, sensed it and knew that something, or someone, was trying to tell him something. Yet, how could he live the rest of his life without her? Making up his mind abruptly, decisively, Navarre closed his eyes. It was still many long moments before he found sleep again.

Kendra donned her clothing as quietly as possible. Navarre had torn the sleeve of her tunic in his haste to press his flesh against hers but she wore it anyway, feeling a dark rush of shame at the promises she had made that night all because of the passion he had stirred within her; promises she had never intended to keep. He had been so insistent, so demanding, and yet, so sweet, declaring his love for her with his words and his actions. How could she have hurt him so right then, so soon after their handfasting? But his final declaration that he wasn't going to let her return to her own time had frightened her and she had lain beside him after their last frenzied coupling, planning how she could get away at dawn.

He had awakened once during the night, startled out of sleep, and had lain there for a long time, staring at the stars. She'd feigned sleep and for a time, feared he wouldn't ever close his eyes again, but at last he had, and fighting her own desire to snuggle up against him and take her own rest, Kendra had maintained a vigil until the faintest, dimmest light began to appear on the horizon. It was then she arose. Finishing her dressing, she gave one last look at her lover, and carefully, quietly, started out of the clearing, her heart feeling as though it were shattering in a million pieces with every step she took away from Navarre.

When she finally cleared the woods she broke into a run. Reaching the camp where Robin slept, Kendra sneaked by him to the horses. Once again she was running away, once again she was on her own. She mounted the horse and straightened her shoulders, refusing to look toward the wooded glade where her husband slept, stricken with the guilt of knowing he would never know, could never know that he was going to be a father. *It was his choice*, an inner voice hissed into her ear. *His choice*. Kendra turned the horse toward Avebury and dug her heels into his sides. He bolted forward and neither of them ever looked back.

Chapter Twenty-two

Kendra was gone. At first Navarre thought she'd walked down to the spring to wash, but after checking there, he realized her clothes were gone too. With a groan, his demands of the night before assailed him. *I will not let you go,* he'd told her. Like a king to his subject, a lord to a serf, but certainly not like a husband to his wife. She'd panicked and run and he could scarcely blame her. Pulling on his own clothing in rough, hurried movements, he made his way back to camp where, as he had expected, Robin remained, rolled in his cloak, sleeping blissfully unaware.

"Wake up!" Navarre shouted, kicking the outlaw in the side. "She has gone and we must follow as quickly as we can."

"Who? Who?" Robin sat bolt upright, sword in hand, blinking both eyes and sounding like a giant owl startled from sleep.

"Kendra," Navarre explained as he stormed around the campsite, putting out the campfire and packing up the supplies. "She has gone to return to her own time and we must stop her."

That woke Robin completely and he jumped to his feet, albeit a trifle unsteadily. "Stop her? Oh, yes, of course. Lover's spat on your last night in England? Tsk, tsk, Navarre." He began helping Navarre load the supplies behind their saddles. "She's gone to Wiltshire, you know. Cennach said that was where her 'circle' would take her back to her own time. I wondered when you would come to your senses. In fact, I found it hard to believe you would leave her behind in the first place, although men react strangely to such things, to be sure.''

"Of course we do, we—'' Navarre stopped and turned with a frown. "What on God's green earth are you blathering about?''

"The babe, of course,'' Robin said in a mild tone, examining his horse's mouth as Navarre stood and stared at him dumbly. "I believe this bit is too stiff for Falcon, what do you—''

"What are you talking about?'' Navarre whispered, frozen in place, feeling suddenly as though the bottom had dropped out of his world.

"This bit, I said I think—''

"Not the damn bit!'' Navarre roared. "You said babe! What babe?''

Robin looked startled, then a knowing smile slid across his face. "Why, your babe, of course. Do not tell me that Kendra has yet to give you the good news. You, old friend, are going to be a father.'' He stepped back as Navarre took a step toward him, fists clenched.

"You knew about this?'' the knight hissed.

"She did not tell you.'' It was a statement, not a question. "Ah.'' The outlaw shrugged. "Well, perhaps there is still time to catch up with her, if you are interested. Of course, you might rather leave the raising of your child to strangers in a strange time.''

"Get on your horse,'' Navarre ordered, the sound of his voice frightening to his own ears. Robin quickly pulled himself up in the saddle. The knight mounted Kamir, and as he did, the black stallion, sensing his mood perhaps, reared back on his hind legs, then brought them down to the ground with a savage thud. "She will not do this to me,'' he whispered.

"Perhaps she thinks you did it to her. After all, she carries the babe, not you,'' Robin said.

"She will not take my child from me!''

"Navarre.'' Robin's voice softened. "Think you that is her desire?''

Navarre felt the crushing turmoil rise up in his throat as

though it would choke him. His baby——a son or daughter, born of the woman he loved. He looked back over at the outlaw.

"I have fought many battles, my friend," he said solemnly, squinting up at the sky, "against kings and peasants, knights and nomads." His eyes narrowed as the golden globe of the sun rose above the treetops, brilliant and liquid against the pale blue backdrop of the sky. He turned back to Robin. "This is one battle I do not intend to lose, and if I must fight time itself, or God Himself, to keep her, never doubt that I will do so."

He brushed his dark hair back from his face with one hand and felt the wind lift it from his head with gentle fingers, just as it had that long ago day when he'd stood outside Magda's hut, listening to her curious prophecy. This strange path had brought both he and Kendra back, full circle, to their beginnings.

"I doubt it not," Robin said, his blue eyes mild. He stroked his goatee softly, his brow furrowed as though weighing his next words. "But there is something you should know before you ride to stop Kendra's journey."

"I know all I need to know."

Robin shrugged. "Ah, that is well then. As long as you know everything then there is no need to tell you that Magda told Kendra if she stayed in our time, she would die in childbirth and the babe with her."

Navarre stared at him, his heart suddenly pounding so loudly he could scarce hear his own thoughts. He started to speak but could not, then swallowed and tried again.

"We ride."

Navarre's lungs were bursting and he knew Kamir's must be near to bursting as well. Against every instinct in his body he slowed the beast from the headlong rush against time into a more sedate pace, ignoring the guilt that assailed him as his faithful horse blew out great wither-shivering blasts of air from his dry nostrils and foaming mouth.

He dared not press him any faster or he would lose his horse, as well as his chance to reach Kendra in time. Navarre dismounted, cursing under his breath as he walked the horse for several yards, then turned as Robin pounded up beside him,

Tess Mallory

his own steed winded, his face flushed with color.

"Matthew and the saints, Navarre!" the outlaw cried. "If you keep up this pace you will kill us both, not to mention the horses."

"We must reach Abury before she leaves," Navarre said, continuing to pull Kamir forward as they trudged across the uneven terrain.

"What will you do if we reach her in time, my friend?"

"Throttle her," Navarre said gruffly, then shook his head. "To be honest, I do not know, Robin. But I must see her."

"The two of you are an odd pair, I'll grant you," Robin chuckled thoughtfully. "I must admit, I still find it hard to believe all this craziness about time travel."

"You won't think so if you see her disappear in a whirl of wind and glimmering blue lights as I first saw her appear."

"Blue lights? Amazing."

"Aye." Navarre stared down at the ground as his boots bit into the moist earth. His pounding heart had slowed a bit and the panic had eased somewhat. In a moment he would mount Kamir and they would ride like hell for another few hours, then stop and eat from their supplies. They would sleep an hour at the most before starting their flight toward Abury once again. And they would reach Kendra in time. That, Navarre swore.

"You think to convince her to stay, but what of the babe?" Robin asked.

"What of it?"

Robin glanced over at the knight, brushing his mustache with one finger as he led his horse beside Kamir. "Kendra says that in her time there are places called hospitals that are very clean and free of—what did she call the things?— germs."

"And what are these germs?" Navarre asked, his interest piqued.

"I know not. Something she swears cannot be seen, yet which cause a wound to rot after a time. An infection, she called it."

Navarre grunted. "The wench has strange ideas."

"That is not all. She said that women have their babies in

344

these hospitals and almost all of them live—to adulthood.''

Navarre stopped in his tracks and stared at the outlaw. "You speak in jest," he said at last, and began walking again. "That is not kind, Robin, when speaking of the deaths of children."

"Nay, nay," Robin assured him, "I speak the truth. Kendra said that almost all children live in her time. There are few born dead and most live to reach their first year and more. And the women do not die in childbirth either. It is rare, she said."

Navarre pondered Robin's words as they continued to trudge along. He did not know a soul who did not have a son, a daughter, a cousin, a nephew or a niece who had not died before they were a year old. He himself had gotten a serving girl with a child when he was only fifteen. The babe had died a few short days after being born. His mother had called it a blessing, but he had wept for a week and sworn to never touch a maid again.

Of course, he had not kept the vow, but he had been more careful than most. He had never spilled his seed inside a wench again, not even Talam, until Kendra. With Kendra he had thrown all good sense out the window and made her his wife in spirit and body even before their handfasting. Now his child grew within a woman again. What if Kendra died in childbirth? What if their baby died?

His heart constricted painfully at the thought. No, he could not bear it. Better she return to her own time where women rarely died in childbirth and babies lived beyond their first year, where both Kendra and his child would have a chance. He slowed his step as a new thought assailed him. If he appeared now at Abury she might change her mind, might decide to stay with him, for he knew Kendra loved him as intensely as he loved her.

"Robin," he said softly, stopping and letting Kamir's reins fall to the ground.

"Aye, Navarre?"

The knight ran his tongue across his dry lips, feeling a new dryness tighten within his throat. "How far are we from Abury?"

Robin glanced up at the sun. "About a half a day, I wager."

345

Navarre nodded, then sank down to the ground upon his knees.

Robin moved to his side, anxiously. "Navarre, what is it? Are you ill?"

The knight knelt in the dirt, his hands clasped in front of him, his golden eyes fixed on a distant goal.

"Robin," he whispered, "God help me, I must let her go."

Robin stared down at the knight for a long moment, then laid one hand upon his shoulder and sighed.

"My friend, you are a fool."

Navarre looked up at him, startled. Robin knelt down beside the knight, their cloaks whipping around them, their gazes even.

"Do you love her?" Robin asked.

"Aye."

"Is there anything left for you here without her?"

"Nay."

Robin slapped him on the back in disgust. "Then what are you waiting for, man? Go after her. Travel with her to her time as she has asked you."

"I cannot," Navarre said, his voice filled with defeat. "I would be thought a fool there, a barbarian, or worse."

"Does she want you to go?"

"Aye."

"Do you trust her?"

"Aye."

Robin sighed and hauled himself to his feet. "Then my friend, all I can say is that if you do not go, you are not only a fool, but a coward as well, and the Navarre de Galliard that I have been fighting beside in England's cause is not a coward."

Navarre stood, his face dark and scowling. It was one thing to think of himself as a coward, it was quite another to have the possibility voiced by Locksley. "And what of England?" he demanded. "How do I know . . ." He stopped and smiled. "Yes, I do know, do I not?" He clasped the other man's shoulder. "Thank you, Robin."

The outlaw returned the clasp and for a moment the two men looked into each other's eyes, acknowledging without words their restored friendship and the separation that lay ahead.

"I shall miss you, old friend," Robin said, squeezing the man's shoulder.

"And I, you. But I shall rest easier knowing I leave England in such responsible hands." Navarre pounded him on the back, suddenly joyful. "Now, let us not waste another minute. Let us ride for Abury and pray God speed our way."

Kendra gazed up at the full moon, which was half hidden by hazy clouds.

Full circle. That was what Cennach had said and he was so right. It seemed an eon ago that she had sat in the fields of Avebury waiting to witness the formation of a crop circle—or a hoax.

Now, as she sat on a grassy knoll with Marian, Friar Tuck and Cennach, overlooking the plains, she knew that if the professor's computations were correct, in a few hours she would find herself once again in her own time. She had arrived at the field at midday, exhausted, hungry, and in spite of her discomfort, had slept for hours, rousing only when Cennach and Marian arrived. Now she sat watching the first stars come out, knowing it wouldn't be long. She could feel it in the air, the same electricity that had haunted her that long ago night.

She patted her ever trusty bag affectionately, wondering if her uncle would believe her incredible tale even if he saw the photographs she had taken of Navarre.

Navarre. At least she would be able to take his image back with her. At least she would be able to show their child what his father looked like. Explaining who his father was, where he was, and why he couldn't be with them—that was a different story.

"Maybe I'm making a mistake," Kendra said, twisting her fingers in the strap of her bag. A brisk wind had kicked up and her auburn hair, worn unbound, lifted to fly about her face in abandonment. "I should have told Navarre. I was just afraid he would try to stop me from going back."

Cennach patted her hand. "You're doing the right thing, Kendra."

"But I could have given him one more chance to come with me."

"He knows where you are."

Kendra shivered. The air had cooled considerably and she pulled her cloak more tightly about her. She looked up to find storm clouds had gathered where only moments before there had been merely wispy clouds.

Friar Tuck sat beside Marian, shaking his round head. "I like this not," he said solemnly. "How Marian ever talked me into this I do not know."

"Think of it like this," Marian soothed him, "what would we do without you here to ask God to protect us?"

Kendra smiled as Friar Tuck continued to grumble and mutter to himself. She turned back to Cennach. "When will I know it is time?"

"You will know," Cennach said softly. "It's almost as though it senses you are here. If you want to wait and see if Navarre shows up, you'd best move away from the field."

Kendra hugged herself tightly. "No. He isn't coming."

"But something else is." Marian's voice was filled with awe as she rose slowly to her feet, lifting her arm to point in front of her. "Look."

From across the broad sweep of the plains they could see the flash and thunder of an approaching storm. Kendra stood, remembering with a small prickle of apprehension the storm that had taken her back in time. What if Cennach was wrong? What if she wasn't taken back to her own time? What if she was leaving Navarre only to be lost in some other time not her own?

She took a step backward and suddenly, the air around them exploded into a frenzy. The wind burst across the fields, surging toward them as though it had a mind of its own, almost flattening the four of them as it pounded down upon them.

Friar Tuck crossed himself and grabbed Marian at the same time Cennach pushed Kendra to the ground. The storm hit in the next instant, rain pelting them as though the gods themselves were gleefully slamming water balloons into the unwary visitors. Kendra huddled on the ground beneath Cennach's weight, then pushed him off of her at last, gasping for breath.

She froze as she realized that the wind had stopped.

"This is the way it was before," she whispered. "This is the way it was just before the blue lights appeared."

Marian's trembling voice came to her as though from very far away. "Do you mean, like those?"

Kendra looked up to see the azure lights, twinkling above the open field as if they were lost in contemplation, or else patiently waiting. Kendra stumbled to her feet.

"Well, folks," she said hoarsely, unable for some reason to find her voice, "this is where I came in."

Quickly she hugged Marian, murmuring words of appreciation and encouragement, though truthfully, she couldn't have repeated a word she said except her admonition to tell Robin good-bye and of course, Navarre. Cennach was next, his calmness a welcome buffer to her increasingly frantic nerves. She clung to his steady frame for a long moment, wordlessly, before Friar Tuck bustled up and she received his good-bye and his blessing. She took one brief look down the road on which they had come, hoping Navarre would arrive. Then Kendra squared her shoulders and faced her destiny.

The blue lights hovered, twinkling above a field of wheat newly sprouted. Kendra walked slowly down the gently sloping hill toward the awe-inspiring sight, her heart pounding fearfully, her palms sweating. Within a hundred yards of the phenomenon, she felt the oddly familiar feeling of a magnetic pull, tugging her toward the lights. As she slowly approached, her eyes transfixed on the sight above her, the blue orbs began to spin, slowly at first, then faster, spiraling downward toward the field where she was walking.

Kendra stopped, or tried to stop, but the momentum of the pull was too great. Involuntarily her legs moved forward, her skin vibrating as though inhabited by a million bumblebees. Panic seized her. What if Cennach was wrong? What if she didn't return to her own time at all? And Navarre—she was leaving Navarre. For what? An uncle who loved her and would want her to stay wherever she was happy? A life she had desperately wanted to run away from, a sorrow that would now be compounded with new sorrow, the loss of Navarre?

No! Her mind screamed as the mystic wind suddenly

whirled around her, as though some heavenly switch had been thrown and the floodgates of time reopened. She wanted Navarre. She didn't care if she had to live without civilization. She could do it as long as he was by her side. Her baby would be fine. Fine. She would take every precaution, tell Navarre exactly what to do. It would work—it had to work!

"No!" she shouted, finding her voice at last as the eerie wind churned around her, lifting her long auburn hair straight up, twisting it, as though giant, unseen hands sought to braid the silken strands. She could hear Marian shouting as the blue lights converged above her and the force wove itself around her, spinning her into an invisible web. Kendra felt her bag being wrenched from her shoulder, and watched as it sailed above her head. The flap on the satchel opened and the gun, hidden within, was plucked from its depths by invisible fingers. The weapon flew straight up—and disappeared. The bag fell back into Kendra's arms and she gave one last desperate lunge against the power holding her hostage. Her legs would not move. It was too late. Kendra threw back her head and wept as the twinkling blue lights descended.

Navarre's joy had quickly faded as the miles passed and time seemed to be flying ahead of him, an elusive quarry he could not catch. He cursed himself as he rode, cursed himself with every breath he took, every mile he crossed. He was a selfish coward, an inexcusable barbarian, a callous knave. If he had only talked to her, heard her out about her time— definitely not ordered her to stay—perhaps she would not have run away from him. Perhaps they would even now be awaiting the circle of time together.

"God help me," he breathed. A storm was brewing. He'd already been drenched with rain, lightning crashing scant yards away from him, and he knew it was not over yet. The clouds above were simply biding their time, gathering to pound out their tumultuous fanfare, no doubt when it would most detain him. Was it God's way of preventing him from reaching Kendra in time? Was He punishing the knight for his selfishness?

But the lightning didn't touch him as the storm broke a second time, and as Kamir finally mounted the crest of the hill that led to the Abury plains, Navarre pulled up on the reins, his vision marred by the sheets of wind and rain crashing down across the fields of wheat below him. Kamir danced beneath him almost in a frenzy, then suddenly the wind stopped, the clouds cleared away, and in the center of a field he saw Kendra, standing alone.

A circle was being woven around her, pressing the budding grain down to the ground by a force of incredible strength. He watched in awe as stalk after fragile stalk of new wheat was bent down around Kendra, frozen in the center of the newly forming sculpture. Blue lights glimmered above her as she stared upward, then the lights began twirling and moving, around and around, circling around her head as a new torrent of sound and power swept over the plains.

Kamir reared up on his hind legs and Navarre almost lost his seat as the horse's hooves plunged back to the earth. Then Kendra screamed, a single word wrenched from her echoing across the valley and up to Navarre. With a cry he had not uttered since Outremer, the knight kicked Kamir into action and tore down the hillside as the blue lights descended upon the woman he loved.

Navarre pounded across the plain, feeling the incredible pull of the circle's power, feeling the frantic buzz beneath his skin he had felt only once before in his lifetime. Kamir slid to a stop as he shouted for her to take his arm. She stared up at him, her eyes unseeing. Frantically he reached for her, but found himself shoved suddenly backward as the blue lights surged downward again, encircling her. He could see her slim form shimmering within the azure glow, and for a moment, part of Kendra was not there. The circle was taking her away.

"Kendra!" Screaming her name, Navarre urged Kamir forward and tried to plunge into the now dizzying whirlpool engulfing his own true love. The power pushed him back again, keeping him from entering the strangely hypnotic pattern weaving around her. The blue lights shivered in perfect synchronization and Navarre could have sworn he heard laughter from somewhere far away.

"Kendra!" he shouted again, and this time, Kendra turned

and looked at him, her eyes focusing momentarily. "My hand!" he shouted. "Take my hand!"

Lethargically, Kendra reached out one hand to him. The blue lights increased their rhythm, the surge of force pushing against him and Kamir increasing as well, and he found he could not reach her. He would not yield. Navarre punched his fist into the current swelling against him, punched again and again until at last he punched through and touched Kendra's hand. Too late, he realized he could not save her. Too late he knew that he, himself, was being sucked into the churning maelstrom whirling around them. Her fingers closed around his and suddenly, without his knowing exactly how it happened, she was in his arms.

The azure lights grew frenzied as their spiraling dance grew brighter and brighter until Navarre could not see the woman beside him. Navarre reached out and twisted one of his hands into Kamir's mane, while the other held Kendra more tightly against him as he felt the surge of power bubble up through the both of them like clear, cold water, a fountain of illumination coursing through their souls.

"Navarre," Kendra gasped, throwing her head back and gazing up into his eyes one last time, "don't let me go."

"Never," he promised, "I'll never let you go again." Navarre pressed his lips against hers, and the world exploded into blue and then black, and finally, into nothingness.

Epilogue

"Marian, Marian—stop that this instant!"

Kendra stood with hands on her hips, her blue eyes flashing in a no-nonsense way that four-year-old Marian should know meant business. The little girl stopped scribbling on the wall and hid the crayon behind her back.

"Yef, Mommy," the cherub-faced mite lisped. She lifted her chin and thrust her lower lip out petulantly, crossing her arms over her chest in a very adult manner. "But Daddy said I could."

Kendra O'Brien de Galliard whirled around and confronted yet another transgressor, this one large and crawling around on the floor, a crowing six-year-old boy on his back.

"Navarre, did you tell Marian she could color on the walls again?"

The tall, broad-shouldered man dumped the boy off, then began tickling him mercilessly. "Do you yield to the Black Knight? Do you?" he asked as the boy squealed, happily hysterical before promptly kicking his foe in the knee. Navarre howled quite convincingly and the little boy jumped to his feet, pushed his father flat, then placed his foot strategically across the back of the man's neck.

"Never! Take that, you old Black Knight. I, Robin Hood, have beaten you!"

"Again?" Kendra said, laughing as she swung the red-headed boy off his conquered foe and up into her arms. "Really, Rob, you ought to let your father win just once."

The boy shook his head. "Nope, that wouldn't be honora-

353

ble, Mommy. A man has to fight his own fights."

"Oh, is that so? I wonder where you heard that."

Navarre rose with a groan and put his arm around his wife, smiling down at her, his golden eyes quickening as his gaze slid over the form-fitting green suit she wore. "Did you want something, darling? No? Well, I do. I'll just get rid of the children and—"

"Did you or did you not tell Marian that she could draw on the wall?" Kendra demanded huffily, refusing to be swayed by the ever more powerful attraction she had for her broad-shouldered husband. He had slimmed down some, since in the twentieth century there was no need to swing broadswords and carry a ton of armor on horseback, but he worked out three times a week at a local gym and rode Kamir every weekend across their farm. She had no complaints.

"Are you not the one who said that children must be given freedom if they are to grow up to be healthy individuals?" he asked, cocking one dark brow in her direction.

Kendra glared up at him. Even after six years of living in the modern world, sometimes a hint of old England reappeared. She loved it. She loved him, though at the moment love was not the first word that came to mind.

"That isn't what I meant and you know it, now—"

"Time! Time!" A gruff voice called from the doorway. Kendra and Navarre turned as Rob and Marian squealed loudly and ran to attack the elderly man entering the room. Arthur Mackenzie bent down to gather his grandniece and nephew into his arms, and Kendra took advantage of the moment to kiss Navarre.

"What was that for?" he said softly, slipping his arms around her waist and pulling her tightly against him.

"Nothing," she replied, lifting her hand to brush a stray lock of hair back behind his ear. "You know, I'm still not sure I like your hair this way."

He ran his fingers through the closely cropped dark hair that was still long enough to fall over his forehead in a rakish way.

"Well, once Mac gives me a new beat I'll grow it out for you. Anything to please milady."

"All right, you two," Mac said, having settled the children

in separate chairs with new coloring books, crayons and a candy bar apiece. "Come on, come on, I haven't got time to sit here and watch you two moon at each other. I swear, for an old married couple the two of you sure take the cake."

Navarre frowned. "Take the cake?"

Kendra rushed in quickly. There were still a few terms Navarre wasn't familiar with, though the list was growing shorter all the time. "So what's up, Mac?" she asked. "What's the big secret about and why did you want us to bring the kids?"

"I happen to like the kids," he said, circling around the desk and pausing to admire Marian's handiwork on the wall. "Hmmm, I think this one's going to be an artist instead of a journalist like her old man and ma."

He spun around and plopped himself down behind his desk. "Yessir, I was never more thrilled than the day that you came back from England with Gally here and announced you'd eloped with a total stranger."

Navarre glowered down at the man. "Mac, you may call me Navarre, you may call me Son, you may call me Hey you if you so desire, but I have told you a thousand times, do not call me Gally."

"Sorry, Son, old habits die hard."

"I seem to remember that day too," Kendra said, sliding one leg over the edge of Mac's desk, her blue eyes mischievous. "I don't think 'thrilled' was exactly what I'd call your reaction," she said. "More like 'insane.'"

"It was a surprise, I admit," Mac said, "but I came around pretty fast, considering. I still don't understand how Rob came to be born only seven months after you met this guy but—"

"Mac!" Kendra jerked her head toward her son, her eyes wide with meaning.

"Sorry."

"I explained that," Kendra said. "Didn't you ever hear of a premature baby?"

"Sure," Mac said, nodding his gray head thoughtfully, then his face split into a grin, "just not an eight-pound one!"

"Mac, I swear I'm going to—"

"Okay, okay, enough. The reason I asked my star reporter and her erstwhile photographer down here is that I have an

355

exciting story I want the two of you to cover.''

Navarre moved forward and stood beside Kendra, his golden eyes alert, his reporter's instincts already thrown into high gear. Kendra watched him affectionately. When they'd returned from England she'd worried about Navarre at first, fearful he wouldn't be able to find his niche in her modern, crazy world. A passport had been an initial problem, but they'd looked up her little friend Sean whose less-than-savory brother had, in return for Kendra agreeing not to turn him in for giving his kid brother a gun, provided everything Navarre needed to prove he existed.

Kendra and Navarre had stayed in England for a few days after their voyage through the circle, but it soon became obvious to Kendra that the sight of his native land, so altered, so different, was more than Navarre could handle. And if London was too much, she was terrified of what he would think of New York. To her astonishment, he loved it. He loved Mac. He loved walking down Fifth Avenue. He loved bagels and cream cheese and delis and he especially loved the movies.

After a few weeks of exploring on his own, and getting into some interesting scrapes, Navarre had begun tagging along with her on the job and had nagged her to teach him everything she knew about cameras. Before long he had surpassed her knowledge and had turned to Mac and any other able-bodied newsman to teach him. About the same time he had started taking a course in government at the local community college, and by the time Rob had been born, she had a man on her hands who was determined to do something to help end corruption in American politics. And what better way than to investigate that corruption and expose it for all the world to see than through photo-journalism?

''America's future is not yet decided,'' he had explained to Kendra. ''So perhaps here I can make a difference.''

The *Galaxy*, Mac's tabloid brainchild, had died a natural death after the first six months and Mac was so happy that Kendra was married and Navarre had promised to keep her out of trouble, he decided to put the two of them on the Washington beat, then sat back to watch the sparks fly. And fly they had, from the beginning. Navarre had a natural flare for his job, and their articles had quickly gotten a great deal of attention. Kendra pushed the pleasant memories aside and turned her attention back to Mac.

"So don't keep us in suspense," she urged, "what's the big deal?"

Mac's blue eyes twinkled beneath his salt and pepper brows.

"It's an unusual scoop and I think the two of you are ideally suited to cover it," he said, leaning forward, pressing his hands down on the top of the desk. "And I have the inside track. I'm sending you to England to cover the find of the century."

Kendra and Navarre shot each other a hesitant glance.

"Did I hear you say the find of the century?" Kendra raised one auburn brow skeptically. "That doesn't sound like you, Mac."

"I know it, but this is different. A friend of mine who is an archaeologist has discovered the writings of an ancient scientist whose theories and mathematics were centuries ahead of anything of his time! He talks of relativity, quantum physics—it's incredible."

"Sounds like a hoax to me," Kendra said uneasily, trying to ignore the alarm ringing in her head.

"Aye, I mean, yes, to me as well," Navarre agreed, taking Kendra's hand and squeezing it gently. "I'm surprised at you, Mac."

"Now look you two, this is on the level, and since the two of you met in England, and since I know you haven't gone back since you came to America, Navarre, I thought you might like a little vacation in your native land."

"This is rather sudden, Mac," Navarre said, glancing at Kendra. She nodded and folded her arms across her chest.

"I agree. Are there any details about this man? Who he was? When he lived?" Kendra asked, feeling an odd sense of déjà vu as Mac shuffled through his papers, then looked up at her and smiled.

Something was going on but she wasn't sure yet what it was. Mac's eyes were twinkling the way they did when he was one up on someone else. She usually got a kick out of it—unless it was turned on her.

"Yes," he beamed. "His name was Cennach and he lived

in the twelfth century. His records begin about the year 1174 and continue until the year 1215.''

Kendra heard Navarre drop something behind her, then felt his arm slip around her, his hand squeezing her shoulder conveying his concern. Somehow she maintained her composure, though her insides were trembling as Mac continued to talk.

''But that isn't the most interesting part,'' he went on.

''Really?'' Kendra said faintly.

''There was a letter along with the papers—a letter addressed to Kendra and Navarre de Gaillard.''

''How—how unusual,'' she stuttered.

''Yes, isn't it?'' Mac circled around the desk and leaned back against it, folding his arms across his chest. ''Not two names you hear everyday.''

''No, you certainly don't.'' Navarre murmured.

''It's certainly an odd coincidence,'' Kendra said, her voice sounding strained even to her own ears. ''Maybe—''

''Save it for the funny papers,'' Mac said flatly.

''Huh?'' Kendra ran her tongue across her dry lips but couldn't seem to speak.

Navarre cleared his throat. ''Now, Mac, you don't possibly think—''

''Never kid a kidder, son.'' Mac's mouth twitched slightly as he nudged Kendra's chair with his toe. ''Isn't there something you'd like to get off your chest—Brat?''

Kendra glanced over at Navarre, who had also sat down as though the bones had been taken suddenly from his legs. He looked at Kendra and shrugged.

''He'll never believe it anyway,'' Navarre said.

''Believe what?'' Mac asked.

''Well,'' Kendra began, ''it all started with a storm.'' She smiled. ''And a knight, and a damsel in distress.''

''Is this a fairy tale, Mommy?'' her son bounced across the room to her, hanging on her arm and looking up eagerly into her face.

''A little different from Cinderella, I'd wager,'' Navarre muttered under his breath.

''Not too different,'' Kendra whispered back. ''I got Prince Charming didn't I?''

Circles In Time

"No, just a knight in tarnished armor."

"Story! Story!" Marian cried, abandoning her coloring book and running to throw herself into her mother's lap.

"Yes, I'd like to hear the story as well," Arthur Mackenzie said, pulling his chair closer.

Kendra sought Navarre's gaze over their children's heads and felt anew her love for him. She gave him a tender smile as she rumpled her daughter's hair and laughingly planted a kiss on top of their son's head.

"What's the story about?" Rob asked.

"*Who's* de story 'bout?" Marian added.

Kendra tossed her long auburn braid back over one shoulder. "It's a very exciting story and it's about Robin and Marian and—"

"*We're* in your story?" Rob demanded.

"Well, in a way, yes, you're in my story," Kendra said, shooting Navarre a hesitant glance. "I really don't know if—"

"Is you and Daddy in it?" Marian asked.

"Yes, Daddy and I are in it too."

Robin and Marian climbed up into her lap and the little girl snuggled down contentedly while Rob stared curiously up into first her face and then his father's.

"Is it a fairy tale? 'Cause fairy tales are sissy."

"Not this one, laddie," Navarre interjected, finding a chair and pulling it closer to Kendra. "This is a fairy tale that I guarantee you're going to like."

"So how does this fairy tale begin?" Mac asked, his blue eyes as warm and loving as the day he'd sent his favorite niece across the ocean to cover a harmless little story for the *Chronicle.*

Kendra gave him a grateful smile, then reached over and took Navarre's outstretched hand. "Well, Uncle Mac, how do all fairy tales begin? Once upon a time . . ."

"Wait, wait!" Marian cried, jumping up and down on her mother's lap. "I know de end of de fairy tale. I know! I know!"

"How does it end, princess?" Navarre laughed, squeezing Kendra's hand and leaning forward to rumple his daughter's tousled hair. The little girl grinned back at him triumphantly.

359

"A fairy tale always ends like dis—" She poked one finger into the air, accenting each word. "And dey all lived happily after."

"Yes," Kendra whispered to her husband softly, "they certainly did."

Navarre gazed down into Kendra's eyes and for a moment, Mac and the children faded away until it was only the two of them, enclosed in their own private circle of time and love. Across time and space they had found one another, battled the odds, and won. No matter what their futures held, they both knew with a surety that their love for one another would never alter, never perish, never die. The moment passed, and the circle extended once again, this time including them all.

High above the Chronicle building in New York, a flurry of mysterious blue lights flickered and twinkled, tumbling over one another in what to the observing eye would appear to be giddy abandonment. Gradually they slowed, then one by one, almost reluctantly, disappeared.

THE OUTLAW VIKING

TIMESWEPT

SANDRA HILL

Winner Of The Georgia
Romance Writers Maggie Award

As tall and striking as the Valkyries of legend, Dr. Rain Jordan is proud of her Norse ancestors despite their warlike ways. But she can't believe her eyes when a blow to the head transports her to a nightmarish battlefield and she has to save the barbarian of her dreams.

He is a wild-eyed berserker whose deadly sword can slay a dozen Saxons with a single swing, yet Selik can't control the saucy wench from the future. And if Selik isn't careful, the stunning siren is sure to capture his heart and make a warrior of love out of the outlaw viking.

_52000-1 $4.99 US/$5.99 CAN

FRANKLY, MY DEAR...

SANDRA HILL

By the Bestselling Author of *The Tarnished Lady*

Selene has three great passions: men, food, and *Gone with the Wind*. But the glamorous model always found herself starving—for both nourishment and affection. Weary of the petty world of high fashion, she heads to New Orleans for one last job before she begins a new life. Then a voodoo spell sends her back to the days of opulent balls and vixenish belles like Scarlet O'Hara.

Charmed by the Old South, Selene can't get her fill of gumbo, crayfish, beignets—or an alarmingly handsome planter. Dark and brooding, James Baptiste does not share Rhett Butler's cavalier spirit, and his bayou plantation is no Tara. But fiddle-dee-dee, Selene doesn't need her mammy to tell her the virile Creole is the only lover she ever gave a damn about. And with God as her witness, she vows never to go hungry or without the man she desires again.

_4042-5 $5.50 US/$6.50 CAN

Dorchester Publishing Co., Inc.
65 Commerce Road
Stamford, CT 06902

Rejar

DARA JOY

Lord Byron thinks he's a scream, the fashionable matrons titter behind their fans at a glimpse of his hard form, and nobody knows where he came from. His startling eyes—one gold, one blue—promise a wicked passion, and his voice almost seems to purr. There is only one thing a woman thinks of when looking at a man like that. *Sex.* And there is only one woman he seems to want. *Lilac.* In her wildest dreams she never guesses that bringing a stray cat into her home will soon have her stroking the most wanted man in 1811 London....

__52178-4 $5.99 US/$6.99 CAN

TIMESWEPT

Christmas Carol

FLORA SPEER

Bestselling Author of *A Love Beyond Time*

Bah! Humbug! That is what Carol Simmons says to the holidays, mistletoe, and the ghost in her room. But the mysterious specter has come to save the heartless spinster from a loveless life. Soon Carol is traveling through the ages to three different London Yuletides—and into the arms of a trio of dashing suitors. From Christmas past to Christmas future, the passionate caresses of the one man meant for her teach Carol that the season is about a lot more than Christmas presents.

_51986-0 $4.99 US/$5.99 CAN

Dorchester Publishing Co., Inc.
65 Commerce Road
Stamford, CT 06902

Please add $1.75 for shipping and handling for the first book and $.50 for each book thereafter. NY, NYC, PA and CT residents, please add appropriate sales tax. No cash, stamps, or C.O.D.s. All orders shipped within 6 weeks via postal service book rate. Canadian orders require $2.00 extra postage and must be paid in U.S. dollars through a U.S. banking facility.

Name _____

Address _____

City _____ State _____ Zip _____

I have enclosed $_____ in payment for the checked book(s). Payment <u>must</u> accompany all orders. ☐ Please send a free catalog.

MIRIAM RAFTERY

Taylor James's wrinkled Shar-Pei, Apollo, is always getting into trouble. But the young beauty never expects her mischievous puppy to lead her on the romantic adventure of a lifetime—from a dusty old Victorian attic to the strong arms of Nathaniel Stuart and his turn-of-the-century charm. One minute Taylor and Apollo are in modern-day San Francisco, and the next thing Taylor knows, a shift in the earth's crust, a wrinkle in time, and the lovely historian finds herself facing the terror of California's most infamous earthquake—and a love so monumental it threatens to shake the foundations of her world.

_52084-2 $4.99 US/$6.99 CAN

DESPERADO

SANDRA HILL

Major Helen Prescott has always played by the rules. That's why Rafe Santiago nicknamed her "Prissy" at the military academy years before. Rafe's teasing made her life miserable back then, and with his irresistible good looks, he is the man responsible for her one momentary lapse in self control. When a routine skydive goes awry, the two parachute straight into the 1850 California Gold Rush. Mistaken for a notorious bandit and his infamously sensuous mistress, they find themselves on the wrong side of the law. In a time and place where rules have no meaning, Helen finds Rafe's hard, bronzed body strangely comforting, and his piercing blue eyes leave her all too willing to share his bedroll. Suddenly, his teasing remarks make her feel all woman, and she is ready to throw caution to the wind if she can spend every night in the arms of her very own desperado.

_52182-2 $5.99 US/$6.99 CAN